MW01273765

What About Barnum?

by

Joss Landry

Book Beatles Publishing Ltd.
260-2323 32nd Avenue NE
Calgary AB T2E6Z3

This book is a work of fiction. Any names, or references of events, past or present, and/or to existing people, living or dead, are purely coincidental and intended only for the message to the reader. All names, characters, places are the product of the author's imagination and used strictly fictitiously to enhance the reader's experience.

Copyright © 2017 by Joss Landry

All rights reserved. No part of this book may be reproduced or utilized in any form or by any means, electronic or mechanical, including photocopying, recording, e-book, or by any information storage or retrieval system, without permission in writing from the publisher.

Book cover design: Dar Albert of Wicked Smart Designs
Editing: Rey Dale of Book Beatles Publishing Ltd.
ISBN: 978-0-9959568-0-3 Print.
ISBN: 978-0-9959568-1-0 (ebook)

Publisher's Cataloging-In-Publication Data
(Prepared by The Donohue Group, Inc.)

Names: Landry, Joss.
Title: What about Barnum? / by Joss Landry.
Description: Calgary, AB : Book Beatles Publishing Ltd., [2017] | Series:
    Binary bounty ; #1
Identifiers: ISBN 978-0-9959568-0-3 (print) | ISBN 978-0-9959568-1-0
    (ebook)
Subjects: LCSH: Divorced mothers--Fiction. | Rescues--Fiction. | Man-woman
    relationships--Fiction. | Kindness--Fiction. | Pacific Ocean--Fiction.
    | LCGFT: Domestic fiction.
Classification: LCC PR9199.4.A54 W43 2017 (print) | LCC PR9199.4.A54
    (ebook) | DDC 813/.6--dc23

VERY SPECIAL MENTION

I am grateful for my husband Gilles' devotion. He is steadfast a powerful motivator and believes in my stories. In short, he has slowly become the voice that drives me.

My children and grandchildren also drive me onward to improve, and not merely to do more, but to become more than I am. My personal cloud of angels.

Thank you to Dal Albert for making this beautiful cover.

Thank you to all the prolific authors, beta readers and editors who spent time on this book polishing away the cobwebs.

Last, but most important, thank you, Rabboni for walking beside me.

Joss Landry is also the author of : Mirror Deep,

I Can See You, Emma Willis Book I

Exhale and Reboot,

Ava Moss,

I Can Find You, Emma Willis Book II

If you enjoyed this book, please be so kind as to leave a review. A review is the greatest praise an author can receive. Thank you!

I wrote this story to promote kindness and acceptance of all those we call strangers.

Keep the faith. When a door closes, there lies beyond another path that will take you home.

Follow Barnum. His story will enlighten you.

Joss Landry

PROLOGUE

Millicent Brewer here, known as Millie to my friends and family or as, *it's Millie Time* whenever my dearest ones choose to laugh at my poor life choices or poke fun to cheer me up. Never did lift my spirits—only ever paralyzed me with inadequacy which only invited more bad choices on my part further lending proof positive to the little jingle.

My father, a college professor of creative writing at Oxford University, married my mother, a law professor at the same university. They first met in a heated freshman debate over their differing opinions and outlandish comparisons as to the reasons behind the success or failure of mixed marriages. Well, as my father likes to tell the story: "There we were, clearly on opposite sides of the debate, English brats with Irish tempers sharing nothing other than a common dislike for one another."

However, years later after their post graduate studies, Alan Brewer proposed to star debater Caroline Stuart. My fate was sealed. I was born nine months later, my birth followed exactly one year after by my sister Denise, whom everyone calls Denny, and who is an odd, yet attractive combination of my father's long face and my mother's sweet expression. And although I'm the eldest, and people say I look like Keri Russell—though I don't see the resemblance other than the curly hair—my sister

What About Barnum?

Binary Bounty # 1

Denny holds the key to my father's heart. "Guts and guile," he called all the antics she pulled. He professed mine to be, "Exercises in futility."

Nevertheless, Denny and I became inseparable the year my father uprooted us to immigrate to the United States—California to be precise where he and my mother found new lives at Berkeley University.

Adapting to our new surroundings was much easier *for guts and guile* than for, *needlessly nervous*. At twelve years of age to my timid thirteen, Denny became my protector. She carved a place for me amongst her friends and kept at bay the many boys who gyrated around me. Their avid glares should have flattered me. However, since I was terrified people might discover me to be an easy prey, their compliments created only worry in a shy young girl who tried her best to be invisible.

Far from the debater my mother has been and still is, I could not imagine following in her footsteps. In fact, I could not picture myself doing much of anything, so I was grateful when my mother spotted my knack for teaching. "You have a wonderful gift to share with others, Millie. You're bright and beautiful, inside and out, not to mention that I've never encountered anyone more able to reduce complex problems to their simplest solutions. You should be a teacher. My hunch tells me you will be a star with all your pupils."

Of course, my mother's gentle words were dogma around our house, even with my stern father. So, a teacher I became.

While Denny went on to become a civil engineer, graduating top of her class, I obtained my master's certificate and later, attended Berkeley for a pedagogical degree. And though academia did not crown me class valedictorian, I did get voted prom queen gliding down the red carpet with Todd Winters, quarterback phenomenon and dreamboat extraordinaire, by my side.

A couple of years later after graduating university, to the head shakes of my father, I walked down another aisle with same dreamboat, one that featured white ribbons and a colorful carpet of confetti. Nine months later, my son Jonah's fate was sealed— born healthy, heavy and absolutely gorgeous.

Four long years later, I faced another of my father's dire warnings. My marriage to Todd became an *exercise in futility*— just as he had predicted. With the help of my mother, I fought and won sole custody of my son's upbringing, and Todd won the right to raise hell and all the skirts he wanted.

Thus began my first solo flight for freedom, dear diary, and although you were gifted to me six months ago last Christmas, as a means of sorting through my painful divorce, here I am— ready to allow the overflow of ideas in my head to spill onto your pages. My very own second chance at a greater life I didn't think I deserved.

What About Barnum?

Binary Bounty # 1

—One—

FRIENDLY GIANT

Denny Brewer tugged on the strands of hair flogging her cheeks and clinging to her lips. Wind encircled her, feral and capricious, and she wished her long black hair was tied or shoved under a hat. Yes, a wide-brimmed sombrero would serve a dual purpose—keep the sun from burning her face and slow the Mexican ocean wind from blowing sand in her hair while loose pebbles stuck to her wet cheeks. At least her sunglasses protected her eyes from the sun and the blowing wind.

"¿Señorita?"

Yes! She thought. Twenty minutes was too long to wait for the two margaritas she ordered from the seaside bar. She grabbed a napkin to spread on the speckled wood counter and dropped her purse on it rummaging in her wallet for the pesos she needed, grateful the thatched roof provided a little respite from the heat and humidity of June in Mexico. *Who the hell schedules a conference this far south in the middle of June*? She'd have to peel off her clothes again when they got to the room.

"¿*Cuanto cuesta*?" Denny asked as she recognized how the price for same articles varied from one tacky tiki bar to another, and she wasn't against saving a few pesos. She dropped the money on the counter and stacked the glasses to leave one of her hands free.

She eyed her sister a short way down under the hotel palapa available to guests. Just arrived, Millie was on the phone walking around their little eight-foot shaded spot and appeared to be arguing with flamboyant gestures. *Damn it, she messed up the towels again which means removing the sand without having to eat it when I do.*

Denny had stretched out two large towels at the foot of two lounge chairs relaxing on the west end of their little haven. The brightly colored terry cloth sheets were for Jonah and his toys, and she needed to dust them often for sand.

Hoisting her bag a little higher on her shoulders, Denny admired her older sister's stance. Tall, slim, well-built her lovely expression and warm smile could grab any man's attention with ease. Why Millie wasted her time chasing after badasses, she couldn't guess.

Millie was alone, and this struck her as strange. Jonah was the one who liked to rumple those towels. Did she leave him with the sitter again?

Careful to dig her feet with each step to avoid the hot sand's burn, her eyes followed the chain of twelve white pelicans flying over the water with a leader a few feet in front.

She did a double-take eyeing the rock face five hundred feet from their thatched roof, a couple of hundred feet from where she stood. Surprise wiped the smile off her face as she spotted Jonah by the water's edge on his knees in the sand. Had to be him with that head of black curly hair, and when he stood, she caught the glimmer of his shiny green bathing suit and the Señor *Frog* logo on his T-shirt.

What was her nephew doing so far from their encampment?

What About Barnum?

Binary Bounty # 1

Jonah used his red shovel to dig wet sand into his little pail kneeling dangerously close to the wave. There rose a steep slope of rocks a few feet away, and their guide mentioned not to go in the water in that area as a riptide current ran through the water while debris and sharp coral scattered the ocean floor. Denny couldn't imagine how Jonah walked all that way without Millie's awareness—*most likely he ran there thinking his mother would pursue him as she usually did.*

A mighty wave rose out of the water a hundred feet from the shore, a high high breaker foaming at the mouth. Denny spotted the rage building in the Pacific hand. Salt water would cover Jonah in seconds.

She dropped drinks, purse and began to run. "Jonah," she yelled over and over again realizing her voice didn't reach. Her heart stopped. She froze to the spot as the wave overtook her nephew covering him and transporting Jonah in one swift move. *He never learned how to swim. Would he think to hold his breath?*

She cried and tried to run again but couldn't get her legs to move although the sand burned her feet. Helplessness overtook her, but when she caught Millie's screams as she ran to her son, Denny managed to shake the stupor from her limbs and began running again.

Precious seconds wasted, and how would they dive into this dangerous part of the ocean? She fought back gushing tears when out of the wave came the outline of a strong man carrying a small child. Jonah still held onto his red pail, the shovel nowhere to be seen. He appeared to be unharmed as he called out to his mother.

Denny stopped running. Glued to sticky wet mud, she wiped her eyes as she eyed Pacific Poseidon get closer and hand Jonah over to Millie while his eyes searched her sister's tear-stained face.

Where did this man come from, Denny asked herself. The slow season rendered this section of beach almost empty, and the bulk of people invited to the convention were not due to arrive until tomorrow. At least the god-like figure wore something, well more resembling a short, skin-tight version of a woman's thong, affording a vision of large potential.

Denny shook herself and bridged the distance between them. Millie held her son against her chest, her arms wrapped tightly around him and didn't notice the man emerge from the ferocious wave standing without moving a muscle. Of this, Denny was sure.

"Jonah, don't ever leave mommy's side again. Is that clear?" Millie could not stop the tears from making her voice tremble, no matter how stern she willed her tone to be. Jonah happened to be her reason for living, her entire world, her joy she thought, biting her bottom lip to remove the dark thoughts of life without him. "You have to promise me, Jonah." She perceived her voice to be pleading.

Jonah nodded, his face full of concern confronted with his mother's tears. "I'm sorry, Mommy."

She kissed him on both cheeks and stared up at Jonah's savior as she released her hold on the boy fidgeting in her arms. He appeared taken with this man.

Jonah slipped out of Millie's arms and turned to the muscular

What About Barnum?

stranger. "Are you a giant?"

The man chuckled and shook his head. "No. I'm only six feet and a couple of inches tall. I don't think this qualifies me as a giant."

"To a small child whose life you've just saved, I guess you are, Mister?" Millie extended her hand. "I'm Millie Winters ... I mean Brewer."

He grabbed Millie's hand and held it as he stared into her eyes. "I'm Barnum. You can call me Barnum."

"Well, thank you, Barnum," Millie whispered upholding his gaze. "Although words can't express." A hand to her heart, she continued. "So that you understand, I was going in after him. I would have fished him out or perished trying."

"I know," he stated in quiet tones. "We couldn't allow that to happen, could we?"

Millie thought how odd the assuredness of his statement sounded. She turned toward her sister. "This is my sister, Denise Brewer."

Denny stepped in and clasped his hand. "So glad you were there. You can call me Denny, by the way." Denny stared at Barnum's bad-boy looks, the broad forehead and the curls down the nape of his neck, the long sideburns and the wide, square smile that held the mischief or a surfeit of adventures too numerous to hide. She worried the black, almond shaped eyes and muscular build might steal her sister's affection. Another bad-boy conquest to notch her bedpost and break her heart. "Tell me, Barnum—no last name?"

He smiled but didn't answer.

"How did you get here? Do you have a boat nearby?"

"Denny," Millie remonstrated. "Please forgive my sister's curiosity. She is grateful for what you did—more than you realize." Millie walked over to rub Denny's back with an affectionate hand. "She likes to keep an eye out for Jonah and me."

"I understand." Barnum turned toward Denny to add, "I enjoy swimming great distances. When I spotted the child sitting by the water, I swam in this direction." He bowed to her from the waist. "Glad I was able to help."

As he made to leave, Millie walked toward him. "Will we see you again?"

He stared at her for a few long seconds. "This is something for you to decide."

Millie held Jonah's hand as they watched the wave engulf Barnum.

—Two—

MILLIE AND DENNY

Millie stood against the balcony rail staring out at sea. In Puerto Vallarta two days, she never missed the wink of the sunset. Dramatic as the star on fire appeared to melt into the ocean's churn the instant it kissed the salty, sparkling waves. A count of twenty was all she managed as the day disappeared—heartrending since she needed sunlight to shed warmth on her lonely life.

Jonah didn't seem the worse for wear from his experience. In fact, all he talked about was the giant who saved him from drowning and how scared he was when the wave caught him and spun him around. All during dinner, Jonah yammered about Barnum and how he just couldn't wait to see him again.

He slept now, would wake up refreshed and, she hoped, rid of the image in his mind of being smothered by the ocean, and no longer smitten with a man they were liable never to encounter again. She sighed. With the day almost gone her first prayer of the evening rose from her lips, "Please God, help my Jonah recover from this experience. I promise to be a better mother from now on, be more attentive."

She dabbed a tear from her eye and wished all her prayers were this simple. Alone to raise Jonah, she hated that Todd never called to ask about his son. Of course, she had full custody, but he also had visitation rights. The thought of being adrift in an ocean with no port of call made her edgy, filled her with questions to which she had no ready answers.

Did Jonah need a father more than she realized? Was this why he often found trouble? Perhaps she needed to be more attentive to his needs to prevent him from bad behavior. He understood he was not supposed to go near the ocean especially without an adult present. Millie covered this rule with Jonah more than once. The promise he made not to stray, Jonah gave her time and time again. Was he merely forgetful and she was fussing for nothing?

She found her way to one of the pastel cushioned chairs around the glass table on the balcony, her legs all at once weak from the weight of her problems.

The door to her room opened, and she caught the reflection of her sister Denny in the mirror that covered a wall in the entrance to the suite. Denny walked in and searched for her. "Millie?"

"Balcony," she called out in a whisper. "Not too loud. Jonah is finally asleep."

Denny sat down depositing a foil-wrapped plate on the table. "You didn't come down to dinner. Is this how you intend punishing yourself today? I tell you, Jed was angry-red when he didn't find you at the star-table when he mentioned you in his speech." Denny rolled her eyes.

"Thanks, but I'm not hungry."

"This is your favorite. Rice and spicy shrimps."

"Do you think I'm a bad mother?"

"You already know my answer. Why bother?"

What About Barnum?

"Be honest." She tossed her sister sad eyes.

"You're not a bad mother. You're alone trying to turn a child into a man—a little boy who can be a handful. Not an easy job. I wouldn't be able to do it, as much as I love Jonah. When I spotted him today about to be taken by that wave, I froze. I couldn't move. You should check the bottom of my feet—burnt bright red."

"Do you think this is why he runs from me all the time? Trying to reach his father somehow? He must miss him, yet he never mentions him."

"I don't think he cares or remembers, one way or another."

"He's five. Todd and I divorced six months ago. Of course, he remembers and cares about his dad."

"Not necessarily. You and Todd were separated two years before you finalized the divorce. And you complained about the fact Todd never came to visit Jonah."

"True. Still, maybe Jonah blames himself for his father leaving since Todd never visits."

You're grasping at straws. Jonah's too young." Denny unwrapped a corner of the foil of the meal she brought her sister and picked at one of the shrimps. "Maybe you should talk to him about it."

"The way he took to that man today."

"Speaking of that man. How odd to find him there at that exact moment? I mean, the reef is rife with rocks and sharp coral and all sorts of debris. A maid at the hotel told me someone died there this winter—drowned because no one was able to reach her—a lifeguard tried. Never reached the girl. Tide kept pulling her away, and he got his feet and legs cut up for the privilege of trying to save her."

"Horrible." Millie wrapped her arms around herself to ward off the shivers. She released a long sigh. "Sad."

"What?"

"In a few minutes, we will have a hard time distinguishing there is an ocean in front of us with the water so dark."

"The man, this Barnum, didn't have a scratch on him." Denny turned to her sister. "Want to do something? Let's go dancing."

"I don't want to leave Jonah with a sitter again."

"He's sleeping. We'll ask for Manuela. She's excellent. And you might like to invite some of the people on your team to come with us. I'm sure they would love a night out on the town."

The suggestion perked up Millie. She got up and reached for her cell phone. "Bill and Diane Hurley would love to go. They were talking about it yesterday. Hoshimi and Emiko might want to come too."

"How many people of your team are attending the convention?"

"Five individuals out of eight hundred." Millie smiled as she shrugged. "Not many. A few more may arrive tomorrow. But this is an online business. So we can practice all over the world without needing to come together—ever."

"Still, eight hundred people since January. A lot of work. Have you made any money with this venture yet? I mean this is a gorgeous room."

"Not as grand as Jed's, the Ambassador suite. See this wall of patio doors? Well, another wall of doors perpendicular to this one gives Jed's room a wrap-around veranda. Flowers along the trellis and an enormous hot tub in the corner."

What About Barnum?

"Wait a minute. Didn't you say Jed paid for your trip?"

"He paid for airfare. I'm paying for the hotel room. But yes, I made some money. Used some of my savings to launch the business, but since I started full time, business is profitable. The herbs sell themselves, and people love to talk about them to everyone. So, I consider my efforts somewhat successful—not enough to give up on Todd's alimony, though I would love to throw the money back in his face."

Millie put the phone down. "Odd, no one is answering."

"They're probably at the dinner downstairs. Didn't you say Jed Swayzee was handing out awards tonight?"

"Oh, shit. I forgot. Jed is going to kill me."

"Let's go, just the two of us. It will do you good to take in a change of scenery."

Millie nodded before she lost her courage and called the front desk for Manuela.

As they got off the elevator, Millie wearing a big hat not to be recognized by any of the members of her party, the sisters headed for the front desk. Worried Jed might need to find her, she explained to the night manager she was going to the Mandala Club should anyone need to reach her. She ran to catch up to Denny already at the front door.

Millie removed the hat and gave it to the concierge. "Thank you for saving this for me." She smiled to express her gratitude. They walked to one of the waiting cabs, and Millie spotted someone she recognized getting out of the taxi parked by the curve.

"Oh, God," she whispered to Denny. "Stand in front of me. I

can't let her spot me.'"

"Who?"

"The woman getting out of the cab hauling a pink suitcase out of the trunk is Jed's ex-wife, Julie."

"You're kidding. Well, Jed's ex is stunning. What is she doing here? Is Julie part of his team?"

"No. Jed hates her. He spends half his time hiding from her. She's trying to prove he has more money than her lawyer found because, according to Jed, she wants to bleed him dry."

Denny shook her head. "A woman scorned. Let's get out of here. You don't want to be in the middle of a scratch fest when she finds out he's living in the lap of luxury."

Twenty-two minutes later, arm in arm with her sister Denny, Millie walked into the Mandala Club renowned for dancing, bright neon lights, and great drinks. They walked to the south side which afforded an open area with views of The Malecon. Millie breathed in the ocean close by and caught the sounds and sights of occasional waves eerily white under the full pink moon. Music blasted while the DJ took a break. Colors flashed with neon pinks and greens from giant reflective balls in suspension. Outside was more private and they shared drinks and long-overdue secrets.

"Just what the doctor ordered." Denny raised her glass.

Millie clinked her strawberry margarita to Denny's piña colada. "Did you tell Dad you quit your job?"

"Yeah. I did," Denny answered while swaying to the music's tempo.

"What did he say?"

"You don't want to know. Had to do it. Threatened senior

partner, Don Grimalsky, so many times I would leave if he didn't make me a partner. Had to. No other way to save face."

"You still haven't told me what Dad said."

"He said it was Millie time and I'd lost my marbles."

"Great! Now he's using my name to make fun of someone else like I'm responsible for all the ills of this world—total disconnect."

Denny laughed. "Dad respects you a lot more than you think. I always believed he is intimidated by you, your independence, your beauty inside and out. So, he hides behind ridicule, the only way he knows how to fend."

Millie rubbed her sister's hand. "So sweet," she enunciated over the music. "But I think you give Dad too much credit."

"Hey, look who's standing by the Buddha bar—inside."

Millie turned to try and spot someone she might recognize in the myriad of colors bouncing around the vast dancing area. "Who?"

"Wait until the light goes pink again. Too dark right now."

Millie couldn't believe her eyes when she got a flash of the silhouette standing with his arm leaning against a counter. "Are you sure? The man looks like Barnum. Though I can't tell, he's wearing clothes." Millie winked at her sister.

"That tuft of hair when he dove into the water stayed with me. Barnum, all right."

"Let's say hello," Millie said. "Do you think the man would mind?"

"I mind," Denny told Millie as she shook her head. "You're not getting ideas about this guy, I hope."

Millie smiled. "How often does it happen for you? Meet

someone you are interested in, or just some man you consider might be boyfriend material? Ever?"

"Okay. I don't fall easily—never as a matter of fact which is a little bit scary, I'll admit." She paused taking a sip of her drink. "Don proposed marriage to me."

"Don, senior partner at your engineering firm Don? He proposed marriage to you?" Millie's jaw dropped.

"Yeah."

"I never realized you two went out. You were intimate?"

"Nope. And I never led him on, either. We were friends, period. We went to the movies a couple of times—the extent of it. Oh, one kiss at the Christmas party. No tongue. Anyway, he said he was smitten and wanted to spend the rest of his life with me."

"Wow. So this was the reason why you quit your three-hundred-grand-a-year job."

"Yeah. I'm not in love with Don. What rocks me." Her shoulders swayed left to right. "Aside from this music, is I never stared at a man and imagined myself living with him for the rest of my life. How can someone do this?"

"I know you're not a virgin—David Shenko, and Matt … what's his name—from your lips."

"Not a virgin. I did my share of the horizontal mambo, vertical a couple of times. I lose interest afterward." She laughed.

"Well, I guess that's one way of finding out if the guy's the one. Unlike some people who imagine spending the rest of their life with a man at least once a day, sometimes twice."

Denny eyed her strangely, so Millie continued. "A temp of a particular age walks into the cafeteria at lunch, receding hairline, a little gut, a charming smile, bashful, and he looks at you with that glint in his eye.

What About Barnum?

Binary Bounty # 1

You consider his kindness, his restraint—for lack of a better word—and know he'll never go chasing the ladies the way Todd did. Might be a good dad for Jonah. Then, some beyond hot older man—divorced parent—father to one of your students, finds his way to your heart on a late afternoon with a cute smile and a cute butt. You realize since he's divorced, and as hot as he is, he may very well go chasing the ladies the way Todd did. Somehow you find yourself spending a few minutes imagining how a roll in the sheets might thrill you with his strong, tanned hands caressing your body, and then your next thought is: perhaps you can change a man like this. You certainly have the experience to do so before you call yourself an idiot and mentally walk away."

Denny laughed. "Much too unique to be a generic story, but this is a good sign, sister of mine. You've grown. You're learning to discriminate. Are you sleeping with Jed?"

"We did a couple of times, last January. He introduced me to his ex-wife as his girlfriend, which was okay. Only, I lost interest when I remembered how unconcerned this *boyfriend* was about my son. Jonah is the only man in my life these days."

"I will drink to that." Denny hoisted her glass. Then she rose. "Let's go say hello. You do the talking."

"We'll lose our table, and the DJ is coming back."

"Forget about this rickety little table. We'll be dancing."

Denny would not take no for an answer. She grabbed her purse and Millie's hand and threaded her way to the bar. "And this is the quiet season. Thank God! Can you imagine how this place might be during Spring Break?"

Mandala Club

Millie glued herself to Denny as her sister needed to plow their way to the bar. Not bumping into people became the mile-long hurdle and staying together nothing but a crap shoot. Nevertheless, they both ended up in front of Barnum, deep in conversation with some other fellow. Millie hesitated to interrupt him.

She placed a hand on his shoulder. Her hand appeared small against the rock-hard, round limb he used to support his lean frame against the counter. She backed up somewhat when she caught him raise his stance and turn to face her. No recognition in those unfathomable eyes mirroring the club's neon colors. This man couldn't be the kind soul she envisioned a couple of hours ago. "Do you remember me? Earlier today?"

Before she could add anything about Jonah or the rescue, he interrupted her. "No. I don't know you. My name is Rick Barry." He eyed her up and down. "Wouldn't mind getting to know you." This got a laugh from his partner.

When Millie couldn't think of anything to say, he smiled at her, and she doubted this could be the same man. "I'm sorry. I mistook you for someone else." She turned and left, this time dragging Denny behind her.

Upset she mistook the wrong man for Barnum, the kind soul

What About Barnum?

Binary Bounty # 1

who saved her son's life, she didn't duck or dodge enough to avoid the bumps of dancers' steps along the way. She lost Denny's hand at one point, but glanced back and noticed Denny behind her. She wanted to get out of there as fast as she could. She headed for the door.

When Millie got in the small foyer, Denny no longer stood behind her.

Denny lost Millie's hand when she felt someone tugging on her purse. She'd secured the bag's strap around her neck, so the tug didn't worry her much. Only when Denny looked down, the straps showed jagged little ends, but no purse. She couldn't believe someone cut away her bag.

Staring up at the gyrating dancers, she spotted a man running and staring back in her direction. She yelled to get his attention to no avail. She searched the area for Millie, and when she couldn't find her, a rage fueled her to run after the man.

"Stop that thief. He grabbed my purse." If anyone heard her, they showed no sign of it bopping to the music and laughing at least as loud as the sound of the DJ's choice of modern techno beats. More like a digital echo than music. Nothing you could sing to or even recognize.

Still fuming someone possessed this type of gall, Denny ran out the door unaware of what street she stood on. More than one entrance to the place, I guess. She didn't think this type of crime existed. What were people thinking?

She yelled out for Millie just in case her sister also searched the area, an empty gesture, but she hated the fact Millie would worry about her. With no wallet, she needed money to go home, although Denny breathed easier knowing her passport was still at the hotel. She spotted the same man eying her and running the minute she did. Almost as though he wanted her to follow him. She hesitated. Could this be a trick they might use to get someone away from the busier streets? Common sense prevailed, and she gave up on the intruder. Denny decided to flag down police to lodge a formal complaint.

Millie spent an hour looking for her sister. Aware they would never find each other in this zoo, she hailed a cab to go back to the hotel. She hoped Denny would do the same once she couldn't locate her.

When she got to the hotel, after stepping out of the car, her heart froze. Three police cars surrounded the hotel entrance, and *policias* refused entry to anyone who could not show a room key or a passport. Her passport was always on her. She displayed her papers, and the young policeman told her to stay where she stood in Spanish.

Addressing him in his language, Millie asked him why the commotion, and explained she had a room on the premises.

His hand on her wrist, he held her there until a senior officer came to see her passport.

"Ms. Brewer. Do you know this man?" He spoke in halting English and showed her Jed's picture.

"Yes, of course. Mr. Swayzee is holding a convention here this week for people from around the world. I am attending the conference."

"He said you could vouch for his whereabouts. Is this right?"

Millie panicked. She remembered Julie Swayzee walking

into the hotel and hoped the woman hadn't decided to get vengeance on Jed. "I left the hotel this evening. My sister and I went to the Mandala Club, and I just returned."

"Where is your sister?"

"I don't know. We got separated. I imagine my sister will find her way back. She may already be inside."

"What is your sister's name, Ms. Brewer?"

"Denise Brewer."

"I am Capitán Ruiz. Please wait here while I verify your story."

Millie waited while all sorts of scenarios created panic in her mind. She had a son and Manuela would wonder where she was. How could Jed implicate her like this? There must have been tons of people who could vouch for his presence at the conference tonight, at the dinner and afterward at the award banquet. Why finger her when he knew she had skipped out, or did he? Perhaps he thought she was in her room and he could use her to give himself an alibi? An alibi for what?

After what seemed like a long wait, Capitán Ruiz returned.

"It appears your sister did not return, Ms. Brewer. The only one who answers your phone is the sitter staying with your child." He made a sign to the officer still holding her wrist, and Millie found herself free.

"Please go make arrangements with someone to take care of your child a while longer. We need you to come downtown with us to straighten this out."

"Excuse me, can you tell me what this is all about?"

He left, while the young policeman told her he would accompany her to the room. He waited outside while she tended to her son.

Inside, Millie checked on Jonah and wiped a few tears seeing him sleep so peacefully. She couldn't believe she had to leave him again, not knowing when she would be able to return.

She explained to Manuela what she needed to do and the sitter's eyes screamed the fear she sensed. She pulled Millie aside to tell her. "Don't go with them. They will keep you there for God knows how long. Say Manuela can only stay for another hour, after which your son will be alone. Worse than this. Jonah will wake up, and you will not yet be back."

"I can't refuse to go with them. The Capitán ordered me to go."

Manuela scanned the area and whispered in English. "Tell them you will pay the fine it costs to have the interrogation here. You understand their time is expensive, and you are sorry, but your child is alone with no one to take care of him."

"Why should I pay a fine to hold the interrogation here? You're right. I should be able to tell them what happened while I stay here, at the hotel."

"Trust me. Offer the money. Police will be more amenable to doing this."

Millie found hard to believe money would smooth things over. "Are you talking about a bribe?"

"*Nunca use esta palabra.* Never. Capitán will arrest you if you do."

Millie considered herself a smart person but didn't understand what Manuela was trying to say. She nodded when the young officer indicated they had to leave with a knock on the door.

What About Barnum?

Binary Bounty # 1

Downstairs tears began to flow when she spoke to the Capitán, explaining she was unable to leave her child because the sitter had to go. She had obligations of her own. "Listen, I understand that keeping your men here during interrogation is expensive as they are not attending any other emergencies, so I am prepared to pay the fine it would cost to interrogate me here. Plus, I am not leaving anytime soon, not without my sister. So you will find me here in the morning should you have more questions."

Capitán Ruiz hesitated. Millie could not believe this argument swayed him.

"Very well. The fine will be two hundred American dollars. I need to compensate my men. I am sure you understand."

"Absolutely." She rummaged in her purse, scoured her wallet and took out four bills of one thousand *Banco de Mexico pesos,* glad she grabbed the money from the safe as she left. "Will this do? It's all I have."

"Gracias, Señorita." Ruiz pocketed the cash and entered the lobby where he sat in the first chair he found. He pulled out a pad and a pen from an inside pocket. He invited Millie to sit beside him. "What is your relationship to Mr. Jed Swayzee?"

"Well, we are friends. He recruited me into the business he owns called Herbal Organics. The products are comprised of essential herbs and lotions from organic plants to give energy and lessen the pain of injuries in some cases. He received permission from the Mexican Government to open his business here and offer the benefits to the Mexican people. Like everyone else, they can partake of the products and take advantage of the income potential should they choose to start a business." Millie thought how robotic this sounded—always trying to recruit.

"I see. Mr. Swayzee introduced you as his girlfriend. Is there any truth in this?"

"If he called me his girlfriend, then no. I am foremost a business associate. We did go out a few times in the beginning—when we first met—months ago, but as you know I have a son, and Jed Swayzee is not the least bit interested in a girlfriend with a child."

"Are you aware his ex-wife, Julie Swayzee, arrived at the hotel tonight while he was giving a conference?"

"I spotted her stepping out of a cab while my sister and I were leaving, and I pointed the woman out to her. She didn't see me. She took out a pink suitcase from the trunk of the cab and wheeled it into the hotel."

"Do you remember what time it was?"

"Well, Manuela arrived around eight fifteen, and we didn't leave right away. Maybe eight thirty?"

"Will your sister be able to corroborate your story?"

"Yes. As soon as my sister arrives, she will tell you the same thing I just did."

"Please remain in Mexico. I will need to ask for your passport. It will be returned to you once this investigation no longer needs your cooperation."

"I am more than willing to cooperate with the authorities and answer your questions. May I know why? What is this all about?"

Ruiz stared at her for long seconds and probably deemed she had no idea of what had taken place because he admitted, "Mrs. Julie Swayzee was murdered tonight while in Mr. Swayzee's room."

What About Barnum?

Binary Bounty # 1

Millie put her hand over her mouth, her intake of breath squeaking as she did. "How?"

Ruiz rose. "We will be in touch, Ms. Brewer."

As soon as the officers left, Millie ran to the elevator, to her son. She couldn't believe the man had taken her money when he could have asked her the same questions without the fuss since his interrogation took all of five minutes. Different country, different attitudes. Now she had a more urgent problem. She needed to find Denny. Then she needed to find representation.

One hour later, when Denny had still not returned, Millie fought the urge to bundle up Jonah, grab a cab, and look for her sister. What could have happened to her? Why couldn't she pick up a phone and call?

Denny waited to speak to someone in authority at the local police station. There seemed to be a lot of blue suits waiting around or discussing urgent matters. She couldn't get anyone to take her statement. She asked directions from a cab driver, and he took her there free of charge after hearing her story. Denny, most grateful, asked for his business card to call on him each time she and her sister might need a taxi. He appeared very pleased with the offer.

She approached the counter as the crowd seemed to disperse and spoke to someone writing up a form. "Excuse me, my name is Denise Brewer, and I was robbed tonight while at the Mandala Club." When she obtained no response, not even a batting of eyelashes, she repeated her question in Spanish. Still, nothing— *nada*.

Someone tapped her on the shoulder. "Did you say your

name is Denise Brewer?"

Denny turned and observed the short man with the beady black eyes staring at her. She hesitated but nodded as her only answer.

"I'm Capitán Ruiz, and I interviewed your sister tonight for one of my cases."

"Thank God, you've heard from my sister. We were at the Mandala Club when we got separated." Denny stopped gushing. "What do you mean you interviewed my sister in one of your cases?"

Ruiz ignored the question. Instead, he asked her the same questions he asked Millie, and she responded the same way. She left the part of Julie Swayzee out of her story. When the officer asked her about this, she replied, "Yes, Millie pointed her out to me. She walked into the hotel carrying a pink suitcase. Can I use the phone to call my sister? I don't have any money to use the payphone."

Ruiz nodded. "First, you say someone robbed you this evening?"

"Yes." She showed the captain the jagged ends of her purse strings still around her neck. "I must admit, I only felt a slight tug. Since the purse was around my neck, I never worried about someone taking it. Even with the tug, I realized they would not be able to remove anything as the clasp is very tight. When I looked down, I was stunned."

"Of course. Did you happen to catch anyone running away?"

"Yes, I ran after him in the crowd, which was how I lost my sister. Then when I lost him, I stopped running, searching the area for Millie. A few minutes later, I noticed a man staring at me. When the thief caught me looking at him, he started running again, and so did I, all the way outside. I called out for my sister, but no one responded."

What About Barnum?

Binary Bounty # 1

"This man, would you recognize him if I showed you pictures?"

"Well, I'm not sure. However, just as I was getting ready to leave the club, I looked up in the same direction, and spotted the thief under a light, staring at me. Why would he wait for me and why wait under a light? I panicked. I thought maybe he wanted me to chase him to lead me in some dark alley."

"Why would you think this?"

"Logical. You hear about these situations."

"Do you or your sister have enemies?"

Denny chuckled. "Sorry, neither of us lead very exciting or dangerous lives. My sister was a professor at Berkeley until recently, and I'm an out-of-work civil engineer."

"Please remain in Mexico a while longer. I will need to ask you more questions."

"Thank you. I will call to reassure my sister and ask her to stand by with money for a cab."

"Not necessary. One of my officers will drive you to your hotel. Juan," he called out.

"Very decent of you. Is there a fee for this service?"

"No. Your sister donated a very generous sum to this department." He smiled and walked away.

Four

AFTERMATH

S itting outside on the patio adjacent to her hotel room, Millie nodded off during her breakfast of eggs, croissants, and ham. She and Denny had spent the night chatting. Subjects abounded from alibis, dead ex-wives, stolen purses to cagey men with hidden agendas, and a humorous policeman— one of whom had charged her two hundred dollars to teach her a lesson. Ruiz would have agreed to interview her at the hotel had she asked.

The story of her payola drew a huge laugh out of Denny. All in all, she derived from the evening a massive migraine, the sort which made her too nauseous to eat. Still, Jonah being rested, rambunctious and roaring to play, pulled on her legs to go collect seashells on the beach.

"Let mommy finish her breakfast, Jonah, okay? We'll go down soon. Why don't you draw a beautiful picture of the ocean and the sand and the birds as they fly by?"

"Okay, Mommy. I'll add a giant in my picture."

Another thing Denny and she discussed the previous evening. Barnum. The identical twin of the man sitting at the bar professed he didn't know them, and while Denny did not believe a word of this, she could not explain why SIMU-Barnum would need to lie about recognizing the two of them.

"Barnum is on the beach this morning, Mom."

"I don't think so, hon."

"Why? Where is he?"

She shrugged and mumbled a small prayer her son would soon forget the friendly giant. By the looks of it, last night's man at the bar did not appear chummy, and she didn't relish getting into another sordid situation with her son in tow. It was bad enough that she needed to contact her mother this morning to find out about possible legal representation in Puerto Vallarta. She didn't bother to ask anyone about Jed's whereabouts and wondered if he would give the training later this morning.

Millie downed the rest of her black coffee, which constituted her breakfast this morning—the strong coffee already serving to relieve some of her migraine. She got up and decided to wrap up the rest of her meal, and popped the food in the midsize refrigerator for later.

She checked her answering machine. She had three messages. One from Jed who told her, "I found Julie dead in my suite. I'm freaking out. Where are you for shit sake? I called police making sure not to touch anything. I told them you would provide me with an alibi."

The next message was from Diane, of Bill and Diane Hurley. "Will there be training tomorrow morning? We understand Jed got into a bit of a fix tonight. Give me a call."

The last message was from a stranger, appearing to be a woman's voice. "Stop pursuing him, or you'll be sorry."

This last message got her attention. The disguised voice sounded like Julie Swayzee's voice.

Her first instinct was to erase the message—the words of a dead woman's voice freaking her out almost as much as the thought of Ruiz coming across the news.

She had nothing to hide, and deleting Julie's message which eventually might leak out, would only serve to make her appear somewhat guilty.

She backed up from the answering machine as though the contraption might become a live grenade liable to explode at any moment.

What was going on? Why did her life suddenly take this *mucho* crappy outlook, and what did she need to do to stop the truckload of rotten luck dumped on her doorstep?

She caught a glimpse of Denny as she entered the room in her bathrobe, her long brown hair tied back in a ponytail.

"Good morning, sis. Oh, and hello, Jonah."

"Aunty Denny, I want to go to the beach. Will you help me build a sandcastle?"

"Sure, honey. What you got there?"

"I made a picture of the water and the birds. And here's Barnum, the big giant."

Denny stared at her aware she hadn't said a word. "Why are you looking at the answering machine like the thing is going to plug you? What's wrong, Millie?"

Millie smiled and indicated Jonah. "Nothing's wrong. I promised Jonah I'd go to the beach with him. Do you want to come?"

"Sure. Give me half an hour to have coffee, and I'll meet you guys down there."

"Good. Before you come down, make sure you listen to the answering machine."

What About Barnum?

Binary Bounty # 1

Denny's smile disappeared, and Millie realized she imagined the worst. Well, she would soon discover her worst might be less significant than the message of a dead woman threatening her to stay away from her husband.

Millie walked along the beach with Jonah by the hand, and her bag loaded with towels and sunscreen in the other. She'd also donned a packsack with bottles of water, and some dried fruits for Jonah to enjoy.

She located the palapa she used on most days and spread the towels on the ground. She dug out Jonah's red pail and new shovel so he could make a sandcastle.

"Let mommy put some lotion on you. I don't want you to burn."

"Ah, Mom. Not on my face. I hate it. Gets in my eyes."

"Mom will rub it all in, and it won't burn your eyes."

After the struggle to protect Jonah with sunscreen, she put some on herself. Even though her hair was much lighter than that of her sister Denny's hair, short, curly and streaked honey blond, and despite her green eyes, she never burned as most fair-haired people did. Still, she slathered on SPF fifty to be on the safe side.

"Barnum is over there, Mommy. I can see him. I'm going to ask him to help me build my sandcastle."

Millie laid her hand in front of her eyes only now realizing she forgot her hat at the concierge's office. The man some two hundred feet away did appear to resemble yesterday's Barnum.

She got up to run after Jonah before he reached him. "Oh, no you don't. You have to stay here, little one." When he pouted and fussed, before he could start screaming his discontentment, she smiled and looked into his eyes. "Jonah, you know how much Mommy loves to give you whatever you need, right?"

He didn't answer. He kicked at the sand tossing small pebbles Millie's way while the wind carried the little dust cloud the rest of the way.

Millie bent to be eye to eye with her son. "Grownups like Barnum have work to do. They can't always find the time to play, not as much as they would love to do so. Why don't we start the castle together and Aunty Denny is going to come down soon to give us a hand. Okay?"

"Okay. But we need to go close to the ocean to get wet sand. What happens if a wave takes me? Barnum is way over there. He won't be able to save me."

"Well, your mom is an excellent swimmer, and I'll be right beside you. Also, remember what I told you? At this time of day, the ocean is at low tide. Low tide means the waves are small and they don't come near the water's edge."

With all the confidence of a five-year-old, Jonah smiled. "Okay, Mommy. Let's build a castle together."

When Denny stepped on the beach, two images sprawled before her eyes, Millie and Jonah building a castle with a moat of wet sand around the first set of walls, and the man they called Barnum walking up the coastline in the opposite direction. She decided to run to accost him, and she stayed in the deep end of the sand not to attract her sister's attention which made running to catch up with Barnum much more challenging.

"Hey," she breathed panting and trying to haul air into her lungs. "Barnum, that is your name, right? Barnum?"

What About Barnum?

Binary Bounty # 1

"Hello again. Is there a problem?"

"You were at the Mandala Club last night. We saw you talking with another man at the bar."

"You mistook me for someone else."

"That was what you wanted us to believe, right? Rick Barry. I can understand you not wanting to give away who you are, but I recognized you last night, I'm sure."

Barnum lost his smile. "I'm afraid you made a mistake."

His eyes pierced through Denny's smugness and she hesitated. "Well, if this is so, let me tell you. You have a double somewhere in Puerto Vallarta."

"Possible," he smiled. "Would you like to see my driver's license?"

She laughed. "Unnecessary."

"How is your sister? How is the boy?"

"They're fine, although there has been a development."

"For instance?"

"Her boss' ex-wife was found murdered in his hotel room. She was interrogated by police last night as the man gave her name for the verification of his whereabouts."

"But she was nowhere near the place. The Mandala Club is a good twenty minutes away."

"How do you know where ..."

"You just told me. I'm sorry to hear about Millie. If I can be of any assistance, please let me know."

Denny wondered what sort of help a person like Barnum might be able to lend. Or was his offer along the lines of the simple rhetoric people often used as a means of sympathy.

"Sure. If I get caught in the surf, I'll make sure to give you a wave."

As she turned to join Millie and Jonah, she distinctly heard him chuckle.

By the time Denny reached her sister and nephew, their sand monument had two full walls erected and a deep-water moat surrounding the digs.

"Wow, this is some big castle, Jonah."

The little boy became very talkative, excited as he ran to the edge of the ocean to collect water in his pail. Slowly as not to spill, he walked to the sandcastle to dump the content of his bucket in the ditch his mother and he created. Every time he got up, he needed to raise his bathing suit caked with wet sand, as the suit would ride down his hips.

Before Denny found a place to sit, he brought back two more buckets of water.

"So, what did he say?" Millie looked up at her sister's sullen features as she stared out at the ocean.

"Who?" Denny turned and eyed the path she just walked and realized Millie spotted her. "Denies he was the one we talked to at the Club. Says his name is Barnum."

"Unbelievable, unless he has an identical twin." Millie sat down in the sand beside her sister. "Did you listen to the tape on the answering machine?"

"I did. You're going to need to call Mom."

"Yep. I also tried to reach Jed. He doesn't answer his cell phone."

"Maybe he's downstairs giving the training."

"I also called Bill and Diane while you were in the room,

What About Barnum?

the only two I could reach. They say they haven't seen or heard from Jed—not since last night when police came to investigate his ex-wife's murder."

"So, by now, everyone knows?" Denny picked up sand in her hand she allowed to trickle through her fingers.

"Pretty much. This sort of news spreads like cheap manure." Millie kept an eye on Jonah.

"Can you give the training?"

"I've given the training a couple of times, to a much smaller group, mind you. Still, to talk in front of an audience that size, a person needs charisma, aplomb. Jed would say balls the size of coconuts."

"You're a professor at Berkeley, and you ooze of charm and confidence. Look at you. Everyone is going to think you're beautiful."

"God, you're an easy grader." Millie rose and brushed the sand off her legs. "I'm going to go check on the status of this meeting. Can you keep an eye on Jonah?"

"Jonah, honey. Mommy needs to go to the hotel for a bit. Do you want to finish your castle with Aunty Denny?"

The little boy stopped and stared at his mom, then at his sand-castle. "I think I'd like to go to the playground inside."

"I'll bring you inside, Jonah," Denny told him. "First, we'll take that cool shower on the beach, then we'll add a top to that bathing suit, and you can play indoors with all your friends."

Her son's big smile confirmed he liked the suggestions. "I'll bring my backpack and leave you the bag with the towel and the bottled water."

"Go, go. I'll meet you in the room in an hour and a bit. Leave your cell phone on."

After a great big hug to Jonah, Millie slipped into her sarong and sandals and walked toward the conference room. The training didn't start for another fifteen minutes, so she took the elevator to the room, and slipped into a summer dress and a pair of shoes before she went down again.

She scoped out the people at the meeting, only a half a dozen or so. *Boy, bad news travels fast.*

She asked the seated group if they knew where everyone else was. One man stood and spoke frankly.

"Most of the people heard Jed might not be here this morning, so they took a free day to visit the city and get some sun. Some went snorkeling, and some went shopping."

"Well, this meeting will be postponed. I was prepared to do the training, but it's not productive to train six people, or is it? What do you think?"

The small group consulted with each other and shrugged. They apparently had nowhere to go.

"So, how about we convene here later this afternoon, and Jed or I will proceed with the training. Everyone in agreement?"

One woman stood. "Is it true Jed's been arrested for murder?"

"I have no information on what happened to Jed. If you exercise a little patience, I'm sure he'll fill you in on all the juicy details when he returns. Also, please make sure you tell everyone you recognize that the training will take place this afternoon."

She smiled and left before anyone else asked her the same burning questions she was not prepared to answer.

She stopped by the front desk asking when the marketing coordinator would be in his office. She needed him to put up an announcement in the lobby with the training's new schedule.

As she prepared to take the elevator, she bumped into Barnum. Surprised, all she could think to say, "Fancy meeting you here." She berated herself for finding him as handsome as she did. Just another man who possessed much too much charisma—bad sign. Dangerous sign.

"Pleasure," he emphasized staring deep into her eyes.

Happy her former beaus immunized her against this sort of behavior. She added, "I guess my sister told you we met your double last night at one of the clubs in town."

Millie picked up the slightest hesitation in his features, in his body language. Being accustomed to the world of students, some of them able to draw lies the size of houses, she realized for the half-a-second he fudged he was the man at the Club.

He didn't deny this. He smiled. "Sometimes depending on who we are with, anonymity is the best policy."

"Thank you for trusting me. I completely understand. Is your name Barnum?"

"Easier if you call me Barnum, for now."

"Sure." The elevator bell indicated all she needed to do was step inside and leave. Somehow his eyes held her, and she could not muscle the courage to break free. *Idiot, leave, just leave—leave.* With gumption she would be proud of later when rethinking about the incident, she turned and stepped into the elevator, even as he continued to stare at her. The only thing she would regret would be her appalling lack of manners. She never said goodbye.

Five

JED SWAYZEE

Millie paced back and forth her hotel room while Denny watched Jonah and a friend play with cars on the balcony.

No news from Jed. What does that mean? Millie stopped pacing and dropped on the sofa to calm down. She could easily lose it with all this trouble going on right now. Through the patio doors, Millie spotted Jonah laughing and smiled. Her son might be a handful, but he also kept her heart in good shape, and right now, he was the only one able to provide her with the courage she needed to telephone her mother. One of the top legal minds in the country, she would be able to give her valuable advice.

A half hour later, Millie stared at her cell phone as though she might wish to change the conversation she had shared with her mother. The sound of the patio door sliding open caught her attention. Denny walked in with concern stamped on her face. "What did Mom say? Did you guys have a bad connection or something? I could hear you through the door. You kept asking her to repeat."

"No. She spoke a little fast. You know how Mom gets when she's nervous or upset trying to solve a situation. She's like a bulldozer tumbling down a hill—so much information bombard-

What About Barnum?

ed me all at once. But mostly my lack of comprehension arose from Dad who kept badgering her in the background, telling Mom to order us back home, laughing at you and your poor decisions, saying I was a bad influence on you. Grueling to pick Mom's bullet -like sentences out of the jumble."

Denny couldn't help a giggle. "Don't let him get to you. You have enough problems right now."

"Oh, right, not the least of them being Mom and Dad threatening to come down here."

"No. *Padres* wouldn't come down here, would they?"

"You know them as well as I do. It was a little early to be calling—I forgot about the two-hour time difference. I told Mom coming down here was unnecessary and we would manage. She did tell me to speak to Ruiz and let him know about the calls on the machine."

"What about representation?"

"She mentioned she would contact a few criminal lawyers but reminded me this was Mexico and they didn't always play fair."

"I think Ruiz is a good man. When you call him, you should ask him about Jed. If we need to pay a fine to let him out, we should know what that is."

Millie gave her the nod. "Can you go out there and keep the little boys entertained. I don't want Jonah catching any of my conversation with Ruiz."

Millie waited on the line for Capitán Ruiz, five minutes or so. When he came to the phone, and she repeated who was calling, she had the distinct impression he did not remember her.

"Yes, Ms. Brewer. What can I do for you?"

She told him about finding the calls on her machine when she came home the previous evening and thought he should know since the voice message might help him with his investigation.

"Thank you. How certain are you the disguised woman's voice belongs to the victim?"

"I'm not. I guess the one person who would be able to confirm this with more certainty would be her ex-husband. I only met her once." She paused, knowing Ruiz was taking notes. "By the way, what happened to Jed Swayzee? He never gave the training he was supposed to give this morning at the hotel."

"He was released early morning. His lawyer flew in last night from San Francisco, so he must be in his room sleeping or plotting with his lawyer."

Plotting with his lawyer? She wondered what the officer meant using this expression. "Thank you, Capitán Ruiz."

"By the way, Ms. Brewer. Mr. Swayzee alleged that you and his ex-wife did not get along. She apparently blamed you for their breakup."

"Capitán Ruiz, I met Mr. Swayzee's ex-wife once. We were dating at the time, but Jed had been divorced well over a year. We became friends after a couple of dates—instead of lovers, and I told you why. I have a son, and he is the most important man in my life right now. We dated for two weeks. Since February, we have been merely friends."

"Beware of slick, well-paid lawyers, Ms. Brewer. I thought you should know." He hung up and when Millie put the phone down her hand shook.

She came close to telling the officer: "The truth is, Jed Swayzee hated his wife. He said she was trying to bleed him dry after

What About Barnum?

the divorce," but she held her tongue. She was not going to stoop to Jed's level.

Millie couldn't even get her feet to move away from the phone. Her back facing the patio doors when she heard her son laugh, she broke down and cried. The door opened, and Millie hoped it might be Denny and not Jonah asking for something to eat.

Denny walked over to her and Millie stubbornly stayed with her face in her hands, unwilling to let her sister see how upset she was.

"Millie, what's wrong?"

Not to let her imagine the worst, Millie turned to relate the captain's warning.

"I can't believe Jed is trying to implicate you. Talk about Mexican police not being fair. Amazingly decent of Capitán Ruiz to warn you. He didn't have to, you know." Denny rubbed her back to get the circulation going again since she had a bad case of the shivers.

"By the way," Denny added, "This type of comportment may mean Jed is scared out of his wits, or he did kill his ex-wife and now needs a patsy. Either way, I don't think he's good company anymore."

"Listen, I appreciate your help. I do. I don't like to jump to conclusions about Jed or anyone. I'm going to talk to him first and find out what this is all about."

"Fine, do what you want. But, if authorities believe I am your only alibi, they might try to blame me for trying to protect you."

Jonah came running in with his toy cars, his friend Jose right behind him. "Look, Mommy, we made a road out on the balcony with bridges and ramps to make them jump."

"That's wonderful, Jonah." Millie eyed the chair cushions and the flower pots in a jumble all over the balcony.

She sighed exhaling the weight of the world off her shoulders.

"Don't worry about the balcony. I'll fix the mess."

Millie walked aimlessly around her hotel room while Denny made a game of picking up the cushions on the patio.

Millie couldn't crank up the courage to call back her mother. Enough parent trauma for one day. The last thing she wanted was her mother and father flying down here in a huff, taking over this volatile situation.

Jed leaves me a message but doesn't call me back. Why? Millie stopped pacing and dropped onto the sofa to contemplate her options. *Maybe I shouldn't call him. But, something tells me this may be a misunderstanding.* Millie tried Jed's number to no avail. After sitting for a while in complete despair, she stood and got herself something to drink. Her mouth was dry and parched, and the stressful situation would ruin her health if she didn't find the means to calm down. She walked over to the patio and signaled to Denny to come in.

Denny must have realized how haggard she appeared because she tried so steer the conversation into another direction. "So, you bumped into Barnum?"

Millie gave her sister a reproving look. "Barnum is not part of this equation. Yes, he admitted he lied last night, but right now I'm more worried about Jed."

She sighed attempting to exhale her troubles. "Can you help me check something before I go up to the man's room and wring

What About Barnum?

his neck?"

"Sure, what can I do?"

"Call Jed's room, let's say from the restaurant? Or from anywhere else than here, and not from your cell phone."

"You think he's not answering because he recognizes your room number? or your cell?"

Millie nodded. "If he does answer, just hang up, don't talk to him. Call me right away, and I will try to reach him."

"Okay, give me five."

Denny left, and Millie waited for her return. While she did, she made the two boys sandwiches and some lemonade.

Then Denny called the room to confirm Jed answered his phone on the second ring and to try him now.

Millie did, but Jed never picked up.

When Denny came back into the room, she found Millie at the little glass table serving the kids their lunch. She threw in a couple of bags of potato chips with this, and they were thrilled, both talking all at once about the big giant on the beach.

"So?"

Millie shook her head side to side while smiling at Jonah blowing bubbles in his lemonade with his straw.

"Listen, honey. The way Jed is acting might mean his lawyer asked him not to talk to you."

"This doesn't make sense. The place is full of people. He can't just ignore them. And when he talks to them, he'll be reachable. Also, I can easily attend the meetings and bombard him with questions."

"If you do, the gesture might make you look desperate and a little bit crazy."

"Wait a minute." Millie looked up at her. "How did you get his room number. I didn't give it to you."

"Well, I called the front desk and asked them to put me through to Jed Swayzee."

"Ah, I'm stupid. No wonder Jed's not answering. They gave him another room by now, most likely this morning when he returned from the police station. His old suite is surely off limits for the investigation."

"My God, you're right."

"He must think I'm giving him the silent treatment or … worse." She stared into Denny's eyes pleading for help.

Denny took the lemonade pitcher from her to refill the boys' glasses. "Call him. Get this out in the open. Start a frank discussion with Jed. You'll feel better, and I'm sure he will too."

"I don't want to discuss this over the phone. I'm going to set up a meeting somewhere on the beach away from prying ears, and I hope you can be there too."

"Arrange this. I'll go with you." Denny took a chair and sat down beside the boys. "By the way, I noticed your sign for training was up downstairs for the Herbal Organics Group. The training starts at three p.m. This leaves you a little wiggle room to set up the meeting, but you need to hurry."

Millie opted for the balcony to make her call to Jed. "Hi, it's me."

"Where the hell have you been? I left you a message, and you never called me back."

"I was calling your old room. And your cell phone is dead. Keeps going to voicemail."

"May as well be dead. I lost it in the commotion last night. I had the hardest time getting a hold of my lawyer. And I'm mad at you. You were supposed to be at the meeting yesterday. Were you sick or something? Last night was a big do. I was counting on you."

She sighed, holding her tongue. "Can we talk about what happened, face to face?"

"I guess we should—if only to get our stories straight."

"You've got that training at three o'clock."

"Yeah. I know. Thanks for doing that by the way—rescheduling the session."

"I was prepared to do it myself, but when I got to the hall, I counted six or seven people, tops. I guess everyone heard about what happened and figured they could take a day off or something."

"Can we meet in front of the tiki bar in five?"

Millie released a big sigh. "Sure. I'll be there."

"Alone, please. I beg you not to bring your nosy sister, Denny."

Millie hesitated. "Okay, in five."

Millie repeated the call to her sister, Denny's terror-stricken eyes assuring Millie, Denny would not let her go alone. "You can't be serious."

"You can't come. We're meeting in front of the margarita bar on the beach. There's no cover. He'll spot you right away."

"Okay. Wait here." When Denny came back from rummaging in her suitcase, she handed Millie a little device.

"What's this?"

"A digital recorder."

Millie's turn to be wide-eyed and panic-stricken. "Whatever

for? You carry this with you?"

"I used it all the time when I visited clients. They were always very impressed about how much detail I remembered about their projects. Not illegal to do this without permission as long as you don't use the information as any proof of wrong doing. Would not be admissible in court, although the information would be enough to sway police to begin an investigation should one be warranted."

"You're more like Mom than I thought."

"I thought of going into law. But, Mom's already the best criminal mind in the country, so how do you compete with that?"

"I have to go. Where do I put this?"

"Little recorder has a long range. You can drop it inside a pocket, and you'll get good reception. Your dress pocket will do fine."

Millie reached for the little recorder. "Is it on?"

Denny flicked a small switch. "It is now. Good luck."

Millie gave her sister a hug. "Please keep an eye on Jonah. He can be a handful at this time of day."

BUMPING INTO BARNUM

Millie walked along the beach in her flip-flops and brightly colored summer dress, having retrieved her hat from the concierge to block most of the glare from the sun on her face and shoulders.

She donned a pair of sunglasses to help with the noon light ricocheting off minuscule glass pebbles in the light cream sand and peered for Jed as she neared the tiki hut. The place lay deserted at this time of day, but an attendant still sat in the shade ready to hand out refreshments and icy treats.

She couldn't spot Jed and wondered if she was too late. Perhaps thinking she wasn't coming, he scurried away, the heat too hard to handle for very long at this time of day.

She did catch sight of Barnum walking out of the sea at the same spot where he saved Jonah's life the day before. She started to raise her hand to wave when she spotted him looking her way but curtailed the gesture. She waited for Jed, and she got the distinct impression when Barnum spoke to her the day before he wished to remain unseen.

Cupping her hand in front of her face to avoid the effect of the breeze swirling the sand up and around her face, she turned and stared at the hotel to see if she could spot Jed walking toward her. As she did, Millie continued to walk a backward trek toward the tiki bar thinking Jed might be waiting at the back of the shack to take advantage of the shade provided by the overhang of the thatched roof.

While her eyes scoured the horizon around the hotel, she kept moving toward their scheduled rendezvous when Millie bumped into somewhat of a wall.

A little scream escaped her. Turning to gaze at the offending impasse, she found herself inches away from Barnum. "God, what are you doing here?"

"Wasn't sure if that was you under the hat. Wanted to say hello."

"Had you known I was the one under the hat, would you have still wanted to say hello?"

He smiled. Something magnetic about him, Millie thought. She held back a sigh while staring into his eyes.

"Of course. I hoped it was you, Millie."

His words brought on the butterflies, full grown with their wings spreading little goosebumps all over her arms and neck in this hot weather. She spotted the tiny bathing suit he'd worn the day before, and shyness crept into her gestures.

"Well, I'm meeting someone here, at the tiki bar." She hesitated, but smiled as she added, "My boss, so to speak, and he is in a bit of a quandary at the moment."

"Is this about the murder at the hotel? I understand police may hold a suspect in hand—a man irate with his ex-wife?"

"Jed is not a suspect. Hundreds of people can vouch for his whereabouts at the time of his ex-wife's murder. Police interrogated him last night and released him." Millie could not understand why

What About Barnum?

Binary Bounty # 1

she provided this information to Barnum, but his proximity made her giddy, and she needed to distract attention from the fact she was melting under his gaze. She also wondered why Barnum called him flat out a suspect. How would he know anything?

"Do you think it's a good idea for you to meet him alone?"

"Well, I'm sure he's not guilty of any such crime. He asked that we meet alone so as not to be disturbed."

She caught Barnum's frown. "I will be close by should you need any help." He gave her a small salute and walked back toward the beach.

Millie watched him go and took off her hat to fan herself with the wide brim. Too much of a hunk for any woman, she would never consider inviting a man like Barnum into her life. *Jonah is smitten with him.* No, she scolded herself for letting the thought creep into her consciousness. For Jonah's sake, this was about avoiding the mistake she made when falling for Todd Winters, the hunk of a man everyone told her would break her heart—and who did. He shattered her confidence, her joie de vivre, and no matter how much she loved Jonah and found solace in her life now, the inkling of failure still loomed. Despite all her accomplishments, Jonah needed to spend his life without the love of a father.

Someone called her name. She turned and found Jed running in the sand, still behind her, the one who was late.

She stayed put as there was no point going all the way to the tiki bar. Looking at Jed running up the shore, she thought: more muscles. Muscles, broad shoulders, broad back, and long, muscular legs. She stared up at the bright blue sky imploring the heavens to answer why. Why did the universe contrive to send her all the wrong men, the gorgeous, hard-to-resist Adonis types who could not hold a candle to Jonah's needs? As for her needs, she wanted a man she could count on come hell or high water. Not someone forever on the prowl and looking to score. As he came closer, she wondered why all he wore was a pair of boxers he used as a bathing suit. He never took the time to slip on a shirt.

"Sorry I'm late," he said a little out of breath. "I took count of what I needed for the meeting. I left my projector in my old room. The hotel marketing manager is still trying to find me a new one."

"Well, I'm sorry about your ex-wife. I know you two didn't get along, but no one should ever meet with that type of fate. What happened?"

"I didn't even know she was coming. She never mentioned it. So I was shocked when I finished downstairs and found her in my living room, dead. I called the police right away."

"Has the investigation revealed anything?"

"Well, so far, they've established the time of death somewhat, between eight forty-five and nine thirty. Tons of people gave testimony I was downstairs until ten." He eyed her slightly morose. "Where were you? I thought you were in your room, sick or something. That's the excuse I gave everyone when they asked why you weren't there to pick up your award."

Millie took off her hat letting it hang down her back. "Jonah nearly drowned yesterday afternoon, around four o'clock."

"What?"

She nodded "If it hadn't been for this man who came out of the surf holding him in his arms, I was going in after him, and I

What About Barnum?

would have saved him or perished."

"How did this happen?"

"I was on a three-way call with Diane and her friend who lives here, trying to explain the product and the marketing plan, and Jonah got away from me. He ran toward the escarpment lifeguards have told us to avoid."

"The one northwest of the tiki bar?"

"Yeah. When that wave grabbed my son," Millie stopped to wipe tears running down her cheeks. "I thought he was a goner. But then this man walked out of the wave with Jonah in his arms and my son appeared to be fine."

"Waves were tall yesterday, I remember. A wave grabbed him, and someone fished him out of the water—where the slope is rocky, and coral litters the ground?"

"Yeah. Don't bother asking how. Denny and I can't answer that question. No one can."

"You should have told me." Jed came closer and gently took Millie in his arms. "I wish you would confide in me more. I realize we're just friends now, but you should unburden yourself more often. I can take it." He smiled and pecked her lips. "Wouldn't mind if we were more than good friends actually, now that my neurotic wife is out of the picture."

Millie took a step back to move out of his arms. "Well, to answer your question, this is not something a person likes to admit. I felt like a bad mother, unsure and depressed. I wanted to hide away and never show my face again."

"Are you crazy? You're a great mother."

"Nevertheless, Denny thought she could cheer me up by taking me dancing, getting my mind off the place, the circumstances. In a way, this helped. Then when I came back around ten thirty, police surrounded the hotel."

"I called them a little past ten."

"Listen, why did you tell your lawyer Julie blamed me for breaking up your marriage?"

"I didn't tell him that. He misunderstood. I said my womanizing broke up my marriage. He assumed the rest. Don't worry. I already cleared this up with Ruiz. By the way, he says you have a strange message on your machine I need to decipher? You told him you thought it might be Julie?"

"Yeah, but now I'm not sure. The message came after yours. Don't voicemails follow the order in which they arrive? I don't know about machines. I never owned one."

"I don't either. Might be an older message you never picked up. Anyway, let's start walking back. I have to hurry, and I hope for all our sakes the marketing team found another projector."

"If they haven't, I gave this training already without visual aids. I can help you."

"Would you? That would be much appreciated."

They walked back Jed's arm wrapped solicitously around her waist, and Millie did not move away, taking pity on him and the hard times befalling him. She tried to imagine how she would feel tripping on Todd's dead body in her hotel room, and since Millie could not visualize the image without gagging and dizziness overcoming her, she held more sympathy for Jed.

Before they entered the lobby, she needed to ask. "Do police have any clues as to what might have happened to Julie?"

"Well, Ruiz says there has been a rash of robberies of late in some of the penthouse suites of the better hotels. Guests seemed to be out when the perps enter the room. Last night, I was out, only Julie's arrival was not scheduled. They think she may have surprised the burglars or the other way around."

"A bullet?"

"Multiple knife wounds."

"God! Did they take anything?"

"No, this is what seems odd, unless they took something from Julie. She had to be traveling with at least a carrying case. We found none."

Millie kept silent about Julie's pink case, and as both entered the lobby, they jogged to the first elevator they found. "You coming up to my room first?" Millie asked.

"Yeah, let's do this. Can't stay, though."

Inside, Millie called out to Denny and Jonah, but no response came. She figured they were downstairs at the pool or in the playroom staying out of the sun.

Millie played the message for Jed, and he asked to listen to it again.

"Not Julie. I can swear to this. Even when someone disguises their voice, you can usually find something familiar to identify them. Not her."

"Well, the only solution left is that someone called the wrong room. I have no idea who this is, and I have not pursued anyone in months—not since you and I were dating."

"Wow, I'm flattered." He came a little closer the sex-crazed expression on his face stirring caution inside her. "You're going to be late."

"Right." He seemed to collect his thoughts. "You going to help?"

"Absolutely. Let me find Denny and Jonah, and I'll be right with you."

Millie went to the pool and found a few people lounging in the sun and wading in the water, but no Denny and no Jonah.

She then went to the inside playroom and when she didn't find them there, hurried to the front desk. "Excuse me, did my sister Denny Brewer leave a note for me, Millie Brewer?"

The desk clerk checked and came back with a smile, handing Millie a note from Denny.

Did you know there is a movie theater in town? Not eight minutes from the Hotel by cab? Jonah, his friend Jose and I are watching the animated feature Jonah and I missed last year. The Good Dinosaur. Hope you don't mind. I will be back in a couple of hours. Thought you could use this time to yourself to get a massage or sit poolside. Please don't worry. Love, Denny.

Millie breathed a little more comfortably. She was dying to relate to Denny her meeting with Jed, but this would have to wait. Instead, she needed to live up to her promise. She hurried to the conference room to help Jed.

***

Denny walked out of the theater with one little boy in each hand. They were exuberant and excited, so she understood they needed strict supervision.

Jonah stopped walking, lamenting about the sand in his shoe hurting his foot when he walked.

Denny bent to check it out. "This is why, Jonah, you should never wear your running shoes on the beach." She undid the

What About Barnum?

Binary Bounty # 1

straps to Jonah's shoes and told him to hold Jose's hand and to hold on to her collar tightly.

"Why, Aunty Denny?"

"There are a lot of people here, and it's easy for a big group like this to sweep you away." She shook the right shoe and couldn't believe the amount of sand that fell on the ground. "I'll have to brush off your sock. Then we'll do the other one."

As she looked up to make sure Jose was still paying attention and holding Jonah's hand, she spotted the man who stole her purse—the one who patiently waited for her to run after him. She stopped brushing her nephew's sock and told him to put his shoe back on.

"I'll have to let go of Jose's hand, Aunt Denny."

Denny kept hidden and crouched on the ground. "Jose, hold my collar with a firm hand," she told him. As Jonah put his shoe back on, she stared at the man. No doubt about the profile and she recognized the jewelry in his ear, the one she spotted during the light flashes at the club and later when he waited for her under a street light. She wouldn't have remembered, but now eyeing the earrings for the second time, she did. Two gold hoops in one ear while one of the circles had some charm dangling from it. What disconcerted Denny most was the man's police uniform—same one worn by Ruiz's officers.

"How's the other shoe, Jonah?"

"It's okay, Aunt Denny. The other one Mom emptied when I came back from the beach."

Denny hesitated to rise. The man occupied one of the exits at the theater complex and was deep into conversation with another policeman. She needed to head back to the hotel without being seen while towing two boisterous little boys.

She picked up her cell and dialed the same number she composed to get to the theater, calling the cab driver who'd taken her to police headquarters the night before. Alejandro was friendly, polite, and very grateful she chose him to chauffeur them around.

When he got there, she rose and quickly shuffled the little boys inside. She eyed the policeman one last time from the safety of the car, to commit to memory all she could about his features.

Seven

Caroline Stuart Brewer

*J*ust as Denny stepped out of the cab, her cell phone rang. She answered while paying Alejandro, thanking him with a big smile. She grasped the hand of both boys in her left hand while slipping her phone into her pocket and turning on her Bluetooth. "Capitán Ruiz, great. What a coincidence. I was just about to call you."

"I have tried to reach you or your sister for the past couple of hours, Ms. Brewer."

"My sister is giving a presentation at the hotel, and I was at the theater with my nephew and one of his friends. What's this about?"

"Evidence turned up in the case of the woman murdered at your hotel. I need to talk to you and your sister, Millie. Please come down to the station as I cannot remove the evidence from the premises."

"We will need to find a sitter for Jonah, and I will locate my sister. I will call you back promptly."

Denny hung up the phone wondering what could be wrong. Worried about Millie, she was dying to listen to the recorded conversation with Jed hoping she had not turned the recorder off after the session.

Millie finally shook the last guest's hand. Having done most of the presentation, she allowed randomly selected people to try the product and ask questions about the marketing plan. Jed finished with his personal sales pitches, and the two recruited quite a few members. As for Jed, he briefly mentioned to the crowd how he found his ex-wife in his room dead and called the police. Police thought this was related to burglaries which had occurred in several big hotels lately. A few questions arose, either out of respect or out of lack of interest. People were more interested in what they offered.

Now, Millie couldn't wait to get back to her room to chat with her sister.

"Listen, before you go, Millie, my lawyer wants to ask you a few questions. Do you have a couple of minutes?"

To Millie, the request sounded strange although not strictly out of left field. "Jed, I need to get back to my son. We are going out to dinner. Then, he's had a big day, so he'll need a bath and a couple of the usual stories to put him to sleep."

"Yeah, I get it. Perhaps after dinner when Jonah's down?"

"Sure. I'll give you a call."

"Thanks for your help today. You saved my ass."

She smiled but left promptly.

Upstairs in the room, she exhaled with relief. Denny was back. "I called you not five minutes ago. I worried when I couldn't get an answer."

"I went upstairs to drop off Jose. His mother appreciates the attention we've been giving him and offered to take Jonah with them tomorrow. The whole family is going on a pirate tour of the islands. The show is for children between five and nine, so it might be fun

What About Barnum?

for Jonah."

"Well, I'll call her later to thank her. With everything that's going on, I don't know if I can accept the invitation, Denny."

"What do you mean?"

Jonah came running in from the balcony and gave his mother a big squeeze. "Wish you were at the movie, Mommy. Best dinosaur ever. You would love him."

"You're lucky, Jonah. Mommy is happy you had fun."

Her son's little face stared at her while his big brown eyes peered into hers. "I don't mind going to see it again if you like?"

Millie's heart melted, and she couldn't help a big smile, hugging him for his sweet offer. "Sounds like fun, Jonah. How about you go color on the balcony, and after, we'll go for dinner."

"Okay, Mommy."

"Don't worry about dinner. The boys had tons of popcorn and two small bags of chocolate candy."

Millie handed the recorder to her sister. "Didn't turn it off. Thought we might get more out of listening to everything that went on."

"Hoped you might do that." Denny reached for the recorder and checked the time span on the screem "Started when you left the room and finished right ... now." She pressed the stop button. She rewound to the earlier part of the afternoon and got a repeat of Jed and his conversation.

"Don't like his explanation about the lawyer. Sounds phony." Denny listened to more of the recording, and almost screamed her discontentment. "He can't be serious—you two as a couple?"

"He talks a big game. Don't worry. I'm not buying."

Denny fast forwarded the presentation except for a minute or two of her sister's performance. "Wow, you're excellent."

"Get to the end quickly."

"What? His lawyer wants to ask you a few questions?" Her sister was outraged at the idea. "No way. Is he nuts? The lawyer who conveniently misunderstood and gave Ruiz false information about you? You shouldn't answer any of his questions." Denny hit her forehead with her right palm. "Oh, I can't believe I forgot."

"What?"

"Ruiz phoned me just as I was coming in. He's been trying to reach us for the last couple of hours. I gave him an account of our whereabouts and …" Denny hesitated. "He said more evidence turned up on last night's murder and he wants to see us both. He said he wouldn't come here because he can't remove the evidence from the premises."

Millie flopped on the first chair she found. "I can't believe this. He's never going to leave us alone, is he?"

"When he called, I remember thinking I wished Mom had made good on her threat—you know about coming down here."

"We're in serious trouble, aren't we?"

"Let's not panic before he gives us the facts. He may need our help."

"Yes, but if we go down there and they decide to hold us, they'll put us in jail which I heard from Manuela is a very unsanitary place."

"Speaking of Manuela how do we get in touch with her?"

"She doesn't get to the hotel before seven. I hope she didn't schedule her time for someone else."

What About Barnum?

Binary Bounty # 1

"If worse comes to worst, we can always ask Jose's mother if Jonah can sleep over after dinner."

"I'll call Ruiz. I want to gauge how serious this is by the tone of his voice." Millie told her sister.

Before she could pick up the receiver, the phone rang.

"Two short rings, inside call," Denny told her.

"Jed. Wanting to firm up tonight's meeting," Millie said before she picked up.

"Hello—Mom? Where are you calling from?" Millie gave Denny the wide eyes.

"I'm a couple of doors down from you, honey. Took the first plane available this morning and arrived this afternoon. I tried to reach you girls for hours."

"Well, your timing couldn't be better. We need to go to the police station tonight."

"Stay where you are. I'm taking my grandson and my two daughters to dinner, and you'll fill me in on all the details."

"Is Dad with you?"

"No. Your dad is preparing study guides for the Creative Writing Department and couldn't get away. It's better your father stays behind. He would only muddle everything."

"Thanks, Mom. See you in a bit."

Jonah came running in to show his drawing. "Look, Mom. This one is for you."

"Wow, this is wonderful, Jonah. You drew a big dinosaur."

"And a baby dinosaur, see? Just like you and me." He hugged his mother, and Millie held on to him, so grateful this kind and thoughtful son was a part of her life.

Denny whispered, "Listen, it might be better to go downstairs right now and get a bite to eat with Jonah. Then when Manuela arrives, she can stay with him while you, Mom and I go to dinner before we meet with Ruiz. We'll be more at ease to talk without little pointy ears listening in."

"Would you like to watch your favorite show on the big TV in mommy's room, Jonah?" Millie asked him. "Starts in a few minutes. I will get you settled in, and after your show, we'll go to dinner."

He nodded his little face utterly happy. "Can I have the chicken with fries, Mommy?"

"Of course, sweetie."

Millie closed her eyes and took a deep breath. Her mother's arrival had lifted an enormous weight off her shoulders. "You're right. Mom said she is a couple of doors down. Please call her room to tell her to come whenever she's ready, and we'll go downstairs with Jonah. Meanwhile, I'll call Ruiz."

Finally tucked away Jonah slept soundly after his big day. The three women left Manuela in charge and headed for the shrimp and sushi bar. "Are you sure you like this type of food, Mom? You don't usually enjoy seafood."

"It's fine, Millie. I do like fish from time to time, quite the brain food I need about now. Tell me, how did you girls ever step into so much aggravation?" She shook her head, her nose up in the air, yet the love in her eyes unmistakably shining.

Millie slipped her arm around her waist and hugged her. "Long story, Mom, very long story—compounded aggravation."

When Millie finished relating the last few days' events, the

What About Barnum?

Binary Bounty # 1

trip to the Mandala Club, including Denny's purse being cut right out from under her, she glanced at Denny who gave her the silent head tilt, meaning she should spill every little detail about the delightful, awful day.

"There is something else, Mom. Not something I like to talk about, but Denny thinks it might be relevant." She took a deep breath and admitted to Jonah's near drowning. Like someone about to receive a punch in the gut, she toughened her stance and waited.

"Well, I'm not surprised. My little grandson inherited my sweet temperament, but your father's penchant for mischief. The other reason I came down here I fear. The man's constant reprimands of you two drove me barmy."

The comment so out of left field had the girls stare at each other and laugh outright. Millie knew her mother reverted to British terms when she was upset and realized Denny faced the same musings she did. Their father, Alan Brewer's puckered face and unruly brows, running around rambunctious in the same way Jonah did.

"Never mind your father. Tell me about this man who saved my grandson's life."

Millie did, not sparing details about his looks and his kindness toward her.

"Can't say I blame him," Caroline grasped her daughter's chin. "Is there any man alive capable of resisting this beautiful face and sweet disposition? I doubt it."

"Mom," Millie protested. "I don't think about Barnum that way."

Caroline raised her chin to look down at her daughter. "This is your mother you're addressing, young lady. I know you inside out. What else do you know about him?"

"Not even a last name," Denny supplied.

"Let your sister tell me, please."

Millie realized Caroline Stuart Brewer, the star debater, interpreted every word she said, including the accompanying body language. No wonder she couldn't hide anything from her mother.

She recounted their meeting at the beach and what Barnum said to her.

Denny leaned forward wiping shrimp from her hands. "Wait a minute. Was this today?"

"Yeah, on the beach."

"When did you speak to Barnum on the beach today?"

"Before Jed reached me. I arrived maybe five minutes before he did and Barnum was coming out of the water at the exact spot where he saved my son's life." Millie turned to her mother. "I forgot to mention. The slope where the wave swept Jonah away is marked off with a danger sign. There are strong rip currents in the area, and debris and sharp coral rocks litter the ocean floor. No one can even walk there."

"You can't have spoken to Barnum today," Denny argued. She rummaged in her purse and pulled out the recorder she loaned Millie. "Since you say you talked to him before Jed arrived, his voice should be on the recorder. It's not."

"Can't be. Here I thought you skipped over this part since Barnum wasn't in our plan."

Denny shook her head side to side, her wide eyes attempting to depict the seriousness of the situation.

What About Barnum?

Caroline stared at them appalled. "You recorded Jed's meeting on the beach?"

"Yeah, Mom," Denny answered.

"Well, I never!"

"It's not illegal to record someone without their permission if the recording is not going to be used against them."

"Denise Brewer," she enunciated her sister's name. "I have never been prouder of you. The fruit did not fall far from the tree, it would seem."

Denny laughed. "Yes. You handed out good advice over the years. I used it to record my clients' wishes with their projects. They were always impressed with my phenomenal memory."

Caroline laughed. She wiped her mouth, having finished her salmon *en croûte*, and added with her hands and both thumbs up in the air, "So summing up, there's a man, a gorgeous one at that." She eyed Millie. "A man with no last name, who can walk through rip currents over debris and coral and whose voice cannot be recorded." She nodded repeatedly. "Now, you have a story, my angels."

"Mom, this is not about Barnum. He doesn't figure in the problem I am facing."

"Oh, and Mom, he was at the Mandala Club." Denny smiled, wagging her eyebrows up and down at Millie.

Caroline stared at Millie. "Was he?"

"Yes. But Barnum refused to be recognized by us when we walked over to say hello. He told me the next day it was because he didn't want his identity revealed to the man he was chatting with."

"I must meet this man. Most interesting. Might be the solution to all your problems."

"Mom. Barnum is not the answer to my problems. Yes, he is the gorgeous man who saved Jonah's life. He has nothing to do with Jed or Jed's ex-wife."

"Sweetheart, I know you're upset, and I don't blame you. But, even you must realize this man seems to appear wherever you are. He might not be able to provide you with an alibi, considering his anonymity issues, but perhaps he's come across the information you seek about this murder."

"Mom comes up with a winning idea." Denny smiled

"I'll have you know, young lady, all my thoughts are winning ones."

"Yes Ma'am," was all Denny dared to answer.

"Mom, please don't tell the police about him. Might jeopardize whatever he is trying to do."

"Fair enough. Now, let's go see this Capitán Ruiz and teach him proper manners."

Millie refused to warn her mother how careful she needed to be, being in Mexico the land where las policías appeared to be always right and able to defend their point of view against anyone or anything. Of course, they'd never encountered Caroline Stuart Brewer. Millie suddenly experienced new respect for Capitán Ruiz.

—Eight—

BREWERS AND CAPITÁN RUIZ

Alejandro stopped the cab in front of the police station, and Caroline paid him and thanked him with a pat on the shoulder.

A hand on the door handle, Denny paused seemingly in no hurry to move.

"What are you waiting for, Denny?" Millie read the concern on her sister's face.

"The man standing over by the door to the police precinct is the man who stole my purse and ran that night," she whispered.

"How can you be sure?" Millie wanted to know.

"You caught sight of him when he stood under those lights, I suppose," Caroline said.

"Yes, and he was also at the door of the theater complex when I came out with Jonah and Jose this afternoon." Denny turned to stare at her sister and mother.

"Did he spot you?" Millie's heart sank.

"I don't think so. But I did. The man wears two earrings on his right earlobe, and one of them dangles some little charm."

Denny turned toward Alejandro whom she had learned to appreciate in the past few days. "Excuse me, Alejandro. Can you make out the man in front of the doors talking to someone? Is he familiar to you?"

"Ah, *sí*. The man is *Oficial de Policía* Jose Fernandez—a friend of Capitán Ruiz. He is on patrol, undoubtedly waiting for his partner."

The three women eyed each other. Millie was first to recover. "What do we do now?"

"We go and have a nice chat with Ruiz," her mother answered. "We make sure we retrieve your passport. In any case, you two will need to let me do the talking, agreed?"

Both girls nodded.

Caroline stared at Denny and nodded toward Alejandro.

Her mother needed something else, but what? Denny gave her mother a sign she understood. "Alejandro, is there another way into the police station?"

The taxi driver smiled the only sign of his curiosity in the raised eyebrows. "At the back, in the alley, but you would need to ring for someone to let you in."

"Bring us there, please." Caroline's tone did not waver.

Alejandro obeyed promptly and waited to leave until someone did answer the door and the policewoman allowed them inside.

"You need to come to the front door next time," she said in perfect English.

"Thank you," Millie answered. "We will."

In the foyer, they waited for Ruiz. While they did, Millie could not peel her eyes off the front door, worrying Jose Fernandez might come back inside. Ten minutes passed, and Millie began chewing her nails. She sensed her mother's hand on her arm and her reproving eyes on the fingers.

What About Barnum?

Binary Bounty # 1

"Thanks, Mom. Nerves are taking over."

Five more minutes with her eyes on the door and an officer came to lead them to Capitán Ruiz.

Ruiz stood when the three came through his door. "Señora, Señoritas." He extended his hand toward the three chairs in front of him.

Then he rose to open the doors to a cabinet. Out of the cupboard, he wheeled the pink suitcase Julie Swayzee had brought into the hotel that night.

"Recognize this?" Ruiz stood the case and reached for the zipper.

"Yes," Millie answered. "The case Julie Swayzee carried into the hotel, at least it looks like it. I never studied the thing up close."

Ruiz opened the case, and inside he reached for an object he handed to Denny. "Go ahead you can take it. We dusted for prints."

"My purse," she said picking up the evening bag with pieces of leather strap jagged and uneven still wound into the gold hoops on each side of the bag. "How did my purse find its way inside Julie Swayzee's suitcase?"

"My question, Señorita."

Caroline put up her hand to prevent her daughter from adding anything. "Quite easy to explain. The man who grabbed the suitcase in Mrs. Swayzee's room and the one who stole my daughter's purse is the same person. The knife he used to cut the straps of this bag may also be the murder weapon."

"Possible." Ruiz indicated they rise and follow him through another door.

After a few questioning stares, Caroline put a finger in front of her lips to remind her daughters to be silent.

Ruiz nodded. "I would like you to follow me to the evidence room where I will ask you to identify some of the things that were in the purse."

But the room next door was not the evidence room. Caroline waited until Ruiz closed the door then said, "Soundproof booth. You do have something to communicate."

"Yes." He sat down and indicated the chairs in front of his desk. He opened a drawer and handed Millie back her passport.

Millie took it with a sigh of relief and a shaky hand.

"We checked with the Marriott and their taxi cab service going in and out. The time you two booked the ride to the Mandala checks out. The time you came back, Señorita Millie Brewer is also recorded and correct. We also verified your story Señorita Denny Brewer, and Alejandro testified that he took you to the police station and his car was able to give us the record of the time and place."

"Now we have something to tell you," Caroline consulted with her girls, and both nodded for her to continue. "My daughter Denny recognized the man who stole her purse. A police officer by the name of Jose Fernandez."

Ruiz eyed the women without showing any emotion.

"May I assume by your lack of reaction that you suspect this officer?" As Caroline waited for Ruiz to say something, he nodded.

"Six months ago, a decorated police officer and my friend infiltrated one of the drug cartels in the area. His role was to tell the cartel bosses he needed extra money and was willing to help

What About Barnum?

them."

"Why was he deliberately allowing me to see him and then running, and stopping for me to see him again?"

"He hoped you would get the message and stop pursuing him. Otherwise, you would have met his partner who would have knifed you in the alley."

"Oh, my God," Millie put her hand in front of her mouth her reaction unstoppable at the thought of losing her sister.

"Luis told Jose to get your purse. Luis encountered you in the course of his activities, but he never said where. Luis worried you might recognize him. He needed to know who you were. Jose knifed the purse strings and ran in a clear way so as not to be pursued."

"So Jose's partner is a member of the drug cartel?" Caroline asked.

"His out-of-uniform partner. A member of the cartel who is exercising a little business on the side and asked Jose to participate."

"If the cartel finds out he's receiving money on the side." Caroline didn't finish.

"They did. Jose had to tell them Luis forced him to go along as Luis threatened his life. They eliminated Luis."

"These people play rough."

"Why can't Jose just walk away?" Millie twisted her hands without realizing this. Her mother put a hand on top of hers to calm her down.

"If he did, they would kill his wife, his children, and any other family member they can find. And, since Jose has allowed us to discover more about these drug lords in six months than we have in six years, he wishes to continue playing his role. His brother was killed by these people last year."

"You have no choice. You need to get to the head man." Caroline stared at her daughters. "Allow me to ask again. How did you little girls get into so much trouble?" Turning toward Capitán Ruiz, she thought aloud. "What does this have to do with us. Why hold my daughter's passport and create all this anxiety?"

"I apologize Señora if I have caused you or your daughters anxiety. We are so used to living with this sort of fear. We no longer recognize when we create such fear in others." He took a deep breath. "However, this is not a drug cartel-related crime."

"True," Caroline breathed. "And the murderer is not your hotel *bandito*?"

"No. The only reason a man such as this animal would ever attempt to do this is money—lots of money. Someone hired him."

"Oh, you can't suspect Jed?" Millie trembled.

"We interrogated him most of the night. Jose surveilled Jed without being seen and refuses to believe Jed Swayzee is the one who put this in motion. Maybe he is right, and maybe he is wrong."

"Why tell us all this? Aren't you worried about us telling someone else?" Millie spotted her mother studying Ruiz's reaction carefully.

"No. Thought never crossed my mind. If you do, you die. They will kill you."

The three women leaned toward the back of their chairs at the same time, the thought of someone killing them over this

What About Barnum?

outrageous.

Millie extracted the answering machine from her bag. "I asked the hotel if I could bring this with me. I want you to listen to the messages. Jed says it's not his wife's voice. He listened to this twice, and the second time, I had the strange impression he recognized the voice."

"My daughter Millie is an excellent judge of human nature—except for the one failed marriage, of course. She inherited her keen sense of people from me."

Ruiz obliged them and listened to the message three times. "Sounds like a man disguising his voice with a mouthpiece."

Caroline stared at Millie. "Of course, if the captain is right, this does not rule out Jed."

"I want to draw your attention to the fact this person's message came after the murder after Jed left his message."

Ruiz nodded while deep in thought. "Thank you for pointing this out, Señorita Brewer. Can you leave this with me for a couple of days?"

"Sure, but why?"

"We have formed a multinational task force with three other countries since these crimes directly affect them also. One of the men helping us gave you an alibi at the Mandala Club, Miss Millie."

Caroline put out her hand to forestall her daughter. "MI6?"

"He does not want his identity revealed. So I will respect his request. None of the people working with us desire their names to be known. I can't say I blame them."

Denny fidgeted with her purse. She pulled out her little recorder and silently interrogated Millie about handing this over to Ruiz.

Millie shook her head making a face, so she put the recorder back in her purse.

Caroline took in a deep breath. "What would you like us to do, Capitán Ruiz?"

If you could stay in Puerto Vallarta a while longer, let me know what your estupendo sense of people tells you. I would appreciate the help." He shook his head. "I cannot ask our man in the task force to help me any more than he has. This crime does not fall within his jurisdiction nor is it any business of his."

They rose to leave. Denny addressed the officer. "By the way, there is nothing left in this purse. Can I throw it away in the trashcan here?"

"I gave you the purse so you could take it with you. Your fingerprints are all over the bag. I will need to lie about the evidence. Say we lost the bag."

Denny realized the size of the favor Ruiz accepted to do for her. "Oh, thank you so much. Of course, I will bring the bag with me."

Alejandro picked them up ten minutes later, and they no longer feared Jose Fernandez—a relief for Denny and Millie.

When Denny turned to her sister asking why she didn't want to release the recorder to Ruiz, Millie explained. "I'm going to need it tonight when I go answer Jed's lawyer's questions, right?"

"Of course you are, good thinking, by the way."

Caroline shook her head staring out the window, and her puzzled frown appeared troubled with more than one question.

What About Barnum?

Binary Bounty # 1

"I was going to recommend you don't go talk to Jed's lawyer. Now, I am suggesting you do, sweetheart, but try not to say anything they may hold against you."

"What do you mean, Mom?"

"You girls believe you are astute using the recorder? I can assure you, they will also record. My advice is to tell them immediately that you are taping the conversation. This way when they ask permission to tape yours, you will be on an even footing."

"Wow, hadn't thought of this." Millie eyed her mother. "Why not come with me as my lawyer?"

"I would first need to inform them of our relationship, and let them know we are taping the meeting." Caroline smiled. "This might be a lot of fun."

Millie called Jed to firm up the appointment because of the lateness, and because she promised she would call him after finishing at the police station.

When they got to Millie and Denny's room, Manuela gave Millie a big hug. Aware of their outing, she feared for them. Millie hugged her back. "Was Jonah any trouble?"

"No, boy very sweet." She brushed a few tears. "I worry *por su regreso*," she told them.

"We were there a little longer than we wanted, but I can attest to Capitán Ruiz being an honorable man. You can trust him implicitly."

"Muchas gracias, Señorita Millie. *Bueno saber*."

A knock on her door and Millie let in her mother who also saluted Manuela. "When is the man expecting us?"

"He said his lawyer would be there in fifteen minutes."

"I just spoke to your father and told him everything was moving smoothly, and we resolved the matter with the authorities."

"He's going to want you to go home right away."

"I told him I wanted to spend more time with my grandson and that we were here for another week ... or so." She smiled wagging her eyebrows up and down.

"Mother, you're incorrigible." Millie offered her a glass of wine.

"No wine." Caroline waited for Millie to focus on her and said, "Barnum."

"What about Barnum?" Millie hated this subject.

"When do I meet your Barnum?"

"Mom, he is not my Barnum. And I can't ask him to meet my mother. I hardly know the man."

"You could introduce me as your ... lawyer, slash mother."

"No." A heavy sigh followed the strong negation. "Denny please talk some sense into our mother."

"I want to thank him for giving you an alibi at the club."

"We don't even know he's the one who did. Barnum was talking to another man at the time, and there could have been some other agent in that Club looking out for me. Look at the mistake Denny made when she jumped to the conclusion Jose Fernandez was the crook who stole her purse?"

"He was the man who stole her purse."

"True Mom," Denny came to Millie's rescue. "What Millie meant to say, was that I jumped to the conclusion Jose Fernandez was a crook."

"Then you girls leave me no other recourse than to beg: please?"

What About Barnum?

Binary Bounty # 1

Millie chuckled at her mother's pathetic expression.

Denny considered, "You might tell Barnum your mother, Jonah's grandmother, is very grateful he set out to save Jonah's life and would love to thank him."

Millie assessed her mother's Cheshire cat smile and conceded. "Maybe—accidentally. If you promise not to talk about anything else."

"I accept the challenge—of remaining silent on all the rest of it, of course." Caroline hugged her daughter.

JED'S LAWYER

O n their way to Jed Swayzee's Ambassador suite, Millie gave her mother some idea of what she might find upstairs.

"Mom, I'm telling you, the first time I walked into Jed's suite, the elegance blew me away."

"Thank you, sweetheart. Your father and I stayed in quite a few posh hotel suites in our days."

"Yes, you have. And your Thousand Oaks home is quite the showpiece. However, best to be forewarned."

"Quite right."

Millie glanced at her mother and thought she spotted nerves in the Iron Lady's demeanor. She hoped all this drama wasn't too much for her, at least not in the same way as this trip which appeared to suck all the energy out of her. She left home to help her girls and relax. Well, the only one resting was Jonah.

During the past few days, Millie found herself leaning on her sister and now on her mother more than she had in the last five years. She prayed to get some of her courage back, worried she might turn into one of those lonely, scared women afraid to leave their house. In the older neighborhood her parents lived in, her mother catered to some of these women who resided in huge homes with no one to talk to for days, sometimes weeks. Caro-

What About Barnum?

line visited them and ran errands for them while the women took turns recounting their sad tales, mostly the same stories repeated with every visit.

"Here we are. Sweetheart, you're rather quiet. Are you all right?"

"Yes. Just lost in crazy thoughts." Millie chuckled to try and change her mood.

"Do we knock or ring?" Caroline asked.

Millie grabbed the door knocker to make their presence known refusing to chew the inside of her upper lip.

Jed answered the door. "Hello, come right in. We were sitting on the patio, but the sun is gone, so we decided to bring the meeting inside."

"Oh, my what a lovely view you must enjoy during the day. Ocean makes for a dark canvas at night, doesn't it?" Caroline smiled as she extended her hand to shake Jed's outstretched invitation.

"Jed, my mother, the famous criminal lawyer I mentioned. Caroline Stuart Brewer."

After the introductions, Millie spotted a tall, slim man enter the room. He wore a dark business suit and a colorful red tie. His presence wheeled a lot of power, his movement toward them slick and quiet like the steps of a large, ferocious cat. As her mother would say, he made an entrance and relished all eyes on him. No smile softened the lawyer's rugged, weather-beaten face, and the coal-like black eyes appeared to assess them quickly.

Jed proceeded with the introductions. "Gregorio Villante, Millicent Brewer and her mother, Caroline Stuart Brewer."

"Ladies," was all Gregorio said as he shook their hands, squeezing Millie's fingers to a pulp. She hated when men exerted too much force in their handshake. She took this as a sign of war.

Gregorio designated the glass table in front of them. "I think these chairs are a good place to sit." The lawyer took the seat at the end of the table. "When Jed mentioned his girlfriend's mother was the great Caroline Stuart Brewer, I looked you up on the Internet. You've won quite a few high-profile trials in your day, quite impressive."

Millie at once regretted not having asked Jed for the identity of his lawyer. They were apparently at a disadvantage. "Excuse me, but I am not Jed's girlfriend." She smiled to remain polite.

Caroline laid a hand on Millie's arm to intimate calmness and continued. "Thank you." Millie recognized her mother's saccharine-sweet smile. "In fact, Mr. Villante, your background is also quite impressive. You've fought and won a lot of money for some of the Argentinian families. You are renowned in your country—and still so young. I'm sure you've mapped out all sorts of lucrative territories for your future."

Millie held back her expression from painting surprise—her eyes and smile in check—and caught Gregorio's eyes become mere slits while his long, tanned fingers flicked his pen.

Villante's eyes veered toward Jed as he turned in his chair to stare at his client, appearing angry that people were aware of his identity.

Jed shrugged, his eyes indicating the surprise Millie sidestepped.

"Don't blame Jed," Caroline continued. "He didn't say a

word about you, respecting your wishes." She paused to allow her words to sink in. "Amazing what information twenty dollars will buy you when a famous cartel lawyer arrives in Puerto Vallarta all the way from Argentina."

"You are misinformed, Madam. I'm not a lawyer for any cartel. I am in commercial law, and I do very well for myself without the lure of tainted money."

"Well, I apologize. What we read on the Internet is not always true, of course." Caroline paused to allow the man to collect himself, Millie presumed. He appeared quite shaken. Only, she didn't know if her mother's words created the conflict present in the nervous tic of his eyes opening wide and narrowing again, or if the fact people were aware of his whereabouts bothered him more.

"There's a lovely cross breeze in here," Millie added to change the subject. "How do you do this, Jed? We need to keep the air-conditioning on all the time. The ocean breeze is salty and refreshing." She took a whiff of the sea air occupying the room.

"I keep both sets of patio doors open all the way which provides me with all the sea air I want."

Millie smiled. His answer explained why noise arose on the dining room side of his suite brought on by the playful jostling around the pool while in the living room the only sound emerged from the dark, turbulent ocean kicking up a dry sinister echo at this late hour.

"So, what are the questions you wish to ask us?" Caroline demanded to know. "And before you do." She nodded toward her daughter. "My daughter will be recording this interview."

Millie rummaged in her purse and stood the recorder on the table.

Jed's eyes grew rounder. "Hey, I have one of those too." He extracted his from the inside pocket of his jacket. "How long have you had yours?"

Millie smiled and got the surreptitious nod from her mother. "I had mine this afternoon when we met on the beach, and throughout the training presentation."

Millie could tell by Jed's face he hoped for a different answer.

"What was your relationship with Mrs. Swayzee, Miss Brewer?" Gregorio asked.

"There was no relationship. I met Julie Swayzee once."

"Were you aware Mrs. Swayzee blamed you for the breakup of my client's marriage?"

This will save us a lot of time, Mr. Villante." Millie turned on the recorder, and since she had already rewound the little machine, she pressed the play button so Villante could listen to her afternoon conversation with Jed on the beach. She pumped the volume to maximum since the noise level picked up poolside when a large helicopter flew ocean-side getting closer and louder. What were people thinking of, skydiving at this late hour?

As Villante mulled over her story coupled with the voices on the machine, the memory of Barnum's voice sounding nowhere on this recorder drew Millie's concern. The oddity of the man scared her. As much of a hunk as she recognized him to be, she hated the thought of introducing him to her mother.

Millie paused the recorder, and Villante turned toward Jed who gave the lawyer his best clown face, the one with the wide eyes attempting to play innocent while depicting the dubious

What About Barnum?

Binary Bounty # 1

smile of someone about to be chewed out.

"May I keep this little recorder for a day or two, Miss Brewer?" Villante made a motion of reaching for it.

"No. You may not. First, the machine is not mine. Second, I might need this." She grabbed the recorder before he could and, in her haste, sent the little machine flying to the floor. "Oh, my God. I hope it's not broken." She bent to retrieve it and as she did her mother yelled, "Jed get down." Caroline pulled the rest of Millie to the floor and had them crawl under the table.

With her mother lying on top of her under the table, Millie heard a hail of fast flying little snaps, giving birth to different sounds. She caught the sound of the glass table on top of them crack as though someone threw pebbles at it.

"Mom, what's going on?"

"They're shooting at us from that helicopter. Don't move. Don't say anything."

Only once the sound of the helicopter faded did Caroline release her daughter. "Are you all right?" she asked as she crawled out from under the table.

Millie took account of her arms and legs and stood to make sure. "Yes. My right arm is sore a little, but I think this happened when you pulled me down."

Then Millie discovered Villante sitting in his chair, a bullet to his forehead, his eyes wide open.

Millie turned to put her head on her mother's shoulder. "Oh, Mom, this is horrible."

Caroline wrapped her arms around her rubbing her back and cried out, "Jed, are you okay."

When no answer came, she walked to the other side of the

table. She turned Jed over when she saw him sprawled on the floor.

"Mom, he's not dead, is he?"

"No. I believe Jed banged his head on the floor when he jumped, and a bullet caught his leg. Find me a towel or a rag or a shirt. I'm going to need to make a tourniquet. He's bleeding quite a bit."

Millie came back with one of Jed's shirts. "Here Mom, will this do?"

"Yes. Now call the front desk and tell the manager to send the paramedics up here. Give them the description of what went on in the room."

Once done, Caroline grabbed her cell phone and called Denny. After a brief explanation, she told her to reach Ruiz.

"Mom, they called for an EMS. Meanwhile, the on-call doctor is on his way up."

"Good."

Jed's moans and cry for help roused them both to action. Millie got to him first. "You're all right, Jed. You bumped your head when you came down on the floor, and a bullet grazed your leg, but my mother made a tourniquet, and the ambulance is on its way."

"What the hell happened. The last thing I remember is your mother yelling at me to get down. I did, but then nothing."

"Someone in the helicopter hovering near the window began shooting at us."

Caroline came over to Jed's side. "Don't think about anything. Don't try to move. You must conserve your energy. The emergency vehicle will be here shortly."

What About Barnum?

Binary Bounty # 1

Millie got up to answer her phone. "I'll tell you about this later, Denny. Is Ruiz on his way?"

"The woman at the precinct says he's gone home, but that she would try to reach him."

Millie hung up before Denny could ask her more questions.

She glanced at the table and noticed her mother had dropped one of the hotel's fluffy towels over Villante's head and shoulders. Less tragic now, as Millie didn't need to stare at the bullet in the man's forehead or at the lawyer's dark eyes laced with the shock that he'd just been killed.

Caroline answered the knock at the door to let the resident doctor into the room. He seemed young, and she hoped experienced enough to know not to touch anything.

"I'm Caroline Brewer. Please consider the room a crime scene."

"Of course, Señora."

Millie stared at her chair, transfixed by what she witnessed.

Caroline walked over to help her remain calm and caught sight of what her daughter's eyes fixated on: three bullet holes in her chair.

"Why would anyone want to kill me?"

"No reason whatsoever. There are two bullets in my chair as well." Her mother released a huge sigh. "Wrong place, wrong time is all. Nothing any of us can do."

"Señora, I gave the man something to ease his pain. Not much else I can do for him. We'll have to wait for the paramedics to get here. You did a good job with the tourniquet." The doctor left.

"Mom, I want to go home." Millie walked toward her mother and knew she would take her in her arms and make her feel better again—now, but what about tomorrow? And all the other days to follow? Whatever happened, she needed to keep Jonah out of this muck.

Millie found her mother staring at the glass table in the middle of the room. She spotted age sneaking up in her demeanor, in her drawn features and her sad, reflective expression.

"Count your blessings this glass table did not shatter. Being covered with glass is a fear of mine. It happened once, a long time ago, and I needed to be hospitalized and treated for infection because minuscule shards of glass covered my legs." Caroline extended her arm for Millie to nestle against her. "I say this because I can spot at least two bullet holes in this table. Thank God, they make these tables out of tempered glass today."

Millie considered they had to build the table to resist all sorts of accidents. Frankly, she was amazed only one of them under the table suffered a bullet wound. And her mother's admission moved her, the fact Caroline used her body to protect her despite her fear of broken glass. She nodded to show her mother she understood.

"Is your little recorder still functional?"

"Yes. I made sure it's not damaged."

The door burst open. No one had locked it after the doctor's visit. Two men came in with a stretcher and prepared to hoist Jed on it. Caroline asked them what hospital they were taking him to.

"San Javier, Señora."

As they lifted the stretcher, Jed woke up. Strapped down he could only turn his head, and he spotted the towel over Gregorio's head and shoulders. "Oh, no. Here goes the last Ambassador Suite available. Now, where am I going to stay?"

Caroline rubbed a hand on her daughter's back. "Please go down and reassure your sister. Give a big kiss to Jonah for me. Don't wake him, though." She smiled. "I'll be down soon. I want to make sure I speak to Ruiz before I leave."

"Mom, they might not be able to reach him."

"They will, and from what I've learned about the good Capitán, he will be here."

"Call me if you need my help." A kiss and Millie hurried to her room, to Jonah's side.

Ten

MURDER AT THE HOTEL

An hour went by before the first officers arrived on the premises. When the coroner rang, Caroline had fallen asleep in the other room. She jumped up to open the door still a little groggy and spent some time explaining how things happened.

While law enforcement officers took pictures, Ruiz walked in shaking his head. "Señora, murder seems to follow you and your daughters."

"Good of you to come, Capitán Ruiz. Perhaps you can enlighten me as to what took place here this evening."

"Well, Señora, Gregorio Villante is a well-known drug cartel lawyer," Ruiz stated as they wheeled his body away. "He has worked for the Sinaloa Cartel settling disputes for Rotsman and his sons. Possibly, the New Generation Jalisco Cartel has learned of Villante's arrival and decided to take him out. Bad blood runs between the groups as they fight to own Mexico."

"The United States suffered through the same growing pains in the twenties. The city of Chicago comes to mind. Drug lords became all powerful. Officials had no choice than to ignore them. Until they realized if they didn't stop them, no one would ever be free."

"*Sí*. Only your people called this growing pains. I call this a

What About Barnum?

disease."

"At least, you have a multinational task force on board."

"What was a man like Gregorio Villante doing here?"

"Mr. Swayzee's lawyer." Caroline eyed Ruiz strangely. "My daughter said you were aware of Jed's lawyer. Wasn't he the one who picked him up from your headquarters?"

"Ties in with the rest of what we found." Ruiz addressed Caroline's question. "Man gave himself the name of Gregg Johnson."

"I see. The lawyer had no choice but to give his real name at the hotel." Caroline admitted what worried her the most. "What I don't quite understand is why these people would try to kill us. We are not part of their feud."

"Señora Brewer, these people make up the rules as they go. We witnessed this during the occurrence of violence last summer in Puerto Vallarta. Drug lords no longer fear the authorities, which is why we recruited help from foreign nations. Also, some of the bigger hotels make sure they hire robust patrols capable of defending their guests. Their roofs are capable of sustaining a helicopter, and the army responds in a heartbeat when danger arises. When the call came in from my office, I touched base with them. They did see the helicopter circling the Marriott around eight thirty—most likely waiting for the cover of complete darkness. The guards alerted the army. Around eight forty-five, the military ordered the unidentified helicopter to leave, or they would escort them off the premises with force if necessary."

"An all-out war."

"*Sí. Banditos* retaliated, said they were on a mission of mercy, but if we interfered they would kill everyone in the room."

"So, this was known?"

"The hotel guards had no idea which room or who they were targeting. Scanning the list of guests—one of the first things the army did—Gregorio Villante drew a red flag. However, his suite was garden side."

"Are you saying the army's threats are the reason they shot at all of us?"

"Well, the army's threat was the reason you are still alive." Ruiz checked out the bullets in the chairs and the ones through the table. "When the army pursued them, they had to leave whether the rest of you were alive or not."

"That's why only two bullets in the table."

"Correction, many bullets seemed to … how do you say re-botó off the table. Only two apparent holes," Ruiz stated.

"Bullets ricocheted off the table."

"They are not usually this sloppy. Might be first-time recruits." As he touched a few of the holes to assess the size of the bullets, more cracks in the glass were heard.

Caroline screamed and jumped back. "I'm sorry. Shattered glass terrorizes me."

"Good thing this table would never shatter as it might have ten years ago. Removing glass from your body can sometimes be trickier than removing a bullet."

"Yes, I am well aware of this fact."

"Where did they bring Mr. Swayzee?"

"San Javier."

"I have a lot of questions for him. So, I will let you get some rest, and I will visit Mr. Swayzee in the morning." He tipped his head and left.

What About Barnum?

Binary Bounty # 1

Caroline realized she needed to leave. The cleaning crew would follow the police, and she suspected her daughter Millie would not sleep until she released the information she gathered. Caroline didn't realize what Ruiz meant when he stated the group vied to kill all people assembled if the military launched a pursuit. She regretted not clearing this up with him.

Military ignored their threat and pursued them just the same. The killers spoke of a mission of mercy. Ruiz thought all they wanted was to get rid of Villante. He might have held something on the killers or forced his beliefs on them somehow. With Villante dead, would they let the rest of them go? Or would they return to execute their threat? Should she mention to her daughters the killers might return to exact revenge? Or should she focus on spending time with her grandson and ignore the rest?

Over by the balcony, Caroline found stray bullets also nicked the furniture and one of the glass tables. Dangling lights delineated the perimeters, and beyond them, the black cloth of the ocean. The mountains had become lumpy specters on this moonless night. The Sierra Madre which lay behind the lovely bay forming the Occidental chain of mountains appeared imposing during the day. Had the deadly helicopter emerged from the hills' crevices? Traveling in the space of minutes to Banderas Bay?

Caroline released a sigh and nodded toward the policeman who requested she leave. One last eyeful surveyed the room before stepping out toward the elevator.

Arriving at her daughters' door, she feared fatigue might not let her make the right decisions. She tapped lightly on the door and waited a couple of minutes before she knocked again. She would tell them she needed to rest and they would discuss the matter in the morning. Sun's warmth would dispel the shivers.

This time the door opened and Millie stood in front of her with a tear-stained face.

"Sweetheart, why are you crying?"

"I've brought you into such a mess, Mom. I'm sorry. I want to go home, and I'm afraid for Jonah." Millie opened the door moving aside to let her mother enter, and Caroline didn't have the heart to refuse.

"I think these people might come back to finish the job, Mom. That's what I can't get out of my head."

Caroline refused to vocalize her fears and answered with a question. "Honey, what makes you think these people want to kill us?" She decided on a half-truth. "Ruiz finally came. He says the military was alerted to the whereabouts of the rogue helicopter. He states the hotel supports first-rate security."

"Of course, he would say this." She tugged at a tissue tucked into her bathrobe's sleeve and blew her nose.

"Where's your sister?"

"Asleep, an hour ago. I told Denny about the evening when I got back, and she thinks we should leave. She doesn't think staying here will help matters. They'll let us go home, won't they?"

"Of course, they will." Caroline took Millie into her arms. "You need to get some rest. Things will look better in the morning."

"I want to go see Jed in the morning, find out why they were gunning for this Villante."

Caroline released a great sigh. "Let's sit on the sofa, and I'll tell you who the man is. No sense tossing and turning all night in your need to get to the truth."

What About Barnum?

"I'll make us some tea, Mom." While Millie did, she thought she heard rumblings on the beach and tried not to pay attention to the wind, the surf, and most likely the few people still down there talking about what happened at the hotel. Twice in as many days. The hotel's popularity would take a hit. Of this, Millie was sure.

"How much does this place set you back, honey? Two rooms, a small kitchen and a dining-living area?"

Millie came back with a pot of tea and two cups on a tray.

"Jed took out a group of rooms and got us a fabulous discount. Three of the rooms were for the top earners, those of us who won an award. The place still costs me a hundred dollars a night, though."

"Phenomenal bargain. Mine is just a plain room and costing me more than twice that amount."

Millie sat down and poured for them. "I'm sorry, Mom. I should have offered you to stay with us. Never crossed my mind. I'm so out of it."

"Not at all. I wouldn't want to crowd you, honey."

"Mom, you wouldn't be crowding us. Denny said the same thing when she got herself a room the first night. Then with her not working and us eating out, well this added up to quite a bit. I told her she could stay with me. This sofa turns into a most comfortable bed and comes with sheets and blankets. Denny used it a couple of nights. Then we moved Jonah to the den and told him he would have his bed. We had a cot wheeled in, and he is quite pleased with the idea."

"Where does Denny sleep?"

"With me. There are two double beds in my room."

"I think I'll take you up on that offer—not because of the money. I think I need to be close to my family."

Millie found her mother's tone ominous. "How about you tell me all you learned from Ruiz." Millie got up to sit beside her on the sofa.

Caroline exhaled a shaky breath and smiled as she patted her daughter's hand. As her mother finished relating everything she learned from Ruiz, Millie thought she heard a noise outside, a woman's scream. Distracted by the sound, Millie got up and walked to the balcony. She hurried to unlock and opened the patio doors and found no one beneath her. The night appeared unusually dark, and she wondered if nightfall prompted the helicopter to hover and wait, to get more nocturnal cover.

"Sorry, Mom. Did you hear the scream?"

"No. I guess my hearing is not as sharp as it used to be."

Or the scream was mine, echoing in my brain. "Crazy that the people might exact revenge on us." Millie had a thought. "Please don't tell Dad about this."

"No intention of telling your father anything, other than we are having a superb time." A deep breath later, Caroline admitted. "Your father's a strong man, sweetheart, kind and generous, although his impetus would put us in a dire situation for sure."

Her mother's tone got a giggle out of her, and Millie dried her tears. "Not knowing drove me crazy. Thanks, Mom. Now I can thrust and parry—or at least imagine I can."

Her mother giggled. "Thrust and parry, one of your father's expression."

"I know. I love Dad too."

"What about that man? The one who saved Jonah's life, the

one who gave you an alibi at the club? I can't remember his name."

"What about Barnum? He has nothing to do with this—or does he?"

"Where does such mistrust originate? I didn't raise you this way?"

"Mom, yes, the man saved my life at least once. I say my life because I would have died if Jonah drowned. And Barnum is handsome, no doubt whatsoever." Millie shrugged. "I just don't trust him."

"Well, you suffered through the charms of at least two very handsome men these past years: Todd, Jed, which might account for your dislike of Barnum."

"No. The man's looks don't bother me. He's a mystery. He never gave us a last name. Is Barnum even his first name? I think what scares me is the fact he is an enigma. For instance, Barnum appears everywhere I seem to be. Denny told me he gazed at Jonah and me building a sandcastle one morning. Didn't even notice Denny coming up to him. She went to ask him questions, and he refused to answer her. He came out of the surf when I met Jed on the beach. I find his behavior unsettling."

"Well, until you know for sure, until you ask him these questions, only natural you experience mistrust toward him."

"I don't think I care enough about him to get into all this."

A knock at the door made them both jump.

"Can only be Ruiz," Millie stated

"I don't think the polite Capitán Ruiz would call at this hour." Her mother rose. "You stay here. I'll see who it is."

"No," Millie laid a hand on her mother's arm. "We'll go together."

Millie opened the door while her mother stood guard holding a heavy object. Millie sensed a giggle coming on, but she made a point of shooing away the nerves.

When she opened the door, she became mute, unable to imagine the smallest greeting. Barnum stood in front of her in a black sports jacket over a black turtleneck and tight black jeans. His hair was tied back, and the dark eyes that stared into hers robbed her of all the questions stringing together in her mind.

Luckily, her mother came to her rescue. She needed to force the door out of Millie's hand and faced with the notorious description given by both her daughters, she attempted a guess. "You must be Barnum." She extended her hand to shake his. "I'm Millie and Denny's mother."

Millie could say nothing as she witnessed her mother's and Barnum's first contact. Then she caught her mother's smile as she invited Barnum inside. "I wanted to thank you for saving my grandson from drowning. My daughter Millie explained."

"My pleasure," Barnum answered while Caroline's cheeks took on a pink hue. Barnum turned toward Millie. "We must go. Round up all the clothes you wish to keep, all your identification papers, money, credit cards, airplane tickets—anything you might need. You have thirty minutes to pack."

"In the middle of the night? My sister and my son are asleep. No way can we pack in thirty minutes."

Caroline shook her daughter. "Do as he says. NOW, Millie." Caroline turned toward Barnum. "I have one bag I will collect in another room down the hall."

"We meet here in twenty-five minutes," Barnum added. He

What About Barnum?

Binary Bounty # 1

followed Millie to her room. "I will help you."

"Why are you doing this?"

"No time for questions."

She had a difficult time waking Denny who kept rationalizing they would leave first thing in the morning. "We need to leave now, Denny."

"I'm not leaving now, Millie," she said half asleep.

"Mom's orders." The words finished rousting her sister. She sat up in bed and caught sight of Barnum helping Jonah get dressed. Jonah was smiling at his favorite giant and listening to everything he suggested. "Wow, Barnum is here?"

Denny jumped up and put some clothes on top of her skimpy pajamas. Then she grabbed her purse and made sure all papers were inside. She threw the rest of her things in the one bag she brought then began to help Millie with hers. Millie had two suitcases aside from Jonah's case and his backpack.

Millie thought to ask, "What about food and water?"

"No need," Barnum responded as he finished by giving Jonah a drink of water and a couple of cookies. "This is for the trip, Jonah."

"How long are we traveling?" Millie wanted to know.

"One hour. On the water." Barnum veered toward Millie. "Weather has dropped down to seventeen degrees °C, and the wind kicks up on the Bay so wear something warm."

He helped Jonah into his jacket and shoes, and Jonah pocketed the cookies but downed the glass of water. "I was thirsty, Mommy."

"I'm bringing Jonah to the bathroom. We need to meet at the door." Barnum left the room.

Caroline arrived with her suitcase, and Millie considered she appeared exhausted. Worried about her son in the hands of that man, she closed her eyes and schooled herself to remain calm. A tall order when given thirty minutes to leave the comfort of a hotel room in the middle of the night.

Eleven

Escape

Millie found their escapade in the dead of night to be surreal. She witnessed three men pick up their bags and carry them to a yacht anchored on the right of a long row of posts where authorities warned them not to swim.

Jonah was excited and talkative, and she wondered with surprise why Barnum did not try to contain his enthusiasm, not that his little voice echoed loudly into the windy night, but she remembered how Todd and Jed would lose patience with Jonah's exuberance.

The three men embarked first, and Barnum followed after having helped the ladies up the hydraulic passerelle while he carried Jonah is his arms.

The yacht's motor fired up, and Barnum led them to the main saloon. There was a shivering breeze, quite brisk over the ocean, and Millie welcomed the warmth of wood fixtures, long suede couches and what she suspected were wall to wall windows on both sides though vertical blinds covered them at the moment. The main deck was well lit, and one of the men brought them hot cocoa topped with marshmallows.

Millie took the cup and clasped Barnum's sleeve before he could leave. "Will you please tell us now what this is all about?"

"Not now. We will reach our destination in fifty minutes. I must take my place up front to help the man at the helm. There is a head—a bathroom—downstairs on the right side of the hallway. Cookies and assorted crackers are in the cupboards in front of this saloon, in the back of our chairs." He left her, but she could still keep an eye on him through the opening between the two captain chairs in the galley.

"Can I go in front with Barnum, Mommy?"

Barnum turned around and smiled at Jonah. "Come on," he told Jonah while the words gave the small child wings. As Jonah skipped toward Barnum, as though just remembering, he paused to look back at his mother and waited for her approval.

"You can go. Just don't get in the way."

Millie sat down between Denny and her Mother as they moved to make space for her. Both turned down the hot cocoa and resembled a couple of zombies with their faces drawn and a severe amount of lassitude fogging their eyes. Too much worry in her raised eyebrows, and sad eyes prevented her from looking like her sister and mother—unless her expression was known as a scared zombie. She took a few gulps of her hot chocolate before setting it down on the table in front of her.

When she noticed her mother closing her eyes, she allowed the sway of the ocean to rock her, hoping the wave might put her to sleep for the short duration of their trip.

Wave did the trick—though the reprieve seemed like mere seconds. Barnum's hand on her shoulder woke her. When she opened her eyes, Jonah's little face smiled right up against hers, their noses touching. "Jonah, what are you doing?"

What About Barnum?

Binary Bounty # 1

"Trying to wake you," he said pulling up one of her eyelids. "We're here, Mommy."

"Jonah, I'm awake. Thank you."

She glanced at Barnum, and he was smiling while his eyes found their way into hers, as usual. She got up, stretched and searched for her mother and sister.

"They're already ashore waiting outside, on the pier."

She followed Barnum who held on to Jonah's little hand and who helped her out with his other hand across the divide between the passerelle and the pier.

"Where are we?"

"*Las Marietas.*"

"I tried to organize a tour here. They stopped all people from coming as of May of this year. I just missed the opportunity to visit these wonderful islands."

"The mountain has come to you it would seem." He smiled as he released Jonah's hand. Her son wanted to run to his grandmother.

She waved back to her mom and sister following the guides out front carrying their luggage.

"Seriously I was told the authorities are forbidding the general public from visiting."

"They are searching for solutions to rebuild the coral and undo the damage years of tourism created. But I own this house, and they allow me to use it."

Millie walked beside him and saw windows and double doors embedded in the flank of the cliff. She couldn't imagine what the place might look like inside since the sides and depth of this house appeared to be encased in solid rock.

As the rock face continued into the water beside the house, a massive door opened upward. "This cave is where I store my yacht. Ocean water flows in and out and always leaves me plenty of room to park."

"Impressive. How do you make sure the tide doesn't fill in the area?"

He smiled. "Astute of you. There is a powerful hydraulic pump at the bottom that helps maintain the water at an even depth."

"I see," Millie breathed while staring at the boat moored at the dock. She stared at her mother and sister holding Jonah by the hand and waiting by the front door. Three men deposited their bags on the stoop and were on their way back to the ship. "Where do they stay? On the yacht?"

"After they park the ship in the cave, they share quarters that do not communicate with the main house. The entrance is near the garage."

Millie smiled at her mother and sister and braced for Jonah running toward her with his outstretched arms threatening to wrap around her legs.

"Are you all right, sweetie?" Caroline smiled.

Millie nodded toward her mother while cuddling Jonah in her arms. Sincere gratitude and a fair amount of pity grazed her when she witnessed her mother's wan features and groggy voice. The woman experienced a lot today and needed to rest.

She turned toward Barnum as he unlocked the front door. "My mother needs to rest. She just arrived earlier today, and of course, you don't know what we've been through."

"I'm all right, Millie. Don't worry about me. I'm more con-

What About Barnum?

Binary Bounty # 1

cerned with what's going to happen to you, to Jonah, to Denny."

Inside the house, Barnum walked in front, and as he did, lights flicked on everywhere. "Room lights only," Millie heard him specify and the brightness of the area toned down, lights represented only in the first room they entered.

"I will give you a tour tomorrow. For now, this is the living room, the place where I like to sit, read, greet people that come here from time to time."

"So, these are the windows we see from the outside," Millie added as she took in the room's fabulous decor. Bright colored canvases adorned the walls, beige leather sofa and matching chairs, and she found the two windows appeared much bigger from the inside, their treatment a white veil. A fireplace surrounded by round stones stood between the apertures and the room's high ceilings displayed two enormous skylights. Millie caught her breath when she spotted what resembled a dark parchment poked with a million stars staring down at her. "Clouds are gone. View of the sky is lovely."

"Where's your TV?" Jonah asked. "There's supposed to be a television in the living room."

Barnum and Caroline laughed amidst Millie's protests. Denny smiled and mussed up Jonah's hair. "This little one needs television," she answered siding with Jonah.

"The house holds a media room where you can watch television or listen to music."

"Let's go see that," Jonah enthused appearing as though he slept enough for the night.

"Sweetie, Barnum told us he would show us the rest of the house in the morning, remember?" Millie kissed his round cheek and sensed her heart melt when his big brown eyes displayed all the love in Jonah's heart. In his mother's arms, he nestled his little face in her neck and nearly choked her with what he liked to call his super duper hug.

"Are there any beds in this house," Jonah whispered in her ear.

Barnum answered. "Yes, there are. You are still quite tired, then?"

Jonah redressed and moved his head side to side, a grave expression on his face. "No. But when you sleep, morning comes faster."

His answer got a roar of laughter from all, and once more Millie gave thanks for this little fellow in her life, this precious little being able to motivate her through any situation.

Upon departing the living area, Millie caught the lights dim and then turn off as those in the vast hallway turned on as they moved toward the back of the house. Millie realized this house was much larger than she first anticipated, at least from what she imagined by the view outside.

True to his word, Barnum showed them to their rooms, two of them. Millie pondered they appeared prepared and seemed to be waiting for their presence. "This is the largest room with two queen size beds, and to your right, there is a separate alcove with one double bed for Jonah. I've closed it off from your room with a sliding door."

Millie put Jonah down on the ground, and as she moved through the large bedroom, lights turned on, pot lights and softly shaded table lamps. Dressers adorned the corners as did tall library shelves stocked with books and what appeared to be

What About Barnum?

Binary Bounty # 1

DVDs. The floors were marble like those along the hallway, and a plush carpet straddled two four-poster beds. Staring up at the ceiling the same breathtaking view as in the living quarters made her gasp, although here the large roof supported five skylights all lined up and providing the light of a blanket of stars more scintillating than she ever encountered. She twirled around the room, catching sight of an archway leading to a gleaming white bathroom. "Wonderful." She smiled. "Which way to Jonah's quarters?"

Barnum asked, "May I enter?"

"Please, this is your house." Millie smiled.

He did, followed by Denny and Caroline. Millie grabbed Jonah's hand to prevent him from leaving the room, and they followed Barnum. He moved to his right and at the end of a little corridor, he opened a door that slid to the right. Inside was a big double bed, shelves stacked with games and children's movies, and at the other end of the room was another bathroom with shower and facilities.

"Do you like this, Jonah?" Millie asked.

"Yes, ma'am. I hate baths. I like to take showers."

His comment got a laugh from everyone.

"I see movies." He pointed toward the shelves. "But no TV." Jonah's little face crumpled.

"There is a television in every room," Barnum answered as he picked up Jonah in his arms. Turning toward the women, he added, "You can also use the screen as a monitor for a laptop or a computer. I will show you how to operate this tomorrow. For now," he smiled at the little tyke in his arms. "You must hurry to sleep to make morning come faster."

Jonah shook his head in solemn agreement. Then at once shy, he added, "But I don't have my pj's."

Barnum put him down and stepped out of the room. He turned once to let them know, "Your bags will be at your door in a few minutes." He eyed Caroline and indicated he would walk her to her room. "Yours is right next door."

Caroline hugged both her daughters and her little grandson promising she would be up at dawn. Appearing forlorn and hesitant, she followed Barnum.

When Barnum left the girls' room, the door slid back automatically.

Jonah jumped up and down and giggled. "Can I go to my room Mommy and look at the movies?"

"Yes, you do that, Jonah." After her son was out of the room, Millie eyed her sister with a panic she couldn't hide. "Are we prisoners here?"

"Millie," Denny scolded. "I might not be awake to the fullest, but I don't think we are being held against our will. Did you see this place and how awesome everything is?" She rubbed Millie's arm. "I don't blame you for being paranoid. Mom filled me in on the worst of what happened in Jed's room. But, honey, you're going to need to separate the bad guys from the good guys."

To try to gain some comfort from her sister's words, and in part to disprove her theory, Millie stepped toward the door. When the door did not open, she stepped in closer. She stared at Denny while her eyebrows raised in a question. "So, Ms. Engineer, how do you open this door?"

Denny lost her smile and walked up to the door to check the frame on both sides. "There doesn't appear to be any mechanism

What About Barnum?

Binary Bounty # 1

I can see. Maybe it's somewhere on the floor." Saying this she began to stomp at different places across the floor and stepping a little to the right, the door opened.

Both girls looked up, and there stood Barnum. A mocking smile swept his face as he caught what Denny attempted to do.

"Your luggage," he indicated as he took the cases off a trolley. Then, he took a circular gizmo out of his pocket that fit in the palm of his large hand and brandished this in Millie's face. "You need to say a long enough sentence into this component to be able to communicate with the house." His smile deepened.

In a truculent mood, as she pondered Barnum might be having fun at their expense, she sighed asking in a petulant tone. "What do I say?"

"How about: 'My name is Millie. I will accept Barnum as my friend, and I will believe everything he says.'"

"Cute," she replied, her mood becoming darker when she caught Denny's choked giggle behind her.

"Repeat, please."

She did while staring into his eyes, deepening her gaze with each word. "My name is Millie. I will accept Barnum as my friend, and I will believe everything he says."

Millie's retaliation dipped in sweet promises did not work in her favor. Instead of seeding shame in Barnum's behavior, as she wanted to do, she spotted his smug expression transform into a hungry glare. Lucky for her, he turned and placed the small sensor component in front of Denny.

"Hello. My name is Denny, and I will make sure my sister and nephew are healthy, happy, and unharmed."

Her defiance brought back a smile on Millie's expression.

Just what she needed about now. A little family support to show Barnum he would not be able to take advantage of her.

Barnum tilted his head her way. He pulled a sheet of paper out of his pocket and gave the note to Millie. "Here is a list of necessary formulas to automate what you will need to use."

"For instance?" she asked, her tone softer.

He pointed to one of the commands and spoke out loud, "Blinds, close."

Both girls' attention flew up to the ceiling as a mechanism slid the blinds to cover all five skylights.

"The sun beams through in the morning. This way, you will be able to sleep a little longer."

"May I try the door?"

Barnum's teasing smile returned. "Please do."

"Door, open," Millie voiced, shyness in her tone. The door slid open.

Barnum walked through the threshold. "Good night, ladies."

Denny laid a hand to stop Millie from giving the door instructions. Then she said, "Door close." And the door did, once more giving them the privacy they sought. "Amazing," Denny added.

Millie suddenly worried about Jonah. "Could he be stuck in his room?" She ran to him and found him asleep on the bed, curled up in a little ball, and holding a copy of the movie *The Good Dinosaur.*

With a gentle hand, Denny pried the movie out of his grasp and put the DVD on the table beside him. "What a darling. He wants to see the film with his Mom."

Rather than wake him, Millie took blankets piled on top of a

What About Barnum?
Binary Bounty # 1

chest by the bed and covered him so he wouldn't be cold. She looked up and noticed two skylights over his little room. She tried the sentence. "Blinds close." And they did.

Back in their room, Millie thought. "How is Jonah going to get around if he doesn't know any of these commands?"

"Well, he can leave his room to come into ours since his door merely slides."

"I guess you're right."

"Let's worry about the rest in the morning. I'm sure Barnum's thought of this." Denny got her bag and took out a nightgown. "I can't sleep in my clothes. Do you want to use the bathroom first?"

Millie sat on the bed a little despondent. No longer having to put on a face, her mood took no time to slip into the doldrums.

Denny told her, "Hey, sis. You go first. I'll wait for you."

Millie thought Denny's suggestion was her means to keep her moving and away from the dark thoughts invading her mind. She got up and smiled. "Thanks, Denny. I'll be all right … and I'll hurry. I know how tired you are."

Both girls lying in bed, Denny admitted, "You know, Millie, I think Barnum is the real deal—someone trying to help us. I sassed him before with that sentence, but I like him, and I believe he likes you, a lot."

"How can you tell?"

"In the sweet way he handles Jonah. In the way his eyes change when he looks at you. He is a smitten man."

"I think I endured my quota of gorgeous men who appear to want me. Something about Barnum I just don't trust."

Twelve

STRANGE HOUSE

Millie screamed when fear yanked her up in bed—her surroundings dark and foreign. She struggled to breathe as though someone tried to strangle her. Millie rubbed her eyes to rid herself of the nightmare—this exotic place without a doubt part of a dream. When she searched the bed with her hand, she could not find her son. "Jonah," Millie said in a low voice. Silence prevailed around her, except for the pounding of her heart, and she fought to rise out of bed wondering why her feet brushed against a carpet.

She walked in the dark and bumped into another bed a few feet from hers. Denny, she thought. They resided in Barnum's house, and Jonah occupied the room in the alcove down the hall. She rushed to his side, feeling her way around by touching the walls. Twice she bumped into furniture but continued until she reached the alcove.

Millie entered Jonah's room, but couldn't see anything. Memories of Barnum's notes he gave her before bed returned and she said, "Blinds open." They did, and the light of a dark sky striated with pink peered down at her. *Must be early morning. Sun always rises around seven twenty. Can it be this late?* Looking down at the bed, she gasped when she found it empty.

What About Barnum?

Binary Bounty # 1

She checked the adjoining bathroom. No Jonah.

She walked back to her room, hands touching the furniture to locate her bathrobe draped over a chair, grabbed her slippers on the carpet, and rather than wake Denny, ordered the door to open. Millie hopped into her slippers and rushed out telling the door to close. Tying the belt to her bathrobe, she ran across the sleek marble floors.

The next room belonged to her mother. Could Jonah have slipped into bed with her? She asked the door to open and found the room in total darkness, her mother still soundly sleeping. Jonah was not there. Her son would have woken his grandmother for sure.

She bade the door to close and ran down the hall. Luckily, skylights along the ceiling released enough sun that Millie didn't have to worry about running into walls. She did worry about where she headed. *Jonah might have found his way to the kitchen. He always likes to eat first thing when he wakes up.* She turned twice around to try and find her bearings. "Where is the kitchen," she spouted in sheer frustration. As she did, she spotted a light trailing along the trim where the ceramic tiles met the wall. She followed the light flashing at a rapid speed making the string appear to shiver. The bright stream had her turn twice, make one turn left, and another right turn before she picked up the sound of Jonah's little voice somewhere beyond.

The place amounted to a maze and she supposed huge. A few seconds later, Millie reached the brightest room she ever entered She squinted inside the dazzling white kitchen, unaccustomed to such bright light a few minutes after waking. From the tall ceiling, a skylight occupied most of the room. A full half-moon window faced the sinks and drew more daylight inside. The huge island in the center of the kitchen appeared efficient, and small trims of mint green and stainless steel appliances were the only other colors to embellish the white gleam. Jonah sat on a stool beside Barnum eating and laughing, as playful as usual.

"Jonah. Why didn't you wait for me? I worried about you when you weren't in your room."

Jonah climbed down from his perch and ran to her. "I'm sorry, Mommy. I was hungry and thirsty. Barnum told me on the boat how to find my way in his big house."

"Good morning." Barnum smiled. "I came in here to find him using the drawers to climb up on the counter trying to find the dishes and the food."

"You taught him how to go through the house?" Millie hadn't meant for her tone to sound reproachful, but she worried Jonah might step outside on his own and drown.

As though Barnum read her thoughts, he said promptly, "Only the four of us can activate the outside door, and the door at the end of the kitchen."

"Thank you," she breathed. Curious, she inquired, "The door at the end of the kitchen?"

"You gotta see this, Mommy," Jonah was already running toward the door. He couldn't wait for Barnum as impatient as a brisk gust of wind. "Door open," Jonah yelled. "Door open," more impatiently this time. The door did not respond.

Barnum slipped a hand on Millie's back when he reached them. "Full of life and quite the happy little boy."

She turned to face him and encountered those eyes wielding enough power to melt her resolve, her decision to stay calm under pressure, to avoid the burn of a good-looking man. Barnum's dark eyes also stirred wariness in the pit of her stomach, although she wasn't quite sure why.

"Did you sleep well?" he asked, appearing unable to redirect his gaze.

Millie nodded, not trusting herself to speak but didn't want Barnum learning this. "Aren't you going to open the door for him?"

"I'm waiting for you to do it."

"Door open," she said, and the door did.

Barnum led her inside with a hand on her back, and the beauty of the area drew a smile from Millie like a little girl on Christmas morning. An Olympic size pool of sky blue water stood before them. The floor shone pristine white while the walls and ceilings stood fashioned of glass. She spotted long red chairs strewn throughout while potted plants adorned the corners. Her gaze remained fixed on the front wall of French doors giving access to the sand and the ocean. "An infinity pool. Amazingly beautiful. How is this possible if you built your house inside the rock?"

"Most of the house is. The pool and a big section of the kitchen are free of the cliff." He took her hand in his and brought her fingers to his lips. He kissed each finger gently.

Too shocked to react, under this man's spell, Millie nevertheless sensed outrage slowly bubbling up inside her. What did he think he was doing? She pulled her hand away, her eyes scolding him as she did.

Instead of being chastised, a smile played over his lips. "Would you like to go for a swim?"

Millie closed her eyes and took a deep breath to ward off more impatience. "At the moment, I want to dress, eat breakfast, and listen to you while you answer my questions."

He bowed his head agreeing to her request. "To return to your room, all you need to do is ask the house for the way there, and the light will guide you."

"Quite a house you own." Nothing left to say to him, she turned toward her son. "Come, Jonah. You can check out the cartoons while mommy showers and gets dressed, after which we'll have breakfast together."

"I want to finish my breakfast with Barnum. Can I?"

Barnum intervened. "Let the boy stay. He can watch his favorite shows while I answer some of those questions you need to ask."

"You're sure he's no trouble?"

"I enjoy his company. Oh, and make sure you wear your bathing suit to breakfast. I'm wearing mine."

He flicked his shirt open, and Millie almost didn't want to look at the small thong he usually wore, but she was relieved—somewhat—when she eyed blue boxers that he wore as bathing attire, snug fitting shorts that fell below his washboard abs.

"Listen …" She was about to tell him off when she spotted Jonah's little face looking their way. "I'm not interested in swimming now. I rather you tell us why you found it necessary to bring us here."

"I'll be waiting," he answered taking Jonah by the hand to go finish their breakfast.

By the time Millie reached the room, Denny was in the shower. She used the Jonah's bathroom for her morning ablutions.

What About Barnum?

Binary Bounty # 1

And since she indulged in a shower at one o'clock in the morning, she decided to dress and move on with her day.

Rummaging through her case, she found one of her bathing suits, top of the pile. She decided to put it on under one of her summer dresses. *No reason to waste such a gorgeous pool or avoid a quick dip in the ocean.*

Millie looked up as the sun poured into the room, which was when the beauty of her surroundings and thoughts of the amazing times ahead contrasted with Millie's agenda. She planned to visit Jed in the hospital this morning, if not to supply him with answers, at least to provide him with a little comfort and some well-deserved encouragement. He would want to know who was tending his group of three hundred and fifty people, devoted enough to his cause to travel halfway around the world for most of them, to learn more about this business. They both worked hard these past six months, too hard to flush Jed's accomplishments without any regard.

Dressed, and with a cell phone in hand by the time Denny came out of the shower, Millie smiled, encountering Denny's sleepy eyes staring at her with affection and indicated she was on the phone. "San Javier?" she asked. "I'm sorry. I don't know the room number. Jed Swayzee was brought in late last night. Thank you."

She spotted her sister rummaging for clothes to wear. "You might want to wear a bathing suit under your clothes. I came across the biggest, most beautiful infinity pool I ever spotted inside someone's home." She nodded to emphasize her point.

The tilt of Denny's head brought on an elated expression. "What I call a vacation," she breathed a smile loaded with gratitude and pulling her face out of sleep mode.

"How is this possible. EMS brought him in late last night with a sizable loss of blood from a bullet wound." Millie put a mute on her phone. "Hospital released Jed already," she told her sister.

Coming back to the nurse in charge, she continued listening to the woman's explanation. "Thank you for the information."

Denny appeared surprised. "They released him already?"

"Yes. The nurse on his floor said his wound was a graze and he's gone home with antibiotics and the advice to rest. He's an outpatient. He'll go back for treatment of his wound twice this week. I have to call him."

"Maybe you should wait."

"Why?"

"We should talk to Barnum first—find out why he brought us here in the middle of the night—make sure this has nothing to do with Jed."

"What?" Denny's remark floored her.

"Well, first his wife is murdered, knifed to death. Rare a burglar would do this. Ask Mom."

"Really?"

"Later, Jed's lawyer is killed, gang-style while Jed gets shot as well. I'm sorry, but someone ordering a hit does not usually demand the killer snuff everyone around the mark. Maybe Jed ruffled some feathers with the business he is doing, and you're an innocent bystander who happens to work and live in the same sphere."

"Do you realize how unlikely that is?"

"Hey, how unlikely is it we're in a house like this?" Denny

What About Barnum?

Binary Bounty # 1

craned her neck toward her while extending her palms, her way of daring her to argue.

"Do you know if Mom's awake?" As she said this, Caroline entered the girls' room.

"Mom is awake, dressed and ready to go," Denny confirmed.

"We didn't mean to wake you." Millie hugged her mother.

Caroline hugged both her daughters. "You didn't. The strangeness of this place did. I haven't had nightmares in years—not since you little girls were young and your father traveled away to some convention."

Denny sighed impatiently. "We need to settle this business—find out what we're doing here which will go a long way to restoring my sanity."

"This morning, I peppered Barnum with attitude. He knows getting answers is what we want, foremost." She turned toward her mother. "I hope you're wearing a bathing suit under your dress," Millie told her with a smile.

"No. Not comfortable. I'm carrying one in this big coral bag I bought at the gift shop when I arrived yesterday. Looks so island like a breath of fresh air." She flicked the little plastic flowers sewn in front of the bag. "A beautiful souvenir when we settle all this awful business." She released a great sigh, and Millie thought she too was fraught with nerves.

"Let's go." Millie grabbed her mother and her sister's arm.

They made sure the doors were closed, and Caroline asked, "How do we find our way around these corridors, and where is all this light coming from?"

"Look up." Millie smiled

"Oh, my God, this is beautiful."

"To find our way in this maze, this will come in handy." Millie secured both her mother and her sister's attention and said. "Where is the kitchen?"

Both family members caught their breath when they spotted the bright ribbon of light indicating the way.

"My God." Denny glowed with enthusiasm as she kept up to Millie's pace. "This house lives and breathes. Do you think the place has a soul?"

"What kind of technical wizardry does one need to engineer all this?" Caroline asked.

"Well, this defrocked engineer witnessed many varied forms of automation in her life, but never to this level of sophistication."

"Defrocked," her mother hissed. "You quit the job you held. You're still an engineer."

"Poetic license, Mom."

Millie recounted how Jonah had found his way to the kitchen this morning and how Barnum discovered Jonah in the precarious position he mentioned.

"The poor boy could have broken his neck."

Denny stopped in her tracks. "What if he opens the door and goes outside on his own. You realize no amount of promising not to do so will never deter him, right?"

"Barnum removed his privileges to the key outside doors and the door to the pool," Millie answered as they took the last lap to get to the kitchen.

"Yep. Quite the sophistication in automation." Denny said.

"Well, at least one can develop a hardy appetite by walking to the kitchen," Caroline gasped.

What About Barnum?

Binary Bounty # 1

Millie laughed at her mother's wit, something she missed these last few months.

They entered the bright, airy kitchen and her mom and her sister drew a breath as they walked in, turning around a couple of times to soak in every little detail they could find.

"There's a butler's pantry somewhere behind those doors."

"I can't even imagine what the upkeep of this place must be," Caroline wondered aloud.

"I think I need to live here," Denny stressed using a sarcastic tone.

"Well, brace yourself," Millie told her sister. "You're about to become even more desirous of living on the premises. I think Barnum and Jonah might be in the pool. Follow me."

When she got to the pool door and requested it to open, the three women entered the area. Denny and Caroline reacted similarly with big eyes and broad smiles.

Barnum had opened the French doors, and when they swam, they could see the ocean's waves.

"Well," Caroline breathed, the first one to recover. "I'm glad I brought my trusted swimming costume in my bag." she patted her coral straw-weaved bag. "I'm going to love to go for a swim."

Denny waved at Barnum and Jonah. as Barnum helped Jonah swim while letting him go once in a while. "He's a quick learner," he told the ladies as he came close.

"Jonah, you can swim!" Millie's smile made his little face beam.

"Yes, Barnum taught me how, and how to float. I can swim under the water. I know how to hold my breath."

"You made his day," she addressed Barnum with a grateful smile, thoroughly happy he took genuine care of her son.

"How warm is the water," Denny wondered aloud.

"Somewhere in the nineties," he answered matter-of-factly.

"Salt system?" Denny asked, always the technical one, Millie thought.

"Yes." Barnum turned toward Jonah. "Jonah, I'm going to need your help to make breakfast for your mom, your aunt, and your grandmother. Think you can lend a hand?"

Jonah eyed the pool, and Millie sensed his disappointment. She was going to add something to Barnum's question to reinforce good behavior in Jonah, but her little boy surprised her. "Sure. Just when I was getting good. Can I come back later?"

"Yes. As often as you like, as long as there is an adult with you."

Jonah and Barnum got out of the pool, and Millie almost turned her head. She found the tall man's clingy swim trunks quite revealing. He reached for a towel and donned his shirt, wrapping the towel around his waist. He bent to shake the water out of his hair.

Denny cleared her throat. "The hunk is more incredible than his house," she whispered in her sister's ear. She pulled out the recorder from her purse. "Take this and tape the conversation. I'll go with Jonah and get him settled in his room in front of his shows."

"Stay and have breakfast with us first. Give Jonah a chance to eat and drink. The swim might have made him hungry."

Denny stared at Barnum. "Yes. Hungry, as in hamana-hamana-hamana!"

—Thirteen—

DISCOVERY

Barnum gave the three women full run of the kitchen and the butler's pantry showing them where he stored everything. All four concocted a superb omelet they filled with grilled vegetables while Barnum prepared his favorite cheese sauce. Coffee flowed, and while each commented on the delicious meal, no one addressed the subject prominent in their thoughts: why Barnum brought them there. Of course, Millie wondered where Barnum got his hands on this much fresh food. The man, his house, his prowess dealing with everything and everyone around him still a mystery she ached and feared to discover.

True to her word, when Denny finished her breakfast, she excused herself taking Jonah by the hand and giving Millie the wink to remind her of the little recorder.

While out in the hall, Denny pivoted and came clean. "I'll be back, Barnum and I asked Millie to record the meeting should I miss anything if this is okay?"

"Not a problem," he answered not seeming the least bit surprised or disturbed in any way.

With Denny's avowal, Millie realized Barnum owned her sister's approval. He scored high on Denny's trust-o-meter for her to admit to her shenanigans. And Millie considered Denny's validation of Barnum might be the more worrisome side of this whole scenario. She counted on Denny's no-nonsense, less-likely-to-take-anyone's-guff attitude. Her sister's acceptance of Barnum meant Millie would need to exercise twice the vigilance around the mysterious man. She would need to be the level-headed older sister for once.

"So, truth time, Barnum." Caroline's sharp words drew Millie from her thoughts, and she thanked God for her mother's arrival. Although a big part of her regretted her mother being mixed up in these improprieties, the rational part of her sensed she might lean on the woman's wisdom and formidable experience.

Barnum stood at the counter scraping dishes to line them into the most massive dishwasher Millie had ever seen. Her eyes quickly riveted on Barnum. After the swim, he'd changed into a loose fitting pair of baby-blue nylon pants, and the white T-shirt he wore depicted a full pair of shoulders while drawing attention to his small waist and lean, yet muscular physique.

He wiped his hands on the dish towel and brought the coffee pot with fresh cups to the table. "What did you learn so far?"

Caroline smiled. "Tactics of a star debater, I see." She raised her hand to prevent his next words. "I understand. No need repeating things twice." She poured coffee into her cup and motioned to refill her daughter's cup, but Millie put her hand over the rim. "What little I know about this situation, I learned from Millie and Denny. And of course, last night when I had a couple of nice chats with the police captain, Ruiz."

"Twice?" Barnum pulled up a chair and sat right next to Millie.

What About Barnum?

Binary Bounty # 1

Millie held back from pulling her chair away so intense became the sensation Barnum invaded her space. She took a deep breath and stayed put when she spotted a smile in her mother's eyes, perceptible only to her.

"Yes. The first time when the girls and I went to the police station, and later the same evening, after the tragic shooting. I sent Millie to the room and waited for the authorities."

"What did Ruiz tell you?"

"First, his staff needed to reach him at home. And I fell asleep in the next room before he arrived. Perhaps this explains why his story sounded so disjointed." Caroline related almost word for word the statement she obtained from Ruiz.

"So, first he tells you the hotel guards alerted the army, and the army's threat becomes the reason you are still alive." Barnum swirled the coffee in his cup, deep in thought. "We've been trying to establish for weeks the people responsible for leaking our information to the cartel." He eyed the two ladies and added, "Once Denny takes note of this recording, I will need to make sure we erase it."

Millie glanced at her mother who gave her a nod. "Of course, we will erase the information. We do not intend to release this to anyone else."

Millie turned to stare into Barnum's face. "You are part of the multinational task force, aren't you?"

He smiled, taking his time to stare back at her. "Yes. I am. The night at the Mandala Club, I was chatting with one of the informants we use. We pay him substantial amounts of money, plus he hates what the gang did to his friends. But, I could not afford to spook him by revealing who you were."

"So, you gave me an alibi," Millie added her tone soft.

He nodded. Turning toward Caroline, Barnum explained. "At first, we believed the hit on Julie Swayzee was done by the man she hired to kill Jed."

He waited until both women's stupor subsided before he added, "Jed's ex-wife didn't know the man she hired was a viper. Still, Luis is probably not the one who killed her."

Caroline's eyebrows rose. "And who was Mrs. Swayzee's lawyer?"

Barnum smiled. "I think you suspect the answer since you ask."

"Gregorio Villante. Unbelievable. But did Jed know this?" Caroline asked.

Millie was shocked. "How can Villante be both their lawyer?"

"Well, it's not uncommon for a divorcing couple to use the same lawyer. The tactic can save the injured party some money, in this case for Julie Swayzee. But to answer your question, Jed did not know she used his lawyer—used being the operative word. In fact, the two of them concocted this plan to get rid of Jed. As his widow, even as an ex-wife—Jed has no heirs, no family and never changed his will—she would inherit everything he owns. Villante made sure of this."

"My God. So what happened?" Millie asked laying a hand on his. "Why would she want Villante dead if he made sure she received all the money?"

Barnum looked down at Millie's fingers stroking his arm and smiled. Millie stiffened at once, wrapping both hands around her coffee cup.

What About Barnum?

Binary Bounty # 1

"The man she hired happened to be a low-life lieutenant in Alfredo Aguado's team, brother of Romeo Aguado, the cartel leader. Jose Fernandez said he overheard Luis' phone conversation with Julie and volunteered to help him. Jose stood guard in the hallway and said Luis entered with his key card. He killed her and made off with her case loaded with the big bills she promised to pay him."

Millie appeared surprised. "Wait a minute, Jose Fernandez, Ruiz's friend and a mole in the cartel?"

Caroline admitted. "Ruiz told us Fernandez sensed himself roped into doing this. That his wife and children's lives would be threatened if he absconded."

"Yes. Fernandez was appalled by Luis' streak of violence, he said, and the fact that he did not respect his word to Julie Swayzee. However, we suspect Fernandez might be taking home a secure paycheck from the police department and collecting money from the cartel he does not declare to his captain."

Caroline chuckled. "Perhaps he sees no need to report the money. Perhaps he shares the money with his captain."

"For weeks now, we've agreed the good captain should receive minimal information."

"This is why he didn't make any sense about the hotel guards and the military," Caroline added

"Exactly. The hotel guards are there to protect the guests, and they never contacted the military."

"Ruiz said they did."

Barnum smiled as he shook his head. "The military is a last resort, and the guards had no way of being sure of anything."

"Why did Ruiz lie?"

"He took a chance with what he thought might be an educated guess. Besides, the last thing he wants is for people to think he is unaware of what's going on in his precinct. Luckily, for some time now, our information to Capitán Ruiz is being weaned."

"This doesn't make sense," Caroline argued. "Why kill Villante and try to kill Jed. Julie was dead. There were no witnesses able to bear any stories. They had the money she promised. I don't understand."

"Now I can see why you are such a great lawyer."

"No smoke, please," Caroline admonished with one raised eyebrow, which was never a good sign, Millie pondered.

Barnum laughed, his broad smile inviting the same smile from Caroline.

Too charming, Millie thought.

"Shortly afterward, someone killed Luis for his involvement in the affair. Any cartel leaders in Mexico realize they cannot tolerate independent contractors within their groups—people who haul their own money through any means. Their dealings are planned and engineered to be surrounded in secrecy. Retribution for anything must first be discussed and approved by the rest of the group."

"Yes," Caroline smiled. "I can imagine how difficult their trading must become when a murder brings them all this unwanted publicity."

"Exactly. When the Aguado brothers went through Julie's case, they found an envelope with the money she had promised Luis. Inside the envelope, they also found a handwritten letter with the directive to kill the lawyer Villante as he was at the heart of the Sinaloa cartel's plan of launching an all-out war on

What About Barnum?

the Jalisco clan in two weeks' time."

"Why would they suspect a lawyer of leading a cartel gang. Lawyers lie inert behind the scene, like snakes collecting all the money they can." Caroline appeared well versed in their procedure, and Millie eyed her with pride.

"A lot of speculation exists about who is running the Sinaloa compound now that Rotsman and his sons are in jail. The rumor circulating is a prominent suit took over, and even if this is a rumor, the fact complies with the letter. The letter also mentioned a few other names needing to be eliminated."

Millie asked, "Why would Julie write down such instructions. A little too compromising, don't you think?"

Barnum rose to fetch a fresh pot of coffee as Denny entered the room.

She took the seat next to her sister. "Don't mind me, you can continue, and I'll catch up with the recorder later."

Barnum returned and reached for another chair. "From the moment the American authorities spotted Gregorio Villante entering the United States, they contacted the FBI. Took no time to get a record of Villante's conversations from his hotel. Once they established a crime was about to be committed outside their jurisdiction …"

"Julie, recruiting Luis to kill Jed," Millie stated to help her sister catch up.

"Yes. FBI turned their findings over to the CIA—to two specific agents working on the drug cartels while residing in Mexico."

"Something in those conversations, right?" Denny asked.

"Yes. Aside from Villante discussing Jed's murder, he also

mentioned he intended to kill Julie once she inherited. At first, we thought Julie found out, either she overheard the conversation or one of the agents conveniently told her. However, when the story of the attack the Sinaloa cartel planned on Jalisco surfaced in the same letter, we knew Julie did not write the message."

Millie's surprise at the turn of events made her ask, "How did you find out—about the letter, about its content."

"The man I met that night at the Mandala Club, an Irish expatriate by the name of Fin Walsh—extremely well connected, gave me proof of what he told us a few months prior. Ten weeks ago, after a particular shootout at one of the restaurants downtown, Fin related what we considered to be a far-fetched story, impossible to believe in fact—one we thought he gave to absolve his friends of well-deserved culpability in the shooting. Two people died, and tons of money went missing. The night I sat with him at the Mandala Club, Fin told me about the letter in Julie's case."

"So fast. How did he know?" Millie asked.

"He knew about the letter beforehand, before the Aguados finding out about this. He also held a picture of two of these men exchanging money."

"Who?" Millie asked.

"One of the CIA agents, right?" Caroline smiled.

"Yes. The two CIA agents are working in tandem."

"Unbelievable." Denny shook her head. She got up and rummaged in one of the cupboards for an empty cup. "This coffee still hot?"

"I believe so."

What About Barnum?

Binary Bounty # 1

"So, Fin's informants about the letter were those two CIA Agents. What do you plan to do? Aren't these men contributing to the multinational task force?" Caroline asked.

"Yes, they are. The next morning, I placed a call to the Director of National Intelligence."

"This wouldn't be your director. Aren't you MI6?"

"I'm on loan to MI6, but I am an American. Anyway, the director permitted me to proceed with caution and to alert the other three in our task force. He also mentioned he was sending two men down to work with us to secure a confession from the traitors—one way or another."

"Oh, that sounds ominous. You men play rough. Wait a minute. What other names did the informant find in the letter?" Caroline breathed. "You said the letter also mentioned a few other names the hoodlums wanted to eliminate. What are these other names?"

"Ah, yes." After a slight hesitation, Barnum gave in. "Names are Millie Brewer and Jed Swayzee. Although by now, Caroline, you are also a target."

The wind knocked out of the three women who sat back in their chairs. Caroline was the first to express shock. "Is this because the men in the Jalisco cartel believe Jed, Millie and I were surrounding the so-called new leader of the Sinaloa cartel and plotted the purported hit?"

Millie's hand shook when she put down her coffee cup. "I'm a single parent raising a son. I can't afford to leave him without a mother."

Barnum stared at her intently. "No one is going to hurt you. I promise." He ran his hand down her back. "This attempt or contract on you three is not handled by the Jalisco cartel. This is the doing of those two rogue agents who recruited a group of known criminals to grow their trade. Men like them, barking up the rear, will use any means at their disposal—even killing innocents and tourists to frighten authorities into looking the other way."

"Here is a thought," Denny announced. "The shooting a couple of months ago at a downtown restaurant was not done by the Jalisco cartel. I bet the two rogue agents organized the bango-rama."

"Right on the money," Barnum smiled. I am meeting tomorrow morning with Romeo and Alfredo Aguado. They say they possess the proof we need."

Caroline shook her head. "Wait a minute. Aguado brothers might be blackmailing these CIA operatives. Why would they want to help your cause? You might be walking into a trap."

Barnum chuckled. "I assure you nothing can hurt me, and I'm not going alone." His glance traveled from Caroline to Denny and to Millie where he stayed a little longer. "I was trained by the best, and you never, ever need to worry about me."

Caroline clammed up. The other girls also did. Such adamancy resounded in Barnum's statement. They accepted the message first hand.

"In fact, the two CIA traitors are becoming dangerous. The Aguados aren't stupid. They concluded this after reading the letter." Barnum hesitated. Then he stared into Millie's waiting eyes and admitted. "Since Julie did not write the letter," he added in a whisper appearing unsure he wanted to add anything more.

Millie stared into his eyes when she added, "Of course, and Luis did not write the letter, which means those CIA agents did,

What About Barnum?

Binary Bounty # 1

and they're most likely the ones who killed Julie Swayzee."

"My, My," Caroline breathed. "Aren't they creative. The two might even spawn the reason for doing so is to decimate the cartel, to remove their power." Caroline stared at Barnum. "This is why you brought us here in the middle of the night. Not because of Aguado's threat, but because of those two demented, rogue agents. They might be the ones who fired at Villante and all of us through the window. The ones in the helicopter."

Millie had never seen her mother this upset. She asked, "Didn't you say Fernandez volunteered when he heard Luis' conversation with Julie?"

"I believe Jose told Ruiz he volunteered while he admitted to the Aguados he was forced into Luis' demand—natural reflex to save his life," Caroline explained.

Barnum nodded slowly, eyeing her with a gleam Millie could not identify. "Correct. What transpired from there and who contacted who, I cannot say. Some of us believe Fernandez walked into the room to find Julie dead and seeing Luis pick up the pink valise thought he killed her. No matter how this went down, we suspect the two CIA men killed Julie Swayzee."

Caroline rubbed her face with her hands. "Of course, they murdered Luis so he could not disavow his culpability of Julie's murder."

"Not to worry. The meeting we have tomorrow will go a long way to restoring the Aguados' faith and their help. Even if they are blackmailing the agents, they understand these agents are more of a threat than they can handle."

"Blackmailing victims often are," Caroline whispered as though to herself. "Of course, they can't get rid of the agents.

Such an action would bring down the whole world on their organization."

"Until I meet with Romeo and Alfredo until they are satisfied with the deal I'm offering they will not consent to help."

"Even with their blessing, I'm sure there is little they can do to help us." Caroline sighed. "Evident that we are still in danger."

"What about Jed?" Millie's voice trembled. "He's out there alone. He doesn't know. I tried to reach him this morning, and he already left the hospital."

"He is still in the hospital. The doctors and nurses were told to say Jed left. I gave him a new passport and a new name for the time being, and when they do release him tomorrow morning, he will be staying with a friend of mine."

"What about our business, the training?"

"Jed said he contacted two people who will finish the training and wrap up the meeting."

Fourteen

WALK ON THE BEACH

Millie kissed her son's cheek. He calmed down when she settled with him in his room to watch the movie the Good Dinosaur. Now, Jonah slept peacefully. They spent a couple of hours in the pool during the afternoon, and she sensed her son to be waterlogged and all out of excitement for the day.

She tried not to think of tomorrow, of all the uncertainty her future carried. If something were to happen to Barnum, what would they do stuck on this island? "No sense crossing a river before you reach it," her mother would say. She was right. Worrying would not solve anything.

Millie sighed and headed to her room. She spotted Denny ensconced in one of the big cozy chairs with a book she picked up off a shelf in the media room. "I think I'm going to go for a walk," she told Denny. "I need to clear my head."

"Clear your head or catch up to Barnum? If your answer is number two, you'll be muddling your thoughts, not clearing them up." She closed the book on her lap, eyeing her sister with a pointed look.

"Denny, what about Barnum? Not everything is about him."
"Really?"
To Millie, Denny's smile proved she was in a mood to tease.

"To tell you the truth, I feel sorry for him—stuck here with the likes of us. Throw in a five-year-old child, and the nightmare is complete."

"My words of caution don't concern you. They concern Barnumf."

"What do you mean?"

"The little machine you gave back to me?" Denny smiled taking in a deep breath. "Blank."

"What? I turned on the recorder. I remember I did. Maybe the little thing got busted. During the shooting last night, the machine went flying off the table on the marble floor."

"I tested the recorder this morning, and it worked fine."

"Might be an intermittent problem."

"No. Yours and mom's voices are recorded."

"You're kidding." Millie rolled her eyes. "Of course, you're not. Would you like me to fill in the blanks of our meeting?"

"Thanks, Mom did a little while ago." Denny laid her head back against the edge of the chair to gaze at all the stars out this evening. "Strange. I told her, Barnum's voice did not record. Mom didn't seem surprised—not one bit. For a criminal mind such as hers, I found this odd."

"Fact is she likes Barnum—likes him a lot. When she talks to him, she loses the I-am-British sort of airs. Talks to him like an equal which is rare since it usually takes Mom weeks, sometimes months before she's comfortable with a new person."

"I'm sure the way we've been corralled together has something to do with it. Just mind your step, sis."

Millie moved over to plant a kiss on her sister's head. "I will. By the way, where is Mom?"

What About Barnum?

Binary Bounty # 1

"In her room. Said she would take in a little telly to help her fall asleep."

"I guess I won't bother saying goodnight. Wouldn't want to wake her."

As she ambled down the hallway, Millie agreed Denny's words served their purpose if only to make her more aware of the indescribable mood creasing her thoughts. Restlessness took on a weird sort of malaise she could not name. A spot of nostalgia mixed in at the moment—not homesickness because she missed the apartment she shared with Jonah. More like a little girl's loneliness. The impression of someone who traveled too far too quickly and has no idea how to get back.

The odd emotion happened whenever she allowed too much time to lapse before mentally tallying the efforts she made to arrive where she stood. She called the introspection measuring star growth against spiritual growth.

The last time she accounted for her life was last Christmas when her divorce became final. Two years before Todd and her going their separate ways proved to be empty years during which she didn't think any spiritual growth occurred. With him chasing every skirt he found, assessing her emotional barometer became frustrating. No point in Todd's denial anymore, not since she caught him in bed with one of her girlfriends—the man too good looking and too charming for one woman—not unlike Barnum.

On her way to the media room, she wanted to get lost in the gist of some movie. Millie sighed with annoyance when a wrong turn brought her in front of the pool door.

She supposed she might grab something from the kitchen and then go to the media room. But when she peeked inside the pool area through the window panes each side of the door, she discovered the area bathed in the light of stars and the towering sphere of a full moon. The enchantment prompted her to enter. A hint of pink lined the western horizon. The faint light would soon be gone giving way to a dark roof permeated with a river of stars flowing to inject emotional warmth.

The door obeyed her request and allowed her to walk inside. As bright as the white room reigned during the day, the place appeared ghostly pale under the pitch of dancing stars.

"Well, hello there."

Millie jumped as she turned and spotted Barnum sitting in one of the red loungers. The other chair, sprawled less than a foot away, did not inspire her to join him. The little glass table next to his chair carried binders and papers, and he seemed to be working on a tablet the only light around diffused by the apparel in his hands. She also spotted the sizable diamond ring on his finger. He always wore the piece of jewelry. Never seemed to worry about someone stealing a rock that size.

He indicated the chair beside him with his hand.

She came close to leaving. She needed to be alone, but the thought of Barnum's meeting in the morning prompted her to be kind. After all, he was going out of his way to help them, perfect strangers, and in such a lavish manner she couldn't find the heart to say no. She stayed glued to the spot while her heart lurched in her chest. Why did the sight of this man fill her with dread—did the mystery of him frighten her? Why did her eyes upon Barnum create such longing for him? How was he able to ignite her desire to run the other way while in him arose the power to fan the burning need to be held in his arms?

What About Barnum?

Binary Bounty # 1

Millie sighed, and her bottom lip quivered when she caught him rising and step swiftly toward her. Try as she may, running the other way was out of the question. She could not move.

He stood inches from her, as though he could not get close enough, and the gesture annoyed her. She opened her eyes and stared into his. He had such dark eyes—dark, disturbing eyes laden with an emotion she recognized but did not want to name. *Impossible. The man is inordinately charming.*

Barnum stepped back and gave a command to the area: "Roof."

Millie looked up and spotted a strange concoction of materials pulling up outside over the immense skylight. "What is this?"

"Leaves, twigs, tree branches—camouflage should anyone fly above us and look down."

"That's why the lights are off."

He nodded. Turning once more toward the area, he ordered, "Sides." Immediately, similar material slid across to cover the sides from the outside.

"Exotic in a way. It appears as though a jungle surrounds us."

"Would you like to go for a walk on the beach?"

She noticed he left the whole front of the atrium still exposed, the doors ready to open at his command, and she couldn't think of a safer person to walk with on the beach once darkness erased the colors and all shadows big and small came crawling in the night. What about Barnum? Would she be safe from Barnum?

With the atrium dark and both exterior sides tucked away, she pondered indoors might not be much safer at the moment, not from his soft breath she caught caressing her cheek. "I never realized lights were installed in the pool area." She didn't know why she said this, more to break the tension and draw attention away from her short breaths, a sure sign of a quickened pulse.

"Lights," Barnum called, and the beautiful glass walls dressed with white sconces became aglow with soft lights transforming the area from spectral to warm.

"What will it be?" He stroked her bare arm. "You and me sitting side by side while I run by you what we intend to say tomorrow during the meeting, or you and me strolling on the beach and talking about anything that comes up?"

Millie certainly had her fill of discussions about the country's regime, yammering about traitors and murderers and whatever else people were liable to bump into during the night. Why she set out to watch a movie. She suspected Barnum somehow agreed with her but afforded her the choice, so she answered for both of them. "I'd love a walk on the beach." Her turn to smile.

"Then a walk it is."

Their feet left no discernible footsteps in the sand as they plodded away from the rock face on the small strip of beach along the back of the islands. Barnum grabbed her hand, and although she found this strange, she didn't have the heart to pull away. She left her shoes inside and welcomed the fact the sand was still warm.

Later, as the night progressed, the pebbles would cool as the world slept while people waited for life to return and the heat from a mighty star known as the sun—a ball of gasses composed of seventy-five percent hydrogen and twenty-five percent helium. She wondered what might be Barnum's composition, and found her musings strange. Where did his charismatic warmth and palpable vibrancy originate? Very few people would ever

What About Barnum?

Binary Bounty # 1

pull off imitating the sun. Did he draw strength from the dazzling ring he wore?

"You're quiet. What's on your mind?" He brought her hand to his lips and kissed her wrist.

A mechanical gesture she expected—or longed to enjoy. She wasn't sure which one applied. "Oh, I teach creative writing and English, or at least I did as of a couple of months ago. I guess sometimes I think I should spend my time writing. My mind runs amok with all these crazy ideas, and if this happened to anyone else, I would insist they sit down and write." She eyed him with curiosity. "I believe some people live to act out their stories, while others remain on the sidelines to write about the adventures others experience."

"I can tell you're part of that first group of people. Why else would you leave your teaching career to be part of Jed's action-packed new business?"

She laughed outright, his wit taking her by surprise. "Yes, action-packed these days, a given. To be fair, I didn't quit my job. I am a professor with tenure, so I took a year sabbatical—always the practical one." She bumped into him to avoid a rock in the sand, and he held her up with a hand around her waist. "I have to be practical," she continued while turning to stare into his eyes. "Raising a child requires me to be sensible, organized, and to let go of being such a dreamer."

He placed a hand behind her neck and caressed the side of her cheek with his thumb. "You may interrupt your occupation of being a dreamer from time to time, but this does not warrant you shelving the dreams."

"Are you a dream? Is this house part of the dream?"

"Is this why you're so jittery around me? You don't believe this is real, that I'm real?"

"Sometimes, I think I'm going to wake up, and you will have never existed. I will no longer be able to find you. But this is not what frightens me. I fear the mystery of you, not knowing who you are."

"I told you who I am. I told you what I do. You know where I live. What more is there?"

"You never told me about us. Why you feel the need to be so close. Why you seem to enjoy staring deep into my eyes. Why you kiss my hand whenever I least expect it." Millie smoothed the hair out of his eyes. "Why I remember you from my dreams. Even when I let go of being a dreamer, the images pour through when I sleep or while I'm awake. If the mystery of us is merely created by my fervid imagination, rather than from bits and pieces still alive—perhaps from somewhere in the past—I need to know."

He came as close as he could his hand securing her from backing up. He bent and kissed her lips in a soft yet sensuous touch. "I'm glad you started to remember," he whispered against her mouth. "The memory of us is both, alive in the past, and in the sweet promise of a future we might share together." He gathered her in his arms, and she realized the soft moan his gesture extracted from her made him tremble.

A noise disturbed their union. The fibrillating sound of motorized blades. Barnum eyed the sky. "A helicopter. Hold on to my arm, Millie." Barnum tapped his diamond ring and closed his eyes and whispered aloud a word she could not repeat if her life depended on it.

What About Barnum?

Binary Bounty # 1

He gathered her in his arms and Millie witnessed the wisps of black clouds turn into the softness of white linen, the helicopter noise disappeared, and the sensation of buoyancy set butterflies aflutter in her stomach. She held on to Barnum for dear life as they floated somewhere far above the ground.

They touched down again once the threat vanished. Millie stared at him, and for the first time, Barnum's antics did not frighten her. "Would you like to tell me about the meeting you're holding tomorrow?" She smiled, stroking the mesh of hair that kept falling into his eyes.

He rewarded her with the ear to ear smile he bestowed on fortunate people now and then. She thanked her lucky stars she was one of them.

"I would love to share this with you."

"Who was in the helicopter?"

"Now, how would I know?"

"If you answer my question, I promise not to ask where you brought us just now, or how you carried us away—or about the power of the ring you wear."

The smile was back. "The helicopter belongs to the Aguados. They are the only ones allowed to take it out."

He flicked her nose gently. "Now, here is my trade. If you kiss me right and proper, I will visit you in your dreams."

She took in a deep breath while steadying her legs. "In my room or my dreams?"

"In your dreams—for now."

"Deal," she said a tad breathless as he parted her lips and allowed his mouth to explore her own. Millie moaned softly and sensed his pulse quicken and his grip tighten while his hands moved provocatively up and down her back—big, gentle hands, and she didn't want this kiss to end.

When Barnum released her, she wondered why his eyes were indigo instead of black. She smiled up at him and admitted. "I held up my part of the bargain, now I will hold you to your promise."

One more of those smiles that melted her heart, and a brief salute of his head tilting to the side. "I never break a promise."

CHAT WITH MOM

Millie and Barnum's discussion lasted a couple of hours. After she politely said goodnight, she walked back to her room thinking she would be alone with her thoughts as her mother and Denny likely slept by now.

In fact, she tiptoed before walking past her mother's room as she spotted the aperture wide open.

"Millie, let's chat."

Her mother's friendly tone caused Millie to jump, and as she turned, she took a few deep breaths to settle her heart. "Mom, you scared me. Thought you'd be asleep by now."

"I was. Fell asleep in front of the news, but then some singing choir on the telly woke me up."

Once inside, Millie pulled a chair closer to the bed. "Don't get up, Mom. I'm not staying long. I'm exhausted."

"How's Barnum?"

Millie guessed the subject—her mother never one for mincing words. "I didn't plan on bumping into him on my way to the media room, but he was preparing his meeting for tomorrow on the deck of the pool."

"Don't care how you met, just want the juicy details of what went on between you two."

"Well, I hoped to find some answers about him—like a name, or why he seems to favor me, and why he appears wherever I am."

"You didn't," her mom exclaimed. "Courting trouble, my darling."

"Maybe you're right because now, I'm more mystified than ever. The man is an enigma."

"A mystery perhaps, yet this mother can spot the intense attraction he harbors for you—the sentiment palpable, and truth be told, somewhat frightening at times. I understand and approve your need to be cautious around him."

Millie shrugged. The sense she learned nothing about the man prevailed over her feeble attempts at communication. "The trouble is he gets me so nuts when we're alone together, I lose my sense of direction. The fact is, I discovered next to nothing of the thick shroud he appears to wear like a glove, no leeway at all in finding out what makes him tick."

"Something to do with that mammoth of a ring he wears, I'm sure."

"Yes!" Millie stared at her mother who waited for her daughter's impressions of the man. "Mom, do you believe in a ... past life?" Slim shoulders hoisted shyly. "The premise we all lived before and tend to reincarnate with the ones we love?"

"God awful question. I believe the debate is still out on that one. Although, I took pleasure in trouncing your father's nullifying beliefs on the subject more than once. However, being faced with the possibility my daughter is pursued by a man who loved her in a past life is quite the spoiler."

What About Barnum?

Binary Bounty # 1

"I thought you liked Barnum?" Millie got up and brought her chair closer to her mother's bed.

"Well, I'm blessed in that both my daughters possess a keen sense of people, although I give you somewhat the edge on Denny in the area. You're a lot like me when it comes to sizing up the people you meet—most likely quicker at doing so than I am being wrapped up in this red flag of caution us Brits deploy when encountering new people. Probably why your sister Denny never married or never enjoyed a long-term relationship that I am aware of."

Caroline drew a long breath, and Millie pondered she'd never caught her mother this fatigued.

"Still, you're right. I do like Barnum. In fact, I would have loved a son of mine to be just like him. So, yes. I like him a lot. I guess my wholehearted approval of someone I know nothing about is what surprises me most, and renders me a tad uncomfortable, as do most penchants this Brit cannot seem to recognize as a part of her demeanor. I'm sorry, darling for this long-winded confession, but in my defense, I'm sixty-two years old, and I never quite befriended anyone as fast as I took to Barnum—whatever his name is."

"What I didn't tell you is …" Millie hesitated.

"No time to be a prude now. Not after I gave you the run-around of my gloomy closet."

Millie chuckled. For a sharp-witted lawyer, Caroline Stuart displayed a poetic heart when she spoke with imagery. "Fact is, I dreamt about Barnum—long before I even realized he existed. Meeting him here, encountering him on a daily basis brought the dreams back. And, Mom, none of them were nightmares, all pleasant, soft and chaste, for lack of a better word."

"How odd. Your sister Denny maintains Barnum brought us all on this forbidden island so he could spend more time with you."

"You can't be serious."

"Well, your sister is a pragmatist at heart, I'm afraid. She gets this from your father."

"I'm sure merman didn't float us all here in this uncanny house just to be with me, Mom."

"Merman?"

Millie laughed. "Just what I call him sometimes—because of the way he popped out of the ocean when least expected and walked on water to bring my son back to me."

"Walked on water is a bit much, don't you think?"

"Mom, lifeguards, and hotel staff told us, again and again. It is impossible to walk on that stretch of beach littered with debris, sharp coral and a riptide current that could carry out a school of porpoises without any trouble."

"I remember you telling me this. Frankly, I don't care how merman did this, snatched my grandson from a watery grave, which come to think of it, most likely accounts for the reason I favor Barnum as much as I do. He saved both my grandson and my daughter's life. Face it. You, my darling, would turn to mush without your son by your side."

Millie nodded at her mother's suggestion. Her life would be over if she lost her son. Some people never quite recovered from the loss of a loved one like a child you love and who depends on you for everything. Without a doubt, she would fit this last category of people.

What About Barnum?

"What did you talk about?"

"We spent the last couple of hours going through what he intends to say to the Aguados tomorrow. He'll be entering their compound with another man in tow, one who agreed not to say a word and let him do all the talking."

"What is he offering them?"

"Immunity on all the charges that arose in the last year or so, meaning he recognizes the attacks on uninvolved individuals came from the CIA rogue agents, although he will not admit to this openly. Barnum is going to try to ask the Aguados to provide the names of those responsible and convince the brothers to testify against them."

"Yes, but Barnum is aware of the two men responsible for these actions."

"This is how he will start. If they refuse to cooperate, he will inform them the United States Government is aware of the traitors, and they are trying to secure these agents' arrest." Millie hesitated. Barnum swore her to secrecy. Still, she deemed it okay to trust her mother. "I learned some anonymous person from the Sinaloa cartel contacted Romeo Aguado to advise him about their supposed invasion taking place in two weeks' time. The caller stated the threat did not come from Sinaloa but, from an independent source."

"Seems to me, they'll have no choice but to agree to Barnum's demands if they do not wish our government to accuse them of collaborating with the traitors." Caroline gave her daughter a sign to come closer. She kissed her on the cheek and smiled. "Get some rest, darling. We'll talk more about this in the morning. The sun will chase away all our dim views on the subject—the Barnum issue that is."

"Goodnight, Mom." Millie smiled at her mother as she tip-toed out of the room.

Once inside her bedroom, she caught Denny sleeping soundly in the next bed. Her sister's face appeared peaceful underneath a ceiling brimming with stars. Denny left the skylights open mentioning earlier how she fell asleep the night before counting stars instead of sheep. However, every time one scintillated a little brighter than the next one, she lost count and needed to begin again.

Millie looked in on Jonah, being careful not to go too close. She did not want to wake him. Luckily for her, once her little boy fell asleep, aside from the occasional nightmare, he remained so until morning.

She slid between the sheets putting her head down on the comfiest pillow she ever found. The bed, soft and molding her body's contours, also made a good impression on her. She smiled at the weird notions invading her mind, of Barnum promising to visit her. As she drifted off, Millie wondered if this might happen? She wondered how someone might project himself into another person's dreams? Of course, Barnum may have been polite—his affirmations an apt measure of wishing her goodnight. She'd dreamt of the tall, hunk of man while living in California, long before she met him. Millie remembered Barnum's question: "You don't believe this is real—that I'm real?" What a strange question to ask when he stood in front of her.

About to fall asleep, she woke, sat up in bed startled by an odd, repetitive sound. *My cell phone.* She rushed to pick it up before the ring woke Denny and Jonah. Grabbing her bathrobe,

What About Barnum?

Binary Bounty # 1

she stepped out into the hall to take the call. Millie uttered a greeting punctured with curiosity, her tone brusque as she didn't recognize the number.

"Millie, Jed. Where are you? I tried to reach you so many times. Called your number but got no reception."

"Jed? This is not your cell. Are you still in Puerto Vallarta?"

"Yes, I'm leaving tomorrow. Where are you, by the way?"

"Staying with a friend of my mom's."

"Did Ruiz give you back your passport?"

"Yes. Technically, we can leave. We'll be returning home too, I guess." She hesitated not wanting to reveal what Barnum had told her. "How is your leg?"

"I'll need physiotherapy when I am back in California. Don't want to waste time with this here. It'll be a while before I return to Mexico."

"Where are you staying?"

"Someone came to see me at the hospital, a CIA agent. Can you believe this? He says Julie's murder was committed by some operative in one of the drug cartels to keep her from spreading some information about our lawyer. Would you believe Villante was also her lawyer and about to rob me down to the last penny?"

All Millie focused on was the word CIA. "What did this man look like?"

"Short, dark, looked like a Mexican, but with a British accent. Strange. Almost didn't believe the creep at first, but then he knew about my new passport and helped me to register at another hotel and provided me with a plane ticket home. He said the same operative who killed Julie was trying to kill me."

"That is strange," she whispered a tremor in her voice.

"I couldn't leave without checking up on you. Someone said you were kidnapped or something and held against your will on some island or other. Glad to hear you're staying with a friend of your mother's."

"So, I'll see you at home. How did the rest of the conference go?" Millie's question sprouted mechanically, as she fought to quash the panic invading her.

"A roaring success—go figure. All this drama allowed the group and me to become closer. Trouble turned out to be a blessing—well not for Julie, of course."

Once Millie hung up, she slid down the wall in the wide corridor and ended up sitting on the floor, fear overcooking her legs like string beans turned to mush.

"Come on, Millie, must be an explanation," she murmured. *No one ever gets the story straight when people play with secrecy. The best way to find out about Jed's claim is to go to the source. Ask Barnum about these allegations.*

Where was Barnum? She rose slowly and considered she didn't even know where Barnum's room was. "Please, indicate the way to Barnum's room," she asked the house. Nothing happened. No light along the corridor, no inkling of where to go. She tried again. "Where is Barnum's room?"

All at once the trusted light indicated the way, and she followed through a meandering of corridors glad she would be able to rely on the string when she returned.

After a ten-minute walk, she arrived at two large double doors and hesitated to open them. What would Barnum think if she walked in while he slept or while he lounged around in less

What About Barnum?

Binary Bounty # 1

than he wore when he swam at the beach—in the buff.

Millie turned around and headed back when she considered she might not be able to sleep if she didn't ask him about Jed's far-fetched story. After all, they were on an island, had been brought without their consent, and given strange explanations of what was going on.

Drumming up the courage, Millie asked the door to open and stepped across the threshold where she nearly fell in the water. She stepped back to secure her balance. When she gazed upon the turbulent size of a small lake, she realized this had to be the garage where Barnum moored his yacht. The turmoil of Bahía de Banderas stirred the water in continuous motion—or did the hydraulic pump beneath the ocean floor create the turbulence? The walls carved of rock appeared as though they'd been erect for centuries, and the open front door gave the place the look of an underwater cavern. Of course, the light of a full moon on the churning sea indicated the yacht was gone.

Millie wondered why the light depicted this area as Barnum's room. Was this where he slept, on his boat?

More importantly, she needed answers to her questions. She made another attempt to communicate with the house. Barnum hooked up this whole structure to some computer. She needed to keep her queries simple as her last question demonstrated, so she asked, "Where is Barnum?"

A computerized voice answered, "Barnum is on board Lunar Five."

Strange name for a yacht. "Where is Lunar Five?"

No answer came from the computer. Millie figured some requests might be off-limits to guests, as Barnum had done for Jonah by securing some of the outside doors.

Following the light to her room, she decided to contact Barnum on his cell phone. He did give her his private number to use in case of emergency—this situation being an actual crisis she pondered.

A feminine voice answered.

"Perhaps I dialed the wrong number. I wish to speak to Barnum."

"You have the right number. However, Barnum is occupied at the moment. Would you like to leave your name, and how he can reach you?"

Millie hesitated. This gruff feminine voice sounded familiar. Where had she heard it before? No accent, just off somehow. "No, thank you." She hung up promptly and continued the walk to her room. She would need patience to sleep through the night

.

—Sixteen—

DOUBTS AND DEVICES

Barnum walked over to one of his men. "Anything to report on the island, Barnaby?"

"A couple of communications broke through since the first morning you brought your guests."

"I am aware of the one from Millie to the hospital."

"No. One to Millicent Brewer's phone from an outside line and another call came to your phone from Millicent Brewer's line."

"What? I asked Helika to monitor this for us."

"Looks like she slipped up again." Barnaby gave him an eyeful of scorn. "Something tells me she is working on an agenda of her own."

"What makes you say that?"

"Helika is too concerned with what you say and do. My feeling is she chose you as a mate and omitted to tell you."

"Don't be ridiculous. Our transformation does not allow us to choose one of our own as a mate."

"Something tells me she doesn't care about the rule and is jeopardizing your mission to your choice of a mate."

"I'll talk to her. Thanks for the warning, brother."

Barnum didn't believe his brother's words. Barnaby had no

idea about Helika's choice of her own—a cattle rancher from a very wealthy family who raised bulls in Barcelona Spain.

"How much longer before we can land?" Barnum asked.

"Another hour."

"We'll need to do this soon, or else we will no longer benefit from the cover of darkness to keep us hidden."

"I'm going as fast as I can. Meanwhile, did you ingest a pod? There are unique pods on the table in the galley."

"Maybe later." Barnum walked toward the console preoccupied with the fact Millie tried to reach him, and he did not get the message. "Who answered the communication I received?"

Barnaby checked the log sheet. "Helika answered. I see here Helika asked for a name and number and offered to take down a message in the system, but the caller did not leave one."

***

Millie woke up to a little bundle of joy jumping around her on the bed, making her nauseous and dizzy as she bounced up and down as though she were on a boat—or a yacht. The thought finished rousing the fog in her mind, and she remembered last night's dilemma and her need to reach Barnum. She also remembered Jed's words which did not make much sense but were too alarming to ignore.

As for Barnum, untrue to his promise to visit in her dreams, Millie realized she would never bring this up. How needy would she appear if she attempted holding Barnum to his promise? She considered herself foolish for believing in such a wild story. She sincerely hoped the rest of what Barnum told them didn't turn

What About Barnum?

out to be irrelevant, and Denny's impression of them being on the island because Barnum wanted to spend time with her nothing other than her sister's vivid imagination.

Still, all things considered, she opted not to tell her mother or her sister about these new developments. No need to worry them. A cold shower to cleanse all thoughts of Barnum happened to be what she needed right now. He would be at his meeting this morning. She'd wait for him to return.

Millie rose and tried to make a call to Ruiz to inform him they were at a friend's house if he needed them for anything. However, she could not get an outside line. Her cell phone would not connect.

She tied her bathrobe and turned to greet her son. "Good morning, my baby kangaroo," she hugged Jonah's little body between two bounces. "Jumping around like a true kangaroo."

"Are you calling me a Joey? That's what they call baby kangaroos, you know," he said his voice tremulous as he continued to jump getting more height now his mother was out of the bed.

"Well, you're getting too smart for me, Jonah." Millie smiled at Jonah. She headed for the bathroom just as Denny came out, Millie's mood souring quickly. What had they gotten themselves into now?

"Hey there, big sister," Denny gave her a play of her eyebrows. "What time did you go to bed?"

"Not too late. Had a little chat with Mom before I did."

"I'll take Jonah to breakfast if you don't mind. Give you some time for your morning ablutions in peace."

"Heavenly." She turned toward her son. "Jonah, Aunt Denny will take you to breakfast, okay? You be good, and mommy will join you in a little while."

When Millie arrived in the kitchen, she found her mother and Jonah seated at the counter, and Denny at the stove preparing breakfast.

Jonah swung his legs as he ate eggs and toast, picking at his bowl of cereal now and then.

Denny poured maple syrup on her ham slices and offered Jonah the same treatment. "I can't believe the amount of food in this house. Anything you think of, you find. Amazing." Denny smiled as she served her sister. "Big slice or small?"

"Just a couple of toasts and some fruit for me. I'm not hungry. Thanks, sweetie." Millie brushed the top of Jonah's head with a loving hand, though a tad unsteady.

"Something's up with my eldest daughter. What's wrong, Millie?"

"Just trying to communicate with the outside world and I can't seem to do so." She turned toward Denny. "Did you bring your cell phone with you?"

"Yeah, clipped to my belt. Want it?" Denny turned spatula in one hand and the handle of a pan in the other. Putting down the pan, she lifted her T-shirt's corner to point to the cell phone hooked to her belt. "My hands are greasy. Help yourself."

"Thanks." Millie tried it but got the same message saying no connection to any network.

"Mom, did you ever give your cell phone number to Barnum?"

"No. The man never asked. Why?"

"Have it with you?"

Caroline handed over the phone she kept close.

What About Barnum?

Binary Bounty # 1

Millie tried the number she knew by heart, and the connection went through. "Hello, I would like to speak to Capitán Ruiz, please."

When he picked up, Millie told him who was calling. A stubborn silence at the other end surprised her. "Are you there?"

"Yes. Señorita Brewer. A team of police officers was looking for you all day yesterday. Someone witnessed you leave the hotel in the middle of the night two days ago constrained by four men and forced to board a yacht. Is this right?"

Millie released a deep breath. Nice to be able to relax again. All this talk of their kidnapping might stem from this eyewitness who spotted them leave. "Stories people will weave," she said with a smile in her voice. "When a friend of my mother heard about the close call we experienced with the shots at the hotel, she suggested we go stay with her for a while. So, her sons picked us up in their yacht and took us to safety."

"Well, thank you for letting me know. We tried to call your cell phone, but the line appears dead."

"I realize this. I just charged the battery." She rolled her eyes toward her mother. "There's another reason for my call. Remember the answering machine I gave you with the information on those three messages I received?"

"Yes, you can retrieve the machine. We no longer need it."

"Thank you. And, do you remember when you couldn't hand me the name of the person who gave me the alibi at the Mandala club?"

"What about him?"

"Well, I met him, and I would like to corroborate his name with you since I am shopping for a little thank you gift. I don't want to write the wrong name on the card." She waited, but Ruiz said nothing, and she hesitated to confirm his name. What if this betrayed Barnum in some way, jeopardized his plans with the Aguados.

"I guess it's okay for me to tell you since you met him. He goes by the name Barnum," Ruiz answered, giving the letter r a Spanish roll.

"No other name?"

"No. All these agents use code names. This way, they cannot be found."

"Thank you for your help. I will keep in touch."

Millie hung up and smiled to herself. "Mom, please don't mention you own a cell phone. I hope you brought your charger as yours is the only phone we can use—for now."

"Millie, what is this all about?" Her mother had those prying eyes which meant her question was a summation rather than a simple demand.

Millie made sure Jonah was well settled and then she proceeded to tell her mother and sister about Jed's call and the uncertainty plaguing her. She detailed going to Barnum's room and finding nothing but the garage.

"Do you suppose he lied to us?" Denny's worry showed in her narrowed expression and tight lips.

"I believe someone at the hotel saw us leave, as per Ruiz, and thought the worst considering the shooting, and this was why Jed thought a couple of men kidnapped us. Although, I can't think how Jed reached me on my phone at that hour after trying for two days, or why I can't call out this morning, and neither can Denny." She gave her mother a dire look. "As I said, you do not own a cell phone." She handed back the phone to her mother. "This way, should we need to leave in a hurry, we can."

"Well," Caroline shook her head. "This is unnerving."

Millie could always tell when her mother wallowed in the grips of doubt or juggled with something she did not understand. A tremor in her neck moved her head, ever so slightly, and she wore little-girl-eyes of a lost child, as though she didn't own a brilliant IQ or possess the best track record in law in the United States.

Denny sat down with aplomb, staring at the table and biting her lower lip. Millie realized she was sulking when Denny threw the words at her. "What if he is a cheat and a liar? Who's to say he dealt with us honestly? If I can't use my phone and you can't use yours, this means we are being held against our will—rumor or no rumor."

"Why did you ask the Captain for the hotel's answering machine back, Millie?"

Millie eyed her mom with caution. She didn't want to say just yet she thought she recognized a voice. In fact, she concluded she should have followed her first impression to not divulge anything disparaging against Barnum. "Well, the hotel is going to charge me if I don't bring it back, right?"

"Right."

"And Denny, please keep an open mind. I intend discussing the subject and more with our friend, Barnum, upon his return."

Millie ate breakfast, and the joy hovering over the kitchen when she first arrived had taken a dive. Even the sun pouring into the place like syrup from a bottle appeared to have darkened and turned sour.

At least Denny now ate her breakfast after making sure everyone else got theirs. Millie dropped a hand on hers to encourage her to be more positive. "You would make an extraordinary mother. Do you know that?"

Took a few deep breaths before Denny smiled, but when she did, the whole room appeared brighter. Whether the change occurred due to her writer's vivid imagination or not, Millie smiled back, grateful to catch the return of her sister's strength.

"Here's what I'd like to do." Her mother took a long sip of her coffee and explained. "We have the run of the house, right?"

Both girls silently consulted with each other and agreed.

"Excellent. Then, we explore every nook and cranny of the place. I want to know why you couldn't find Barnum's room last night."

"Maybe, Barnum only owns the two rooms he shared with us. Now, he sleeps on his boat?" Denny raised her brows.

"Good assumption," her mother answered. "Although this place has plenty of other rooms, you'll agree, I'm sure. The house could have told Millie to head toward any one of those rooms."

"Houses don't talk, Mom," Denny rubbed her mother's back as she said this. "Man's most likely got an ultra-sophisticated computer system that records everything we say, we do, and we ask." Denny raised her eyebrows as she stared at Millie and her mother.

"Well, I'm way past caring what he thinks of us or what his demands might be to keep us safe," Millie bracketed the last word— bravado shaping her facial expression with a little more anger than she wanted to show.

"Still," Caroline added with poise and a Mona Lisa smile she delivered with perfection. "Let's not antagonize our only way off

What About Barnum?

this island. In fact, I believe Barnum is well intentioned in restricting our cell phones. After all, someone using their phone to get to yours can easily ping your phone to pinpoint where you are. Today, people can provide these services at little cost, using the guise of a child-find solution." She eyed her daughters with a hoisted chin and a slanted stare suggesting diplomacy.

"Trust Mom to be up on recent technology." Millie drained her cup of coffee. "So, where do you suggest we begin?" She caught her son, playing in his cereal, stacking the little corn-colored rings in his milk. "Jonah, sweetie, are you finished with your breakfast? We don't play with our food, right?"

"Not a game, Mommy. I'm putting the little circles on top of each other to stop them from drowning."

Sadly, Jonah's thoughts of submersion still affected him, although she thanked God the experience did not make him scared of water. He learned to swim since his accident and Jonah's enthusiasm for the pool made it easy to forget he almost drowned in the ocean a few days ago.

"Well, if you're not hungry anymore, we're going to go visit the rest of the house. Interested?"

"Sure, Mommy. Can we invite Barnum to come with us?"

"Barnum is at work, Jonah. When he returns, he can accompany us, right, Aunty Denny?"

"Yes. The first thing we do is tell Barnum all about this."

Caroline chuckled as she rose from the table. She picked up the empty plates and laid them in the sink. "Something to do later."

Seventeen

THE HOUSE BREATHES

Jed reached for his travel bag and called the front desk for the bellhop to pick up his two suitcases to bring down to the waiting cab. He looked around the room, hating its diminutive size, the dingy furniture, and the fact the hotel stood in the middle of Puerto Vallarta's tourist district where noise and merriment kept him awake these last two nights.

Warned to stay away from the Marriott, he still popped in there once or twice to talk to his group and make sure they were on the right track. As advised, he scoured the space around him wherever he went. Only once did he suspect a car of following him back to the hotel, but the driver moved on once his taxi left him by the curve.

Now, at the airport, he searched behind him as per the instructions he received to make sure no one tailed him.

He would be glad once he sat on the plane and watched the tarmac roll underneath their aircraft while he surveyed Mexico's skyline shrink in the background.

He checked his bags and hopped on the mobile walkway to get to the gate marked on his boarding pass. He checked the area his head bobbing left, right, not quite a circle—except with the help of his legs—like one of those goddamned weathercocks. *What was wrong with these people and their morbid dose*

What About Barnum?

Binary Bounty # 1

of paranoia. Why would anyone want to kill him? He didn't even speak Spanish. He had no political ties, no untoward agenda, and all he wanted was to be left alone to return home.

Once more observing his surroundings, Jed caught someone dodging behind someone else, as though the man's wish was to hide—from him? He turned around and waited while counting to sixty. Once more looking in the area, he spotted the same man from the corner of his eye. He'd changed his position and ran while trying to avoid the people—as if the man didn't care anymore whether Jed spotted him.

Jed began his dash along the moving aisle which gave him a distinct advantage. Then, he spotted the sign for the women's washroom and ran inside, occupying a stall. He then took his cell phone and punched the number the CIA agent gave him in case of trouble.

"I'm being followed. Man, not quite six feet tall, Caucasian with a big nose and wearing black pants, a black shirt and tie, and a beige sports jacket. Oh, and he sports curly brown hair."

"Where are you now?" the voice on the phone asked.

"In the woman's washroom, closest to my gate. I'm flying to LAX leaving at two twenty-four by way of Delta Airlines."

"You're early."

"Couldn't stay in that hotel room another minute. Besides, I thought this might be a good way to fool anyone who might be waiting for me to leave. All planes leaving for Los Angeles depart after two p.m."

"Stay put for another ten minutes. One of our men is following you. We did spot the man on your tail. So, in ten minutes exactly, leave the premises and go toward your gate. We'll be right behind you."

Jed hung up and didn't recognize who he talked to, though the voice reminded him of the British bloke he first encountered. And, the plan did nothing to reassure him. Nevertheless, he would do as told.

***

"So, where to now?" After two attempts to locate Barnum's room brought them to the garage, Caroline looked to Millie to choose another path.

"Too bad I didn't bring Jonah's skateboard. His little legs will tire soon."

"Don't worry, Millie. We can each take a turn carrying him," Denny smoothed her nephew's hair. "Are you getting tired of walking, Jonah?"

"No," he answered in his most bored voice.

Millie considered he needed something to do. "Let's ask to see Barnum's office." When she got the approval from the others, they asked the house to point them in the right direction. When they turned into the next hallway, Jonah bumped into his little skateboard.

"Look, Mom. We didn't forget to bring it. I can use my skateboard."

"Whoa. Where did that come from?" Denny whipped around to stare at her sister. "Did Barnum give this to Jonah so he might go faster up and down the corridors, perhaps?"

Millie eyed her mother and her sister. "I hope so. I didn't bring Jonah's skateboard." Millie called her son. "Jonah, show

What About Barnum?

Binary Bounty # 1

Mommy, sweetie." She grasped the little toy and checked underneath. Jonah's full name was on the bottom in black indelible marker. "This is his all right. No helmet, he doesn't ride. No way. To roll down these marble halls is dangerous enough. Do you know how many times he falls off this thing—which is the main reason I didn't bring it." Millie knelt to explain to her son, "Jonah, you can't ride without your helmet. I'm sorry. Did you put your skateboard into mommy's bag before we left?"

Jonah shook his head, the pout on his face evident. Then he jumped up all excited. "Look, my helmet is over there. I didn't see it before."

The three women caught the protective gear now lying on the floor where Jonah had found his skateboard.

Jonah didn't wait for permission. He donned the red and blue helmet and grabbed the skateboard from Millie's limp hand. He raced halfway down the hall. "Come on, you slowpokes. You need to follow the light to Barnum's office. We're going to see Barnum."

"How sweet. You said Barnum was working, so he thinks he is in his office." Denny exhaled as she smiled. "Such a sweetheart. Was I ever this young?"

"Younger." Caroline posted a teasing smile for Denny. "Could Jonah have packed the skateboard when you weren't looking?"

"I just asked him. He said no." The three women witnessed Jonah stop to tighten his helmet.

"More than an ultra-modern computer controls this house." Caroline's whisper sounded ominous.

Denny paled when she stared at Millie. "Science fiction?"

They picked up the pace not to let Jonah get too far ahead of them.

"No." Millie's negative seemed affirmative and unwavering. "As a matter of fact, I'm prepared to concede Jonah packed the damned thing himself without my knowledge and doesn't want to admit it—rather than revert to science fiction." Millie didn't care how frightened she sounded.

"Still doesn't explain the helmet." Denny called out Jonah's name. When he didn't answer, she ran on ahead. "I'll get him."

"Wish we had boards so we could move a little faster," Caroline voiced. Both women continued jogging, hoping a skateboard might wait for each one of them at the next turn, but when they reached the end of the corridor, they spotted Denny holding on to Jonah while waiting for them to catch up, but nothing else.

"I'm a little disappointed," Caroline muttered. "How wonderful would it have been to find a couple of boards right here waiting for us?"

When Denny's eyes seemed to bulge with curiosity, Millie explained what Caroline tried to do.

"Maybe, this thing we wish for has to be in our life. None of us has a skateboard in real life. Perhaps, the computer may only retrieve an item when the object is already a part of the things we own—bringing it forth." Denny touched her index to her nose, judging her answer more than plausible.

"Let's try this," Millie suggested. "Jonah, if you had your tricycle, you'd be able to get farther so much faster."

"No, I wouldn't. I'd still need to wait for you guys."

All three women laughed. When they looked up, they found Jonah's blue and red tricycle with tassels hanging from white handlebars and the scuffed-up back-step his friends would stand

What About Barnum?

Binary Bounty # 1

on now and again.

Not a word echoed from either woman as Jonah yelped with glee when finding his bike. He jumped from the skateboard and hopped on his tricycle. "Come on, Mom. You people will need to run to catch up with me."

"Not so fast, little one." Denny jumped on the skateboard to trail behind him.

"Mom, what does this mean?"

"Wish I could tell you, sweetheart." She rubbed Millie's arm. "I always provided you with any answer you needed in the past. Now, I'm sorry. I'm at a loss."

Millie started running again. Grateful her mother was in such great shape. She hoped the exercise would not exhaust her.

"How far is this office," Caroline demanded. "We've been ambling down this maze for ninety minutes."

Millie laughed and turned toward her mother. "That's because we walked in circles to find Barnum's room, remember?"

"Sort of wish we hadn't."

Millie grabbed her mother's hand to help her along a little faster. "I'm so glad you're here, Mom. Otherwise, I might think I was going crazy seeing all these things appear out of the blue."

They spotted Denny ahead with Jonah. They'd stopped in front of something, maybe a door.

"Well, I'm not certain that counting three insane people amongst us instead of one is a whole lot better."

Millie giggled, and relief washed over her, glad her mother proved to be a good sport. "You found a door?" Millie asked.

Denny had shed her sour mood most likely deciding she would enjoy these anomalies. "Yep." She laughed. "Only this is not a door. We are standing in front of a flight of stairs."

"No!" resounded from Caroline as she looked up a staircase made of glass. "How is this possible? Has to be acrylic or something, not glass, I'm sure."

"What amazes me is we found another floor. On top should be, the grounds, outside the rock? My impression tells me Barnum keeps this place hidden." Millie attempted the first step. "Jonah, leave your bike, sweetie, and hold Mommy's hand. We're going upstairs."

Denny grabbed Jonah's other hand. "Hold on tight, Jonah." She turned toward her mother. "Come on, Mom."

Caroline began the climb. "Are you sure? I don't like to invade anyone's privacy. Still." She defended their behavior. "Barnum did give us the run of the house."

"Might be a small, camouflaged observatory. Not to worry, Mom," Millie said as she reached the top stair and grabbed her son's little body, so afraid he might tumble down. She held her breath.

"Door open," Denny pronounced. When nothing happened, she inverted the command, "Open door." She shook the handle, but the door remained locked.

"Maybe you're right, Mom," Millie conceded. "Certainly doesn't look like he gave us access to this room."

Denny's eyes rounded as she told Millie, "You try."

"Why me?"

"Can I go back down to my bike, Mommy?"

"In a minute, Jonah." Realizing her mother also appeared eager for her to place the command, she did. This time the door opened.

What About Barnum?

Binary Bounty # 1

"Well, I'll be," Caroline murmured. "Seems the man trusts you, Millie."

"Yeah, and we're about to violate that trust."

"Nonsense. The fact the door opens is Barnum's permission for you to enter."

Releasing a huge breath and avoiding chewing on the inside of her lip, Millie took a few steps inside the room. She gasped, only making the others curious. Nothing could have prepared her for what she encountered.

Millie stared in awe, pivoting on the spot to catch the full effect of a twenty by twenty square foot structure made entirely of glass, all the way up to the ceiling.

"Miles and miles of ocean, Banderas Bay, and the Marietas Islands," Denny enthused. "Hey, we can see the Marriott from here. A speck in the distance, but visible just the same."

"How can this room be made of glass and we're not cooking at this time of day or our eyes itching or burning from June's tropical sun." Caroline walked around to survey the desks and chairs also looking like glass. "This is right out of a storybook." Caroline caught her breath.

"Reflective glass, Mom," Denny explained. "Today's reflective glass now features a broad range of pleasing effects. Gone is that boxy look that used to prevail. A metallic coating on the glass allows us to see out but prevents others from looking in, also during the day. And, the glass allows the right amount of natural light into a building while reducing glare and the need for window blinds and other types of window treatment. With solar control, the glass can reflect incoming solar radiation, which limits heat penetration into the building lowering HVAC usage." Denny rattled off the explanation while looking around the big room.

"This from the defrocked engineer," her mother said with a mocking curl to her lip.

"You're right, Mom. I'm not a defrocked engineer, just a discontented one. All these years of slaving to make a career and the man who is supposed to be my friend says he would rather marry me than make me a partner."

Caroline did a double-take with her head shaking, her mouth agape, words seemingly stuck in her throat. "Don Grimalsky asked you to marry him? Don't tell me. You said no."

"Of course, I refused. The man's been promising me partnership for the last two years, and now he says he would rather I become his little wifey than promote me to full-time partner. No way, the prick."

"Want me to talk to the man? I mean his actions might be construed as sexual harassment, Denny."

"No, Mom. He had a ring and everything, a ring he'd been carrying around for the last six months. And if you'd seen his sad, puppy-dog eyes when I declined his very romantic proposal—dinner at Corso Trattoria with champagne and all the trimmings—you might have felt sorry for him."

"Oh, I love that restaurant," Millie said. "What did you have? And by the way, you never told me Don went through all this trouble."

Denny shrugged. "Grilled Mediterranean sea bass."

"Your favorite dish," Caroline added.

"Yes, my favorite." She stared at her sister. "I never told you, Millie, because the man made me angry. After his proposal I was

What About Barnum?

Binary Bounty # 1

seething, anger oozed out of my pores—ruined my appetite and soured me on the food and the place for a long time to come," she finished in one long, drawn-out breath.

"Can we leave soon, Mommy," Jonah whined.

Millie bent down to her son's level and planted a kiss on his cheek. "Soon, my love. Here are a pencil and some paper. Want to make a drawing?"

"Yeah, I can do that," he said without enthusiasm.

Millie mussed his hair and continued surveying the outside through the glass. "So beautiful," she breathed. Something bumped up against her arm. "Ouch. Oh, my God. Look what I found," she moved aside to allow her mother and sister to gaze upon the telescope she discovered. "Not a big one, though."

"This, my sister, is a reflecting telescope, and though this one appears to be deceptively small, I have no doubt it serves Barnum very well." Denny adjusted the lenses before she peeked at the Marriott Hotel.

"How do you know so much about telescopes?" Caroline asked.

"My passion for many years. And although I don't own one—the one I would like too much for my budget—they fascinate me." After a minute or so, she called Millie over. "Take a look at the beach in front of the Marriott."

Millie applied her eye to the lens and caught her breath. "We can see perfectly. Right down to that cliff where Jonah almost …" She omitted the word not wanting to disturb her son's peaceful moment.

"This is how Barnum keeps track of you." Caroline took her turn to have a peek.

"Doesn't make sense, Mom. He would never be able to reach us in time, would he?"

"Millie, park your eye on Banderas Bay, over to the left," her mother said handing her the telescope.

Millie did and spotted a familiar looking yacht. "Barnum. I can see him on the boat. There is a girl with an arm wrapped around his."

"We need to get back to the main house, and fast," Caroline recommended.

All three hurried down the stairs while Millie picked up Jonah in her arms. When they reached the bottom of the stairs, the tricycle and the skateboard were gone, as was the helmet. "How are we going to manage to get back?" Caroline asked.

Millie thought. "Instead of asking where a room is while we follow the indicator light, why not ask to be brought to our rooms or the kitchen? I'm sure Jonah is starving by now, aren't you, son?"

He nodded, his big brown eyes huge.

Millie asked, "Please, return us to the kitchen."

Caroline rolled her eyes, and Denny shook her head. Almost right away, the floor began to move.

"See," Millie gave both her mother and sister a look of triumph. "Not anything more sophisticated than those airport treadmills, right?"

"Except that at the airport, it's a mobile walkway, and this floor is marble," Caroline debated.

"Might just be a thin cover appearing like marble while the traveling rollers lie underneath the floor, and like everything else, is connected to a command center. In any case, it moves

What About Barnum?

Binary Bounty # 1

faster than the one at the airport—and much more comfortable on the legs." Denny squatted to sit on the floor.

Jonah began to fidget in Millie's arms saying he wanted to sit on the ground too. After ensuring her son's stability, she allowed Jonah to run and sit beside his aunt. His eyes riveted to the walls, Jonah took in all the familiar sights.

Caroline shook her head giving a rueful pair of eyes to her surroundings. "I've never heard of anything like this in today's technology, so I hope you have a frank discussion with Barnum, Millie."

"I will, Mom. Don't worry."

Denny mused, "Actually, our technological advancements have come a long way and may not be so far from what we discovered here today. Stranger feats may exist in certain parts of the world. The fact we are not aware of them might mean those in power, control freaks who would rather these tools remain a mystery, render them unavailable to the rest of us."

BARNUM EXPLAINS

Millie cleared the dishes and breathed easier now she'd fed everyone. She put Jonah down for a little nap, he being unusually cranky, and changed into the bathing suit she kept poolside as she decided to do some laps. Denny wanted to finish the book she started the night before, and her mother retired to her room to rest. She hoped the swim might excise some of the doubts and demons assailing her with all sorts of terrifying thoughts.

As Millie swam back and forth, feeling the water's energy dissolve her physical weight and invigorate her soul, she waited for Barnum's return. Before this charade continued, she needed a frank discussion with him. Asked, Denny refused to take part in the talk her sister considered a private one between Millie and Barnum. "This concerns us all, and whether or not we are allowed off this island, for instance."

Still, Denny agreed with their mother saying the discussion would be best served within the chambers of a closed session of the two main characters; a sentence she spoke with the verve of someone addressing a jury, something Millie recognized.

"Sweet, Millie, you are the most diplomatic spokeswoman of our little group. Trust me. Your talk will fare much better

What About Barnum?

Binary Bounty # 1

without us bombarding the poor man with questions left and right."

Her mother did make a point, although Millie did not consider Barnum, in no way, a poor man. However, Millie sensed the inadequacy of her teenage years surface whenever she and Barnum spent time alone in a room together, or when the two of them strolled on the beach. Something magnetic in his presence curbed all rational thought in her, and she would need to call on formidable focus to remain on target and not get lost in his eyes.

On her tenth lap of the twenty-five-meter pool, Millie climbed out of the water to rest a while and catch her breath. With a clear view through the French doors and surrounding windows, she witnessed the yacht slowly turn to meet with the bay a little way down the beach—the bay where the computer sent them each time they asked for Barnum's room. *So much for catching my breath.*

Millie remembered he sailed with a crew so he would be in rather quickly. She toweled off and opted for one of the comfortable chairs. She wondered if the woman she saw on deck, the one with her arm around Barnum's arm, would also disembark on the island.

Millie sat deck side resting her eyes. She'd dozed off without realizing this as Barnum startled her when he entered the atrium.

"Hello," he said. "Where is everybody else?"

She checked her watch and spotted she'd been lounging in the chair for thirty minutes. "Jonah is resting, so is my mother. Denny is reading in her room. How did your meeting go?" She stretched the pins and needles out of her right arm as it had fallen asleep against the back of the chair.

Before Barnum answered Millie's question, she caught him removing his T-shirt. He unbuckled the belt to his pants and slipped out of them. Barnum wore a boxer-type bathing suit under his pants and dove into the pool. "Sorry," he muttered coming up for air. "I've been waiting to do this all morning."

"You couldn't swim in the ocean?"

"Two others from the task force accompanied me, and we had a lot to discuss."

He continued his swim, and with patience, she waited until he finished a couple of laps. He came out, grabbed a towel and opted to sit in the chair next to hers.

"Where are they now—the other members of the task force?"

"We dropped them a little North of here, to another yacht along the coast." He towel-dried his hair and reached for a drink in the side-by-side refrigerator behind them. "Would you like something to drink?"

Millie avoided his eyes and nodded. "An orange juice would be nice."

Barnum gave her the juice bottle and twisted the cap off his beer. "The meeting went as we expected with our team making most of the concessions."

"Meaning?"

"Well, turns out Costa and Marcos, the two rogue agents, are the ones blackmailing the Aguados. They copied the documentation we painfully amassed during the last year and a half, and promised to keep it quiet in exchange for a significant portion of the cartel's monthly profits."

"So, you're back to square one?"

"Not quite. We agreed to forget about the charges in return

What About Barnum?

Binary Bounty # 1

for their testimony against the two agents. The good news is they also made concessions. They will not grow their territory for the next year or so, and they agreed to release Jose Fernandez from his obligations to them who, as you are aware, infiltrated their organization to obtain information on their operation. Since we cannot use anything Jose collected, they agreed not to harass him or any member of his family or friends."

"That's wonderful. Jose got his life back. Was he on the take?"

"Turns out he was not. The younger Alfredo Aguado allowed the rumor to circulate to keep Jose Fernandez from wanting to reintegrate the police force full-time."

"In other words, they set him up for police and authorities to think he was collecting from them as well."

He smiled. "Something like that." He took a swig of his long-neck and hesitated. "Of course, there is a lot of work to clean this up and obtain permission to seize Costa and Marcos."

"Does this mean Capitán Ruiz can also be trusted?"

"Yes, which is more good news."

"I'm glad the meeting was not all bad." Millie smiled still refusing to look into Barnum's eyes. She sensed hesitation in his body language as he kept switching the bottle from hand to hand. When she glanced at his expression, she found an unusual frown across his brow. Before he continued, she couldn't help saying, "I tried to make a call this morning. My sister tried also, and we had no connection."

"I'm sorry. I omitted to explain the procedure for calling. I put an electronic blockage over the house, and the only way to penetrate this is to tap the zero on your keypad three times which brings you to an operator who will connect you to any number you like. The precautions are to avoid anyone pinging your cellular activity since this way, you are linked to a central phone system and not to your own."

"I see. Thank you. For your information, I called Capitán Ruiz this morning, with my mother's cellular phone—since I found no other way to make a call." She stopped and considered her sentence and wondered why her words appeared so defensive.

"Don't worry about this."

"Anyway, I'm glad I reached him. He seemed to believe we were kidnapped on the night you came to get us at the hotel."

"You didn't tell him where you are, did you?"

"No. Of course not. I told Ruiz we are staying with my mother's friend."

He smiled, stroking her arm with the back of his hand. "Good girl!"

"When I spoke to Jed, he also believed the same story, and he thought we were being held against our will." Millie found she now had Barnum's full attention.

Putting his beer down beside him, he sat up and bent toward her. "You spoke to Jed? When?"

"Last night. He called me." By the set of Barnum's jaw—uppers clamping down on his molars twice in the last few minutes—Millie deduced he accounted for the breach of his security.

"Did the conversation last long?"

"No. Jed mentioned about us being prisoners here, and that he was leaving today."

Barnum picked up her hand resting on her lap. "I hope this

What About Barnum?

reassured Jed, the fact you are not prisoners."

"I told him the same story I gave Ruiz. I don't mind telling you when I became unable to communicate with the outside world, and when nothing we did could reach you …"

"Millie," he grasped both her hands in his. "You need to trust me. You know how I feel about you."

"No, I don't." She pulled her hands away from his grip. "You're using a code name. Other than you working on a secret task force to bring down the cartel, I don't understand the first thing about you." When she witnessed Barnum drop his face into his hands, and shake his head, she thought she might try another way to reach him. "I mean we just met, and you admitted to this profound affection for me—one which can only be derived from years of happiness and mutual respect. I'm asking you to please consider where I'm coming from. I would rather you concede you know me from somewhere … even if it is in the past than profess your undying affection for me now. Appears disproportionate."

"What if I told you I did?" He sat back in his chair, and she figured he worried about spooking her more.

"We met in a common past, in a time long gone."

"Why don't I remember?"

"You told me you did, in your dreams."

"Yes. You also promised you would come to visit in my dreams." She stopped, regretting the words.

He blessed her with his broad square smile, the one that set his eyes on fire.

"I didn't say when, did I? As for why I remember, and you don't, long ago memories are more embedded for some than others."

"I can give you that. But, surely you must understand I don't hold for you the same familiarity your memories about me bring forth."

Barnum rose and invited her to do the same. "Of course, you are right." He wrapped his arms around her waist and brought her closer. "I love that you are here with me. Your presence will allow me to create memories for you, or better still, jog the ones you harbor of long ago—not discarded, merely dormant."

He bent to kiss her lips, but she pulled away. "I rather you explain to me the past you mentioned."

The broad smile illuminated his expression. "This is what I am attempting to do, explain." Before she pulled away again, he pressed his lips against hers, and Millie heard the soft moan Barnum emitted, felt the tremor moving through his arms, the same arms that crushed her against him. The kiss, long and heartfelt, did seem familiar to Millie, like some long-lost sensation she craved without being aware of how sweet the touch of this man's lips might be.

The kiss lasted, his embrace chaste and gentle, and when he released her, his eyes remained closed for a second. When he stared into her eyes, he whispered, "Did I awaken some memory in you?"

"There is familiarity in your kiss, in the tender way you hold me," she said haltingly.

The broad smile returned. "What I like to hear. The veil will soon lift."

She nodded moving out of his arms. Not quite believing his statement, Millie decided to change the subject to one dear to her

What About Barnum?

Binary Bounty # 1

heart. "Now that you made this arrangement with the Aguados, we can leave—leave Mexico and return to our lives, right?"

Barnum turned to stare at the water and took a few steps in that direction. The long hand on the clock facing her on the wall had time to do two complete turns when he pivoted to stare at her, walking toward her as he did. "We were unable to secure the Aguados' help in protecting you, your mother and Jed."

"What do you mean?"

"According to Romeo Aguado, Costa and Marcos are planning to eliminate all three of you. They extracted money from the Aguados so the CIA might compromise the Sinaloa gang for the murders. Romeo claims if he were to interfere, the other two, and the people helping them, would realize something is up and stir all-out war between the two groups."

"This doesn't make sense. We're innocent bystanders. Why us, of all people?"

"Just as you said, innocents up for grabs." Millie's perplexed expression prompted him to explain, "With the murder of Villante, CIA agents weren't able to drum up a lot of support for the reason behind the killing, to eliminate the possible leader of the Sinaloa gang. Villante was crooked, bad to the bone, his murder the punishment by one of their own—family business. However, with the murder of three innocent people, supposedly terminated by members of the Sinaloa cartel, the world would take a dim view of the deed. Federal agents, as well as Mexican authorities, would descend on the lot of them—leaving the Aguados in charge."

"And if the Aguados help you?"

"The corrupt agents will eliminate all three of you, and make sure both gangs are arrested and charged."

"Isn't this what the task force has wanted all along?"

"Not at the cost of innocent lives. These two agents are now our priority. They killed unknowing tourists last spring, and now they bear no qualms about killing again, all for their benefit. We needed to make a choice, and although this is a setback, we made the right decision."

Millie wondered if he needed to fight for the respect of his decision. His arguments appeared well rehearsed. "How will the CIA agents benefit if both cartels are eliminated?"

"They've already recruited a bunch of people. They planned this takeover for two years. They would become the new leaders in charge of selling drugs and reaping in the money—a major coup—and one of the reasons Felix Costa and Brandon Marcos must not get wind that we're on to them. Being as well trained as they are, they would disappear and never be held accountable for their actions."

"So, they can't find us here, right?"

"Correct." Barnum released a huge breath. "You say Jed called you. Do you remember the exact time?"

Millie fudged with her memory of the call. "I'd just gone to bed. Sometime after midnight, why?"

He nodded as though expecting the answer. He answered nothing, becoming tense.

"What's wrong?" Millie feared the worst. No smile in Barnum's dark eyes, only a deeply lined forehead portraying how much he worried.

"We lost Jed." He waited for her reaction.

Only the words didn't register as anything she needed to fear.

What About Barnum?

Binary Bounty # 1

"Lost Jed as you don't know where he is? He is flying home today." She glanced at her watch. "Probably already gone. His plane took off at two—two twenty. I forget what he said." Millie sensed her face drain of color while staring at Barnum's enigmatic expression. "Please don't say they killed him, please." Her words trembled, and she braced herself for the worst possible news.

"We don't know where he is. He has a new passport, and my partner gave him a phone number and taught him how to look behind him and make sure no one followed him. Mitch said he was a quick study and smart. Jed spotted someone at the airport, and he used the mobile walkway to run and lose the man long enough to hide in a woman's washroom. He called Mitch from there. Jed gave him a description. We were following this man. In fact, at some point, tailing him became too easy—giving us the distinct impression another person followed Jed much less conspicuously."

"Did you arrest this man?"

"Of course, we did. Only we had nothing to hold this person. He said he witnessed a man fleece his wallet and thought he was running after the right man. We ran a check on him and found he was once part of Aguado's lieutenants but was let go because of theft."

"What could have happened to Jed?"

"We're not sure. Jed might have come out of the washroom and spotted someone else waiting for him and decided to stay put."

"Which means he missed his flight."

"No. The chase took place early morning."

"They would have been waiting for him at the boarding gate." She began walking, wringing her hands as she did. "Jed is smart. Knowing him, he'll change his ticket to somewhere else."

"He apparently checked his luggage early this morning."

"That wouldn't stop him. He'd just have someone pick it up."

"Where to, do you know?"

She exhaled as she tried to remember some of Jed's habits. "Well, if he believes they know about his mother and brother in San Francisco, he's not going to risk going there. I remember once, he was coming over to see me, but the flights were all booked. He hopped a plane to Monterey and rented a car, and drove the two hours and twenty minutes to my apartment."

"Okay, I'll find out when the next flight leaves for Monterey. We'll have a few agents standing by at the airport."

"Jed wouldn't fly to Monterey. Too far to drive to LA. Maybe you should check out the four, five airports within a two-hour drive of Los Angeles."

"I'll have the agents verify this."

"So, all this is real." Millie eyed him with a little more respect. "I was going to ask you to take me to Capitán Ruiz. I need to retrieve the answering machine I left with him."

"Listen," Barnum walked over to where she stood and took her hands in his. "If I were in your shoes, I would most likely harbor toward you the same doubts you bear toward me. Don't deny it. You wouldn't be normal if you didn't think me a little strange—the type of strangeness most folk associate with suspicion." He raised both hands his head turning to encompass his surroundings. "This house is more than a little crazy."

"More like science fiction or at least, eerily cooperative?"

He flashed the smile she loved so much. "Tell you what, I need to go out again. I'll pick up the answering machine for you."

DEEP WATER

Barnum and Millie spent the rest of the afternoon walking on the beach. She'd given Denny and her mother notice, and they'd promised to take care of Jonah—their contribution to help her get to the truth. After Barnum explained why the house indicated the garage when she asked for his room, she understood a little better.

"I'm used to sleeping on the yacht, and when the Captain parks the big boat in the water grotto, it gives me easy access to the Master Quarters, the entertainment center, the galley, and leaves you four the run of the house."

The long walk on the beach took them to a small cave on the other side of the island. Once there, he invited her to go swimming. "Come. I'll take the bag with me on my back, and we can swim through the opening you see, the one that looks like a tunnel."

"How long of a swim is this?"

"Ten, fifteen minutes. We will go slow and easy. Don't worry."

They dove into the deep waters of Banderas Bay, and Barnum led her through what appeared to be an opening in the mountainside. Once they allowed the current to push them through a small tunnel, they found themselves on the *Playa Escondida*, the hidden beach.

"I can't believe how beautiful this is," Millie breathed as she emerged on the sand. "So this is the wonder one searches for in the *Islas Marietas*. Why so many people visit here."

"One of the wonders, yes. Unfortunately, this beach, though private and secluded, has been exploited without mercy."

"Now, we can enjoy the islands all to ourselves." She stared at him and couldn't help an enthusiastic smile, the one she spotted reflected in his eyes. Millie caught him put his bag down. "What did you pack?"

"Snorkeling gear. Have you snorkeled before?"

"Yes. I gather there's more to see in the water?"

"An understatement. During the winter months, the humpback and gray whales migrate south from Alaska to give birth in the *Bahia de Banderas*, which is the sixth largest bay in the world. Dolphins, sea turtles, rays, and octopus populate these warm waters."

"Wow, but this is June, right? We're not going to come face to face with a humpback whale are we?" The reticence of meeting up with such large underwater occupant held her back.

Barnum laughed. "No. You'll spot sea urchins, pufferfish, cucumbers, turtles, and perhaps a few jellyfish, amongst others."

"Pufferfish more lethal than cyanide. Pray, we don't encounter one of those." Millie rubbed her arms shivering in the hot Mexican sun.

"Here I thought you'd be more worried about jellyfish," he said with a smile. "You know your fish, but don't worry. Stay in my wake, and you'll be fine."

What About Barnum?

Binary Bounty # 1

Millie watched as he opened his bag and the first thing he pulled out surprised her. "Sunscreen?"

"Waterproof sunblock 60. You will need it with your back exposed to the sun as you snorkel."

"You've thought of everything, haven't you?"

"Spending a couple of sleepless nights with severe burns on my back made me a wiser man."

Millie's turn to chuckle.

He pulled out the tube and spread a white blob in his hands. "Turn around."

With gentle hands, Barnum massaged the creamy protection on her back and shoulders, and Millie closed her eyes loving his hands against her skin. Unknowingly, she moaned softly from the deep-seated pleasure of his strong fingers stroking her back.

"Will you do mine?" he asked a sensuous edge to his tone, she thought.

"Sure," Millie answered a little breathless. When she took the tube in her hands and gazed at the length of his back, she hesitated. His suit fell below his waist, and she wasn't quite sure where to start.

"Just my shoulders, and the upper portion of my back. The rest I can do."

"Of course." Her turn quickly ended, though she did add lotion to the middle of his back finding his frame taut and firm, and she handed him back the tube of sunblock.

Barnum gave her a pair of fins and a full mask.

"When you use someone else's equipment the borrowed material rarely fits." She took the gear from him.

He stroked her cheek with his hand. "This gear will fit you."

She tried the mask with the pipe in her mouth and was pleased the plastic hook did not make her gag. Also, the facial cover felt extremely comfortable. As for the fins, they fit flawlessly.

She took out the mouthpiece. "This is perfect. Fits so much better than the gear Todd used to rent for us."

"Follow me and stay close. If you need to let go of my hand for any reason, you can signal me to wait by tugging on my suit," he told her as they flopped on the sand to the water's edge with their fins.

Tugging on his suit? Images of Barnum's naked body—a particular portion of his naked body—emerged in her thoughts. She imagined him on top of her and realized she would not tug on his suit as this would make the removal of the damn thing far too easy.

They submerged once they walked in far enough, and Barnum held her hand.

As they made their way across the bay, she recognized damselfish, giant blue damselfish with white spots on some of them. One, in particular, peered at them with its right eye as the resident fish swam to stay put beside a huge red coral bush. She found her hand squeezing Barnum's a little harder, also wishing she brought an underwater camera. More beauty flowed beneath the surface than found on dry land. Varied schools of fish in all sorts of colors against the blue of the water took her breath away. She had to haul in more air than she thought—the excitement taking its toll.

At one point, Barnum indicated they would go down to spot something dark green lying in the sand. She looked at the top of the water and realized her tube would not give her any air that

What About Barnum?

Binary Bounty # 1

far down.

He indicated she should inhale deeply and hold her breath for one minute as he held up one finger—at least this was what the signal appeared to be. Could she hold her breath that long?

Begrudgingly she inhaled as much as she could from the small tube. When they approached the sandbank, the creature they spotted moved, and Millie recognized a giant sea turtle lying near an open cave. She witnessed Barnum apply a hand to the turtle's mottled back smeared with blue and white patches. At once, the turtle jerked toward her, and she let go of Barnum's hand kicking up her feet toward the top where she would breathe again, panic having forced all the air out of her.

Inexperienced in snorkeling, Millie took a deep breath as soon as she sensed she might be in shallow depth only her tube held nothing but water. And the more she inhaled, the more the pressure against her lungs prevented her from getting the oxygen she needed. Millie wanted to throw up. She emerged on the sand and collapsed on her stomach feeling water trickle out of her mouth. Barnum picked her up and brought her to the shade of rocks. There he gave her mouth to mouth while applying pressure to her chest to rid her of the water she inhaled.

At once, Millie sensed the water gushing out of her lungs and pouring out on the sand as a hacking cough shook her. "I'm sorry," she managed to say. "I feel like such an idiot," she added in a cracked voice.

Barnum helped her stand and trapping her against him he applied a hand on her back bending her slightly while he wrapped his other arm around her waist. Relief came at last when she threw up the rest of the water.

"Didn't think I'd inhaled this much water."

"I'm the one who is sorry. You had no training snorkeling in deep water." He stared at the pupil of her eyes and checked her abdomen. "Can you breathe better now?" He smiled and asked her to take three deep breaths, releasing them through her nose.

She did as he asked. "I'll be all right. The pressure is gone."

"Well, we'll need to monitor this for the next few days, make sure you're not a target for second-hand drowning."

She eyed him with curiosity but shrugged not wanting to ask. "Doesn't hurt when I breathe. I'm fine. I just forgot my air tube was full of water."

She had a few more coughs. "Too bad, because I loved being down there. So calm and beautiful."

"I'll take you back down—after I teach you how to scuba-dive."

She smiled at him. "I would like that." She continued to stare at him and realized worry still lurked in his expression, the tilted eyebrows, the downturn smile. She stroked his cheek and thumbed his lips slowly, eyeing their luscious slant with wonder. When she looked up into his eyes, she shivered from the meaning lurking in their black depths.

He bent and waited once his lips grazed hers, giving her the chance to pull away. When she didn't, he kissed her tenderly then deeper as the heat between them grew to a sizzling fever.

"Ah," he breathed clutching her in his arms. "Please say you remember—even if it's just a bit."

She nodded more to please him than to speak the truth. Some moments in life demanded a little fudging, at least when needing to please a man like Barnum. In time, she hoped she would re-

What About Barnum?

Binary Bounty # 1

member, or she hoped he'd help her remember. Somehow Millie considered he might possess the power to do so, but knowing how gentle this giant was, she pondered he might not want to force her to recall some far away past any more than he deemed necessary. Might be more of a boon for Barnum if Millie conjured the past events on her own.

She abandoned the noxious riddle. She cared more about basking in his charms as they returned to the other side of the island. His arm around her waist, he held her close and rained kisses in her ear and on her cheek. She rested her head against his strong shoulder and sensed something akin to love filling her to the brim. This slow walk back would be the favorite part of her trip and would become a part of their past she *would* remember—for a long time to come.

***

Puerto Vallarta's police station stood as one of the busiest places in the square. Barnum walked in, and the receptionist recognized him. She paged Capitán Ruiz as per his instructions.

Barnum realized Ruiz would put aside whatever he did and scramble to meet with him.

"Good to see you, *señor* Barnum. We have lots to discuss," he said barely rounding the corner. Ruiz threaded his way back to his office and told his secretary, "I do not wish to be disturbed—for any reason."

He sat behind his desk and offered Barnum the chair facing him.

"You appear to be agitated. What happened?" Barnum asked.

"I tried the emergency number you gave me, *pero no obtuve respuesta*."

"When?"

"Earlier this afternoon."

Barnum's recollection of snorkeling with Millie provided him with a warm sensation, enough to ignore the paranoia of a Spanish speaking Ruiz—the captain reverting to his language whenever frightened. "What emergency?"

Ruiz handed him a folded piece of paper.

When Barnum unfolded the note, he found a letter-size sheet covered with words and figures, appearing as though scribbled in a hurry. He checked the bottom of the page. Signature belonged to Jed Swayzee. On the flip side were instructions to bring the note to Capitán Ruiz at the Puerto Vallarta police station and to give it to no one else.

"Who brought this in?"

"Some woman holding two children by the hand. When she used the bathroom, after her plane touched down, she found this note pinned to the mirror with a piece of chewing gum. She read the instructions to bring the letter here. She said she also noticed today's date below the name and thought this to be *muy importante*."

"How did she get here?"

"Taxi. We offered to pay for her ride here. She refused. I also asked her not to tell anyone about her trip here or the note she gave us. She said she was visiting her sister—an expat living here for the last five years and had no intention of telling anyone about this. She also said she did not read the letter's content."

"American?"

What About Barnum?

Binary Bounty # 1

Ruiz nodded.

Barnum read the letter out loud. He figured Ruiz might not have caught half of the note's meaning. "I hear commotion around me. Whistles blowing and people yelling. I think they arrested the man who followed me. Still, I peeked outside the woman's washroom, and I caught a man hands on hips, searching the area. Broad build, tall, black curly hair thinning on top and the sides. A wide nose and a huge mole on his right temple. He wears a ring on his middle finger with a diamond the size of a fist."

Barnum eyed Ruiz to see if he drew the same conclusion he did, but he said nothing seemingly waiting for Barnum to finish. "I am going to wait here for as long as it takes. I changed my tickets online to go to Monterey. I have some friends there. I'll take the taxi directly to the Presidio where an old friend of my father's, Colonel Pope, will provide protection. I've texted him and mentioned the situation." At the bottom, numbers of his flight, time of departure and time of arrival Jed also scribbled.

So, he did go to Monterey. Barnum eyed Ruiz. "How much does Jed know?"

"Very little—at least from our position."

"I'm sure my partner Mitch never told him anything of value, just that he needed to stay low for a while."

"Man has guts. He can care for himself."

"Appears he can. He goes on to add he would like us to contact him once we resolve the situation."

"What's troubling you?" Ruiz asked.

Barnum didn't want to mention the fact Jed's description described Felix Costa. He briefed very few about the defectors.

"Well, if the perps can't find Jed, they're going to come after señora and señoritas Brewer. We will need to keep them hidden for a while."

"They are staying at one of señora Brewer's friends."

Barnum rose. "By the way, do you have Miss Brewer's answering machine? She needs to give this back to the hotel."

Ruiz opened a drawer and gave the machine to Barnum.

"Why do you have this?"

"Three messages on the recorder seemed to worry the Brewer family. We listened to them, and I had an expert analyze the voices. Miss Brewer thought the third message on the machine might be from Julie Swayzee. Jed gave us a recording of his wife's voice while he was in hiding. My expert made a comparison, and he assures me the voice does not belong to Julie Swayzee."

"Why so much fuss about this one message?"

"Came after the others, after the murder."

"Why was I never informed about this?" Barnum sat back down as did Ruiz.

"Not sure."

"After the murder?"

Ruiz nodded. "The first message was Jed Swayzee, stricken with panic, explaining what he found in his room and wondering where Miss Brewer was and for her to call him. The second call from someone unrelated, a woman in their group. The third one came after the deed. A threat uttered. We did not dismiss this as the call happened to be an inside call."

"From inside the hotel? What sort of threat?"

"This last call came from inside the room—Jed Swayzee's

room. As for the threat, content is still there. We erased nothing."

"Any idea who this caller might be?"

"Experts think a man who is disguising his voice to sound like a woman. We thought this person might be Villante. Now, we'll never know."

Barnum eyed the answering machine with discontent. Too many holes lately which explained why he suspected Ruiz of dishonesty. Now, staring at the man behind the desk, rocking back and forth in his chair with a dull gleam in his eye, Barnum realized he expected too much from the chief of police. He deemed honesty to be synonymous with the likes of Jed's smarts. Instead, Barnum conceded he needed to take the man's qualifications at face value. "Thanks for all your help, Capitán Ruiz. I will be in touch."

Twenty

HELIKA

Dinner out of the way, the three women agreed to give Jonah a tour of the yacht. He expressed the wish to visit inside the boat, and Millie suspected he missed Barnum whom he had not seen in a while.

However, when they got to the bay where Barnum stored the yacht, the dark churn of the ocean returned the eerie echo of water lapping the walls and reaching all the way to the ceiling carved in rock—no boat moored on the premises.

"Where's Barnum, Mommy?"

Millie stepped back to avoid getting wet and gave her sister and mother a disappointed glance. She bent down to her son's height giving him a great big smile. "I suspect he had to work."

Denny chimed in, "Of course, didn't you say he needed to go to town and was going to pick up the answering machine from Ruiz?"

"Yeah." She stood and smoothed Jonah's hair as he wrapped his little arms around her legs.

Her mother rubbed her back. "The only way off this island is the yacht. He'll be back."

Millie did her best not to wonder about Barnum, trying to imagine where he might be after seven thirty at night. The sun

What About Barnum?

Binary Bounty # 1

had set, and she felt sure Ruiz had gone home for the day. She never obtained any news about Jed and considered this might be the emergency which presided over Barnum's lateness. He mentioned he would be at the house for dinner. The tone he used told her he wanted to confide in her, but whether his confidences concerned them, their attraction for one another, or whether he needed to talk about the investigation, she couldn't guess.

Once she put Jonah to sleep, a longer process than usual, Denny announced she was going to do a few laps in the pool.

"You go ahead, sis, I'm bushed. I'm going to rest in front of the television." The outing today took a lot out of her. She needed to develop more stamina—her efforts over the last six months consisted mostly of working online while using the help of her creative brain to succeed. She desperately needed a more physical regimen of exercises.

A knock on the door ousted the thoughts away. "Come in."

Her mother stood in the doorway. "Want to go take a walk on the beach? Is this allowed?"

"Of course. I just need to rest for fifteen-twenty minutes."

"Excellent. Give me time to call your father."

"Don't forget to do the 0 three times, Mom to obtain an outside line."

Her mom nodded as she disappeared, and Millie's eyes closed of their own volition, but not wanting to fall asleep she mentally berated herself. *Don't close your eyes, you ninny. You mustn't fall asleep. Come on. You can do it.* Then, she spotted Barnum standing in front of her.

"What are you doing here? Am I dreaming?"

"No. Your eyes are closed, but you are not dreaming. You

need to round up your sister, your mother, Jonah and ask the house to bring you to the observatory. This will help avoid the long trek with the many detours."

Millie nodded, Barnum's tone terrifying her.

"From there, you go up the stairs, step outside and walk along the beach toward the Playa Escondida—a ten-minute walk. Before you reach the hidden beach, you will find the yacht moored to one of the piers. Step inside. In approximately forty-five minutes, all trace of the yacht will disappear, camouflaged. No one will find you."

"From the Observatory? Isn't the place surrounded by rock?"

A pause. "You went to my office," he breathed wearing a big smile.

She nodded. "Yes."

"The observatory is quite high and level with the rock face. Once you walk across the stones and the grass, a slight hill will separate you from the beach. Turn right and walk as close to the wave as possible until you detect the ship. It is unlocked, and the captain and crew are standing by should you need anything. I will explain in the morning."

"We will do as you ask," Millie answered thinking that by walking close to the shore any footprints they left would be erased.

Finally able to open her eyes, she hurried and changed into a warm pair of pants and a warmer sweater. She went out in the hall and knocked on her mother's door. "Mom, sorry to rush you, but can you go get Denny? She's in the pool. Barnum just communicated we need to leave as soon as possible. I'm going to help Jonah dress."

"Righto, darling. Sounds alarming." Caroline got up and jumped

What About Barnum?

into warmer clothes and a long sleeve sweater. She grabbed a bag and packed some emergency clothes and toiletries.

"Hurry to get Denny, Mom. She needs to do the same. Bring a jacket or something. The wind's picked up on the beach, and we'll need to walk close to the shore, getting our feet and legs wet."

"I understand."

Millie went to wake Jonah.

***

Barnum occupied another ship, a starship named Lunar Five. Binar, his birth planet and their people, the Binars, were almost destroyed by the dangerous work of overzealous scientists, not quite nine hundred years prior. Lunar Five stood hidden from human radars behind a shield of clouds and magnetic dust from space. Barnum waited for the people he cherished to be safe on his yacht before taking up a fight with a dear one, a battle coming on for centuries which he avoided for the sake of old friendships, and to maintain family ties.

Barnum turned toward his brother. "Barnaby, is she back yet?"

"No." Barnaby tabulated on the board's computer the angle of Helika's departure and when she expected to return. He rose and stared at his brother. "You're doing the right thing, Barnum. I spotted jealousy grow in Helika over the centuries. Now her animosity measures an all-time high. Your decision will be the only way to replace her unhappiness with some form of comfort."

"I realize this. Being the only female could not have been easy for Helika."

"Binar females need to nest, make a home. They are not what humans call career women."

"Still, going back to our new reformed planet, she'll need to be stripped of all her powers and will have to obey their new rules."

"Not so different from the rules we observed before the surge," Barnaby said.

"She will have a one-hundred-year lifespan at best. She will not bear illness or other forms of misery, which technicians eliminated for all Binars."

"What good did these tests do? Over time, at least fifty of our people decided to return to this new planet to live out their lives. Not everyone wants to live forever and use all these powers."

"Granted. Before I found the love of my life, I too thought of returning to the new world." Barnum turned toward Barnaby. "Have you found someone you can share your life with, my brother?"

"No. I'm in no hurry. A lot of females to choose from on all these planets." Barnaby sat down. "Well, one hundred of us are left—all men and all sharing the same DNA, like twin brothers. The crazy bunch of technicians had us sacrifice quite a bit for eternal life and all the powers we can muster."

"When they gave us the ships and told us to leave Binar's orbit to find an alternate planet where we might locate a life partner to procreate …"

"We should not have brought a woman with us. High priest Brandish told us not to, remember?"

What About Barnum?

Binary Bounty # 1

"Perhaps. Still, finding a life partner also meant waiting for her between life cycles. Something our brilliant minds never mentioned."

"Strange how we Binars do not reincarnate. Why do you suppose that is?"

"Can't say. Maybe we do. Maybe everything and everyone begins again, only we don't remember." He thought of Millie who battled empty memories at the start of each one of her new lives. The same void launched each one of her incarnations. If he refused to remind her, would she manage the recall on her own?

Barnaby adjusted one of the screens. "Here are your friends, needing to run into the night."

Barnum stared at the screen and witnessed a strange scene, a terrifying, lonely scene he hated to serve to the people he loved.

***

Millie, Denny, Jonah, and Caroline followed the wave on the beach by the light of a few stars and a mostly cloudy sky. Unaware of the reason they needed to run other than Barnum advised the four to do so, they readily obeyed realizing he understood the dangers besetting them.

As told by Barnum, the house brought them quickly to the observatory where they went outside and traveled across the stones and the grass. The four wore running shoes and carried backpacks with emergency supplies. Millie hoped none of them would need these supplies, wishing them to be no more than prevention. Denny carried Jonah on her hip for a while. Now, Millie held her son in her arms.

"Want me to carry Jonah, Millie?" Caroline asked.

Millie heard the shortness of breath in her mother's offer and answered with a shake of her head. "We'll soon be there, Mom. Don't worry. He's a little too heavy for you."

"I can walk, Mommy," Jonah mumbled with his head resting on her shoulder.

"Look," Millie enthused. "I can spot the ship."

"Like one of those fairy tale sightings, glistening in the night and all lit up. Quite inviting," Caroline muttered appearing tired and drawn.

Millie conceded this was not the vacation her mother desired. "What did you tell Dad? Is he still demanding you come home right away?"

"Well, you know your father. When Alan Brewer is left alone, to his own devices, he's like a little boy. Quite suddenly he can't cook, can't do the dishes. I told him you girls needed my help and I would stay as long as we found this necessary."

Millie hoisted Jonah a little higher in her arms. She looked around at the dark beach, and down at her wet pant legs and her wet feet, her running shoes soaked by now, and told her mom, "Bet you wish you had listened to him now."

"Don't be silly. I'd be home rested, in dry slacks and dry shoes, but would be sick with worry. I much rather be here contributing to my daughters' and grandson's welfare."

When they came close to the yacht, two men came toward them, and while one picked up Jonah, the other one took their bags. They entered through the stern on the well-polished step at the back of the yacht where warm slippers waited for them except for Jonah. Luckily, his running shoes weren't wet.

What About Barnum?

Binary Bounty # 1

They took the stairs to the cockpit where a lovely padded bench contoured a circular table tastefully set for them. A flower vase and a few candles decorated the embroidered tablecloth. The captain came to greet them, bringing with him a bottle of champagne and lovely finger food. The other two men soon filled the table with more crudités and delicacies.

"If you are cold, we can serve the buffet inside," the captain told them with a smile.

"Are we going anywhere?" Millie asked.

"I was told we are to remain stationary for now." He bowed from the waist. "I am Captain Ramon Villalobos. Please, call me Ramon. I'm here to serve."

The women consulted silently, and Millie told him they would remain outside for a while. The view, enchanting and picturesque, displayed the scintillating lights of Puerto Vallarta in the distance. One of the men bowed and spoke in halting English. "I will help you with your meals. My name is Luis." He reached into the fat pouch around his waist and supplied them with a pair of binoculars. "They are very powerful. You will catch the dolphins jump out of the water, and you can see the hotels along the Bahia de Banderas."

He left discretely, and Millie wondered how she might find them should they require anything else.

"Champagne is delicious," Denny enthused. "Say what you want about this marvelous intrigue. Everything oozes with style. I don't think I've ever been this titillated."

"Watch your language," Millie covered Jonah's ears.

"Nothing wrong with the word," Denny argued. "But, I'll say one thing. I would love to shove this lifestyle in Don's face.

Would he ever freak. Imagine him here this minute?"

"Think of him much?" Millie asked as she poured champagne into long-stem crystal glasses. She poured Jonah a glass of orange juice from the pitcher on the table.

"Nice try," Denny countered. "I'm never going to let Don concede victory, so give it up."

"I see." Caroline's turn to comment. "Fascinating selection of words. Hear wedding bells, anyone?"

"Mom. This is not what I meant."

"Let's enjoy this beautiful, impromptu, utterly rich snack for lack of a better word." Caroline grabbed a plate and filled it with delectable treats. "There are lobster tails, for heaven's sake, and sautéed shrimps, even little sandwiches for Jonah."

Millie rubbed her son's back. "Would you like an egg sandwich, Jonah?"

"Do they have peanut butter sandwiches," Jonah asked.

"I don't think so, sweetie." Millie rose and investigated all the plates. Fruits, vegetables, nuts and dried almonds, raisins, even figs, but all at once a new platter appeared at the end of the table. She knew it wasn't there previously as the dish pattern differed from the others. She peeled back a couple of slices of bread, and found peanut butter in the sandwiches and some with strawberry jam. "Here you go, Jonah. Just what you wanted."

Millie eyed her mother and sister, but no one else caught the stunning party trick.

Caroline took in a deep breath. "Such purified air here. Your father would love this place. I'm going to return with Alan. You can be sure of that."

Once satiated, the captain showed them to the saloon, and to

What About Barnum?

Binary Bounty # 1

their rooms. He picked the master quarters for her and Jonah, the ones Barnum showed Millie, the master guest room for her mother and the smaller guest room for her sister.

"If Don accompanied you, you two would be getting my room," Caroline delivered with an impish smile.

Millie worked hard not to chuckle at her mother's quirky attempt at enticing Denny's thoughts toward Don..

Denny rolled her eyes, and Millie realized her sister regretted her words about Don.

All in all, everyone seemed satisfied. The steward also showed them where they could replenish their water supply and other drinks in the mini-refrigerator in the master quarters and the master guest room and upstairs in the galley.

***

"They're all right." Barnum smiled at the screen depicting his guests. A wave of his hand and the screen turned off. "I see Helika just materialized on board."

"You're going to talk to her?"

"I'm going to make her aware of the decision I made. The council approves and are awaiting her arrival."

"Please find out what sort of hand she had in the violent death of that woman at the hotel, even if your inquiry means the end of the world for us all."

"Of course, I will. As for Helika's rage, she will gather a storm of a tantrum if, as you suspect, her jealousy grew from centuries of misery." Barnum stopped at the door and added, "Please make sure all our guests' wishes are provided."

"Already done."

Barnum left to have a much-needed discussion with an old friend, dreading the pain his decision might cause her but knowing this to be the best solution for her and everyone in fact.

—Twenty-one—

MAGIC

When Helika came into her quarters on Lunar Five, Barnum waited for her, and she jumped startled to find him on the premises.

"What are you doing here?" She smiled, her eyes attempting to entice him. Now that he understood more about Helika's wiles, he realized her friendliness leaned more toward seduction, a scene he did not want at the moment.

He took out a small pod from his jacket and played back the voice he copied from the recorder. "Is this you?"

Barnum caught the answer in Helika's body language, in her panicked eyes.

"Where did you get this?"

"From the local authorities." He stopped the recording and calmed her with his hand. "They don't realize this is you. I was shocked when I caught your voice on this machine. You had to be in the room when they murdered this woman."

She breathed out noisily while shaking her head. "I hid when noise arose in the hallway. Didn't realize what was going on until they did the deed. When the men left, and I came out of hiding, I found the woman, dead."

"You could have stopped this with a flick of your hand. But

you didn't. You thought Julie was Millicent Brewer, didn't you?"

"Of course not. I am well aware of who Millicent Brewer is."

"Were you hoping they might implicate her in this horrible act?"

"Why do you suddenly believe the worst of me? Why? What did I do to make you so angry? You no longer trust me, why?" Helika's squinting dark eyes threw daggers at him. Anger grew in her. Her red lips curled in a thin line resembling some feral cat about to pounce on its victim.

"Why did you go to Jed's room?"

"You sent me to surveil Felix Costa and Brandon Marcos, remember?"

He nodded.

"I overheard them discussing the crime. Thought I would be able to catch the two in the act."

"How about the real reason you stationed yourself inside the room?"

"Okay, okay. I was going to impersonate Millie Brewer and yell at Julie Swayzee, make people think the two had a big fight. I would have made sure a couple of maids stood in the hall to witness their quarrel." Helika wiped her eyes as tears poured down her face.

"Then these men would have killed Julie Swayzee and authorities might have blamed Millie, even though she was miles away—innocent of the crime."

"I lost my nerve. When Julie entered wheeling her pink suitcase, I shuddered at the thought of those men killing her so, I didn't cause a scene and remained hidden. I was going to enter the room and wave my hand, but the man you call Costa was

What About Barnum?

too quick, acted too swiftly and when I rushed out of hiding, I caught the back of him and Felix running away and realized I was too late to do anything for Julie. So, I left."

Barnum breathed a sigh of relief. Through the suspense, Helika remained true to their heritage of no violence and not usurping another's property or taking someone else's life. "Not before you left this message threatening Millie."

"Didn't think my voice would record. Yours never does, neither does your image."

"I programmed it this way."

"How convenient you never told me how to do so."

"I spoke to the council. Binars agreed to take you back. I believe you belong on the new planet—deserve to make a new life for yourself."

"What?" Helika's instinct to back up while she veered to stare at her surroundings indicated she prepared to flee.

"Since you did not harm this world conducting yourself as a true Binar, they will give you a hero's welcome, increased status. You are headed toward a fantastic life."

"Yeah, right. After the council strips me of my powers, and provides me with a lifespan of one hundred years, at best."

"You will not know illness."

"No. But I'll grow old. It's not fair," Helika pleaded. "You and I became engaged to be married before the fusion. The vile fusion that plagued us all with the same DNA."

"In a sense, we were the lucky ones. Thousands died from the poison we were asked to ingest."

"I may as well have died. I lost you."

"When they gave the survivors ships to travel the galaxy and find a place to live out our lives and procreate, I brought you along."

"All the while knowing we could never be together."

"You needed to find someone with whom you would live out the rest of their life. We agreed on this."

"Come to Binar with me. After we take the antidote, we can be engaged again."

Barnum shook his head in a deliberate refusal.

"I still love you, Barnum, and I don't understand your wish to stay here." She approached him slowly. "Yes, all Earths are formidable. But why this particular version? Humans here are horrible. They murder each other steal from one another while hate and envy prevail. How can you live like this?"

"Thousands upon thousands of beautiful souls are abloom on this version of Earth. They need help to awaken, learn how to live in truth and solidarity. We can already sense their future depends on our being here at the right place, at the right time. High priest Brandish has seen humans come of age and unite to impart survival to several galaxies."

"Brandish died of the poison, not long after we left."

"I saw him in a dream in the top half of the last century."

"When you contemplated returning home?"

Barnum nodded. "You must go home, Helika. I will not change my mind. Only one hundred of us remain, and we're in for quite a ride. You realize this."

Helika clenched her fist. "I will not," she yelled.

Before Barnum could stop her, she disappeared. Barnum radioed Barnaby. "Brace for impact. She's on the move."

What About Barnum?

Binary Bounty # 1

***

Jonah finally slept in his mother's king size bed, and Millie smiled at his sweet little angel face. Jonah refused to go to sleep without his purple hippo called, Hippo. The plush animal was small, and although he followed Jonah everywhere, Millie forgot all about the toy in their haste to escape. Then, like for the peanut butter sandwiches, she pretended to take a second look in her bag and wished the hippo's presence. She found the toy nestled at the bottom of the bag.

Jonah squeezed the hippo against him and fell asleep with a big smile on his face.

Millie tiptoed out of the room and climbed the stairs to the main level. She wanted to step out along the balustrade that led to the cockpit to breathe some of the invigorating ocean air.

Barnum said he would camouflage the yacht to remove the boat's sight from prying eyes, although inside the ship all of them were able to gaze as far as vision permitted and take pleasure in the splendid evening. Clouds having dispersed, a million stars peered down from the sky, and she wished Barnum stood by her side to teach her about the many different constellations. Somehow, she figured the yacht's owner might be able to define all of them for her.

"Hey, Millie." Denny dragged her by the arm. "Come see what's going on."

Something in Denny's tone hurried them to the other side of the ship. She stared into the distance at the cove from where they came. She witnessed a strange red light turn blue and create some soundless explosion in different areas. A few seconds passed, and another blue flash ignited in front of them.

"Appears as though something or someone is destroying the house we just occupied—Barnum's house." Denny wrapped an arm around her sister's shoulders. "Do you suppose this is the reason he asked us to evacuate the place?"

"Yep. Must be the reason. Too bad. One hell of a unique house."

"Wait a minute. I still have clothes and things in the house. So do you. Both our laptop computers, our tablets."

Millie couldn't help a smile. "Do you remember everything you left at the house?"

"Of course, I do. Not happy. Not happy at all."

"What would you say are the things you need most at the moment?"

"My tablet and my laptop, all my clothes."

"Well, if you go down to your room, you will find what you need on the dresser, and the clothes you didn't bring are in your closet. Meanwhile, I will find all I need in my room and my clothes hanging in my closet while Jonah's clothes will be folded away in all the drawers."

"What? Millie, are you drunk? Too much champagne?"

"This from the girl who said the house could not bring us to the observatory." Millie gave her the slanted eyes and the side smile meaning for Denny to open her mind.

"You're nuts, and I'm going to prove it," Denny uttered as she took the stairs to go below.

Millie waited, hoping the shock would not encourage her sister's denial. She and her mother discovered what a romantic at heart Denny appeared to be a little earlier when she wished Don

What About Barnum?

Binary Bounty # 1

sat beside her—oh, to shove the surroundings in his face, but they knew better. Something about the man had caught Denny's attention and, to a cynical I'll-do-it-myself career woman, a romantic sentiment might be unforgivable which happened to be the real reason she ran away from her job.

When Denny didn't return, Millie watched the last blue flash raze paradise and took the stairs to find her sister.

Denny sat on the bed in her room fingering her laptop computer. Her tablet stood propped against one of the pillows while the open closet door showed all of Denny's clothes neatly hung and prepped to wear, and she kept shaking her head in disbelief.

She looked up at Millie with such youthful eyes, the sort not encountered since their family sat in Heathrow Airport after having waved goodbye to all their friends.

"How did you know?"

"Small, yet important events like Barnum walking out of the ocean with my son in his arms. Us, unable to record his voice. Jonah finding his tricycle and his skateboard in a place where I brought none of his toys. The place reminded us of science fiction, yet seemingly stood invisible to everyone else."

"What do you mean?"

"Well, don't you think if a house like this became visible, discovered on *Islas Marietas*, the news would attract tourists—even marauders? Plus, Barnum doesn't quite blend in with our culture, does he?" Millie hesitated. "As though he's not from here."

"An Alien? Why didn't you ever say anything?"

"Didn't know if talking about this was even allowed."

"Well, I refuse to believe this. There has to be some other

explanation."

"What about Ellen, the actress you like so much saying, 'The only thing that scares me more than space aliens is the idea that there aren't any space aliens. We can't be the best creation has to offer. I pray we're not all there is. If so, we're in big trouble.'" Millie smiled at her sister's nod.

"Yeah. Except until this moment, this was just a saying by one of my favorite celebs. Now, might be true."

At least her sister considered the possibility. A triumph considering how far Denny needed to emerge from pragmatic boundaries. "You believe Einstein is considered one of the most intelligent scientists of our time, right?"

"Of course."

"Well, he theorized astounding facts about our universe. He also sensed we were not alone in the cosmos. Moreover, Einstein speculated the reason we did not encounter any aliens was that our search methods were not ideal for the quest, a diplomatic means of saying 'there are none so blind as those who will not see.'" Millie spread out her hands as a means of a result. "Apparently, we found a way to communicate."

"Yeah. Absolutely. Put a beautiful, wonderful woman like my sister Millie in front of the radar, and boom, aliens are coming to help us."

Millie laughed at Denny's witty sarcasm. "So glad you're my sister." She continued laughing. "I've wanted to tell you about this for days."

"Don't you think I realize this? You come up with something by Ellen, and wise words by Einstein. You swam in this muck for a while."

What About Barnum?

Binary Bounty # 1

Millie laughed again, glad for the release of her nervous tension. "Probably best we don't tell Mom about this," she whispered. "Come to think of it. I never realized Mom to be this tired before. You?"

"No. But you're right. Mom's often out of breath. Needs bouts of rest for small, ordinary tasks. I hope she's not sick."

"I don't think she would tell us if she were."

"Think she might keep an illness from Dad?" Denny eyed her with worried eyes. "Still, I don't believe we should talk to her about being sick. She'll only blame her fatigue on the trip and on the many moves we needed to make from place to place."

Millie nodded. "Okay, so we don't tell Mom about any of this."

Denny lifted her hand for Millie to clap it with hers. "Deal. Not a word." Denny rose and closed her closet door. "You need to promise me something, Millie."

Millie attempted to decipher what Denny might expect from her. "What?"

"The next time you talk to Barnum about all this, can you include me in the conversation? Don't get me wrong. I'll be like the fly on the wall. You won't hear a sound out of me. But, I would like to be in the room."

"Sure. If the decision is up to me, I'll include you. You realize I'll have to ask Barnum if you can attend such a meeting."

"Yeah. Do what you can."

"What do you think Don might say about all this?"

"Don Grimalsky? He's an idiot. I would never tell him."

"Well, you could shove all this in his face." Millie smiled rubbing Denny's back.

"Listen, if you or Mom got the idea I'm smitten with Don because of what I said, forget about it. Yes, it's difficult not to think about the man. We were friends for all those years. I spent more time with Don than I did with you—or Mom. Doesn't mean I approve of him saying he would rather I become his wife than being a partner. A modern man like Don, wanting a little woman at home to do all his bidding. What kind of relationship would that be?"

"Of course, you're right. I know Don, and I've got to tell you, his attitude surprised the hell out of me." Millie heard Jonah crying, so she squeezed her sister's shoulder. "Goodnight, sis."

FORGIVENESS

Barnum found Helika sitting on the beach in front of the rock face where he owned his home.

He came up beside her and sat next to her on the cool sand. "Got it out of your system?"

Helika stared at him through misty eyes. "I'm sorry I demolished your home. I only did so when I noticed you'd evacuated your guests."

She appeared despondent, so Barnum reassured her. "Yes. I moved everyone out before our conversation."

"You knew I would react this way? I'm so ashamed."

"You have the right to be angry. Besides, you didn't destroy a home, merely a house, and I can have it up again with a wave of my hand, the same way it stood."

"What you just said is what I'm going to miss the most once I'm on Binar. No more powers. Do you realize how wonderful it is to wave your hand and obtain anything you wish?"

"To a point. Waving your hand won't bring you love, genuine, honest, no-frills love."

"This is important for you, isn't it?"

"Loneliness takes its toll, which in no way says life will be better once you're gone. Luckily, Barnaby and the others understand what it means to be Binar."

"In a way, having me around only served to emphasize the loneliness, right?"

He nodded.

"I believe this is what happened to me also. Plus, I never managed to mesh with these humans. Although, during all the centuries on this planet, your Millie is the one person I might have befriended. She is a gentle soul." Helika smiled as she rubbed his arm.

Barnum nodded, an unhappy expression marring his handsome features. "Even during our happiest moments, as much as we were in love, she never discovered my true identity—more loneliness."

"You never told her?"

"How could I? Telling her would mean scaring her out of her wits."

"Are you going to mention who you are? She discovered quite a few clues this time around—you saving her son from drowning." She turned to eye the rock face. "The crazy house." Helika chuckled. Her hand on his, she asked. "Before I go, may I?"

"Yes, you can."

Helika waved her hand. Once more the house would be the same, unchanged, the duplicate of what the former one represented. "Yep, I'm going to miss the wave."

"You'll own full powers for another couple of weeks, months at least. I'm told losing the powers is very gradual."

"Of course. I hear from Brian on a regular basis."

"Brian? The young man who left the ship five years ago?"

What About Barnum?

Binary Bounty # 1

"Yeah. He held on to his powers for almost a year."

"I remember you two were good friends."

Helika rose, shaking the sand off her jeans. "He wanted me to go with him. He said he would wait for me. Now, he'll be the right age, and he is waiting for me."

Barnum rose and smiled. "You little sneak," Barnum admonished taking her in his arms. He held her for a long time and when he released her, Helika's appearance slowly faded. "Goodbye, Barnum. I hope you find the love you're looking for."

She was gone. Barnum wiped the tears coming down his cheeks. He and Helika had pushed and forged their way through the crusades, forayed through two world wars and pulled people out of the fire in numerous other battles—their hearts bleeding with compassion, their minds a blank as to how people endured such hardship. Worse, how were humans able to inflict such suffering on other humans? This particular question remained unresolved, and in a way, he appreciated the thought this treatment of other people would soon become nothing more than a vague memory for Helika. The only catharsis for this type of violence and pain happened to be love, pure, universe-gifted love.

Barnaby had not found this, yet he seemed content with his life. As for himself, if he couldn't dig up the courage to tell Millie who he was and what he did, he would not be able to profess love to her while living his actual life in silence—not this time. He needed to delve into her eyes and show her the treasures he held all these centuries. Barnum hoped she might remember their love from previous times. He wanted past-life memories to remind Millie of their happiness together, triggering some precarious visions of other reincarnations. This time, however, he mapped out the wrong course. How could Millie remember when he never accentuated where he came from or the fact he was Binar, not human.

Barnum gazed at the dark ocean, at the ship in the distance being the only one able to visualize the yacht and decided he couldn't face Millie yet. No more than he wanted to board Lunar Five and rehash the last thirty minutes with Barnaby or be draped in his brother's pity. His eyes gazed at the house on the rock face, one thousand feet ahead of him, and he walked toward the temporary shelter. Illusory walls erected to comfort an imaginary man. A befitting end to his lack of courage.

***

Millie stretched in bed, welcoming the sunny day outside. She forgot to draw the curtains, and the sun found its way into her eyes its presence entering from the beautiful porthole beside her bed. She turned to greet Jonah, but when she didn't see him, panic arose inside her. "Jonah?" He wasn't in the head, and worry grew. She didn't like him wandering about the boat without an adult. He could fall overboard and no one would ever know.

Then she remembered this was Barnum's ship. She had to concede nothing untoward would ever happen to them on a yacht he owned. Even in absentia, his presence lingered in the crown moldings, the furniture tastefully arranged, the subtle promise about the place that all things would unfold to engender a beautiful day. Still, she hoped Barnum would have the courage to show up today, sooner rather than later. She needed to clear up many points with him, and she wouldn't be able to secure Den-

What About Barnum?

Binary Bounty # 1

ny's presence. Her sister would need to entertain her son while this discussion took place.

Showered and dressed, Millie found Jonah with her sister eating outside up in the flybridge lounge around a big table adorned with food.

Denny pulled a chair for her sister and smiled. "Tried your little trick this morning and Jonah and I are enjoying an excellent breakfast with all the trimmings."

Millie's panic returned. "You didn't …"

Denny rose and whispered, " Not in front of Jonah."

"Thank you," Millie mouthed with a smile. "So what are we having?"

"Mom," Jonah got up and ran to hug her as though just now noticing her. "These pancakes are good. They melt in your mouth."

Always a penchant for food, Millie thought as she gave her son a big hug—for delicious food. Very picky about his eating habits, Jonah did recognize a good meal when he sampled it. "I'm going to have some of those," she cheered. Then with a little toss toward Denny, she added, "Are there more pancakes for me?"

"Tons, Mommy," Jonah spoke with a big blob of dough visible in his open mouth.

"Jonah, don't eat so fast, and no talking with your mouth full."

He nodded.

Denny added, "I told him the reason the stack doesn't seem like it's going down is that of how thin the pancakes are."

"The best maple syrup," Jonah yelled once his mouth was

cleared for takeoff.

Denny laughed, while Millie rolled her eyes as she poured herself coffee, the first sip proving to be the best brew she ever sampled. Her sister, obviously smitten with this new development intended making the most of the situation. She scanned the table and spotted a pot of orange juice in a clear pitcher, a hot plate of croissants she could only imagine rivaled those of the best restaurants in Paris, and all sorts of exotic fruits lining the buffet. "Won't the Captain on the ship find this strange? At least our steward Luis will wonder where we obtained all this food, right?"

"Luis is the one who served us, Mom."

"Really." She eyed Denny with an incredulous raise of her eyebrows.

"Absolutely." Denny stretched out her arms her hands indicating her surroundings. "Illusion." She nodded. "So is the help on board. You put platters in their hands of whatever you want, and they'll bring them to you."

Millie couldn't help a chuckle. "Seems you've taken the situation to heart."

"Hey, I'm not a cockeyed optimist. I don't have an award-winning imagination. I'm a realist. Now, you give me a proven blueprint of something that works, as you did last night, and this engineer is on it. Will be on it for as long as I'm on this ride. Best vacation ever," she finished swooping a forkful of syrup-laced ham into her mouth.

Millie laughed. Turns out Denny appreciated the magic, although she threaded through the sorcery as though forbidden and disallowed. She didn't mind using the illusion when her back

What About Barnum?

Binary Bounty # 1

was against the wall, but she could not bring herself to exercise the right to obtain any wish she wanted. "Why isn't Mom here?"

"Still sleeping. I knocked on our *madre's* door, and she said she would be up in a little while. I didn't insist."

"I'm worried about her. We'll need to have a talk with her."

"Better you than me. I wouldn't know what to say."

"Speaking of talks, sis. I'd like to have a private conversation with Barnum, and I was hoping you might entertain Jonah while I do."

"Okay. I'm not going to ask you to bring the recorder. I am sure how that will end, but try to remember everything you discuss. Anyway, I may have a few questions of my own later."

"Thanks, Denny. I'll check on Mom when I pop down."

"Why check on, Mom?" a stern voice asked from the stairway to the flybridge.

Both girls turned to catch Caroline making her way toward them. Millie couldn't help thinking how worn her mother appeared with the dark circles under her eyes and her cheeks drawn in as though some force had shrunken the smile out of them.

"Good morning, sleepy head," Denny teased. "Just in time, we are displaying a feast fit for royalty this morning."

"Coffee, strong coffee. I believe this aroma woke me up, prevalent on the ship like some form of stimulus pumped through the vents."

Both girls chuckled. Millie considered she spotted no shrinkage of her mother's spirits.

As they finished breakfast, the unthinkable came up those stairs—Barnum. "Here you all are. I was looking for you downstairs."

Millie's heart began to race, Denny's head turned around, and Jonah jumped up from his seat to jump into the man's arms.

"Hey, there buddy." He hugged the little body thrown at him like a splat. "I missed you too, Jonah," he answered to Jonah's mumbled words.

Millie wondered how they would ever get to talk now, unhindered by everyone else.

Barnum put the boy down and told him he would teach him how to snorkel later in the afternoon. Then he eyed Millie. "I think you and I need to have a conversation."

Not so difficult to do after all, and Millie considered Barnum's direct approach sounded like a business proposal. "Of course," she answered. Then as an afterthought, she offered, "Would you like to have breakfast first? We ate already."

He smiled. "Thank you, but I also sdid."

Jonah was jumping up and down. "Can you teach me how to snorkel now? Please, Barnum?"

Millie rose and walked to the small child and tall man standing by the flight of stairs. Barnum did not come any further, as though he avoided their presence. She rubbed her son's hair as she reiterated Barnum's promise to snorkel later.

Jonah pretended to hold a little pout, but skipped back to the table, happy to sip his orange juice. Millie also wondered about her sister's persistence in giving nothing but a little wave to Barnum. Newfound fear perhaps or guilt for fulfilling all those wishes at breakfast?

Surprising her, Barnum turned to her mother and asked, "How are you feeling this morning, Caroline?"

"Better, thank you. Amazing what a good night's rest will do for the human spirit." Caroline smiled, and Millie thought Barnum made her day—her mother smitten with the man.

Barnum turned toward Millie, "After you." He indicated the stairs.

She took them, her breathing a little shallow. She found Barnum distant and different this morning, not as gentle or even as amorous toward her as during the past few days.

Once on the main floor, he opened the door to the starboard walkway. They reached the lower cockpit still shaded despite the glorious sun.

Instead of reaching for the seated area, he leaned on the guardrail along the yacht's ramp and watched as the water lapped the boat's flanks leaving salt behind on the hull.

Millie stood beside him and waited for him to release whatever occupied his mind. She sensed formality in what he needed to say.

Barnum straightened and turned toward her still leaning slightly toward the guardrail. "I have good news," he stated the smile not quite reaching his eyes. "Romeo Aguado has agreed to help us mount a coup against the other two and their band of merry men."

"That is good news. How many men are we talking about?"

"How many are in Costa and Marco's group?"

Millie nodded.

"Well, not as many as last week. Quite a few defected when the men brought information to Meo Aguado which was what convinced him to give us a hand. Learning Felix Costa and Brandon Marcos planned to remove him from the equation and take his place stirred courage in the man everyone calls a big baby."

"What are your plans?"

"The task force and I organized a storming of the Aguado's headquarters—phony of course based on pretexts and lots of preparation. Nevertheless, when Costa and Marcos show up tomorrow, taking their rightful place in our organized task force, we plan to arrest them instead, presenting them with all the testimony the Aguados have collected—extensive."

"I hope no one gets hurt."

"I communicated with Jed telling him it is safe to go home."

"This means we can go home also," she stated trying not to sound too disappointed. "When?"

"As soon as you're ready. You may, of course, remain here for as long as you like," Barnum added.

For the first time, Millie noticed an ardent wish in his eyes. Now, she wondered how she might begin what she needed to say to him.

—Twenty-three—

FEARFUL DECISION

Millie, standing with Barnum on the starboard side of his yacht, somewhere between the saloon and the cockpit, sensed shyness overtake her as she considered not talking to Barnum about her doubts and fears. Perhaps if she let all her questions ride and went home without ever voicing them, all this beautiful, magical vacation would dissipate into oblivion, giving her the right to an ordinary life again. If Meo Aguado was known as a *big baby*, her moniker was *needlessly nervous*. Somehow discussing her feelings with Barnum did not enchant her.

"What happened to your house? Denny and I saw your place being destroyed last night."

"Family squabble. The house is up again this morning, same as usual."

"Convenient." Millie could not understand why her voice trembled.

As though sensing her nerves, Barnum came closer, and when Millie straightened, more to protect her space, he took her in his arms before she could recoil.

He held her in his arms until he discovered she still held her hands by her side. He let her go, a question in his eyes as he stared into hers.

"I'm not sure how to begin," she told him. "First, I'm sorry you and Helika weren't able to come together all these years."

"What?" Her comment seemed to push him back.

"She came to me in a dream last night."

"She had no right to do that."

"It's okay." She applied her hand to his chest as though to soothe the agitation she sensed churned there. "All she did was sell you, and tell me how lucky I was to find someone as wonderful and devoted as you are." She worried about lingering anger in his expression. "She kindly showed me some of the lives we shared." She smiled. "They inspired me. I remember most the last one, being a Polish nurse during world war two, part of a group of people called, Żegota, I believe. We helped to smuggle Jewish children out of the Warsaw Ghetto. At one point, one of the hospitals overflowed with these little ones waiting for their papers from the Government. You protected us. I didn't quite understand how you were able to fake out the Nazis at the time, or why they walked by our hospital during their regular inspection. They were always looking for stowaways. I realized from what Helika showed me you camouflaged the hospital, and made the soldiers forget the structure's presence." She exhaled as his face softened and his smile returned.

"She should not have brought back such horrors for you."

"Horrors? Benevolent times during a deadly war? We saved all those children, and you and I got together—became husband and wife. Didn't even wait for the war to end. She also showed me I died of typhus three years later. My death happened while you attended the Nuremberg trials."

What About Barnum?

Binary Bounty # 1

"I left for less than thirty days," he whispered. He stroked Millie's arm with such hunger. She couldn't prevent a tear.

"How broken you must have been, loving each other as we did and you lost me after a few short years. Although, I imagine loneliness crippled you so much more not being loved for who you are, for what you can do. All these centuries and I never understood the man I loved so much."

"You do now."

"No. I don't. I know where you're from—I also learned why you left your planet. And I know you can return. Why would you want to spend your life with me? On Earth? Misplaced loyalty? Fear of breaking your promise to me?" She didn't want to appear indignant or shrill, he accomplished so much for her, and she worried her comportment made her sound heartless. "Barnum, you don't owe me anything. I absolve you of all your promises. You've done enough for us—for me. You can now return home." She smiled and stroked his cheek. "Where you belong."

He smiled back and tilted his head to approve her words, and something died inside her. "Thank you for releasing me. Now, we can both go on with our lives." He picked up her hand and kissed it fervently. "I hope you will allow me the time to teach Jonah how to snorkel."

She nodded taking back her hand, eyes down on the deck. "Of course. We can leave tomorrow if that's okay. I will need to arrange things with the airlines."

He rummaged in his pocket and pulled out four tickets. "These will take you back home safely."

She looked up at him while she took the tickets, shocked he thought of everything.

Gently, he brushed her lips with his, then walked toward the saloon, opened the door, and disappeared.

Denny found her. Millie didn't realize how long she stood, gazing at the ocean while angling in desperation for some calm not to allow her heart to shred into small pieces. She told Barnum what she thought he might long to hear at this stage, words which might give him the courage to walk away should he prefer to do so. He filed in with her arguments swiftly and wholeheartedly, as though tired of the chase. Perhaps he just wanted his life back. He would be able to return home once he accomplished this last mission.

"Are you all right, sis? Barnum's in the jet ski with Jonah. He's teaching him how to snorkel. I thought this would be okay." Taking hold of her arm, Denny shook Millie to get her attention. "What happened between you two?"

"I never seized the chance to tell Barnum I wanted a normal life for Jonah, hoping he might say he wanted the job." She veered from staring at the ocean to gaze at her sister. "I explained to Barnum how I knew who he was. I thought he might be happier going back to his home planet."

"He is an alien?"

"Yes. And, Barnum is eight hundred years old to my measly thirty-three." Millie's mouth stretched side to side in a stab at humor. "In fact, don't know if you can still call Barnum an alien. He's lived on Earth for eight hundred years."

"Why didn't you tell him how much you love him?"

"Do I? Love him? I admit I'm disappointed. I thought he would give me more of an argument."

"And if he had?"

What About Barnum?

Binary Bounty # 1

"He might have persuaded me we belong together. You'll admit. Heartbreaking to say no to a handsome, kind, nurturing man like Barnum. In time I would grow to love him. Maybe I did the right thing. He deserves someone who is crazy about him. A woman who eyes him as the beginning and the end of her world."

"You're crazy. For someone who says I'm in denial about Don, you're way past denial where Barnum is concerned."

Millie closed her eyes to hide the tears, but they still poured out. Her whole body began to tremble. Denny stopped her remonstrations and took her sister in her arms.

"Things will work out. You'll see," Denny told her hugging Millie for dear life.

Once released, Millie added. "Besides, I'm not sure if Jonah and I are ready for a clickety-click lifestyle where everything is resolved for us. Where we may obtain all the things that we need."

"Scares you, right?"

"More than some of those lives I endured."

"What is that supposed to mean?"

Both girls caught Caroline coming to join them through the saloon.

"Later," Millie added.

Caroline came through the door and smiled at them. "Ah, my beautiful daughters. You should see your son, Millie, on the raft with that angel of a man. He put a life jacket on him, a bright yellow helmet, and is showing him how to snorkel. Exciting how Jonah is getting the hang of snorkeling quite fast."

Millie tried to remain calm and smiled through her statement.

"Great, Mom. I'm glad he's enjoying himself." She fanned the tickets she still clutched in her hand. "Good news is we can leave tomorrow. Barnum cleared us to go home. They drew a plan together to work with the Aguados and trap the two rogue agents."

"Thank, God," Caroline uttered. "I'm overdue for a doctor's appointment."

The two girls eyed each other.

"And your father is upset it's taking me this long to return home. You understand how he is."

"Mom is everything all right, health-wise?" Millie asked.

"Of course, I'm all right." Looking at the exchanged looks between her daughters, Caroline added, "What did you two invent? Is this why Barnum wants to chat with me before we leave?"

Millie grabbed her mother's hand. "He said that?"

"Yes. Barnum seems to be aware we're leaving tomorrow."

Millie released a long breath. "He provided the tickets."

Denny grabbed one of the tickets. "You didn't tell me that. Where's the time of departure on these things? Wait a minute." She paused her jaw dropping. "First class." She shook the tickets in the air and yelled, "Yeah, baby. We're flying home first class."

"Denny, can you put these in your bag. I'm going out back to check on Jonah."

When Millie got to the cockpit, she spotted Barnum and Jonah sitting on a jet ski. Why had her mother called this a raft? A jet ski was a lot more fun for a little boy like Jonah and much more dangerous even though he wore a lifejacket and a helmet. Then she remembered, there could be no danger since he was

What About Barnum?

Binary Bounty # 1

with Barnum. She exhaled a long-troubled breath. Imagining Jonah never being hurt with this man around—this angel of a man her mother called him—made her regret she treated the matter with such haste. No, she stood by her decision. No more exercises in futility and no more settling. She refused to lead this man on since he was sweet, and at the moment, he was also vulnerable having lost the love of his life, Helika. She yelled out to Jonah. "Hey, sweetie, looking good."

"I can do this, Mom. I can breathe in the tube under water," Jonah yelled.

She heard Barnum's instructions to Jonah to hold on, and he rode close to the side of the boat. "Put on your bathing suit," he told Millie. "We'll go for a ride, the three of us."

"But you don't have a helmet for Mom," Jonah whined.

"Yes, I do." Barnum reached underneath the console and pulled out a white helmet. Of course, Millie realized the protective wear materialized out of thin air—grateful Barnum kept up appearances not to disturb Jonah with his feats of power.

"I'm wearing my suit under my dress." Saying this, Millie unbuttoned her summer frock and slipped it off. She wore a light green two-piece bathing suit with white trim, and Barnum whistled at her to make her realize how beautiful she looked. "The hat matches the white trim of your bathing suit."

"Okay, okay," she protested. "So how do I climb on this thing?"

He floated close to the back of the ship. "Two choices. You can jump in the water, and I'll help you climb on, or you can swing your leg over and drop down behind Jonah. Hold on to my shoulders to keep your balance."

Millie picked the second choice. She thought it might be easier to hang on to Barnum's shoulders than climb on the jet ski from the water. And she was right. The second solution fared well. Only she found herself digging her fingers into Barnum's shoulders for fear of falling and hoped she didn't hurt him.

"Sorry," she said as she settled behind Jonah. "I didn't mean to squeeze your shoulders so hard."

"Don't worry, Millie. You are familiar with the saying, 'no pain, no gain.'"

What the hell does that mean?

"Hold on, we're going to visit *Bahia de Banderas*, and this may be a bumpy ride," Barnum yelled over the noise of the jet ski's motor. "The water flows with unexpected currents, and this has a tendency of tossing the jet ski around." While they rode slowly, the jet ski obeyed Barnum's words bouncing them from side to side as well as up and down.

Millie tried in vain to interpret the sense of no pain, no gain. She tried applying the idiom to their particular situation but could not come up with anything. Was he talking about his shoulders? Or was this about her telling him he did enough for her, and to go back to his planet where he belonged. Her words drawn like this resounded inauspiciously to her.

The Pacific Ocean did not let up. The ride was bumpy all the way to the Marriott which was where Barnum docked the jet ski and locked the engine before they began their walk on the beach.

"You're not worried someone might take our ride back?"

He produced the square smile she loved so much. "What do you think?" He chuckled at the roll of her eyes. "You have nothing to worry about."

What About Barnum?

Binary Bounty # 1

"This sand is hot," Jonah complained.

Barnum bent and picked up her son as though he weighed nothing more than a straw. "We should have brought your sandals, Jonah." Turning toward Millie, he offered. "I will take you to the boutique nearby, and you can choose something to wear over your suit, sandals for your feet, and a T-shirt for me and one for Jonah."

"And some shoes for me too," Jonah said as he bounced up and down in Barnum's arms. "I think I'd like to have some of those flip-flops, Mom."

When they entered one of the boutiques' courtyard, Millie chose a simple summer dress and a pair of beige sandals. She helped Jonah pick out a shirt and flip-flops he liked. Barnum picked a visa card out of his bathing suit pocket, and Millie refused to ponder how it got there.

As they left, Barnum suggested. "We should take a cab to Rosita's Hotel. *El Malecon* begins there, and I want to show you interesting findings."

"Okay. Thank you for the clothes, by the way."

"My pleasure." Turning to stare into Millie's eyes, he asked, "Do you four still have belongings at the Marriott?"

Her turn to inveigle him with her smile. "How thoughtful of you to ask. The last time I checked, I recognized all our things conveniently stored on the yacht."

He chuckled. "You're welcome."

She bent close to his ears her lips whispering. "Except for Jonah's tricycle and skateboard. They may still be at your house."

He gazed into her eyes. "I'm sure you'll find them amongst his other things tomorrow when you arrive home."

She held his gaze, although she wondered whether he toyed with her. Didn't he realize the thought of home unnerved her since he would not be with her? His deadpan reaction depicted nothing other than a friendly smile and kind eyes she imagined to be a tad wistful.

"Look, Mommy. There's the man who walks on the beach with the ice cream."

"Here, sport." Barnum gave him a few bills. "Go and get us three ice cream bars."

As they walked toward Jonah and the cart full of goodies, Barnum stopped her and caressed her face with his eyes. "I am going to miss you, Millie, more than you know."

"Does this mean you're going back home?"

"Well, I'm a reasonable and accommodating fellow, and you did say home was where I belonged."

Millie heard him chuckle as they neared Jonah and his favorite cart. All she could do was roll her eyes at him which only made him laugh more.

When Jonah motioned to give him the change back, Barnum mentioned to Jonah how he should tip the man and let him keep the difference.

Millie witnessed her son going back to give the man his change saying this was his tip. The man bowed his head and thanked him, and Jonah came back his expression proud and as happy as if he presented her with a beautiful drawing he drew.

"Thank you," she whispered accepting Barnum's gift of a cold treat. "A good lesson for him to learn."

"My pleasure. Little time left to teach Jonah all I know, but I will do my best until tomorrow."

What About Barnum?

Binary Bounty # 1

Though she tried, Millie was unable to read this man, this enigmatic, gorgeous angel of a man. She hoped a living her life without him would not someday be construed as *Millie time*.

Twenty-four

BARNUM'S INSTROSPECTION

B arnum stood on the yacht's starboard side to watch a pod of bottlenose dolphins interact with the antics of what appeared to be a smaller pod of spinner dolphins. Seven in the morning painted a palette of pinks and blues while a dash of yellow rose above the horizon to provide blessed light over Bahia de Banderas. Barnum enjoyed the sunrise, almost more than he did the sunset, and he made a point to catch the scenery as often as time permitted. Sunrise offered promises of enticing days and a little respite for his lonely heart. On the other hand, sunsets for Barnum suspended all actions wise and purposeful, and darkness prevailed bathing the smallest corner with intrigue and suspicion—a fanciful impression, he realized.

Barnum had brought Millie and Jonah back to the pier the night before where he'd parked the jet ski, same place where the captain sailed the yacht during their outing.

With the Marriott at his back, he grabbed some fish in a basket next to him and attempted to mimic the dolphin's whistle. Of course, no one could. Even other dolphins could not imitate each other's cry—all of them distinctive signatures.

Nevertheless, three of them came around and Barnum threw mackerel in the air toward the dolphins. Of course, he would not recommend any ship captain to provide food as he did. Dolphins would remember and come around for more, swim in the boat's wake.

Once he'd gone through all the fish, Barnum made a gesture with his hand, and they seemed to understand. Chirping grateful little squeals, the three left to rejoin their pod.

Dolphins, gentle and intelligent creatures of the sea, did not exist on his planet. Over the years he came to appreciate them and enjoyed their innate sense of people. Some marine biologists professed dolphins to be telepathic and intuitive when it came to people. Barnum had no difficulty believing this. Made him wish he possessed more telepathy toward humans. He benefited from centuries of knowledge amassed through various junctures of interactions, wars, illnesses, famines, many types of challenges and conflicts. Except he did not understand women, their thoughts, their likings when they said one thing and meant another—a situation for which Barnaby once told him Earth females were famous.

During all these centuries, Helika's jealousy escaped him. He believed she thrived happily elsewhere. Perhaps this explained why she ranted about human nature, and why Helika never formed any real ties with any of them.

He believed Millie to be different. Not one to say one thing and mean another. Throughout time she always spoke her mind, too honest to be anything other than forthcoming. Now she gave him the advice to head home to Binar. Did she care they would no longer be together? Perhaps she did, but not with the same intensity, at least not with the same undying love coursing through him. Raised to believe unconditional love demanded you release the person should she wish to be free, he wondered where he would find the courage to let Millie go.

He walked toward the master suite as his thoughts brought him to her bedside. Avid eyes caressed the contour of Millie's face as she slept. She moved her head, and he wondered if she sensed his presence. Jonah lay curled up against her and the woman owned little wiggle room to spare, even in a King size bed. In other circumstances, Barnum envisioned Millie curled up against him while her head might rest on his shoulder and her arm would wrap around his torso. What a privilege, a sensuous, exciting concession since he had waited so long to claim her—to sense her stretched beside him in total adoration. However, now that he found her, and Millie understood where he came from, she no longer wanted to spend her life with him. A tear rolled down his cheek. Too difficult to stay in her presence, he left. Reaching the cockpit, he boarded the jet ski and lowered it to the water. He would take this mode of transportation to ride to Playa Camarones. A helicopter would pick him up on the beach to bring him to Playa Garza Blanca, where the Aguados owned a summer home.

***

Millie opened her eyes and smiled at the vision of her son nestled against her, still sleeping soundly. They returned to the ship late last night after enjoying an excellent dinner in town. Barnum brought them shopping on the *Malecon,* and she bought a little souvenir for her sister, her mother, and her dad. She bathed in Barnum's caressing looks all evening, and this morning, couldn't wait to see him before he left to meet the Aguados.

What About Barnum?

Binary Bounty # 1

Barnum was scheduled to take them to the airport, and though she would be heartbroken to say goodbye to a man she still knew so little about, she made up her mind to allow him to live his life his way.

She got up and tiptoed around Jonah hoping not to wake him. At times he proved to be a bouncy little boy, and the flight home would be hard on them, so the extra sleep would do him good. Saying goodbye to the stunning Mexican resort while having encountered such wonders as to keep them dreaming for a long time to come would quickly be upon them—her legs weak each time she considered time away from Barnum.

Once she showered and dressed, she paid particular attention to her hair and makeup which she never did. Nevertheless, her heart skipped a beat imagining Barnum's welcome this morning. The sentiment prompted her to look her best.

As she prepared to leave, Jonah called out to her. "Wait for me, Mommy. I'll be ready in a jiffy."

"Oh, my little boy." She smiled at him. "You go wash your face and hands and brush your teeth, and then we'll go upstairs to eat."

When Jonah finished in the bathroom, with super speed, he hurried to put on his bathing suit.

"Jonah, I don't think you should wear a bathing suit right away. We'll come and change after breakfast."

"No, Mom. I have to hurry. Barnum is going away early this morning, and I want to go snorkeling before he leaves."

"Well, at least put a shirt on, you can keep it on when you snorkel to keep your back from getting red."

After he donned a shirt, Millie took her son by the hand.

"Barnum told you he was leaving early this morning?"

"Yes. Don't you remember? Last night at dinner. I asked him when we would snorkel again and he said I would need to get up early in the morning because he had to run an errand really, really early."

Millie frowned but didn't answer, Jonah, knocking the wind out of her. Of course, Barnum would have breakfast with them. Only polite to wait before he left.

Upstairs, no one was at the big table in the flybridge lounge. *Denny might still be in her room.*

"Where's breakfast, mommy?"

"We'll go in the saloon. Maybe your aunt Denny is there with loads of food."

They went down, while Jonah chirped about the pancakes he had the day before.

In the saloon, still no Denny, but her mother seated at a table for four sipped coffee, her eyes locked on the horizon.

"Mom? You're up early."

Caroline smiled a calm and relaxed smile, the sort that reached her eyes, the smile Millie had not spotted in her mother in quite some time. She didn't remember how enchanting her regaled expression could be.

"Something about this salt air. Most invigorating. Liable to make an old woman young again."

"Is that all you're having? Coffee?"

"No. Luis is bringing us pancakes and syrup, eggs Benedict, and all sorts of delectable fruits."

"You placed an order with him?"

"I did. When I asked what the yacht's galley offered, Luis

What About Barnum?

challenged me. Said to order anything I wanted and they would be happy to supply this—why I ordered the eggs Benedict."

"Where's Denny."

"I knocked on her door to see if she needed help. She overate yesterday. I knew the gourmandize would catch up to her. Lobster, caviar, your sister downed all sorts of exotic food." Caroline chuckled as she shrugged. "She took a couple of pills and opted to remain in bed, trying to rid herself of a migraine."

Luis brought the food and Jonah jumped up and down to welcome him. "Great, my favorite pancakes, Mom. And the orange juice I like."

Millie got up to help Jonah in his seat again, tucking the napkin into his shirt. "Remember not to eat too fast." She sat back in her chair and wondered aloud, "I wonder what's keeping Barnum?"

"Barnum is gone, sweetheart. I thought you knew. He told me he got a phone call while at dinner with you and Jonah. Something about Romeo Aguado concerned about some of the information they received with regards to Costa and Marcos. He wanted Barnum to be at the meeting place very early this morning. Aguado felt they needed to change their MO to catch those men."

Millie's heart dropped as though falling off a cliff. "Strange. I don't remember this, yet Jonah informed me of Barnum's early departure this morning."

"You may have been away from the table when he took the call. The subject veered to other things when you returned." Caroline made a place on the table as Luis arrived with their breakfast wheeled in on a cart.

"He told you this last night?"

"Knocked on my door after the three of you returned. Wanted to have the chat he mentioned earlier."

"Why would Barnum need to talk to you?"

"Don't worry, darling. Our talk had nothing to do with you. Just a friendly chat to get to know each other better." Caroline smiled.

Somehow, Millie figured Barnum's need to chat with her mother had to be more than friendly conversation—more like a heart-to-heart, only she couldn't insist, not when her mother's adamant tone brooked no chance to pry. "He told me he would be here for breakfast," she answered instead.

"I'm sure he planned to be here with us."

Millie gave her son the pancakes he wanted and poured him the juice he clamored for by holding his glass in front of her face. "I wish he would have told me. There are a few things I need to … clear up with him."

"I want some syrup, Mommy."

Millie poured syrup over her son's pancakes and proceeded to cut them for him.

"He'll be back to drive us to the airport. You can tell him then." Caroline laid a hand on her daughter's arm and smiled.

Millie figured that like Denny, her mother thought she might be in love with Barnum. She nodded to close the subject. Millie didn't want her mom to ask any questions. She didn't quite understand the frazzled thoughts assailing her and didn't want to risk tears surfacing when she tried to sort out her sentiments.

She turned the conversation to a more practical agenda. "I packed my bags last night. The only way I can go around this

What About Barnum?

morning and make sure we have everything we need."

"Denny and I did the same. We're ready to go," she said as she savored the rich fare on her plate. "I don't think I have ever eaten better eggs Benedict in my life," she added with a groan of satisfaction.

"Yes, no question about it. The food is delicious, as is this coffee." After taking a sip of the brew in her cup, Millie wondered aloud. "I hope Barnum doesn't get into something he can't handle. Did he tell you about his plans?"

"No. And I didn't ask." Caroline gave her a conspiratorial smile. "I wouldn't worry if I were you. After all, this is Barnum, right?"

Millie eyed her mother wondering what her smile meant. Had Barnum revealed to Caroline some of his secrets, advised her of what he could do?

***

On the beach, waiting for the helicopter to pick him up, Barnum had plenty of cause to worry. He headed to the enemy's lair, to the men they tracked down for the last two years and on whom they recorded enough material to put away for life.

The jet ski parked in front of the pier at Playa Camarones, Barnum stared up at the deep blue sky hesitating with the action he agreed to take. He recognized the emotion making him uneasy and a bit queasy. Having lived through two world wars, and a whole bunch of other monumental shifts of power, fear played a familiar role in his life, and though the unwanted guest invaded his existence too often, his apprehension had nothing to do with his life. He dreaded the planned retribution on Millie and Caroline and Jed. The rogue agents and the Aguado Family did not believe in sparing lives, only advancing their business at any cost.

He realized the task force a few agencies had formed to help local authorities and the Federals curb the drug cartel terrorists did not quite measure up. Since 2006, over sixty thousand people had perished due to the war on drugs, many of them innocent of these crimes—bystanders, students, women, and children. The worst development showed the cartels no longer committed murders to shield their activities or protect their anonymity. Instead, the members now used killing people as a propaganda tool whenever they wanted to spread fear and terror to hold the authorities at bay. Barnum found the more their task force made inroads, the more violent the gangs became. No wonder. With the drug cartel earning an estimate of sixty-four billion dollars per year, the members fought everything and everyone to protect their loot—and yet the cities they resided in were some of the most impoverished ghettos in the world. Robin Hood and his band of merry men they were not.

Barnum hated to make these concessions to the Aguados merely to catch two of their own. Unthinkable. Also unbelievable, the cartel now recruited women—widowed because of the wars, these women needed to feed their children or ailing members of their family. Women jailed because of drug trafficking in Mexico had increased by more than four hundred percent in the last decade.

As he sat on the beach, his knees between his arms, dark thoughts churned as fast and as loud as the blades of a helicopter

What About Barnum?

Binary Bounty # 1

rotating overhead. The chopper came down on the wet sand, and he was forced to tread water to hop on as a passenger.

Two people from their task force were already aboard, and he saluted them as he sat down beside Joan Crenshaw and Matt Hayes.

"To Playa Garza Blanca?" Barnum asked.

Joan bent toward his ear to speak. The motor was infernally loud, and since the courier did not supply headsets with microphones, she didn't want to yell for the others to hear. "Yes. As I mentioned yesterday, Romeo meets with dignitaries and such at his summer house."

Barnum nodded to show he understood. He wondered where Joan received her information.

When they landed on the beach south of where he parked, Barnum stepped out and gazed in wonder at the spread before him. "This can't be Aguado's home," he breathed.

"I understand what you mean," Joan told him.

Two men came out of the front section fully clothed in army garb wearing black cloth over their faces as masks and sunglasses to hide their eyes. Both armed with several weapons hanging on different parts of their bodies, each held a Russian-made rifle, AK-104. Barnum wondered why so much firepower seemed to be required.

"*Espera aquí,*" one of the men told them.

The two men stood back with a hand on their rifle as the helicopter took off. Joan mumbled under her breath. "Meo uses this summer house as a meeting place. The surroundings—extremely well-guarded. Take a peek at the roof."

Barnum allowed his eyes to glance briefly above the second

story mansion and caught sight of a man crouched low, as only his head appeared above the small parapet around the flat roof on which rested the butt of his rifle. Only one man was visible, yet he sensed others might be lined up in surveillance as well.

Another five minutes passed before Romeo Aguado came forward waving to them from the open patio that gave access to a dining room while they could spot the vestibule and the open bar inside the mansion.

"Buenos días, señors, señora. Welcome to my domain." He walked over to them, and released the men with an abrupt command of, "*Vete*," and the wave of his hand. The armed soldiers disappeared somewhere inside.

"I apologize for the heavy security, but with what I learned, we can no longer trust our original plan. We will need all the protection we can muscle. Come inside, please. I will show you around mi casa." A broad smile illuminated his ordinarily dark face. Barnum considered the thick, bushy eyebrows and full black beard darkened his appearance—not to mention the unstable temperament and periodic fits of rage that could kill a man in an instant.

JALISCO DRUG CARTEL

R omeo Aguado welcomed Barnum, Joan Crenshaw, and Matt Hayes to his summer house, the place where he brought people when he wanted to make a good impression. The four of them walked past the enormous infinity pool along the stone patio and crossed the threshold of an open portico that led to the living room with bar and dinner nook.

"There are five bedrooms all with their private bathrooms, and two of the rooms are downstairs."

"Do you keep this wall leading outside open at all times, Mr. Aguado?"

Meo smiled at Joan. "Please, call me Meo. We are all friends here." He offered them to sit at an elegant mahogany table for six and stepped behind the bar. "I will tend bar for you. What would you like to drink, Señora Joan?"

"Just water, thank you."

"¿Cerveza, Matt?"

"Sí, Meo, gracias."

"I'll take the same, Meo," Barnum said.

Once Meo sat at the table, his brother Alfredo came down the stairs to join them. Barnum was anxious to hear what they had to say. "Why did you mention the agents discovered our plan?"

Meo turned toward Joan. "Oh, and Joan—may I call you

Joan?" he asked.

"Please do." She smiled.

He gestured toward the portico. "A sliding panel comes down when we need to keep people out, or when we are not here or busy elsewhere. Not to worry." He chuckled. "I like the open air, the scent of flowers and the sound of the ocean."

Barnum became uncomfortable. For some reason, Romeo Aguado seemed to be stalling, but why? "Alfredo," Barnum acknowledged the other man's arrival at the table. Alfredo held a glass of hard liquor in his hand, what looked to be a dark rum, and Barnum couldn't help thinking it was early in the morning for a drink, neat. "What's this all about, Meo," he asked again.

"Simple. One of my men called me yesterday. Said he spotted *el loco vago* who told us Costa and Marcos were planning to take over our operation. The bum didn't recognize my man. He sat at the table with Felix Costa and Brandon Marcos along with a few of their associates."

"Doesn't mean they are aware of our plan to arrest them. This vagrant may have been fishing for more information."

Meo smiled. "We are not the police, and we are not the government which means we are thorough, and we leave nothing— nothing to chance," he finished a little louder.

"Your man followed him after dinner, right?" Matt Hayes supplied.

Meo bowed his head. "Of course, but my man made sure he was not alone. Let's just say *el pobre tipo* will not be saying much of anything anymore." He made a gesture of slicing his throat. "I apologize for my words, señora, but such is life and death." He laughed outright, and this reminded Barnum

What About Barnum?

how dangerous these traffickers were. They cared about making money, protecting their turf, and staying alive. They did not care about the chaos they created.

For the first time, Alfredo spoke. "The man, named Miguel, accepted mucho dinero from us for his information. Then, he turned around to ask the agents for mas dinero when he confessed about your plan to arrest them."

Barnum rose and paced alongside the rectangular table. "This means they will never show up here today if they are aware of the trap we set for them."

Alfredo laughed. "My brother told you. We are not police or government *idiotas*. We made certain we knew where to find them before we killed their man."

"Thank you, my brother," Meo answered. "We needed to plan an ambush. One with enough men so that we are sure none of them escape."

"Wait a minute, Meo. The three of us need to bring these agents back to stand trial for their crimes. They will be put away for a long, long time, but we don't want them dead." All at once, Barnum realized they would never be allowed to bring back Costa and Marcos alive to face a judge in the United States, or under any circumstances. Of course, Costa and Marcos knew too much about their secrets, and they couldn't afford this information to circulate in the courts in America.

Meo laughed, and Barnum could almost see him raising his chess piece with the cry of *checkmate*. He wondered if this story of a man catching sight of another man with the two rogue agents was true. Perhaps the only truth about their story was their trumped-up charges stating the two rogue agents had to die. But then, what was stopping them from killing the three of them?

To keep matters from escalating, to give himself more time to find a solution and try to save at least the lives of the two agents accompanying him, Barnum capitulated. "So, what's your plan, Meo?"

"Well, I'm glad you ask, dear friend." Barnum found the emphasized words and tone to indicate without a doubt that the Aguados planned to eliminate them all. "These men are the worst scum alive. They pretend to be agents of your Government, come here in our country and destroy our business, our families. We cannot stand for this any longer. The fact we have put up with this for so long makes us scum too." He pretended to spit on the floor. "When I look at my face in the mirror, I no longer recognize who I am, the proud Mexican man I am supposed to be." His gestures were meant to convince them and himself that the actions he was about to take were warranted.

Alfredo laughed nervously. "Tell them, brother."

"Miguel informed us they own a small compound in the foothills of the Sierra Madre. A few tents where they meet with their men when they prepare a coup. And, my friend." His dark eyes stared into Barnum's eyes. "They are preparing an uprising against us, against our families, our homes. We positioned many of our men, and a half-dozen of Federals we can trust. My people surround your formidable agents and their gang. These loyal men wait for us so that we can take our land back from these sharks." He paused and stared at the three of them, one after the other. "You are with us, or you are not?"

Tension ran in the room. Barnum understood if either of

What About Barnum?

Binary Bounty # 1

them admitted they did not agree with Meo's tactics or asked him to stop his insurrection, they would die on the spot. After the three exchanged glances, Barnum answered for all of them. "We would prefer taking these men to our Government, Meo. However, we support your quest. No doubt these people endanger all our lives."

Alfredo jumped up. "*Siente mi corazón.*" He beat a hand over his heart. "This day will be a great day of liberation."

They clinked their glasses together, and Barnum saluted Meo with a smile.

"To you, my friend," Meo responded by raising his glass.

Once they were alone, Barnum whispered, "Joan, in the helicopter when we near *Playa Camarones*, you will make a pretext that you need the washroom, violent stomach cramps. They will land, and you will not go toward the hotel. Instead, you will head for the blue and red silver top jet ski parked at the pier, and head for *Islas Marietas*. You know where the house is?"

"Yes, of course."

Barnum reached into his pocket and surreptitiously gave her the key to the jet ski. "Simply ring the bell out front, and staff will take care of you. You can hide there."

"For how long?"

"Might take a while. In time, someone will come and get you, and this will be your cue to leave."

He stared at Mark. "You and I will keep our fingers crossed and mix with the fray."

"Why are we doing this?" Joan asked.

"I know men like Meo and Alfredo. I have spent a lot of time with their sort. As sure as we are here, once they deal with Costa and Marcos, they will kill us."

"What? Are you sure?" Joan was appalled though she kept her expression serene.

"Positive."

"No honor amongst thieves, right?" Matt rendered.

"None, whatsoever." Barnum attested. "Lift your glasses and cheer." When they did, they attracted Meo and his brother's attention who came to join their little triad.

"What are you three so pleased about?" Meo demanded to know.

"Well, Meo, my friend, seems my colleagues and I agree with your methods. They don't believe these two men or their cohorts would ever come quietly, and would most likely want to take us all out in a war to remember rather than submit to the American authorities."

Meo smiled outright. He toasted Joan and Matt with his glass. "Happy you see things my way. I salute true *conquistadors*."

Meo brought the three and his brother to an elevator. "This elevator goes to the top of my mansion. I have a surprise for you."

When they reached the roof, Barnum recognized the X3 Eurocopter, a machine he'd only read about as futuristic. The giant helicopter built with two hybrid wings, each one with mounted propellers, could travel faster and hold a more significant cargo and people load than any other helicopter. "Has this been released? I thought they were merely running tests."

"Three were purchased at a recent auction in Russia, and I am the proud owner of one of them. The chopper is going to be very useful to me this morning."

What About Barnum?

Binary Bounty # 1

"You have a man who can drive this bird?" Matt asked.

"Two of them, señor Hayes," Meo added fanning with his right arm a one hundred and eighty-degree area.

Helicopter aside, Barnum now spotted the six men standing on the roof and armed to the teeth. He sensed Joan step in a little closer to him.

"Pedro, Johan, prepare the helicopter for departure."

The designated men attended their duties with precision and efficiency.

"Where are we going?" Barnum demanded.

"Monterrey," Meo told him with a smile.

"That's more than one thousand kilometers away, Meo."

"Barnum, I assure you with this helicopter, the trip will be a mere two hours. We possess all-terrain vehicles waiting for us when we land at the border of the city."

"You plan to attack these people in broad daylight?" Barnum thought if he made him talk, Meo liking to brag as much as he did, he might discover more about this junket and be in a better position to protect all their lives.

"Of course, many of the authorities in that city would love to clean the filth out of their territory. They will turn a blind eye. Plus, the chief in the area offered his support."

Just as he thought, the Aguados did not plan this attack in one day. He paid him lip service while he went about forging his deadly plans.

Once inside the helicopter, Barnum nudged Joan. She had little time to spare to give them notice of how she felt.

She moaned immediately, and Barnum thought the noise she made entirely credible. "Meo, you need to let Joan off here.

She's in pain. Perhaps something she ate."

Meo eyed Joan bent in half and screaming in pain, while she apologized for this delay.

"No problem, Joan." He smiled an unctuous smile. "No delay." He gave the pilot a command on his walkie-talkie, and a panel slid open on the floor close to her feet. She stayed in character despite her surprise.

"We will fly real low and stay put while you jump down into the water. There is a ladder fashioned of rope attached to the rim. All you need to do is unhook this and let it hang."

"Unacceptable, Meo," Barnum said with a firm glint in his eye. "There is a mile to the shore from here."

"Very well." Another few words on his radio and the pilot took a dive to their right to get closer to the beach.

Joan grabbed her bag, dropped her shoes into it and prepared to descend. "Good thing I have a waterproof phone," she whispered.

"Go down as far as you can," Barnum told her. "The water might be on the shallow side here."

She nodded. When her feet touched the water, she jumped and was glad she waited. She was submerged up to her waist as she waded her way to shore.

The helicopter continued its route.

"You're not waiting for her?" Barnum asked while knowing Meo would never delay his plans.

"We will gladly pick up beautiful Joan on the way back. This fight is no place for such a lovely woman," he added with a smile.

Barnum caught Meo and Alfredo looking down, and both

What About Barnum?

Binary Bounty # I

protested. "Where is she? I lost her," Alfredo said visibly disappointed.

"Don't worry," his brother mentioned. "We will locate señora Joan on our way home."

Barnum spotted Joan. He was the only one who could, having distributed a cloud around her as camouflage. She carried her purse and ran toward the pier where the jet skis were anchored. She would be fine, away from the Aguado leeches.

Now, he needed to take care of Matt and himself. He sent a signal to Ruiz via his phone texting him to let him know what was going down and to alert the others in the task force, also giving the name of the city where the helicopter headed.

"What are you doing with your phone, Barnum?" Alfredo asked. "We do not allow the use of cell phones while we fly."

"Trying to text Joan to find out where she is."

"Excellent," the younger Aguado answered.

"Ah, she says she will wait for us in the hotel lounge."

Thoughts of Millie entered his mind as he checked the time on his watch. She ate breakfast about now, perhaps wondering why he left so early. Not only would he not be sharing a meal with her and Jonah, but he also considered he would not be able to take the four of them to the airport. He hated the way he left things with her. So much he wanted to tell her only he feared her rejection. Most of all, he worried about influencing her decision. Now that she understood about his race and his planet, he fretted the knowledge might skew her perception of him. He wanted the love of her graceful heart and gentle soul. If he needed to walk away to prove his love for her, he would do so. Only, he would prefer affording the time to explain his intentions. He hoped she would understand and forgive him, allow him the chance to declare his sentiment when she better comprehended what sort of emotion her heart elicited toward him.

—Twenty-six—

BLOODBATH

The helicopter traveled for a couple of hours when Barnum caught the Chihuahuan Desert sprawled west of the oldest capital and largest city in the state of Coahuila. The thriving town of Saltillo comprised of eight hundred thousand people enjoyed the supreme appeal of the Sierra Madre. The chain of mountains rose east of the city providing its inhabitants with a homey sense. Aside from their spectacular beauty, the mountains' snow-covered peaks always had an ample supply of fresh water the town folk appreciated.

Barnum also noticed the helicopter tilt and start its descent toward the east rim of the City. "Didn't you say we were headed toward Monterrey? Still thirty minutes away, isn't it?" Barnum questioned Romeo.

"Just another surprise. Not Monterrey. Saltillo." He laughed taking in Barnum's raised eyebrows. "We will find the bastards in the foothills of the Sierra Madre just outside Rayones."

Barnum glanced at Matt. Nothing they could do. These men were armed, well-financed, and possessed the help of numerous, invisible friends. He checked his phone and still had no answer from Capitán Ruiz. He wondered what this meant. Then he checked the time and realized it was only nine in the morning.

The good captain was most likely on his way to work, his cell phone still not powered.

They disembarked on a large abandoned farm. As they walked toward the jeeps parked and waiting, Barnum asked what they once cultivated in the fields.

"Coca plants." Romeo smiled. "The Federals destroyed all the plants when they found them. My friend moved. We helped him and his family with money. He has four children."

Perhaps Robin Hood to some people, Barnum thought. He and Matt were handed a couple of water canteens and told to take a seat in the back of a jeep. Barnum realized this would be a bumpy ride. As many as twenty men boarded five vehicles. The green and black cars appeared built of reinforced steel with roll bars instead of roofs.

Since the accompanying men stood decorated with firepower, more so than the worst dressed mercenaries, Barnum thought he might mention, "Why are we here? We can't help you with your fight. We have no weapons."

Romeo laughed. "You are not here to fight. You are here to observe." He laughed again. "I will assign a man to stay behind with you."

Barnum exchanged a glance with Matt and realized they would need to take care of themselves.

When the jeeps pulled to a stop around an old abandoned wooden cabin, the men scurried inside.

Romeo ordered one of the men to remain outside with Barnum and Matt. The soldier in green fatigues did not argue. He hoisted the rifle on his shoulder and stood to face them.

The strategy Meo wanted to discuss with his men seemed to

What About Barnum?

Binary Bounty # 1

last a while.

Barnum became restless and tired of waiting. He signified to the man that he wanted to smoke. "May I grab my lighter and cigarettes in my shirt pocket?" Barnum asked in Spanish.

The man nodded. Carefully, Barnum extracted a cigarette pack from his pocket and shook one out. He removed one to put to his lips. He blew into the small cylinder, and a dart reached the man's neck. The soldier never had time to react. He fell to the ground.

"Is he dead?"

"No. He'll be out for a couple of hours. Long enough for us to leave." Barnum took the man's artillery and picked his pockets. He found the key to one of the jeeps, their jeep. He handed Matt a couple of pistols.

"God, where do these people get their weapons. H&K P30, the 9mm pistol can fire 15 rounds with little recoil." Matt seemed impressed as he caressed the two weapons in his hands.

"You've got a total of 30 rounds in the magazines, so use them wisely." Barnum pulled on the man's shoulders. "Help me put him behind the boulder."

As Matt helped drag the man behind the nearest rock, he added, "I didn't know you smoked."

"I don't."

"You just carry the little trick pack in your shirt in case?"

"Hey, I realized how deep the hole might be before I met up with them this morning. Never thought the Aguados would kill us like dogs, though."

"Well, very James Bond of you, 007." Matt smiled, seeming grateful Barnum was resourceful.

Matt redressed after helping Barnum dump the soldier in the moss behind the rock and complained about his back. "I'm getting too old for this shit."

Barnum took a deep breath and eyed him squarely. "Truth or dare. Twenty-some men are coming out of that cabin soon with one purpose on their tiny brains—to kill or be killed. We've got two choices." He brandished the jeep key. "We can make a run for it, or we can hide until they leave and follow them from a distance."

Matt made a face of a scrunched nose and narrowed eyes. "Truth: the logical side of my brain shouts to run, or better yet hurry and drive away. Dare: wild side of me cries out to follow them. Although what can we do? Aren't we better to leave and alert the authorities?"

"Think authorities will believe two CIA agents saying a Mexican drug cartel leader and his men are about to eliminate another drug cartel leader and his men?"

"Of course, they will. But *oficiales* won't care."

"Yes. What I think." Barnum gave him the key to the jeep. "Go to Saltillo. There is an airport in the city. Board the first flight you can."

"What about you? I'm not leaving you here alone."

"I've got all I need to take care of myself. Trust me."

"If I go to Puerto Vallarta, can I hide in your house on *Islas Marietas*?"

"Absolutely. Where Joan is."

"Okay. Don't forget. The three of us are witnesses to what went down here. So, good luck, man."

Stealthily, Matt bent low to crawl through yellow tufts of

grass and dirt patches while trying to avoid the rocks. He swung himself over the jeep's door and started the engine. He waited thinking someone might come running after him, but when no one did, he backed up and left.

Barnum communicated with Barnaby tapping the ring on his finger. "I need your help. Can you stand by?"

"What do you want me to do?"

"Keep the yacht and the house camouflaged at all times."

"Will do. Anything else?"

"I'm in a bit of trouble. My guests aboard the yacht need to take a plane at two this afternoon. They need to be at the airport before noon. The prototypes I programmed on board are incapable of taking them while making sure no harm comes to them."

"Do you need an armed escort?"

"Yes. But the four can't know about this."

"I'll fix it. I'll select a van to pick them up with several untouchables inside all going to the same airport and on the same flight. They will protect from afar."

"Great."

"What do we do about you? You're in some impasse, aren't you?"

"I'll need you to monitor this frequency and follow me. I'll use my camouflage cloud whenever I can, but I'll also need to come out of hiding when I want to interfere. I might need a few of your untouchables to back me up, fully armed. I will let you know if I do."

"Need me to go down there?"

"No. I need you to monitor things where you are." Then Barnum thought of a winning idea. "Send me a clone capable of resembling Matt Hayes. You know the man, right?"

"Yep. On my console. The clone will be there in ten minutes."

The clone's appearance coincided with the men coming out of the cabin, Meo leading the group. Barnum didn't wait, he hid the guns and the rifle in the bushes and told the phony Matt, "Come on let's go meet with these guys. This way they won't immediately discover one of their jeeps is missing."

"Meo, I'm a little disappointed you're not taking us with you. Matt and I could do a lot of damage." Barnum stood in front of the man with hands on hips.

Meo stopped to think. He glanced at his brother Alfredo who shrugged and added, "We can use the help, my brother."

"Very well, you stay between Miguel and Jorge. They will do the shooting for you, and they may share some of their weapons if they think you might be able to help." He nodded toward two of his men who took their place beside Barnum and the cloned Matt. Meo searched the area. "Where is the other Miguel, the one I assigned to stay with you?"

"Went out in the bush to take a leak. He'll be back."

"Useless piece of shit," Barnum caught Alfredo mumble under his breath.

The men started on foot which Barnum found odd, but he decided not to say anything for fear of angering anyone. Barnum found nerves taught in the men's strained eyes and worried expressions. Where was Romeo Aguado? He and his brother, and a good bunch of the army disappeared. At the moment, he worried more about securing Costa's and Marcos' safety.

The terrain, dry and mountainous displayed rocks of all sizes

What About Barnum?

Binary Bounty # 1

strewn everywhere as though falling from higher echelons of the mountains on an hourly basis—almost made Barnum want to look up to avoid a hit on the head.

Grass resembled dry weeds from lack of water, and even the few trees extended bare arms. They walked for fifteen minutes under the hot sun, getting hotter with each passing minute, before they began to climb. The rock face appeared smooth and unscalable, so, they followed a roughly beaten path up the hill.

Barnum knew not to ask questions, not to talk. All the men understood. To utter a single word might give them away long before they ever got to their goal. Echo around these mountains played tricks on people bouncing sounds at unusual angles in the rock face while sometimes landing in all the wrong places.

When they got to a plateau and a small clearing, Barnum spotted tents, perhaps ten or twelve of them, surrounding a windowless log cabin not much bigger than an outhouse. Only, he knew this had to be where Costa and Marcos were hiding.

The peaceful encampment appeared abandoned, and the doors to each tent were open. Barnum thought everyone scattered, perhaps aware of the ambush.

A soft series of clicks followed by a muffled sound of pain came up behind him. Barnum dove to the ground. Costa and Marcos were aware of the ambush and trailed behind them. He camouflaged in a hurry and a good thing he did. The two men assigned to protect him also fell.

A man yelled. "Hit the ground. The *locos* are behind us."

Barnum crawled away, thinking he wouldn't need to protect Costa and Marcos provided they took care of Meo and Alfredo. Suited him since his mission was to bring those men back to the

United States.

Soldiers from both sides fell to the ground. A waste of good people, and a bloodbath. Glad he sent Matt away when he did, he tripped over someone's body, corpses strewed everywhere. He chose to be visible again.

The shooting continued unabated, deadly but silent, except for minimum noise from the rifles equipped with silencers. Barnum tried to find Meo and Alfredo but failed. They escaped somehow or were part of the carnage lining the dried-up countryside. He did come across the bodies of Felix Costa and Brandon Marcos, both shot in the back.

As Barnum walked through the clearing back to the path going down the mountain, he wondered where Meo and Alfredo had gone. They must have foreseen this scenario, which explained why they had a few of their men walk in front of the group while they followed a good distance behind them.

He spotted the cloned Matt on the ground and rifled his pockets for any identity. No need to worry, Barnaby would bring the clone back to their ship. A dry twig broke under someone's weight, and Barnum turned in time to spot the brothers surrounded by five of their men.

"I am surprised you are still here, *amigo*." Romeo's tone sounded laced with danger, while a threat lurked in his eyes.

The small group approached Barnum, and he hoped Barnaby kept monitoring the situation. The two brothers did not have their guns aimed at him, but somehow, he didn't trust the situation.

"Why this bloodbath, Meo? Who is going to clean this up?"

"These people were dangerous, a nuisance to their com-

What About Barnum?

munity and a threat to everyone around them. They defend their actions with the Almighty now, someone higher and not impressed with guns, even less impressed with what they did."

"What about the day you go to the Almighty. What will he say about the Aguados?"

"That is between me and my maker, *señor* Barnum," his tone became small and purposeful. He picked up his gun slowly, relishing the knowing he read in his eyes, Barnum thought.

"You understand. We cannot leave any witnesses behind. Señor Matt Hayes was graceful enough to bow out without causing us the terrible duty of doing this ourselves."

As Romeo raised his pistol and aimed at him, Barnum closed his eyes and braced for the pain and the fall. The 9mm went off a few times, yet there was no pain. He opened his eyes and witnessed Romeo and Alfredo fall to the ground. Three of the five others scattered while the other two writhed in the field in pain.

"Who are you?" the leader of a group of people with their faces covered by ski masks demanded to know.

"You have just shot the head of New Jalisco cartel—and his brother. They were about to kill me." He hesitated. "Barnum. I am a Federal Agent. Who are You?"

"We are vigilantes, militia who have come together to take back our land. We belong to the self-policing community of Rayones." The four men came close. "We have been trying to get rid of Felix Costa and Brandon Marcos for months. So, thank you, New Jalisco cartel."

"Do you always shoot first and ask questions later?"

"You should be thanking us, *señor*, for ridding Mexico of the scum-sucking drug lords. You should be grateful that we have saved your life."

"I am. *Muchas gracias*. What I mean to say is you lead dangerous lives."

Another series of whistling clicks, and this time—pain. From somewhere behind him, some man still alive shot Barnum.

As he fell, before he lost consciousness, he tapped numerous times on his diamond ring.

Going Home

Millie eyed her watch, frantically searching the horizon for Barnum. "Where is he, Mom?" The rhetorical question echoed in Millie's mind as no one would call out Barnum's whereabouts.

Denny, Jonah, Caroline, and Millie stood on the quay near the Marriott Hotel. The yacht's captain told them a van was on its way to pick them up and would arrive promptly to take them to the airport.

"Didn't you say he would drive us to the airport?"

"Sweetheart, I thought so. He told me his meeting with the Aguados was a planning strategy, nothing more."

Denny added, "Do you suppose the meeting turned into more than a huddle? Perhaps an outright raid on the agents and their people?"

Caroline shook her head, sadness invading her eyes. "Don't know what to tell you, my darlings."

Jonah yelled excitedly. "There's the van, Mommy."

Millie smiled at her son. She couldn't allow despair to color her expression. She just spent the last hour consoling Jonah about not being able to snorkel before they left for home. Then he cried about not saying goodbye to Barnum. More tears she needed to mop while swallowing her own. She could have cried a torrent herself when discovering she would be unable to stare into the eyes of the man with the reassuring smile—at least one last time.

As they climbed the van's stoop, Millie first to help Jonah up the high step, Caroline told them, "No worries, my lovelies. I gave Barnum the means to reach us last night. He'll be contacting us, I swear by it." She gave them all a reassuring smile.

The van offered three places left. The big cargo vehicle transformed into a nine-place taxi happened to be full.

"Surprising so many people are going to the airport at the same time," Millie whispered to the others as she gathered Jonah on her lap. The driver had loaded their suitcases into the bin on the roof.

Denny bent toward her mother and Millie. "Especially since I spotted the inside of the bin and our bags are the only ones in it."

Caroline agreed. "Strange. Perhaps these people are part of a group going to Mexico City for the day."

"Yes, maybe," Millie whispered. "Luckily, our direct flight to San Francisco will last one hour and forty-five minutes."

"First class, don't forget," Denny added with a smile.

Millie thought the group of people, who all resembled each other, might merely be workers on their way to the airport.

She didn't care about any of them. Millie wanted Barnum to contact her. She needed to learn he was in good health and nothing untoward occurred. His lateness and lack of presence proved to be out of character for the man she came to accept as reliable and trustworthy. She prayed silently he did not meet with an enemy he could not handle.

What About Barnum?

Binary Bounty # 1

***

Following Barnum's couple of text messages, Ruiz contacted the task force and required the army's help. Two Lockheed & Martin Hercules combat planes launched. One from Chihuahua and another from Zapopan, Jalisco.

Jose Fernandez asked, "Why not send the plane from Apodaca, Nuevo León? Much closer. They would be able to help these guys so much faster."

"A hunch tells me fighting is over. A shootout like this lasts fifteen, twenty minutes. Going to be a cleanup operation and a roundup of strays." Ruiz shrugged. "I inquired about Apodaca. Nothing parked on the tarmac. Chihuahua's plane will be there in an hour and a half."

"Why do you suppose we had so little warning from Barnum and Matt Hayes?"

"Joan Crenshaw is also with them." Ruiz raised a pair of helpless shoulders. "Barnum is a dedicated worker and usually on time with his information. If the Aguados screwed with him like they did with you." He left the rest unsaid. "Come on, let's go. Lieutenant wants us on board."

By the time Ruiz and Fernandez arrived in Rayones, clean-up crews had gathered the bodies and tagged known victims. The vigilantes had removed their masks and helped in any capacity they could.

Ruiz approached one of them. "Did you happen to see a man named Barnum when you first arrived on the scene?"

He hoisted a shoulder, but one of the men holding a pile

of machine guns answered for him. "There was a man called Barnum. He identified himself as a Federal Agent. The Aguado brother was about to kill him when we interfered and killed them both."

"Where did he go?"

Two of the men exchanged glances. "I was one of the first ones here, Capitán, Ramon Gomez." He extended his hand, to shake Ruiz's hand, and the captain did so reluctantly. "We heard shots behind the man after he identified himself and he fell. We checked, and we could not help him. He died."

Ruiz's discouraged breath almost let the fight out of him. "Do you remember the name, Matt Hayes?"

Another man spoke. "Aguado—and we found out they are the Aguados because this man Barnum identified them by name when talking to them. Aguado mentioned lucky Matt Hayes had the good sense to remove himself and save them the trouble of killing him which was when we fired on them."

"Thank you."

Ruiz left and searched the grounds for an army representative. "Where are the bodies you assembled? We can help with the names and tagging. The reason why we are here."

"We are not finished, but those we retrieved we laid to rest in the bunker underneath that big tree." A young man with an earnest expression gave him the answer and Ruiz couldn't help thinking how difficult this must be for him.

Ruiz and Fernandez entered the bunker taken aback by the twenty to twenty-five bodies lined up in a pile. The gun fighting reverberated in the distance and Ruiz realized the army's weapons did not possess silencers like most of the cartel rifles scat-

What About Barnum?

Binary Bounty # 1

tered about the place. Their mission comprised of hunting down strays. Warned that these *banditos* presented a severe threat to everyone, the men received their orders to shoot first and ask questions later.

Ruiz hurried through the ones he recognized and told the young chap writing up the bracelets the few names he uncovered. Ruiz did not come across Barnum or Matt Hayes. Had it not been for the testimony of the few vigilantes who were helping, he would not have realized both had been shot and killed.

He turned toward Jose Fernandez. "You are familiar with a lot of Aguado's men. Stay here and help these people. I am going to look for answers." Ruiz left the compound in search of the lieutenant in charge. When he found his tent, he went inside and asked, "Are there bodies you haven't retrieved yet?"

"We're still fighting with half a dozen of them maybe more. These men won't give up until they run out of ammunition or until we can fit them for a stretcher."

"I mean, any more bodies lying around?"

"We don't know. We've got a couple of dogs helping us. The corpses cover quite a wide area. Why do you ask?"

"Three Federal Agents are missing. People here told me two of them are dead. I went to the bunker with my undercover man, and we were able to identify some of the bodies. We didn't find the Federals."

"Well, most likely means they're still out there. I'm sorry. As long as this fighting continues, it will be difficult to get to those who perished."

"I understand, Lieutenant. Thank you."

As Ruiz was leaving, two young men ran into the big tent.

"Lieutenant, you'll never guess what we found?"

The Lieutenant's somber expression prompted his men to speed up their information process.

"An X3 Eurocopter."

"In good working condition?"

"*Si.*"

"This may be what's holding up the fighting. The men can hope to escape in such a helicopter."

"How?" Ruiz asked.

"Chopper is faster than any plane we own. A hybrid of a plane and a helicopter—worth millions of dollars."

One of the young men stated, "We're in the wrong business." He laughed nervously.

The Lieutenant eyed him gravely. "The men who owned this fabulous bird are dead. Would you want to trade places with them?"

The young man lost his smile and looked at his boots. "No, sir."

The other young man stated shyly, "We found the registration inside as belonging to Romeo Aguado."

"Arrogant bastards. Most likely thought no one would be able to drive this thing other than themselves." He addressed the young men. "Hope you didn't touch or remove anything from that machine." He received two adamant denials.

Ruiz asked, "Do you employ anyone who can drive the helicopter, Lieutenant?"

"Not on the premises. We'll need to send the request for someone to fly it back."

"Back where?" Ruiz wondered who would benefit from this

find.

"Lost and found, I guess." The chief smiled and hoisted a shoulder. "We'll need to locate Aguado's next of kin and offer some form of exchange, or perhaps buy it from them." He prepared to leave the tent. "At this point, the rogue helicopter is the least of my problems."

Ruiz followed him outside. "Did you contact the local police force in Rayones?"

"No. So far, relief is just us, and those vigilante militias who are helping at the forefront."

"I'm just asking because our task force has an ongoing investigation on the local law enforcement authorities in certain areas, and this sector happens to be part of the ones we are investigating."

"Good to know. I will put this in my report, Capitán Ruiz."

***

Once at the airport, Millie, Denny, Caroline and Jonah checked their bags and obtained their boarding passes. Their plane did not leave for another hour and a half, so Caroline suggested they grab lunch before they boarded. "You know there will be nothing worthy to eat on the plane. Jonah will be hungry. May as well bring him some bottled water also."

"Good idea, Mom," Millie answered preoccupied while her head swung back often enough to give her pain in the neck.

"Why do you keep looking behind you?" Denny asked also looking down the wide corridor they just walked.

"I swear I spotted two men following us a while back and

they're still a mere few feet away."

"You're right. I remember those two. These weirdos came around when we hired the man to help us with our bags," Denny stopped in her tracks and deliberately stared at them.

"Did these men board the van with us?" Caroline asked. "If so, they could be going to the same place we are."

"No. Not in the van with us, Mom."

"Well, Denny," Caroline said. "If you don't want to attract attention, please don't stare at them."

Denny turned around to look at her mother. "Committing their features to memory. We may be interrogated about them later."

"Mom, do you suppose something might have happened to Barnum, and these men are the direct result of this—trying to harm us in some way?"

"Let's not get paranoid. We're going to have lunch, and if the strangers are still around after we eat, we'll find someone in authority and complain about being followed."

As they made to leave the busy intersection of corridors, two people came up to the men following them and asked for their papers.

"Now, these two men were in the van." Denny smiled. "I distinctly remember how they all wore jackets and identical-looking trousers. They are police officers." She turned toward her sister. "Barnum sent them to protect us. How much do you want to bet?"

A skirmish ensued as one of the men following them pulled out a gun at the officers. In a couple of short movements, the man found himself disarmed and the two slapped with handcuffs.

What About Barnum?

Binary Bounty # 1

"I think you may be right, Denny. Barnum did send them to protect us." Millie smiled at her mother. "No way are those two regular police officers—able to move that quickly?"

Caroline shook with an involuntary shudder. "Let's get out of here."

Upon landing in San Francisco, Caroline wondered why Barnum had not reserved tickets for them going to Oakland International Airport. "We would have saved a good forty minutes traveling time."

"Mom." Denny protested. "I checked. We wouldn't have been home before midnight. No direct flights left Puerto Vallarta to go to Oakland International."

"I guess forty minutes of a taxi is better than an eight-hour delay."

"Mommy, I want to take BART home. More fun than a car."

"Jonah, you're right. The Bay Area Rapid Transit is fun, but with all our bags, sweetheart, we need to take a cab home."

Denny's glance appeared fixated ahead of her. "Did you call Dad, Mom? He might want to come pick us up."

"No. An hour and a half round trip. We'll take a cab."

They lined up for a taxi, and when their turn came, two men took their cab ahead of them. "Sorry ladies, you can have the next one." The man responsible for the allotment of resources spoke loudly to be heard by the pushy men. "Some people own the world—they think."

Denny felt like telling the men off when she noticed something strange. "Hey, these men were in the van with us too. Why do you suppose they shoved us to take that cab?"

"Are you sure, Denny?"

"Yes, Mom. I'm sure. I spotted most of these people on the plane."

They were directed to the very next taxi, and this time no one showed up ahead of them to usurp their ride.

"Well that does it," Caroline said as she got into the cab. "Any other time I would disregard these conspiracy theories, but not now. Too evident someone is trying to tag us. You girls are staying with me for another week. Denny, you don't have a job to worry about, and Millie, you're on sabbatical. Jonah is on summer holidays. We've got the park where Jonah can play and ride his bike, and that big swimming pool out back which is only ever used by your father. We should stick together for a while, at least until we hear from Barnum."

Once they all agreed, Caroline gave the driver their address on Thousand Oaks Boulevard.

—Twenty-eight—

ALAN BREWER

Millie found the week at her parents' house went by quickly. She and Denny spent most of their time talking and reliving some of their youthful days. Having each their own ensuite seemed familiar and comfortable. Even Jonah had his room and play area.

They would come together for breakfast and stroll to the park to watch Jonah play with other children. Before long, lunch would be served on the patio table, and they spent the afternoon in the rose garden, either swimming or reading a book in the shade of the awning or chatting the hours away.

When Denny announced she would be going back home on Sunday, Millie thought it might be time for her to go back. They never heard from Barnum which troubled her no end. She couldn't ask about him or mention him to her little clan. The one time she had, Jonah cried and cried to see Barnum, and that night, he woke up from a doozy of a nightmare—more tears Millie needed to nurse. Thoughts of Jonah recuperating faster from the Barnum ordeal in his room at home prompted her to say on the day of Denny's departure, "You know, Dad, maybe Jonah and I should leave as well. Might be easier for him to forget about this vacation in a familiar environment." Millie lounged in one of the comfortable chairs surrounded with roses from the garden while her father swam a few feet away.

Alan turned toward her leaning his chin on his arms by the side of the pool. "Well, not the time to discuss this, Millie. Jonah will be bouncing back here after his bathroom break. Still, your mother has a doctor's appointment next week. I am sure your mom would love for you to be here when she returns."

"Why, Dad? Is anything wrong with Mom?"

His eyes widened and his smile gelled. The sound of a tooting horn announced Jonah's arrival—his new way of making his presence known these days. He ran through the garden tooting incessantly and jumped into the water wrapping his arms around his bent legs to make as much water as possible when he hit the surface, the way his grandfather taught him.

Millie stashed her book under the towel right before getting splashed. "Jonah, must you make a water bomb every time you jump into the pool?" This time he took advantage of a running start which created a bigger splash.

"It's fun, Mommy. Grandpa said if I do the bomb super well, and I splash you, you'll have to come in the water with us."

Millie laughed as she caught her father roll his eyes. Luckily, the concept of keeping a secret had not yet touched her son. She berated herself for hoping it never would. Of course, he would become more secretive with age, only natural. Everyone did. Perhaps this inclination to conceal thoughts created misunderstandings between parents and their children or between friends. In fact, this happy week revamped all her old views about her dad, chasing away staid impressions she harbored about him. Yes, her dad was a tease. But watching him in action as he taught

What About Barnum?

her son different types of swimming strokes, she sensed the patience and the understanding he held for Jonah. Millie spotted the child in her father. His attitude also brought back fond memories of when she was a little tyke, and how congenial Alan Brewer always managed to be with her and Denny.

She made a point of remembering this lesson when Jonah grew up. They would need to frequently talk about their likes and dislikes, so she wouldn't unknowingly hurt him in any way. Familiarity did breed contempt at times, although she always hated the idea. In a sense, one needed to nurture close acquaintances with respect and honesty, like the closeness of marriage.

Millie put down her book and rose. "Okay, you turkeys, my turn to splash you." She ran, cupped her legs with her arms and jumped as close as possible to both of them. The big wave bounced Jonah around and made him laugh. Surprisingly, her father laughed also. She hadn't heard the sound in years and wondered if her mother's health might be the factor in making him cranky and sad. He often said how Caroline Stuart happened to be his one true love and life without her would not be worth living.

"I'll stay, Dad. I'll stay another week."

The week went by fast, and with Denny gone, Millie fell into self-introspection, her attention directed solely toward Jonah. She felt like the shy, introverted teenager again without any means to release the thoughts she held dear. No wonder her parents didn't comprehend what went on inside her. Did she even understand herself?

Not hearing from Barnum drove her crazy. His promise to

visit her never happened. No dream of him or at least, none she recalled. Each day, the hurt deepened like a wound uncared for and festered with regret, empty wishes, remorse and more grief. Why didn't she tell him how she felt? Why did she believe because Helika returned to their home planet, he would soon miss her and want to return also? Why didn't she at least mention her concerns about fathering Jonah? Barnum possessed all the makings of a terrific parent for Jonah. She never said this to him.

Her mother came downstairs early one morning, and Millie made an effort to be agreeable. "Where are you heading to at this ungodly hour?" Millie smiled to show how much she cared even though she didn't often make the first step.

Caroline put an arm around her daughter's waist and told her. "Thank you for staying. Dad said you wanted to leave last week." She took a deep breath. "I have a doctor's appointment this morning."

"The second one this week? Mom, what's going on?"

"Where's Jonah?"

"Still sleeping." Millie sat at the table with her coffee while she offered to pour her mom a cup.

"I don't even have time for coffee. I have to leave right away."

"Just tell me. Why twice in one week? More tests?"

"You understand how doctors are with their tests. They didn't believe Tuesday's results. Here comes Friday and they want to be certain."

"I'm going with you."

"Millie, I already called a taxi. What about Jonah?"

"I'll get Dad to look in on him."

"You'll get Dad to do what?" A stern voice sounded from

What About Barnum?

Binary Bounty # 1

around the corner.

Caroline smiled shaking her head side to side. "I thought you were sleeping."

Alan kissed his wife on the cheek. "And miss saying good morning? Not on your life."

"Can you look in on Jonah and make sure he has breakfast when he wakes up?"

"Sure. I'll make the boy my celebrated bowl of cereal with maple syrup instead of milk."

"Dad. Please don't. He'll be bouncing off the walls all day."

Alan laughed. "Don't worry. I'll make him sausages and eggs and lots of vegetables."

"You can cook?"

"What cook? Your mother has tons of platters of everything stacked in our refrigerators and freezers ready for any Tom, Dick, and Harry that comes here and needs to eat."

"Is that true, Mom?"

"Alan. Millie is coming with me. So, you need to take care of your grandson. And please keep your good eye on him. He instinctively gets into trouble faster than any other child. Trust me."

Millie chuckled. "Afraid Mom's right, Dad. He is a handful."

"Ah, you ladies don't understand us, Brewers. We are as good as pureed when handled properly."

A car horn sounded outside.

"Taxi's here." Millie caught her father take her mother in his arms and deciphered the whisper he dropped in her ear. "Keep your fingers crossed."

What surprised her most was her father scooting over to her

and planting a kiss on her forehead. She backed up unable to stop her eyes from rounding.

"Take care of your mother."

"I will." She bent and planted a kiss on his cheek.

In the hospital waiting room, Caroline skipped through pages of a magazine faster than a child skipping rope, nothing catching her attention her mind apparently stuck on the troubles ailing her. "Mom, what is this all about, please?" She put her hand on her mother's arm to draw her from the magazine. She appeared stuck in an indeterminate loop of events, a worse mechanism than her longings for Barnum.

Caroline released a drawn-out breath as she put the magazine down. "Where to start?" She turned to glance at her daughter. "I didn't want to tell you or Denny, didn't want to upset you." Still, she hesitated. "Two years ago, I found a lump in my breast. I went to the doctor, and after a biopsy, they determined the lump to be malignant."

"Mom, I can't believe you never told us." Millie rubbed her mother's back, afraid of what she might learn next.

"They took out the small lump, and I had several sessions of chemotherapy. Afterward, tests revealed the cancer was all gone."

Caroline paused as she stared at Millie's hands holding on to hers. "A couple of months ago, I began combatting extreme fatigue. Couldn't stay awake. I went to the doctor, and because of my history, they knew where to look. They found the cancer cells had spread to my lungs."

Millie put her hand in front of her eyes.

What About Barnum?

Binary Bounty # 1

"Please don't cry, child. The night before we left Puerto Vallarta, Barnum came to see me. He said he knew I had cancer and that he understood this disease to be lethal to our human bodies."

Millie sat back in her chair—the wind knocked out of her. "Did he tell you who he is?"

"He did. Said you were the next person he needed to tell. Said he was in love with you. He wanted to spend the rest of his life with you."

Millie started crying. She realized her mother thought the tears were for her predicament, but they were a tribute to her cowardliness, not telling Barnum how much she loved him.

"Anyway, he pulled a small vial from his pocket and told me to drink it. He said by taking the one dose, I would no longer be stricken with cancer—ever."

"Oh, my God, Mom. Barnum did this for you?"

"Yes. He did. When the doctor could not find any cancer on Tuesday, they thought this was all a mistake. I showed them the vial I took. Did what Barnum said I should do. I told them it was a bitter potion drawn by a shaman, fruits and special herbs I ingested while in Mexico. I also mentioned I didn't think the concoction would work which explained why I ignored its content."

"Good one." Millie rummaged in her purse for a tissue to wipe her eyes. "So now we wait for the results of these second tests?"

Caroline nodded. "I didn't want to spend a few more days waiting and hoping their first analysis wasn't a mistake, so the doctor is speeding up the process for me. Why we're waiting."

"Unbelievable. Barnum cured your cancer—told you where

he comes from, who he is."

"What happened between you two that morning."

"I admitted to Barnum that Helika came to me in a dream that night telling me who she is, who Barnum is, and from which planet he comes. She even showed me a small part of the past four lives Barnum and I spent together. All the while I never realized who he is. She said he never found the courage to tell me."

"Well, love gave him wings, and he found the courage to explain this time. He even told your mother, and although I doubt Denny knows all the details, I'm sure she is aware he comes from elsewhere." When Millie still wouldn't say, Caroline asked again. "What happened, darling?"

"I don't know what came over me. I stood there all smug, mostly worried. The thought of spending my life with an alien upset me. I toyed with the idea he might not be a good role model for Jonah. I don't know what prompted me to tell him he should go back home which was where I thought he belonged."

"What did he say?"

"He seemed to agree with me. He didn't argue, insist or contradict me in any way. He continued to be kind and gentle that whole day."

"Well, knowing Barnum, even as little as I do, and sensing how much he truly loves you, he wouldn't want to influence your decision in any way. One should never force true love upon another."

Millie started crying. "Maybe I was jealous of his relationship with Helika. I thought he brought her with him for a reason, and perhaps now she was gone he would miss her. I can't

What About Barnum?

put Jonah through another one of my doomed relationships. But, Mom, I love Barnum so much. I didn't realize how much until now."

The loudspeaker called Caroline Brewer for her consultation with the oncologist. She handed her daughter a tissue. "Don't cry, Millie. We'll get it all sorted out, I promise." Caroline took her daughter's face in her hands and kissed her tear stained cheeks. "Smile. I'm sure he is still here on Earth. We'll find him."

Millie nodded and wiped her eyes. Faced with her mother's courage with regards to her illness, she considered her problem to be much less critical. The fact Barnum took the time to cure her mother brought tears close again, but Millie swallowed them refusing to allow her mother's new hope to be spoiled by her stupid tears. She was the one to blame for having handled the matter so poorly.

She waited patiently wondering if she shouldn't have gone with her mother to meet the doctor. What if cancer still lurked in her body? She would be devastated. Ten minutes went by, and her mother stood in front of her.

Millie rose and stared into the eyes she cherished so much. She detected tears in her mother's kind eyes, and she brandished a hesitant smile. "So?"

Caroline brushed her forehead with a shaky hand and bit her bottom lip not to cry. "The cancer is gone," she whispered. "Barnum cured me, which means your father will worship the ground he walks on." She chuckled through her tears. They both did. She exhaled a tremulous breath. "Silly tears. I'm relieved, sweetheart. I'm going to get to see my grandson grow into a handsome, wonderful man."

Mother and daughter each slapping an arm in back of each other for support walked out of the hospital, and Millie looked up to the sky saying a grateful prayer for an angel like Barnum. "No wonder you liked him the moment you met him." Millie smiled, tears replaced by deep gratitude. She had her mother back.

CELEBRATIONS

T he evening they returned from the hospital, Denny visited, and the four exchanged many secrets. Serving the best champagne, and bubbly orange soda for Jonah, they celebrated Caroline's newfound health. They toasted the man who gave her mother the gift of life while Caroline tearfully thanked Millie for needing her in Puerto Vallarta. "Strange how the tiresome, surreal decisions we sometimes choose for ourselves change our life. The last thing I wanted to do back then was, leave for Puerto Vallarta. As fatigued as I was, I didn't know how I would make the trip, especially after your father forbade me to go. He did."

"My way for you to never leave my side. I worried this trip would shorten what little time we had left. Yes, I'll admit. I am selfish when it comes to your mother. Want her all to myself." He smiled as he raised his glass. "Never dreamed some man would present himself as a healer of sorts."

Millie realized her father didn't quite know how to react to the notion of an alien. So, he naturally found another way to praise Barnum—as close as he dared to recognize Barnum's differences. Talented was what Alan Brewer called him.

That night, they also celebrated Denny and her newfound

love, Don Grimalsky. Denny found numerous calls upon her return from Puerto Vallarta, from the man's apology to his undying affection, to him making her a partner. He never put through her resignation and dubbed her as being on sick leave.

"To be clear, I didn't go back to the firm because he made me a partner—well, not the only reason." She paused waiting for the laughter to subside. "I am in love with Don. In fact, I never realized how all-consuming this sentiment could be, yuck." More laughs, her family knowing her as well as they did. "I was hoping he would be here this evening, but he had to work."

"We can all meet him on Sunday." Caroline smiled. "I will be serving late brunch here with all sorts of goodies. I'll even invite some of my less fortunate friends." When the girls stared at her with an inquisitive curiosity, she added, "Educated, well-to-do, lonely women who never seem to get any visitors other than your father and me."

Her father made a sign to specify not to count him in when her mother became preoccupied elsewhere. Laughter rose, and Caroline stared at her husband. "You accompanied me on several occasions, Alan Brewer."

"Twice—to help you carry the damn platters." He turned toward his daughters. "You would be as mortified as I was, shocked for lack of a better word, to catch these older women drool as they stared at me—not at the food I brought with me, no, no. Make no mistake. They wanted me."

Her father's words and expression generated the most significant kind of laughter, the one that stops you from breathing and hurts your ribs. By the time they dried their eyes and took a

What About Barnum?

couple of big gulps of air, Millie stared at the triumphant smile on her dad's face. The picture superimposed Alan Brewer as a younger man, and she remembered how handsome and bigger-than-life he appeared to her in his youth. Staring at him with affection brought on her dad's glance. He smiled, and her heart melted. She glanced at Denny and thought Don Grimalsky resembled Alan Brewer somewhat. Not necessarily with the features, but with the sound, down-to-earth character and vibrant personality. In fact, nothing deterred Don from the woman he loved—commendable, she thought.

Yes, her mother considered love should not be forced upon a person, but did this make Don's efforts to secure Denny's heart unjustified? Of course not. People, at least humans, enjoyed fighting for what they wanted. At times, men garishly chased the woman they loved until she reversed an adverse decision to a positive one. Why didn't Barnum do this for her?

After Denny left, Millie helped her mother put away the dishes and clean up in the dining room. "Mom, I'm going home tomorrow. I love spending time here. Your place is so much bigger and better situated than my little apartment, but somehow I take comfort in my things and my little area. You understand, right?"

"Of course, I do." Her mother placed an arm around her shoulders. "Tomorrow your father and I will help you settle in. No worries." She placed a kiss on her forehead.

***

Settling in for Millie was quick and painless with her parents' help. Jonah ran around their two-bedroom apartment with glee, checking all his toys and talking to his stuffed animals as he told them about all the adventures he enjoyed.

With her parents gone, began the more challenging portion of the program. Living alone again, and contemplating on what to do with her life. She retrieved eight phone messages. Although everyone had her cell phone and she did leave the number on her answering machine, she forgot to keep it charged for the last week she stayed at her parents' house. So now, she needed to get busy. But how would she return three calls from Jed? How would she talk to Diane Hurley, one of her team members? She could always chat with her friend Holly. Holly would understand why she didn't call her back. She didn't even answer her emails, had not posted anything on Facebook in ages—at least during the last two weeks which happened to be an eternity in internet minutes. Worse, she had two calls from Anita Gray, Administrative Secretary to the university's English Department reminding her of the two weeks of remedial classes she agreed to give starting July fifth.

She enjoyed a one-year sabbatical, why had she agreed to such a ridiculous demand? Of course, she remembered the reason. The Dean summoned her to his office, put on the show of his life, and pleaded with her to give up the month of July to please, please help. When this didn't work, he asked if she earned any money during the first half of her sabbatical? "Against university policies. You know that."

"I took an unpaid sabbatical, Dean Fleck to take courses, learn new marketing techniques to help my writers, and start my novel. I'm a single mother who just got a divorce. I needed the time to myself, and you agreed."

What About Barnum?

Binary Bounty # 1

"Millie, I approved your sabbatical, knowing full well what you intended doing. You were above board and honest with me. Therefore, my turn to be honest. We received an extremely poor tally this year of volunteers to give the remedial classes. I hate to do this, but we need your help."

He smiled and accepted her offer of working two weeks with a handshake.

She couldn't backtrack now, even though the Dean promised her one more month in her sabbatical. To find it cut short this way caused her grief.

Anita was the first call she returned, and though the worst to receive, the easiest to lay to rest. "No problem, Anita. I promised Dean Fleck I would be there."

"Most gracious, Millie. I'm surprised he asked you since you're on sabbatical and all. Oh, I almost forgot. A new professor we hired will sit in on a couple of your classes to get the gist of what your theme is since he will finish the two-week term—if this is okay with you, of course."

"No problem. I'll be in class bright-eyed and bushy-tailed day after July Fourth."

"Talk about ruining your Independence Day celebrations. Looking forward to seeing you again, Millie."

"Thanks, Anita."

Millie took the time to write down what she wanted to say to Jed. The words failed her. She now understood how much she valued her tenure at Berkeley and didn't wish to jeopardize this by starting any business, even a networking opportunity.

She armed herself with a cup of coffee and lots of deep breaths. "Jed, it's Millie. Sorry I didn't call you sooner. I was staying with my parents, and my cell phone stayed in my bag," she read off her piece of paper. A light pause marked her words, and she braced herself for Jed's reproach.

"Well, if you're wondering what happened to me, I spent a long time away from home too, on an army base to be precise. Anyway, I'm back in Los Angeles after the agent confirmed to reintegrate normal life."

"I understand what you mean, Jed. People call this a return to normalcy, only how do you deal with the ghosts?"

"No kidding. I still can't leave my condo without first glancing at the faces of the people I spot outside or checking the parked cars idling in my neighborhood. Last week, I called the police to tell them a man was following me. He seemed to be stopping when I did and kept staring in my direction."

Millie breathed again. No recrimination from Jed and she realized the situation fared much worse for him being alone to cope with the threats. "Don't know how you managed to go through this alone. Without my mother and sister, I can't think how I would have managed." She left out Barnum's name. He was the most helpful of all.

"Easy. I communicated with my top leaders with words of encouragement and motivation about the business. To teach is to learn and this helped me stay focused and on track. By the way, your team has grown despite all the shenanigans. I made sure of this."

Millie could not imagine a worse time to let Jed know about her decision. He expected gratitude and excitement, and she offered him a cold shoulder. "Thank you so much, by the way. I spotted the check coming into my account and thought it ap-

What About Barnum?

Binary Bounty # 1

peared bigger than usual." One deep breath later. "Jed, I made the decision to go back to teaching come January. I'm not going to continue with the business."

Silence prevailed, and Millie wondered if she still had the line. "Jed? Are you there?"

"I'm floored. You just sucker-punched me from here to hell. Why are you doing this? The business treated you more than fairly, and you're doing so well? You're a natural. I don't understand? A little craziness in Mexico and you're done?"

"No. Mexico never factored in with my decision. The truth is I'm not cut out for this type of business. I need to raise my son, and although networking is an adventure in meeting people, going places, making tons of cash in a hurry, I find networking is not designed for coping with a child as a single parent."

"What are you saying? Some women take up this business because they are single parents."

"Yes. I understand. However, as great an opportunity as Herbal Organics presented to me, I cannot pursue my original goals. I'm going to take some courses during the next six months, sit down to start the book I always wanted to write and devote most of my time to my little boy. Children grow up so fast and if you don't give them your undivided attention when they're young, the moment is gone forever."

"I see. So, there's nothing I can do to talk you out of this?"

"Afraid not. I'm happy, Jed, with the way things are. I'm sorry. I don't mean to let you down, but I need to be a full-time mom to Jonah."

Another few seconds of silence. "Can I still call you once in a while?"

"Of course, we're friends, aren't we?"

A slight pause. "Goodbye, Millie."

At that moment, Millie realized she would never hear from Jed again.

Her conversation with the top leaders in her group fared much easier. They understood and sympathized with her. As for the others in her downline, she would send an encouraging email to all concerned.

***

Sunday meant back at her folks' house to greet and meet the boyfriend. Millie spent time with Don at some of the office parties where Denny invited her big sister in the hopes she might hook up with an eligible bachelor. Of course, as fun as they were the parties never produced the inkling of romance for her. She found Don to be perfectly suited to her sister on the first day they met. Long talks on the subject did not convince Denny her Don might be her Don Juan. She needed to be without him for a while to truly appreciate the man's attributes. A little like discovering she loved Barnum with all her heart and all her soul now he was gone and no longer interested.

At least, Don remained loyal to Denny which she thought might be the best testimonial to their sentiment. More than pure glitter, Don's affection shone like the sparkle of the beautiful diamond he gave Denny. Genuine love should never come undone.

Their father seemed to take to him. He shook his hand vigorously and was not only happy Denny displayed a gorgeous

What About Barnum?

Binary Bounty # 1

ring on her finger, but he also raved about one of his daughters making partner in the well-known engineering firm.

Don stood as tall as their dad, and possessed some of the same rugged features, although his eyes were a softer brown— less stubborn perhaps? He spent the evening smiling and relating how he missed Denny thinking she might have signed on with another firm. Millie wondered if Denny would ever admit to Don about her time spent in Puerto Vallarta, especially the week they devoted to the magical *Islas Marietas* where the house had a soul and sensed how to replenish itself with anything they needed.

She brought some of the dishes from the dining room to the kitchen and started to rinse them to stack in the dishwasher.

She spotted her father coming in to help with more dishes he picked up. "Dad, why do you own two dishwashers? There are only two of you."

"I told you. Your mom makes dinner for whoever needs to eat and so, there are always dishes to wash and pots to clean and put away. We hired someone who comes in twice a week to help with this."

"Wow. Just like Mom to keep busy."

"And this when she thought cancer invaded her body." Her father stood beside her at the counter. "Millie?" He waited for her to turn and face him. "Your mother tells me you lost someone dear in Puerto Vallarta—this man called Barnum who performed a blooming miracle on your mother's health."

"She told you, Dad?" She eyed the mountain of pots and pans. "I fell in love with him, but I never said anything." She tried to think of something else, decided not to cry, but ended up snuggled in her father's arms weeping all over his T-shirt.

"Hey, it's okay. I realize I poked fun at your boyfriends in your young life. Since I'm an old coot, you need to forgive me."

She grabbed a tissue from her jeans and blew her nose. "I don't hold any rancor toward you if that's what you're asking."

"How serious are you about this man?"

She couldn't answer, words failing her. She never took part in a heart-to-heart discussion with her father about anything. She shrugged, tears too close to comment.

"Here is an idea. Since your mother recovered, and I would very much like to meet the young man who cured my wife, the same young man my eldest daughter is in love with, I propose you, and I go to Puerto Vallarta."

"You're not serious?" Millie eyed him disbelief rounding her eyes.

"Dead serious. I'm so glad you gave Jed Swayzee the boot, going to Puerto Vallarta is my way of celebrating."

"Dad, I'm not going back to teaching because I dumped Jed. I dumped the business not him. Jed and I were partners, not lovers. In the last six months, I've come to realize how much I love teaching."

"You should love teaching. You're terrific at it. Glad you realized this, Millie."

"Speaking of teaching, I have to run a remedial class at the University in less than a week, July fifth."

"We'll be back by then. We just need a couple of days, right?"

She nodded. "What about Jonah? Denny's going to start working again."

"Not before September. I heard her mention to Don that she

Binary Bounty # 1

wanted the summer off." He smiled. "Jonah will be with his grandmother and his aunty Denny."

"We would need to leave soon."

"I'll make all the arrangements. Leave them to me. Hope you didn't unpack yet." He chuckled.

"Of course, I did. We'll only be gone a couple of days, right?"

"Long enough for you to show me the sights and introduce me to your young man."

"Have you discussed this with Mom?"

"I'm a grown man. She followed her daughters to some fancy schmancy hotel in a foreign country. I can too." He exhaled a long breath. "Of course, I discussed this with your mother."

Millie chuckled and gave him a hug.

MILLIE AND DAD

The plane landed in Puerto Vallarta, and Millie's heart jumped when the wheels grazed the tarmac—not because of fright, but because she now breathed the same salty, warm air Barnum did.

Her father reserved the tickets, paid for them while refusing to take her money, and she promised Jonah she would bring him back a stuffed toy. So, all guilt neatly stored away, she needed to deal with sweaty palms and a racing heart—soon she would be in Barnum's arms again.

Her father bent toward her to stare out the porthole. "So, this is it, huh? The jewel of Mexico, Puerto Vallarta."

Millie chuckled. "Best viewed from outside the plane's porthole, Dad. Did you plan an itinerary?"

"I did. I thought we might first go to the hotel and then you can take me to the island you mentioned."

"Well, we'll have to rent a couple of jet skis and circle the island. There is a place where we can land. At this time, authorities closed Islas Marietas to tourists. They are redoing the coral and attempting to fix years of activity on the islands." Grabbing her overnight case from the overhead bin, Millie preceded her father off the plane. "I read they are thinking or reopening the beach at the end of August this year. They are trying to strike an understanding with the local tour organizers to limit the number of passengers each day."

After they breezed through customs and walked outside, Alan indicated to Millie they should get in line for a cab. "Of course, if they reopen the islands, all the better for us."

"Although, snorkeling in the hidden beach with a significant other when no one else is around is quite the thrill."

"I haven't been snorkeling in years. Would be fun to give it another try."

When they walked up to the reception counter, the front-desk clerk recognized her.

"Back so soon, Señorita Brewer? Most enjoyable you are staying with us again." He smiled.

"Thank you. So kind of you to remember." She pointed to her dad. "This is my father, and he's the one who made the reservations."

Alan's confirmation was a simple nod.

"Buenos días, Señor Brewer." The clerk flipped through his book and reached for two keys. "You are both on the same floor a few rooms down from each other. I hope you enjoy your stay." He stretched to look over the counter. "Are these the only bags you carry?"

"Yes," Alan answered. "We do not need a porter. Thank you."

Before they retired to their rooms, Millie told her dad to wear swimming trunks with a shirt on top. "No matter how much you try, you'll get wet with the jet ski spraying water everywhere."

With little unpacking to do, they met downstairs in the lounge area where Alan suggested they eat and drink a little something.

"Your mother raved about the fresh fish, and I've been dying to sample the sushi."

"We can go there for dinner. Chefs cook fresh fish teppanyaki style, delicious. La Estancia is the resort and spa here, and they serve the biggest breakfast and lunch around. Plus, we can take a table by the ocean. The place is wide open, except for the roof, and is so enchanting."

"Lead the way." Alan smiled, and Millie thought he enjoyed himself. Of course, she needed to be congenial and not race through everything to find Barnum.

Millie took her father by the arm and brought him to the table where she had spent charming hours with Denny watching the ocean as they ate.

Both chose a concoction of fruits and eggs with ham slices from the buffet. Her father added prawns to his lunch.

The breeze of salt air came to relieve the sun's heat, already high in the sky, the gazebo style roof providing shade and privacy.

White linen tablecloths and tall glasses of iced tea decorated with lemon wedges welcomed them both.

"This is an exquisite decor. No wonder your mother did not want to leave. I'll have to come back with her—make this our little winter getaway."

Millie smiled. She didn't quite know what to say to her father. Shyness crept in as she enjoyed only a modicum of conversation with him in the past.

"Your mother tried to pass Barnum off as an alien, believe it or not."

"Well, Dad, Barnum is an alien. Like you, I found difficult to

What About Barnum?

Binary Bounty #1

accept the notion."

"How long has he been on earth?"

"I'm not sure. Around eight hundred years."

"After five years, immigrants can apply for a green card. I would say, after eight hundred years, the man's no longer an alien." He took a sip of his coffee. "She never explained the circumstances of how he came to Earth. Did Barnum tell you?"

"Some of their scientists discovered a potion to be used with an electronic pulse that would make them live forever, annihilate death. When they tried their formula on a group of a few hundred people, they responded positively. Of course, they waited for more side effects to manifest which was when they discovered they also gained enormous powers. Another thousand people applied to receive the same formula and only a hundred or so of this new group survived."

"What went wrong?"

"No one was able to tell. Worse, all those who took the formula and remained alive now shared the same DNA, as though they were all identical twins."

Her dad finished his mouthful as he expressed surprise. "Wow. But why were they sent out into the universe?"

"They stopped producing the formula to work on an antidote. However, after a while, people began to fear these new, all-powerful beings. This was when their council supplied five starships for them to find suitable planets where they might live and procreate."

"We're talking hundreds of these beings then."

Millie nodded. "A few ships ended up on Earth. They found the people charming, and since all the travelers were men, except for one woman Barnum did not wish to leave behind, they made their home here marrying human females."

"They don't age, though. What happens?"

"Well, when they marry they age, at least artificially. When their spouse is gone, they're young again and find another woman to love."

"This means that Barnum wedded many women in the past eight hundred years."

"No. Only me."

"What?"

"Humans reincarnate, as do Binars, I'm sure. They just didn't realize this before coming here. Barnum was devastated when I died after the first life we spent together. He didn't remarry. Then one day he met up with me again. My hair was a different color, and I was taller than my former self, but he said he recognized my soul. He purported them to be the same. He still loved me, so he married me again."

"How is this possible? I understand mathematics and science, but this is outrageous. How many lives did you experience?"

"Dad, this is proven science. Trees, flowers, all rejuvenate and start again. You also enjoyed many lives. Now, imagine if you could spend them all with Mom? Would you want to?"

"Quite the question." He paused staring out at the ocean and the waves the wind grew and spun into a foam. Turning toward Millie, he took her hands in his and answered, "Human life is a bit like the tide rising and receding." He smiled. "In answer to your question, I believe I would."

She smiled pushing her plate to the side.

"So, Barnum's been trying to find you, life after life."

What About Barnum?

Binary Bounty # 1

She nodded. "And this time, I came back faster than Barnum expected, and well, you are aware of my awful timing with Todd. Slowed him down. He thought he would need to live without me this time around."

"Listen, without Todd, I wouldn't be blessed with Jonah, a beautiful and caring little boy. Reminds me of myself when I was his age." He chuckled. "Let's go rent those jet skis. I haven't been on one in a long time. You'll need to show me how to navigate."

They reserved two jet skis for the rest of the afternoon, and the supplier explained in Spanish how to use the machines. Alan asked his questions in Spanish, and Millie found her dad's language skills excellent.

When they sputtered out of the quay area, Millie shifted to go faster. When she searched for her father, she spotted him some distance behind her. She slowed and allowed him to catch up, so they idled beside each other. "Do you know how to speed up, Dad?"

"I do. I don't dare, but I do. No brakes on this thing and when I let go of the throttle, there's no way to turn." He winked at Millie. "Had a tumble once at high speed."

Millie laughed. "You're right, I'll go slower."

When they got to the islands, Millie began to coast and taught her father how to do the same to minimize the noise and avoid attracting the coast guards. They came in at the back which was where Barnum's house was situated.

When Millie secured her jet ski pushing it up on the sand, she waited for her father to catch up.

Meanwhile, she searched the area and could not see the

house usually depicting the two main windows and the high stone levy in front of the watery garage where Barnum kept his yacht. Only rock face. The wild beach appeared inviting—the one where Barnum and her strolled in the moonlight and kissed so tenderly that she now sensed shivers crawling over her body in the hot sun.

However, Millie found nothing else except for vegetation which appeared to grow fiercely. Listening intently, she caught the landscape's heartbeat, nature's protective hand overseeing the birds, the fish, down to the tiny insects and anything that moved as though no human had caressed this place in ages.

"Ahoy!"

Millie realized her father experienced trouble with his gears so, she ran down to the water's edge to lend him a hand.

When he rose, he took in the small beach, the rock, and commented, "Are we in the right place?"

"We are. Only the house is gone."

"How can a house disappear? The one your mother mentioned was enormous and extraordinary, I believe she added."

Millie stared into her father's eyes. "Yes. Extraordinary is an understatement, living and breathing and attentive to all our wishes. Since it's no longer present, I suspect Barnum went back to his home planet."

"He can just remove a house with the flick of his hand?"

Millie nodded, sensing her dad's disappointment. Her mother must have described the property in length. "Yes. Barnum can remove a house if he decides he no longer needs the place or no longer cares. He can execute this with the flick of his hand—with a mere thought."

What About Barnum?

Binary Bounty # 1

Tears hovered, but she kept them at bay. "This might mean Barnum decided to go home." Concerned with her dad's sullen expression, she considered Alan Brewer had come all this way to witness magic, and as a whimsical female, the magic passed him by—much like she did to Barnum. She had played the role of a capricious woman.

Alan put a smile on his face, his tone measured and solicitous, and Millie realized he set aside his letdown to care for hers. "We'll find him, Millie. I'm sure he's still here, on Earth."

"Well, Dad, if he isn't, if he did go back home, I can't blame him. I have to respect his decision and move on with my life. I have a son to raise and a dad to whom I promised a tour of Puerto Vallarta." She smiled at him. "We can take these jet skis we've rented for the afternoon and go all the way to town. There's a restaurant where they make the sushi fresh, right in front of you. You never tasted anything like this, Dad. Delicious."

"What are we waiting for?" he thundered.

She laughed, well aware of his love of raw fish. They spent another hour riding around Banderas Bay.

Then her father pulled up beside her. "How about we stroll down the *Malecon*? Your mother never had the chance to do this, she told me, and she would have loved the experience. We can bring her back pictures and souvenirs."

"Wonderful suggestion. We can leave the jet skis at the pier near Hotel Rosita. The *Malecon* begins there."

"Didn't we take our jet skis at the hotel?"

"Same owner. Barnum introduced me. A nice man." She took a deep breath. "The last night Barnum and I spent together we walked along the *Malecon* with Jonah."

"My grandson must have been tired."

"Barnum carried him most of the way. *Malecon* is only a mile. Takes anywhere from ten to sixty minutes to walk the distance, from Rosita's to Cuale River maybe fifteen city blocks."

"I would enjoy this." He stopped to add, "I imagine the sixty minutes is when you visit the surrounding boutiques and art fares."

"Sometimes, much longer. You can take pictures, and we can shop until we drop." Millie chuckled. "Afterward, we can go to Chez Elena to dine in front of the sunset. Phenomenal."

"I suggest we go back to the hotel, return the jet skis, change and take a cab to Rosita's."

She nodded. "Sure, let's do that."

When they got to the hotel, going through the terrazzo at the back, Millie spotted a face she recognized. She stared at the woman having dinner with a man. The thin, very short red hair and the big eyes rounded over a turned-up nose could not be mistaken. She had spotted her on Barnum's yacht through the binoculars while in the house's observatory.

She caught the woman rise when her companion left bills next to his plate. "Excuse me, Dad. A woman is leaving the restaurant, and I need to talk to her." Millie ran in that direction and grasped the woman's arm. "Excuse me, my name is Millie Brewer, and you work with Barnum, don't you?"

The thin, tall woman looked prudently around her, almost with fear Millie pondered. "You must be mistaken. I don't know any man called Barnum."

Without the terror-stricken expression, Millie might have believed her. "Sorry, I thought you were part of the task force

What About Barnum?

Binary Bounty # 1

working with the authorities to stop the drug cartels."

"You do know Barnum." She exhaled and smiled, extending her hand in friendship. "I'm Joan Crenshaw. Of course, Barnum and I both work for MI6."

Millie clasped her hand, hope building up inside her. "We were supposed to meet here. We didn't connect. I'm worried about him."

"Well, I just left his house on Marietas, last night. I heard the Aguados were dead, shot, both of them. I thought it might be safe to leave the house. I fly to England in the morning. Our Bureau Chief called us back."

"Did you meet with Barnum? Since you stayed at his house?"

"No. I was hiding on Marietas while Barnum fought with the cartel. Matt Hayes and I don't know what happened to …" Joan hesitated as she stared at Millie, and took a few steps back.

Millie turned and spotted her father. "Oh, this is my father. Dad, this is Joan. She works with Barnum."

"Please to meet you, young lady."

"I have to go. All I can say is on the day I escaped from the Aguado's helicopter a shootout resulted in carnage. The army and several municipalities' police force participated in the cleanup. Sorry. I'm not privy to where Barnum is."

"What about Felix Costa and Brandon Marcos?"

"Ah! You are briefed. What country do you represent?"

Millie pondered Joan assumed her to be a member of the task force. Not to get Barnum in trouble, she answered promptly, "The United States."

"Ah, well, both dead, as are most of their men—the rest are in jail. If you hear from Barnum, please tell him the Bureau Chief is looking for him." She waved and hurried away, eyeing both sides of the grand piazza before she entered the hotel.

"What's that all about?"

"Joan hasn't seen Barnum either." Millie stared at her father trying not to betray more worry than necessary. "Shall we go?"

—Thirty-one—

BACK IN PUERTO VALLARTA

M illie and her father took a cab to the north end of the *Malecon* and walked toward the wide promenade lining the beach. Millie tried not to think about Joan's words. Yet, somehow they churned in her mind popping up at the oddest moments. And although she smiled and made up her mind to enjoy herself as she and her dad strolled along the beach, Millie failed to erase the term *carnage* from her thoughts or that everyone appeared to be dead. She wished she remembered more about what Barnum told her when he said he would live forever. Did living forever include someone trying to kill him, or didn't that matter?

He couldn't be dead. If he were, authorities would be aware of this, and Joan would not be searching for him.

"Wow, what is this statue?" Alan ran his hand on the sculpture on the beach and wondered what it entailed.

"Well, this is called, *The Millenniums*, a bronze tribute to all the millenniums. The artist's name is Mathis something. I forget. Barnum told me the first part represents life originating from the sea, then you have three different representations of Christ and the third is a woman holding out a dove representing the whole of humankind searching for peace."

"Amazing. All those sculptors and painters that are showing their wares. I must bring your mother here. She wouldn't have enjoyed this, as fatigued as she was. But now, I'm looking forward to accompanying her this winter."

They stopped and sampled shops where artists displayed their sculptures, where precious jade mingled with bright lucite and statues made of sand and stone.

At a stylish jewelry store, her father purchased a necklace he knew her mother would love. Even insisted Millie pick up the small broach she admired.

When they arrived on the south side of the *Malecon*, after Alan Brewer sampled the best sushi he ever ate, Millie indicated she was taking him to Chez Elena for dinner. "A restaurant that serves authentic seafood and delicious Mexican fare as well as a wonderful margarita. Plus, they own a rooftop area called *El Nido*, the nest, where we can watch the sunset. The best place in the city to witness the transformation of day into night."

While enjoying his dinner, Alan thought out loud. "Millie, what was the name of that police captain your mother raved about. She imitated him a couple of times to make me laugh."

"Capitán Ruiz?"

"Yes. Ruiz. Why not go and ask him what happened to Barnum. He must be well informed. I'll go with you, first thing in the morning."

"Deal. Forgot all about him. You're right. He would be aware of Barnum's whereabouts."

They savored their eight-course meal slowly, having one of the best tables in the place right by the edge of the rooftop seeming as though they were perched above the ocean, and watched

What About Barnum?

Binary Bounty # 1

as the atmosphere dispersed the last light of the setting sun into separate colors.

Millie's chest took in all the air she could, the sight not merely bringing vivid memories of Barnum, but so beautiful, the sun's dip brought a tear to her eyes. She glanced at her father and caught him enthralled by the spectacle. As the last bits of sunlight broke into striae of vibrant colors, a flash of green became exaggerated and visible to the human eye just before the sun's orange candle melted in the ocean's lap.

"Did you spot that green flash? Or were my eyes deceiving me?" The waiter understood Alan's expression and came over to explain the refraction phenomenon in succinct sentences.

"You are lucky Señor, Señorita. This evening presents ideal conditions to witness the *green flash*. We will issue to both our special drink by the same name. Enjoy your evening."

"This place is magical. I've got some crow to eat when we return."

"What do you mean?"

"Your mother kept telling me about the magic house, the magic yacht where you ordered any food you wanted and be spoiled for consuming it anywhere else. Using my most prosaic tone, I told her there was no such thing as magic."

Millie laughed. "You should know by now, Mom is always right."

While they enjoyed their drink, and some of the toasted nuts served in a caramel sauce, giant firecrackers illuminated the now darkened sky.

"Where are these coming from?" her father demanded. "A barge on the ocean?"

"There is a pirate ship north of here, moored at the pier along the Malecon. Every night, at least when weather permits, captain thrills the tourists and those living here with the bright display of colors."

"A warm people who thinks of everything. Love their joie de vivre."

The next morning, Millie was in a hurry to talk to Capitán Ruiz. She thought it might be better to discuss the matter in person.

Father and daughter readied their little carrying cases as their plane left in the afternoon, and after a leisurely breakfast at the hotel, they took a cab and headed downtown.

"Sorry I couldn't secure two tickets returning on Saturday. I guess people booked all the places to spend the fourth of July in the United States. The fastest return was Tuesday the fifth."

"Which is when I begin work." Millie smiled and nudged his arm. "Don't fret. We both agreed this short jaunt was more than worth the trouble, right?"

"How unfortunate that you allowed yourself to be talked into working—in the middle of your sabbatical. Dean Fleck can be quite the pushy tight ass sometimes."

Millie chuckled as they boarded the taxi the hotel doorman flagged for them, and Millie gave the driver the address of police headquarters. "It's okay, Dad. Anita mentioned I'm also training a new professor. Someone they just hired."

"Which department?"

"English. He or she is moving from Harvard. Had tenure at Harvard."

What About Barnum?

Binary Bounty # 1

"From Harvard to Berkeley—as big a difference as New York and California. Still, a student is a student, and if this professor is coming from Harvard, he or she is going to be an asset."

When they arrived at headquarters, dragging their suitcase behind them, Millie led the way. The receptionist recognized her and called for Ruiz to come and meet them.

Ruiz was shocked to see Millie. He invited her to his office. When he spotted the man behind her, he asked for identification. "This is my father, Capitán Ruiz. He wanted to witness how beautiful Puerto Vallarta is." She smiled.

Ruiz appeared tired and in no mood for pleasantries. He sat down and indicated the chairs in front of him. "What can I do for you, Señorita?"

She had rehearsed in her head how to form the question. "I ran into Joan Crenshaw yesterday, on the grounds of our hotel."

She now had Ruiz's attention. He leaned on his desk toward her. "*¿De Verdad?*

"Yes. Both Joan and I want to find out what happened to Barnum. She states she left the Aguado's helicopter on the day of their meeting and lost track of him. Matt Hayes told her how the place was in shambles and what ensued between the two cartels became a bloodbath—a carnage the word she used."

"Where is she now? I would love to interrogate her. And Matt Hayes is alive?"

"Yes. Both were taking a plane back to England this morning. Her Bureau Chief called the three agents back. This was why she wanted to know about Barnum."

"Well, when Jose and I went there to assist in the cleanup

operation, someone from the militia told us Barnum was shot down, killed by one of the cartel members."

Alan reached for Millie's hand to give her strength. She realized she couldn't cry and scream in front of this man. She had no intention of letting go of her control.

Ruiz paused his eyes in the distance. "He also told me witnesses attested to Matt Hayes being killed by cartel members, but you say Joan was leaving for England with Hayes?"

Millie didn't trust herself to speak, she nodded.

"Captain, were you able to find Hayes and Barnum's bodies?" Alan asked.

"No. We accounted for everyone, except for those two—and Joan, of course. Now, we know what happened to Ms. Crenshaw and Mr. Hayes. Only leaves Barnum unaccounted for."

Alan also asked, "Is it possible there are still bodies somewhere in the bushes?"

"No. We used dogs, several of them. No one left in the field."

Millie rose quickly. She didn't know how long she would be able to hold the tears from pouring out of her. She gave Ruiz a brave smile. "Thank you so much for your help, Capitán Ruiz." She turned toward her dad and explained. "The captain was most helpful to us. Made sure we were well protected," she added.

Alan rose and shook the officer's hand. "My wife and I will be back to your wonderful city, Captain. We found the people here extremely warm and helpful. Beautiful city Puerto Vallarta."

"Ah, yes. When our fair city is not invaded with drug lords, we enjoy a wonderful life."

He walked away from his desk to escort them out. "I hope

What About Barnum?

Binary Bounty # 1

you and your family return to Puerto Vallarta. You will always be welcomed here Señorita, Señor. You can ask Valeria at reception to call you a cab."

Outside, waiting for the cab, Millie could no longer hold the tears. She clutched her father's arm and bit her bottom lip to stop the torrent of hurt and disappointment from shrieking out of her body.

"Millie. I'm sure Barnum is fine. You heard Ruiz? They never located him among the wounded or the deceased." He hugged her toward him, and Millie realized he tried to instill courage in her. "Imagine, the authorities thought Hayes had been shot and killed. He's up and about, and well."

She nodded taking a deep breath. "This could also mean they haven't found him because he decided to go home." She swallowed a hiccup.

"Nothing stopping him from going home for a visit, right? Doesn't mean he won't be back on Earth?"

Millie opted to remain quiet. No arguments left. She'd rushed down here at the advice of her dad, and even though grateful for the walk down memory lane, the warm landscape and friendly people simply reminded her how she allowed happiness to slip through her hand like sand—before she sent the love of her life back to his planet.

Nevertheless, for her father's sake, she had to hold her own. Plenty of time to grieve once she was home alone.

"Dad, what do you say we head out to the Malecon. Our plane is not for another four hours. We have time to have lunch and tour the place once more."

He smiled and took her by the waist as they walked to the

curb.

"Dad, good thing you swam for a couple of hours last night at the hotel. I'm sorry this trip is so short. So many more places I wanted to show you."

"The infinity pool at the hotel, especially at night, with the outdoor kiosks dispensing those yummy, decorative drinks? Honey, last night crowned my day." He smiled. "This trip may be short, but we packed it with excellent choices. So, don't worry. Just a preview."

Ever since she became a teenager, discussing any subject with Alan Brewer appeared impossible—or at least improbable. Could the difficulty have sprouted from her adolescent perception? She didn't possess a whole lot of self-confidence and didn't fare well with people making fun of her choices. She now understood her father offered more than teasing or making her feel subpar. Millie stumbled upon his kindness and compassion, and she also found they shared a few character traits. Somehow, Millie needed this small triumph in her life. At a time when the love of her life evaporated like a distant notion, Barnum pushed away by her thoughtlessness, she located another love in her life, her dad, who proved to be a staunch ally.

***

Leaving any vacation spot to return home usually sparked calm and the welcome of familiar surroundings inside Millie. Yet, twice she departed from the paradise of Puerto Vallarta, and twice her departure robbed her of joy—any joy, even the simple one of settling in her home with her son and her hopeful views

What About Barnum?

Binary Bounty # 1

of the future. This time, however, not only did her return not provide her with exciting prospects for tomorrow, the plane's ascent left her bereft of ever meeting Barnum again.

Sitting near the window with her eyes in the clouds, Millie turned to glance at her father. Mute for the last hour, she smiled when she spotted Alan sleeping with the headphones askew on his head. He appeared to be plunged into a deep sleep, his chin down and his mouth slightly open.

Just as well. Millie doubted she might find the strength to discuss trivia with her dad or anyone else. Perhaps she would head home and never speak to a soul, except for Jonah. Of course, Millie needed to give a class Tuesday morning and didn't quite grasp how the teacher in her would manage to be congenial to all these people preparing for a makeup test— twice a week for two weeks. Her mother had volunteered to stay with Jonah, but she assured Caroline she would bring Jonah with her and leave him at the daycare across the street. Millie found more comfortable to drop her son off and pick him up when she headed out. The truth was she wanted to head home and wallow in sadness rather than be forced to maintain a conversation at her parents' house. Much easier to entertain Jonah by going to the park or to the community pool or have a few of his friends over for a movie or to play with his computer games.

What was in store for her? She'd stepped out of her comfort zone to adopt Jed's business liable to keep her busy and on the move for a long time to come, not to mention positive and thriving. Now, she refused Jed and his business and returned to the life she once wanted to escape. She brushed a tear away with the back of her hand. Staring into the clouds did not comfort her, only rendered her small and insignificant. She closed her eyes and wished for sleep. She too deserved an hour of oblivion, the precious commodity of peace before stepping off the plane and into her usual life.

ON THE JOB

Millie examined her new suit in front of the full-length mirror, a light salmon waist jacket over the same color dress. Slimming and complementing the tone of her skin, she no longer worried about the expensive price tag. She would encounter plenty of chances to wear the outfit, and the dress went a long way to boost her morale, also giving her the confidence she needed to proceed with her class.

She and Jonah spent the Fourth of July at her parents' house—a full house with the four elderly ladies and the two older gentlemen her mother invited. Of course, Denny and Don attended, and she and her sister shared a long conversation about the trip with her dad and Barnum's disappearance. Denny's thoughts aligned with her father's opinions. She went one step further by mentioning Barnum might be recuperating on his home planet, and she had no doubt he would be back to Earth for the long haul. Millie refused to allow herself to think about the possibility of Barnum's return. Her current occupation involved raising a little boy into a man, which meant getting reacquainted with her life as a university professor, a single mother, and in time, thoughts of Barnum would become ghostly memories.

Jonah yelled from his room. "Mom, can I bring my bike to

daycare?"

"Not today, Jonah. You're not going to be there long enough. I'm only teaching for a couple of hours."

Millie stared out of her room window. As usual, the sweeping views of the bay from her top floor apartment inspired her to rise and accomplish her tasks with all the heart she could muster. The view didn't score as high on her list as the one from the building's rooftop, though. The roof, covering the full surface of the apartment complex, displayed beautiful wood floors, and containers decorated with shrubbery and flowers. Divans and comfortable chairs furnished the area to welcome guests, and even several fire pits offered the tenants extra leeway to celebrate special days.

After the scrumptious dinner at her parents' house, her immediate family drove over to her apartment. They took their places on the rooftop of her building, right by the shallow estuary of San Francisco Bay where the city of Berkeley and San Francisco combined resources to present a breathtaking spectacle of fireworks that left everyone dreamy-eyed and smiling. Denny and Don glued together like the perfect lovers near the roof's balustrade exchanged kisses during the bigger colorful blossoms of peonies and diadems. To Millie, the sight of her sister happy and in the arms of the man she loved represented the most significant swell of the evening.

Jonah and Millie took the elevator to the garage where she parked her car. She made sure he was buckled up in the backseat before she left. As red lights and stop signs littered in front of them, she ran a quick mental check of the items she needed for her class. Briefcase, purse, glasses, coffee cup and water bottle.

What About Barnum?

Binary Bounty # 1

She smiled at Jonah in the rearview mirror. He kept looking at her from the back, and she wondered if he forgot something.

"Do you have everything you need, Jonah?"

"I don't have Barnum," Jonah said with sadness she'd never encountered on her little boy's face.

Millie's heart flip-flopped in her chest. Barnum happened to be the missing item on her list as well. Strange how Jonah sensed this. "I told you, sweetie, Barnum is all tied up with work. He works in Puerto Vallarta." She smiled, though her heart ached. Not just for the loneliness that she spotted in her son's eyes, but for the fact that Barnum would never be a ghostly memory nor did she want him to be.

"I didn't even say goodbye, Mommy. Why can't he work here, with us?"

Millie spotted Jonah's daycare around the corner. "You know what, Jonah. When I finish teaching, after I pick you up to go home, we'll talk about this, okay?"

He nodded disenchantment still apparent in his brooding expression.

However, by the time she left Jonah with the daycare attendants, once he ran toward all his friends, his smile bright again, she breathed a little easier. Enough that she was in the throes of heartache, she would do everything in her power to keep Jonah from experiencing the same pain. She watched him play and settle in for a few minutes before she left.

Proceeding gingerly through traffic, Millie hoped she would not be late. Luckily, Anita sent her parking permits for the ten days she agreed to teach. She entered through Sather Gate, went by the Department of Comparative Literature where she frequently taught

Joss Landry

and took a right on South Drive to park at the back of Wheeler Hall.

As Millie walked the halls of the English Department, her short square heels making quite the raucous as they echoed loudly in the vast, almost empty corridors, she heard the soft sound of another pair of heels in her wake, and they sounded as though they were catching up to her fast.

Millie turned to face her pursuant. She paused to gaze at a tall dark-haired man with a great deal of facial hair, something she did not like. She preferred a well-groomed individual. He wore a tweed sports jacket over jeans and a blue T-shirt. Wired spectacles dangled loosely on the bridge of his nose, and over a broad forehead she spotted a tuft of black hair short and sleeked back.

"Are you Millicent Brewer?" He asked in deep tones.

"I am, and you are?"

He extended his hand. "I'm the professor you kindly agreed to initiate to the university's dos and don'ts."

Millie eyed his smile, stared deeply into the man's dark eyes behind the glasses and sensed a clutch grab hold of her senses. She remembered those eyes, she thought, ones that accompanied the heartwarming smile she missed so much. Would every man remind her of Barnum for the rest of her days? Was she doomed to relive the few moments she shared with him over and over? She took his hand in hers. "Pleased to meet you. I'm happy to assist you with the initiation to a few of your classes here. As for the dos and don'ts, you'll need to consult the policy manual. I'm almost embarrassed to admit I only understand the policies as they apply to my students and me. Sorry," she added when humor did not deter his stare. "Follow me then." She turned and

What About Barnum?

Binary Bounty # 1

walked away wondering why she had to face down so many good-looking men lately. At least this one opted for facial hair. Falling for this one would not happen nor would she imagine spending the rest of her life with him. Barnum still occupied her heart, and she found herself wondering if she would ever be free of him.

She opened the classroom door, and all noise subsided as students hurried to catch sight of the teacher in their midst.

"Hello, please be seated." She smiled. "I'm your teacher for the next two weeks. This gentleman is a new professor just arrived from Harvard University. He will begin with us during the fall semester." She looked at the teacher who sat down in a comfortable chair at the end of the first row. "I'm sorry. I didn't catch your name."

He rose and looked at the class. "Richard Barry."

Part of her wondered how she missed asking for his name while the limbic part of her brain wondered why the name sounded familiar. Of course, the professor's name was a common one, not as ordinary as John Smith, but nevertheless quite typical.

"So, let's begin." She took chalk and wrote her name on the board. "You may call me Ms. Brewer."

She checked the attendance sheet and noticed all thirty students were present. "So, let's start by discovering why you need to take this makeup class. As I call your name, please give me a quick sentence stating the class and the test you need to redo."

Once she finished, she sat down and eyed the students earnestly. "Of course, English 298 is a must for those working toward their doctoral degree, which is most of you here. However, those needing English 375, I counted eight of you, and you should be going toward a degree in pedagogy?"

Five of them raised their hands.

"Will the other three who cited this class raise their hand, please?"

"John Harlow, Ms. Brewer. I was told I could take English 375 to substitute another English course made up of a substantial writing assignment."

"Any teaching experience, John?"

"As a matter of fact, I do, at the high school level."

"Well, you may wish to petition the Graduate Chair to seek your teaching experience as credits to replace your course. It's up to you. I say this because whether you decide to take it or not, the course is a good refresher and an easygoing class."

She stepped from behind the desk and leaned against it. "Ladies and gentlemen, we have thirty days to turn your unsatisfactory term paper into a satisfactory one." She stopped to answer the raised hand at the back. "Yes?"

"Paul Miller, Ms. Brewer. I received an unsatisfactory grade on my writing assignment for English 250. I asked the Chair to go over the details as another teacher assured me my paper was quite good. The Chair told me to take this up with the teacher providing the makeup class."

"I see. Well, Mr. Miller. I cannot reverse another teacher's grade. Where is this teacher now?"

"Away for the summer. I did try to reach Mr. Hancock before he left."

"Ah, yes. Mr. Hancock."

The professor in training, Richard Barry, stood and asked permission to speak. "If I may?"

What About Barnum?

Binary Bounty # 1

Millie nodded.

"I can read Mr. Miller's paper and make some suggestions. The subject is one I taught at Harvard, different numerology for the course, but the matter and references are the same."

"Thank you. Most helpful of you, Mr. Barry." She turned toward Paul Miller. "If you'll be so kind as to make arrangements with Professor Barry before you leave, he will be able to help you." She continued her train of thought. "Therefore, because our class is made up of several groups of people taking different subjects, I suggest you pair up with your respective groups. You should exchange phone numbers, meet outside the class if necessary, and discuss ways to better your papers to obtain your credits."

Millie showed them the books she had brought as material, suggesting they acquire the tools as soon as possible. "I recommend you use the three books displayed on my desk. For English reading assignments, best to obtain the latest edition of the questions at the end of each chapter. They are in the same style as those asked in the makeup exams. We will discuss this in class more at length once you've all turned in your first assignments."

"Jenny Logan. I just acquired last year's edition for directed readings. Is there a big difference, Ms. Brewer?"

Millie thought a bit then asked, "Can I see a show of hands for those who own the latest edition of the reading assignments?"

The majority of people raised their hand. "If you don't wish to purchase a new edition, Jenny, I understand as the book is quite expensive. I suggest you team up with one of these people to view the questions and answers at the end of each chapter."

A couple of hours later, once they decided on their first assignment, she let everyone go.

Millie was the first to leave as most students stayed behind to confer with each other as she had mentioned they do. Richard Barry remained in the classroom to take Paul Miller's information and arrange to read his paper.

Millie took a stroll along the broad avenue leading to the bookstore. She wanted to get some supplies while she was here. Her purchases in hand, Millie walked toward her car and unlocked the doors, but before she got into the driver's seat, someone called her name. She spotted Richard Barry running toward her. She waited for him to catch up.

"I wonder if I may trouble you for a ride? Someone dropped me off, as I don't know the city very well, and I thought if it's not too much trouble you might be able to point me in the right direction."

"Yes, of course," she breathed out a tad annoyed he expected her to drive him home. "I have to pick up my little boy at daycare if that's okay. If not, Anita Gray could call you a cab."

"No. No. I don't mind the detour. We can become better acquainted during the ride home."

Just what I don't need, a clingy professor. She smiled as she boarded the car. Since Millie could not think of anything to say, silence rode between them. They got to Jonah's daycare without the exchange of a single word.

"Excuse me. I'll go get my son."

"Need any help?"

"No. Best if you stay here."

When she returned with Jonah by the hand, and a bag of his

What About Barnum?

Binary Bounty # 1

toys dangling from her arm, his pout showed he was not ready to go home yet. Playing with his friends he wanted to continue his game. "You came too early. I didn't finish my game."

"Sweetie, I told you today was a short visit to daycare."

Millie dropped the bag of his toys in the back and tied him into the booster seat.

When she got into the car, the sound of her five-year-old questioning the new professor produced an eye roll out of her and colored her cheeks pink.

"Who are you?" Jonah asked.

"Jonah, your manners please."

"Hello, my name is Jonah. May I have your name, please?"

Richard chuckled as he turned to eye Jonah. "You are quite the polite little boy. Pleased to meet you, Jonah. My name is Richard, and I am a professor like your mom."

"Do you know Barnum?" Jonah asked with a child's limited vision of the world.

"Jonah," Millie protested. "You understand by now that we don't all know each other."

"Yes. But this man looks like Barnum."

Millie turned to Richard and apologized. "Jonah and I just came back from Puerto Vallarta. We spent a couple of weeks there, and he liked one of our friends, a lot."

"I understand," Richard answered while his eyes caressed her face.

She couldn't remember why she didn't start the car, why they weren't leaving. Millie stared back at Richard her eyes glued to his. "Oh, I forgot to ask. Where do you live or at least, where do I drop you off?"

"I'm not even sure of the street yet. Avalon apartments." He smiled.

"I live in Avalon Apartments." Millie realized her tone was one of shock, but she couldn't help herself. "How long have you lived there?"

"A little over two weeks. A friend told me about the place. Talked about the lovely views of the Bay."

"Yes," she responded still stunned. "This is quite the coincidence. I bought a fourth-floor apartment. I've been there a little over a year."

Millie started the car and realized her hands shook. What was wrong with her? Such a concurrence of events could easily be explained. Both professors in English might mean they shared other familiar tastes and habits. Those apartments were new and spectacular. Plus, they were minutes away from work. She remembered this being the main reason she moved from San Francisco with Jonah—to be closer to Berkeley University.

NEW PROFESSOR

Millie struggled with the dilemma of sharing a building with Richard Barry. His apparent clingy nature prompted her to want nothing more than a working relationship with him. She would tell him about being in love with another man—the cold shower apt to protect her and force him to stay away.

"Here we are, Avalon apartments." She clicked the remote to the garage door on her visor and found her parking spot. "What is your apartment?"

"I'm on the third floor. Apartment three twenty."

"Oh, my God. My apartment is four twenty." *I live on top of this man. What are the odds?* Millie got Jonah's bag out of the car, her purse, and her briefcase. Her hands still shook. When she turned, Richard stood right in front of her.

She stared at him, and a familiar sensation stirred her. She encountered the grin she loved so much, the pleasant promise that told the world nothing untoward would ever happen to her.

"Here, let me take the toys, at least until we get to the elevator."

"Thank you," she mumbled.

Jonah pulled on his mother's sleeve. "Mommy, can the new Barnum have dinner with us?"

"Jonah. The man's name is Richard." She eyed Richard with a smile. "He's just a little boy. He doesn't understand."

"Quite all right. Why is this Barnum no longer in your lives?"

She chuckled. "Too much time to explain while waiting for an elevator."

"Perhaps Jonah's right. Allow me to take both of you out to dinner, ease up on your load a little."

"No, thank you. Very kind of you. I brought home papers to read, assignments to prepare. Quite an extensive amount of work in these makeup classes."

"Too bad. I don't know a lot of people in the city."

"Maybe we can do it some other night?"

"Friday?"

"Yes, I think that might be okay." *Insistent, especially when he lassoed me into going out to dinner with him—something I didn't want to do.*

"All right then." Richard pressed the elevator button. Before stepping out on his floor, he mussed up Jonah's hair. "See you soon, sport."

Before the doors closed, Jonah expressed surprise. "Did you hear that, Mommy? He called me, sport. He said, see you soon, sport the same way Barnum did."

Millie had to admit Jonah's excitement pleased her, happier than he had been in a long time. "Jonah, why do you think Richard looks like Barnum?"

Little shoulders went up. "Maybe because he smiles like Barnum. Mussed up my hair like Barnum used to do."

Millie smiled and cradled Jonah in her arms—the innocence of children. Did young ones' lack of guile allow them

What About Barnum?

Binary Bounty # I

to recognize a familiar soul? At least, better than their adult counterparts might do?

During the following days, the work involved in beginning a brand-new class while taking care of her five-year-old kept Millie busy, and she scrambled for a little rest early in the evenings.

By Thursday night, she was bushed. When Holly called to chat and to propose a sleepover for Jonah on the following night—as Millie caught the sound of Holly's five-year-old Ben jumping up and down in the background—she agreed to Holly's request.

"A chance for you and me to catch up," Holly told her. "So looking forward to hearing about your adventures in Puerto Vallarta, Missy Millie. Your hints are more than juicy if you catch my drift."

Millie chuckled. She and Holly were best friends for many years, having each given birth to a baby boy on the same day, at the same hospital. The only difference being Holly divorced her man one year ahead of her.

"Yes, it will be fun."

"Oh, and Ben would like to speak to Jonah."

"Jonah is sleeping. I left him at the daycare this afternoon. Didn't pick him up after my class, as he requested. He was almost the last little guy picked up, and this time, he was glad to see me. I gave him an early supper then he fell asleep in front of one of his movies. Can you hold, I have a beep."

She took the call and recognized Richard Barry's voice on the other line. "Richard, how are you? We missed you in class today. How is your assignment with Paul coming along?"

"Well, I've read his copy, and he's right. His work is excellent. I don't know about Berkeley, but at Harvard, I would have given this an A."

"Wow, quite a discrepancy. Can you run Paul's copy by the University's app that checks for plagiarism?"

"Already did. I used the same program Harvard uses. The application will find anything vaguely familiar out of the most obscure novel. Who is this Hancock he referred to?"

"Professor Hancock. He's quite the character. If for whatever reason he does not like a student, he will become an impossible grader for this person. If you hand me your report in writing, I will go to the Chair. She's a woman who has crossed swords with Hancock before, so she'll be sympathetic to our cause— one down, twenty-nine to go."

"Of course, I'll do this. By the way, I had previous appointments today I could not postpone, but I'm looking forward to our dinner tomorrow night."

"Oh, my God. I'm sorry, Richard. I forgot all about it, and I allowed Jonah to go to his friend for a sleepover." She took a deep breath remembering Holly on the other line. "Can you wait for a second? I left someone on hold on the other line." She switched to Holly's call without waiting for his permission and told her she would call her back.

"Sorry, I told the person I would call her back. About tomorrow night."

"Listen, I'm sorry Jonah won't be there, but I'll take you with or without Jonah."

Millie hesitated. Perhaps this was the perfect time to tell Richard she was in love with someone else. This way they would keep their association friendly and professional. "Okay, might

What About Barnum?

Binary Bounty # 1

be a sound idea. Guess we can dine without Jonah this time."

When Millie hung up, she called back Holly. "Holly, tomorrow night will only be Jonah. Sorry, I forgot all about saying yes to having dinner with the new professor, Richard Barry. He just reminded me, adamantly."

"Oh, I envy your life, cutie pie. Another lover in the wings?"

"No. I agreed to dine with Richard to warn him I'm not available. I fell in love with Barnum, and I'm not ready to do so again. I'm not sure if I'll ever be ready."

"Once more." Holly sighed heavily. "What about Barnum? When are you ever going to tell me about Barnum?"

"Saturday morning. When I pick up Jonah, you can come back to my place. We'll go to the gym, and then we'll sit on the roof and chat. How's that?"

"Sounds like a plan."

Millie hung up the phone thinking she was never going to be able to tell her best friend all about Barnum. Meager details would be allowed.

Not ten minutes into her assignments, another call rang to pull her away from work, and she considered taking the phone off the hook.

"Hello," she answered a little short.

"Millie, it's Denny. Am I interrupting anything?"

"Hardly. I'm putting together reading and writing assignments. I'm out of practice, and you're the third call in the last half hour. So, what can I do for my little sister?"

"Well, your sister's not little anymore, but she still misses you. Used to be Mom, you and I spent a lot of time together. Now, I don't know what's going on with your life. Don's working tomorrow and I'm spending the day at the parents' house. I thought you could join me. We haven't had a chat in a while."

"Good idea. I need to run a few things by you."

"How's Jonah? Mom says he went to daycare twice this week."

"Yep. He's fine. Still talking about Barnum. Oh, do you remember this makeup class Dean Fleck pressured me to give? Well, I drop Jonah at the daycare on my way to class, and he loves being with his friends. I believe this is a healthy distraction for him at the moment. Keeps him from thinking about Barnum."

"Really. Poor little fellow. Any news of Barnum?"

"Nope. Although," she didn't want to continue. "What do you say we save this topic for tomorrow, sis. I need to get this work done or else I won't be able to go to the parents'."

"Sure. Get to work, slave." Denny chuckled. "Can't believe you agreed to this right dab in the middle of your sabbatical."

"Please, a subject best left aside forever. When Dad learned about this, he called Dean Fleck a tight ass—a pushy tight ass."

Denny laughed outright. "That's our dad." She smacked a kiss on the mouthpiece. "Catch you tomorrow."

Millie wiped her eyes, fatigue catching up to her good intentions. Nevertheless, when she looked at the time and found it was still only seven forty-five, she decided to work for another forty-five minutes.

When eight thirty-five came around, she closed the books and reached for a bottle of white wine in the refrigerator, a wine glass, and the child monitor she kept since Jonah was a baby—a restless sleeper up until the time they moved here. She wondered if she might attribute the situation to her divorce? Millie had

What About Barnum?

Binary Bounty # 1

never drawn the conclusion until now. He slept without night-mares ever since Todd was out of the picture, a strange observation she thought.

She took the stairs leading up to the rooftop avoiding the elevator and hoped for solitude.

The place appeared deserted. Millie slipped toward the front of the building and aimed for the corner divan with the coffee table in front—by far, the best spot to catch the sunset.

She sat down amidst the cushions and poured herself a glass of wine. The best way to unwind after a hard day's work.

"Well, hello."

The deep voice prodded her out of her skin. Her glass over-flowed, and an excess of wine trickled from the stem's rim to the table and on her pants. She even dribbled a few drops down her blouse. She rose quickly to wipe her hands down her jeans and dabbed at her shirt with a tissue.

"You scared me, Richard. Thought I was alone up here."

"I'm so sorry," Richard said as he came closer to help her wipe the table with his tissues. "I felt sure you saw me. You looked right at me," he chuckled.

"I was admiring the sunset. I often come up here about this time."

"There should be lights, pot lights or lamps of sorts. Gets kind of dark here when the sun is setting."

Millie put the cap back on the bottle. She pointed toward a structure a few feet away. "On the column, the one with the fake tree in front of it, you will find a few switches at the back to turn on the lights in some areas."

He returned, and the lighting arrangement was perfect. They

could still admire the sunset without stepping on each other's feet. "Had I known you were here, I would have brought an extra glass."

He stepped out of the shadows with a mug in his hand. "I carried my cup with the rest of my coffee up here. Cup's empty. You may pour a little wine in it if you wish."

She did, and the two clinked glass and porcelain together. "To friendship and a good working collaboration," Millie toasted.

"To our friendship," he added.

"Come to think of it, the last sunset I admired took place in Puerto Vallarta. Breathtaking."

"Is Puerto Vallarta where you met this friend Jonah can't seem to forget?"

She nodded taking a sip of her wine. "Yes. Where we met Barnum. Have you ever been to Puerto Vallarta?" Millie eyed him with sharpened antennas directed toward his expression and his body language. Something about Richard spooked her or pulled at her heartstrings. She couldn't be sure which emotion prevailed.

"Yes, I have."

"Part of the time, we stayed on his yacht. Quite beautiful."

"I own a yacht. It's moored on the Pacific Ocean in Mexico."

Millie caught her breath as she stared at him. Cranking up her resolve, she refused to interpret anything in his words. Many people living in California owned boats and yachts, and Richard was calm with a warm smile. He appeared steady and in control of his emotions. "You're lucky. They're quite comfortable. Is it a big yacht?"

"A seventy-five-footer."

What About Barnum?

Binary Bounty # 1

Another little catch of shallow breath, so she smiled to calm down.

"What happened between you and this friend?"

"Hard to say. And I don't think I would call us friends. We barely knew each other. He saved Jonah from drowning, and his gesture, his beautiful, kind gesture made me feel like a terrible mother—this from the person who suffers from low self-esteem. Thus our relationship began, me at a disadvantage, and him the perfect angel. I couldn't understand why he liked me as much as he did. I kept searching for the angle, the reason," she stressed. "The men in my life have not always been there for me, which did not help my assessment of Barnum."

"Couldn't you discuss those feelings with him?"

Millie stared at the sun about to disappear into the Bay. "There's something so familiar about all this."

"Well, the sun descending in Frisco Bay or in the Bahía de Banderas is a common occurrence."

"I'm not talking about the background." She indicated him and her with her index finger.

"You didn't answer my question."

"Well, we scheduled a time to chat, share our feelings," she shook her head and gave him a rueful smile. "I started with the wrong words, fear with a little jealousy mixed in."

"Jealousy?"

"His ex-fiancée was going home. So, I told him perhaps he should go home also, and that was where he belonged."

Richard stared at her with such gentle eyes. She couldn't understand where the inclination to air all this came from or where she got the courage to continue.

She wiped a tear trickling down her cheek. "I expected him to deny he wanted to go home. I allowed fear to shape my words. I guess I needed Barnum to reassure me." Millie raised her shoulders and eyebrows over sad eyes. "Barnum agreed with me. He smiled and changed the subject. He produced four airline tickets for us to go home. That day, he spent with Jonah and me was the last time we saw him."

"I'm sorry you were so misunderstood. Some men cannot decipher women—at all."

"Oh, I don't blame Barnum, I blame myself, just as Jonah will one day when he finds out about all this." She used the tissue on her eyes. "Can we please change the subject?"

"Of course. I'm glad you told me. Brings us closer, don't you think?"

Millie wondered what he meant, what he tried to say. She didn't feel close to him—Richard Barry, the English professor who just arrived at Berkeley. And if he thought them to be closer, she would need to set him straight on what transpired in her heart. Whatever emotions shook her to the core did not belong to him. Her love—all her love—belonged to Barnum.

"Listen," he suggested. "For me to be more productive in our classes, what do you say we share the work?"

"What do you mean?"

"Well, you're working out of three manuals and taking care of three makeup classes. I could address two of those subjects. Still, this would include less than half the students, and you could work on the main course."

"You would do this? That's so sweet, thank you. I don't mind telling you—this would be a big relief."

What About Barnum?

Binary Bounty # 1

"So, it's settled. I'm glad I can help. I'll have to be in charge those last two weeks."

"Well, I rethought my position on this two weeks bit. I spoke to Anita today telling her I would be there until the end of the month." Richard appeared surprised but pleased. "I taught many of these classes before, and I know what the exams resemble. The ideal objective is to get all the students to graduate—not hold anyone back."

Richard raised his mug to her glass and stared into her eyes as he drank his wine. Millie sensed the burn of his eyes but stared at the sun losing some of its power, losing some of its warmth. Richard might turn out to be a good friend someday.

Thirty-four

RICHARD BARRY

Relaxing in one of her mother's comfortable cushioned lounge chair, Millie would have fallen asleep under the shade of the rose bushes by the pool if Denny had not prattled on without stop, slinging at her one question after another.

"Why would Jonah call this new professor Barnum?"

"Richard. Richard Barry is this new professor's name." Millie reapplied sunblock and repositioned herself on the chair. "And you've asked me that question before—twice."

Out in the pool, Jonah yelled at his mother to look at him, so she rose on her elbows and smiled at him. Her father was helping Jonah perform aerial acrobatics to render the biggest possible splashes—though the water missed their chairs by a couple of inches each time. Nothing to worry about—*missed by an inch missed by a mile* crowded her mind for whatever reason. "Wonderful, sweetie. I'll be in the water in ten minutes."

She lied back down, enjoying her moment in the sun while trying not to think about Barnum.

However, Denny kept talking. "Richard Barry! Where have I heard this name?"

"Ten minutes, seven minutes and five minutes ago, each time I answered the question you asked."

What About Barnum?

Binary Bounty # 1

"Oh, my God, Millie I just remembered."

Millie breathed out her frustration and remembered to do this lounging at home on her rooftop next time. Since Denny would not reveal what she knew without obtaining her full attention, and she needed a little peace and quiet, she cranked up the lever on the side of her chair to a sitting position. She looked at her sister with raised eyebrows. "What?"

Eyeing Denny's smirk on her pleased expression, Millie couldn't believe she needed to ask again. "What?" A little more impatiently this time.

"Richard Barry, Rick Barry was the name Barnum gave himself. Remember?" She raised her hands to make quotes. "His phony double. Yep." Denny chuckled in triumph. "What does your professor look like?"

"No. A mere coincidence. He can't be. Yes, Richard has been to Puerto Vallarta, and yes, he owns a yacht, a seventy-five-foot yacht moored in Mexico."

"Aha." Denny shrieked with glee. "I bet you he's Barnum. Richard is Barnum."

"Will you please stop. I'm trying to forget about Barnum, but I can't if you regularly bring him up. And Richard can't be Barnum. He looks nothing like him. Richard comes from Harvard, a professor at Harvard."

"So, you and I both know Barnum can do anything he likes and be anyone he wants to be, right?"

"I suppose. No. No. Doesn't make sense. Why would Barnum put on this elaborate charade when he finally came clear about who he is after centuries of lying about who he is."

"Perhaps because you rejected him when Helika told you

who he is. Maybe he would rather be with you and support the loneliness of you not knowing his real self. A compromise I can understand."

Millie leaned on the arm of the chair, covering her eyes with her hand. "You understand," she answered, her mood swinging between teary disappointment and frustration of not having Barnum's arms wrapped around her.

"I do."

"You're saying you wore a disguise to approach Don?"

"Well, not anything physical, but an emotional disguise, yes." Denny picked up a rose fallen on the patio and twirled the bloom in her hands. "When you're too ashamed to find the right words and when you don't know how to apologize without losing face." Denny dropped the rose and eyed her sister. "I called Don. I told him we came across difficulties in Mexico with the law, with the cartel. He left work in the middle of the day and rushed over. I think he thought I might be hurt. Not sure why." She smiled. "Didn't know what to say when he showed up. Luckily, he'd done some thinking himself, and when he took me in his arms, I started crying." Denny picked up Millie's hands in hers. "Love makes us do crazy things. We can't always understand why, or explain why we do them? If you care for a man, you accept the craziness and love the rest of him."

Millie bent toward her sister, placed her hands on her cheeks and kissed her on the forehead. "Thank you. Only, you're the crazy one, not him." Millie sat back in her chair. "Here's me being honest. I can imagine this man might be Barnum. When I do, fear takes hold of me again. As much as I love him, as much as I'll never be able to love anyone like him again, ever, I wonder

What About Barnum?

about his powers and what they mean for Jonah and me. Not an ordinary life to say the least. More like a disruptive one."

"Hey, Don and I will be earning close to a million a year. The money gives us all sorts of powers. Power to hire anyone we wish, to splurge and take the holidays we want to enjoy. The fact is, there is a ton of power in this world. Nothing more than a tool. You need to learn how to use power cautiously, for good, for your happiness and those of others. Something tells me Jonah would become a better man because of Barnum."

"You're right. What would I do if you weren't in my life?" Millie waved at Jonah as she wiped the tears pouring down her cheeks.

"Gramps says it's more than ten minutes, Mom."

Millie laughed. "I'm coming, Jonah." Millie rose from the chair and dabbed more sunscreen on her arms and legs. "By the way, I agreed to dine with Richard Barry this evening." Millie walked away chuckling when she sensed Denny running behind her.

"What? You wait until now to tell me this?"

Millie dove into the water and surfaced beside Jonah. "Hey there, sport."

"Mommy, don't call me that. It's Barnum's name for me."

"You are in the water, and swimming is a sport. So, since you're a good swimmer, I'm allowed to use it."

"Okay," he said with a smile. He climbed on his mother's back. "Throw me in the water like Gramps does."

***

Millie checked her little black dress in the mirror. Three times she changed for this dinner date. Excitement took a permanent hold on her, a strange, burning type of fever. She blamed this on the fact Richard Barry lived and breathed in the apartment underneath her. However, the actual reason for her nerve endings tingling resided elsewhere. On the way back from driving Jonah to Holly's place, she surmised two reasons still caused her alarm: the partially dissolved anxiety of raising Jonah amidst Barnum's powers, and what she feared the most, discovering Richard Barry was not Barnum.

Precisely at the time convened, Richard knocked on her door. Taking two deep breaths, she opened, wearing a smile. "Hello. You look handsome," she said surveying a dark sports jacket and trimmed black pants. He wore a blue cashmere turtleneck. She could tell cashmere a mile away. "Elegant," she added. She almost wished she wore more than her little black dress, even though her dress fit appropriately in all the right places.

"And you look beautiful, as usual."

"Thank you." A little frisson coursed through her. Perhaps she imagined Barnum's tone of voice. With all the talking Denny and her shared, deciphering reality from fantasy became worse than finding a solution to a Sudoku puzzle.

"Would you like to take your car or mine?" He asked.

"You have a car?"

"Of course."

"When I drove you home the other day, I had the impression you didn't own a car. I don't mind if someone else drives for a change."

When they got to the garage, she followed Richard to a light

What About Barnum?

Binary Bounty # 1

gray, convertible Jaguar. "Top up or down?"

She smiled, thinking this expensive, gorgeous car had to belong to Barnum. "Down please." Her curly hair would always bounce back from anything the wind or weather might throw her way. "Where are we going?" She asked as she buckled her belt. "I thought you didn't know the city all that well."

"No worries. The GPS will bring us where we need to go."

"Which is?"

He laughed. "I'm taking you to Chez Panisse. Ever heard of it?"

"Heard of it? I've been trying to get in there ever since I moved to Berkeley. My father and mother raved about the place, but they got in maybe once or twice. You have to make reservations months ahead of time. How did you manage this?"

"A friend of a friend."

"Oh, sure." Millie stared out the window praying that the charming man beside her might be Barnum, driving a fancy car, taking her to a fancy restaurant. The question as to why Barnum played this game with her, she could not answer. Why the disguise? Why not tell her he returned to discuss his feelings with her?

She glanced at the man beside her and hung her head. No way was this man Barnum. Denny owned a vivid imagination, as did she. Millie decided she would remain cool, calm and tell this man she could not pursue any relationship other than collaboration with their school work.

When Richard led her inside, she smiled as she glanced at her surroundings. The restaurant displayed the warmth of wooden floors and country charm. Tables strewn with white lace tablecloths glowed under the muted light of wall sconces. She breathed in the scent of freshly baked bread, welcoming the rustic appeal. "The place looks more like someone's home than a famous restaurant."

Richard gave Millie the choice of going downstairs or upstairs. "Upstairs you will have menu selections. Downstairs is a fixed menu they change daily. This being Friday, tonight's downstairs menu is seafood."

"Then seafood it is."

He took her hand and escorted her downstairs to a table tucked away in a little corner. His hand was big and warm, yet gentle. A long time since someone held her hand. Then she remembered Barnum holding her hand as they walked on the beach.

When they got to the table, Millie pulled her hand away. "I'm sorry. I can't have dinner with you."

"Would you like to go somewhere else?"

"I just want you to take me home, please?"

She noticed his eyes became sad, and his expression changed to one of hesitation. "Did I do something wrong?"

Millie looked around the place. "I don't want to talk about this here."

He placed an arm around her waist and marched her toward the door. They left quietly, and Richard briefly explained they would be back.

The silent ride home drew them apart. Millie questioned her stupid sentimentality deploring she ruined Richard's evening. She tried to imagine what Denny would do in this type of situation but gave up. Perhaps she acted too quickly. No rule said she couldn't have friends, whether she was in love with Barnum

What About Barnum?

or not.

She turned toward Richard and gazed at his set profile. He seemed to be ruminating on dark thoughts, perhaps contemplating how she decimated the magic out of their evening and left it all in shreds. "I'm sorry." She tried to stop the tears, but they came anyway.

Richard said nothing as he pulled into their garage. When the car came to a stop, he sat behind the wheel and pushed the button to have the top rise. Still, he didn't look at her or add anything else. He remained in the driver's seat and waited, as though she might run out and head for the safety of her apartment.

"Would you like to come up to my place and talk?" She let out a tremulous sigh and figured he no longer wanted to have anything to do with the crazy lady. He didn't answer. Perhaps he waited for her to leave.

As she clasped the handle while sobs swelled up inside her, she prepared to leave. Heartbroken and lonely, she thought probably best to nurse this overwhelming pain on her own. No one else would understand. A couple of weeks of acting normally, going about her everyday routine, served to bunch up all emotions she harbored for Barnum into a tiny corner until they could no longer be ignored. "Well, good night." Before she could swing her legs out the door, she felt his hand grab her arm.

She waited not wanting to let Richard see her tear stained face.

Richard strapped an arm behind her seat and turned her head to stare into her eyes. "If you want to talk, I'm a good listener." His expression became illegible.

Millie nodded.

In the elevator, she grabbed tissues from her purse and wiped her eyes and face. She needed to find calm somewhere, or she would only blubber unintelligible words, and Richard would think her even crazier than he did right now.

When it came time to choose one of their apartments, he hit the third floor, and she said nothing. Too distraught to argue, sobs too close to speak, she let him guide her with his hand on her back. He unlocked his door and invited her in with the sweep of his hand.

She went to the familiar view of the bay in his front window, realizing his place was exquisitely furnished with all the right trimmings. She sat on the sofa wringing her purse while he rummaged in the kitchen.

When Richard returned, he brought with him a platter of crackers and cheese and a bottle of champagne in a bucket of ice. He popped the cork and poured into each glass.

"You're too kind, Richard. I don't deserve all this attention."

"Take a sip of the champagne. You'll feel better afterward."

She nodded. She brought the glass to her lips and took a big gulp. "Light, dry, excellent champagne."

He sat down beside her, not entirely committing to the sofa. Sitting on the edge, he turned toward her. "What happened? Millie, what brought this on?"

She took a couple of shaky breaths and bit down on her lip to stop it from trembling. "In the restaurant, you held my hand—all came crashing down around me." She looked at him. "I'm sorry. I can't ever be more than your friend because I'm in love." She took a couple of deep breaths to steady her voice. "I'm in love with someone else." She stroked his arm over the sports jacket

What About Barnum?

Binary Bounty # 1

he had not removed. Gazing into his eyes, she added, "I'm in love with Barnum. I went back to look for him with my dad."

"When?"

"End of June."

She watched Richard shake his head and roll his eyes. He seemed more upset than she was disappointed. He appeared angry as he muttered to himself.

"We couldn't find him anywhere. Ruiz said he died."

"Millie, sweetheart."

Richard rose and pulled her up with him. He gathered her in his arms and like once before on a summer night on the beautiful beach of Puerto Vallarta, the apartment disappeared and her surroundings dissipated into the softness of white linen while the sensation of buoyancy set butterflies aflutter in her stomach. She held on to Richard worried she might fall as they seemed to float somewhere far above the ground. When they touched down again, Millie looked up at the man holding her against him and found the love of her life, Barnum.

"It was you, all this time. Denny said you were Barnum. I didn't believe anymore. No more games. I want to be with you."

A soft moan escaped Barnum, as he bent to kiss her lips. Gently, he was swept up in her vibrant passion. The kiss lasted, and Millie felt as though they were one person, one soul, two hearts beating loudly and in synchronicity.

When he released her, she asked, "Why the charade? Why didn't you tell me right away?"

"I thought you feared me. Feared Barnum, the alien from a distant world. I didn't believe you trusted me to do right by you. When I learned of Helika telling you about me that morning, I was angry, seething—One of the reasons I couldn't trust myself to speak. Then I died in Rayones from a handful of bullets, and death was painful. Barnaby brought me back to the ship, and within five minutes I was alive again with no wounds, except for one. You didn't change your mind about me as I thought you might. You took the plane and left. You didn't want me, and the thought became more painful, more insidious than any death I ever experienced."

She stroked his cheek. "You never came after me—to convince me."

"You can't force someone to love you. You would have resented me after a while. So, I decided to let Barnum go and become someone else. Start fresh. Even if this meant you would never know who I really am."

"You were prepared to do this for me?"

He nodded and gave her that smile she loved so much.

"I love this residual image of you much better than the one of Richard Barry, by the way."

"Perfect. This is my true human self. You and Jonah are the only ones who saw the borrowed Richard Barry image. The image would not have become permanent until I was sure you were in love with this other version of myself. Strange how Jonah saw through the Richard persona."

"With their innocence, children can detect a lot. What's going to happen at the university?"

"Nothing. I will retain the official name of Richard Barry, although everyone at the university visualized my residual Barnum image."

"That's good news. Can I still call you Barnum?"

What About Barnum?

Binary Bounty # 1

"Yes. I don't know if I am allowed to ask the following question. If I'm out of line, please tell me."

She nodded.

"Would you be so kind as to spend the night with me, the first of millions?"

She smiled, a soft sigh escaping her. "Yes. You're allowed asking this question, and yes, my answer is yes." She whispered, "I love you."

He kissed her ear and whispered, "You are my soulmate, my one true love. The one woman I wish to be with for eternity."

"Eternity is impossible to measure. A moment such as this one can be our eternity."

He backed up and stared into her eyes. Caressing her face with his hands, he said with a soft moan, "Yes, such a moment can last an eternity. Only, you'll need to tell me when you've had enough."

She pulled a deep breath and released a soft sigh when she realized he would be a tireless lover. As they clung to each other, Millie never had to tell him she had enough. In time, she fell asleep in Barnum's arms, exhausted and exulted.

Thirty-five

FINDING BARNUM

T he soft motion of Barnum's breath tickled Millie's ear, and she woke to a blissful smile. She slept on her side facing the window. Millie sensed Barnum wrapped around her while his steady breathing indicated he slept soundly with one of his arms stretched underneath the pillow while the other reposed around her waist.

Foggy blurs of their whirlwind lovemaking came back to her, got stronger as she focused on the memories which embarrassed her with their intensity. When she moved, wondering how she might step out of bed while still in Barnum's arms, she felt a kiss on the lobe of her ear.

"Good morning, my love," he whispered.

She turned, as tricky as this was to do, to gaze into his eyes. A few times during the night, by the light of the lamp, Barnum's eyes turned indigo. What color were his eyes this morning she wondered? Face to face, she smiled at him. "Checking your eye color."

He chuckled. "Why?"

"They change color when you kiss me."

He kissed the tip of her nose and pecked her lips." Did their color change?"

What About Barnum?

"No," she breathed.

"They lighten when our souls become one." As he said this, he removed his arm from her as though on cue.

"I'll be back. I need the washroom. I want to freshen up." Sitting on the bed, she mechanically searched for her slippers then thought out loud. "I'm at your place. I don't have any of my products."

He tugged on her arm. "Really?"

She lay back down facing him. "Right, I forgot. Does this apartment provide the same luxuries your house did on the Marietas?"

Barnum pulled her up against him. "Of course, it does."

"For everyone?"

He smiled as he pecked her lips. "For you and me." He searched her eyes. "If this bothers you in the least, make me a list, and I will go to your apartment to retrieve anything you need."

"You would do this?"

"We are going to live our life according to Millie, okay?"

"Thank you." Millie caressed his chest down to the taught ripples of his stomach. "I guess it wouldn't be so bad if I asked for my things this time?"

"From me or the Universe?"

She turned and rose. "Get some rest. I'm sure you need it. I'll use the universe's kindness this time."

He smiled as he closed his eyes. Millie realized Barnum's offer represented a considerable change, and a significant sacrifice for him, he who could ask for anything he wanted with pure thought.

When Millie returned, wearing her silk bathrobe, her slippers and carrying a tote bag of her products, Barnum appeared to be sleeping. He opened his eyes and smiled at her.

"No silk bathrobes to bed, my love."

"I can't find the time anywhere. What time is it?"

Barnum stretched on his nightstand to grab his watch. "Eight-thirty."

"Oh, my God. I need to pick up Jonah. He'll be waiting for me. I told Holly I would pick him up around nine. I also said she could come back here—not here, upstairs, my place—to go to the gym, and then we would spend some time on the roof to chat about my trip." When she didn't get any answer from him, when all he did was smooth the bed where she slept as a clear signal he wanted her to join him again, she added. "Barnum, she's my best friend, and I haven't told her about my leaving Jed, going back to teaching."

"Did you tell her about me?"

She nodded. "Not anything she wouldn't understand. Only that I fell in love with you, and Jonah also. She's been asking, though. She cares about me."

He let go of a huge groan and sat up in bed. "I understand. I'm anxious to see Jonah also." He got up and walked over to her side taking her in his arm.

Millie pondered that Barnum wasn't troubled by his nudity, not as much as she was shy of her own nakedness. She squeezed him tightly. She would need to be more in tuned to this man's needs. To accomplish this, she wondered aloud, "I hope I didn't disappoint you, as a lover I mean."

"Disappoint me?" He shook his head. "Never. You can never

What About Barnum?

disappoint me."

"I shared my bed with two other men in my life. My husband Todd and Jed a couple of times. Not much experience."

"I wouldn't be able to compare. I only shared myself with one lover in my life, human or otherwise."

"But you were engaged to Helika. She said so."

"Yes, but we never bonded. On my planet." Barnum seemed to hesitate. "On Binar, we have evolved beyond physical bonding. When we love someone, we join with this person for life by merging our souls. When we wish to procreate, we are able to do so with a simple touch and special blessings—an all-encompassing sentiment most of us enjoy thoroughly."

"Is this why you kept searching for me, life after life?"

He nodded. "I bonded with you a long time ago. Our souls joined, and I can never love anyone else."

As hot as he is, Barnum is the one man who will never go chasing the ladies the way Todd did. "So, is what we did last night repugnant to you?"

He scooped her up in his arms and giggled, caressing her with bold hands. "Not repugnant, simply unnecessary, yet enjoyable as you and I used the physical pleasure to merge our souls."

"Yes. I did sense us become one. I wasn't quite sure until you mentioned this. Still, you're quite the lover." She stared at the affection in his eyes and added, "Of course you're proficient at everything you do, aren't you?"

"I try to live my life with passion. Although sometimes, human nature can trip me up. The Aguados, for instance. Didn't see that coming."

"Or me? Admit it. I may not be in the same league as the

Aguados, but I did trip you up without wanting to, didn't I?"

"I don't care about the step we missed when we first started dancing. I want to marry you—at least a human wedding."

"What do you mean?"

"Well, when you're ready, and after we're married in the human tradition, we can also be married on Binar. Binars would welcome you to their home."

"I can go to your planet?" Millie backed up as though panic seized her.

"Not necessary." He reached for her to hold her close. "Only if you wish to go. And this would merely be a visit, not a reintegration into life on our planet." He kissed her, a deep kiss to make her relax, she figured. "After all you almost went to Binar twice."

"I did, when?" Before he could answer, Millie did. "When you held me in your arms, and we lifted above the ground. Thought we were in the clouds."

He nodded. "Yes."

"What would be the point of a Binar wedding?"

"Not important. Not now."

"Please, I want to know. We can't keep secrets anymore." She stroked his hair and sensed him shiver. "I may panic in the future, become scared now and then, but I will never leave you. You are a part of me now. I trust you implicitly."

"That is the point of a Binar wedding, right there."

"Explain, please." She smiled.

"The high priest would pronounce us as one, and you would acquire my powers and the equal privilege of the long life bestowed upon me."

What About Barnum?

Binary Bounty # 1

Millie almost backed out of his arms again but curbed the fright. "You mean, I would be able to wish as you do?"

He nodded.

"I would live without needing to die?"

Again, he nodded.

"Not necessary to do this now, right?"

"I promised you. We will live our lives according to Millie. What Millie wants, Millie gets."

"Millie wants you. I want to please you, give you everything in my power you may want and need. I will find the courage somehow." Tears rolled down her cheeks. "I will. I promise."

"I don't doubt you will. It took us eight hundred years to get here. We'll make it all the way there—eventually. Time is on our side."

"Time—oh, my God. I need to call Holly."

A short time later, they were on the road. Holly understood and told Millie she should spend the day with her two fellows.

"Something I don't quite grasp, Barnum. I remember this Jag as having only two doors yesterday. I am sure 'cause I wondered where Jonah might sit. Now there are four doors and room in the car for five."

Having lowered the top down, he smiled as the wind ran through his hair. "Well, we needed a bigger car to give a ride to the boys and your friend, don't we?"

"Of course. Why do I bother asking?"

He picked up her hand and brought it to his lips. "Please say you don't mind. I apologize. I wanted to impress you with my little roadster yesterday. Hadn't figured we would get together so fast. This way, I would have had time to tell you. I traded my car in for a better one."

She turned in her seat to face him. "Please don't do this. I am aware of you now. You need to be honest with me."

"Of course, I will."

It was her fault. She realized this. She cornered him with the question. "What do you mean my friend and the two boys?"

"Well, I thought we might bring them back to the apartment. You can proceed with your friend to the gym while I entertain the boys. I thought I might bring them to the community pool."

"You are a lifesaver. As a warning, takes Jonah a long time to get into the water at the pool."

"Why?"

"Water is so cold. He hates cold water. Other kids don't seem to mind. He does."

"Good to know?"

"Why? What are you going to do?"

He smiled. "With your permission, of course, water doesn't have to be cold, does it? At least for Jonah and his friend—and myself. I also hate cold water."

"As if you need my permission."

He gave her the raised eyebrow glance over his sunglasses.

"Of course, you have my permission." She nudged his arm with her hand. The sound of his laughter made her laugh until she remembered. "We're having dinner with my folks this evening. I forgot."

Barnum glanced at her and smiled. "Just can't wait to see Caroline again—a formidable, kind woman. Will also be nice to see Denny, and I hope your dad will be receptive to me and my

What About Barnum?

Binary Bounty # 1

ways."

"Are you kidding, Dad is bowled over with the fact you gave my mother a potion, and she got rid of cancer. I guess you don't have cancer on your planet?"

"No."

"What about AIDS or Ebola or that new virus that just sprung into our lives the Zika virus?"

"No, no such diseases on Binar."

"In other words, no one raced toward biological weapons on your planet."

"We also have no pollution, no poor—no one is left out."

"I'm amazed you chose Earth as your home planet."

He laid his hand on her lap and stroked her hand with his thumb. "Here is where my love is."

She gazed into his eyes and the world around them seemed to disappear. She witnessed his eyes turn a soft shade of indigo. When Millie searched the area, she found them parked at Holly's semi-detached and caught sight of Jonah running to the car.

Jonah eyed his mother then stared at Barnum mutely for a few seconds. The moment he realized who drove the car, he yelled Barnum's name repeatedly while jumping up and down on the sidewalk—his mother grabbing hold of his arm so he wouldn't run into the street to get to Barnum.

Barnum got out of the car and flew to Jonah's side. First, he helped Millie out of the Jaguar, then, he scooped up Jonah in his arms, her little boy cooing as he hugged his friendly giant, "I knew you'd come. I told Mom you'd come. Barnum, I missed you so much."

Holly and Ben looked on while Millie quickly wiped the tears budding in the corner of her eyes. Her son had adopted Barnum as his hero. Now, this hero would become his father.

Millie rushed to Holly's side. After a big hug, she told Holly what Barnum suggested.

"I missed you, Millie. This sounds like fun. I'll just round up Ben's bathing suit and towel and my gym bag."

"Wait, I want you to meet Barnum." Millie couldn't wait to introduce him.

"Pleased to meet you, Holly."

Holly smiled, and Millie recognized in her smile how Barnum impressed her. "Anyone who can make my friend and her little boy this happy is surely a friend of mine," Holly took the hand he extended.

Barnum put Jonah down, and Jonah ran to encircle his mother's legs with his little arms. "How did you find him, Mommy?"

The adults laughed. Millie bent down to kiss his chubby cheeks. "Barnum found us, sweetheart. He knew exactly where to look." Jonah jumped into his mother's arms while she was precariously balanced. Millie would have fallen had she not felt invisible support in her back. She attributed the last-minute juggling to Barnum's help and figured this was not such a frightening arrangement.

As they left Barnum's apartment to go to her parents, Millie pondered out loud. "We're going to have to find better living accommodations fast—or decide on which apartment we wish to keep."

"I agree. We can't have Jonah spending his time up and down the elevator each time he needs to tell me something or be re-

What About Barnum?

Binary Bounty # 1

joined with you." Barnum smiled at Millie. "Besides, I need to be with the woman I love, at least, living in the same house."

"Okay, so Barnum, you are in charge of finding us a place." Millie realized her request gave him her silent permission to materialize a house to his liking.

"You sure?"

"Yes. I'm positive. Hope I can help decorate."

The big square smile he gave her was her favorite. And she sighed. No more silly notion of half empty receptacles she needed to visualize as half full. Her happy cup overflowed, full to the brim.

After they parked in her parents' driveway, Denny ran out to greet them. Don followed behind her at a more leisurely pace.

"I came out to gawk at this car, but now I'm gawking at the driver. Barnum! About time you came back. What took you so long?" Denny gave him a hug as he closed the car door.

"A hug from Denny. A notable moment for sure," Barnum laughed.

Millie gave her sister a hug and shook Don's hand. Then, as Barnum and Don exchanged handshakes, she asked Denny with mitigated words if Don was aware of who Barnum was.

"He is. I couldn't keep it from him. Too momentous. He's happy. Says he understands that to tell anyone would bring DHS at our door, and put us all in hell."

"Does he know what he can do?" Millie asked.

"No. Best never to tell anyone about that." Then she turned toward Barnum. "I might have known this fancy car carried a fancy owner," she winked at him.

Framed in the doorway, Caroline yelled out. "May I ask why

you two are bringing the reunion outdoors when your father and I are waiting indoors?" Caroline waved to them—the gesture meant to invite them to move faster.

Barnum picked up Jonah and wrapped an arm around Millie as they gazed into each other's eyes.

Denny and Don followed, and Denny sighed. "Remember when you and I used to be lovers like this?"

"Used to be," Don said, squeezing her toward him. "Would you like a demonstration here and now?"

"Just joking, my sweet. You know I'll always be in love with you, and no one else," Denny kissed his lips.

When they entered the vestibule, Barnum put Jonah down for him to greet his grandparents. When Jonah moved from his grandmother's arms and ran to his grandfather, Barnum approached Caroline. "How are you feeling?" He smiled.

She pinched her lips and gave him the smile of someone trying not to cry. "Never better." She hauled a big breath to curb tears mostly. "Life is good again, thanks to you," she released a huge tremulous breath. "Thanks to you," she whispered.

"I'm happy." He took Caroline in his arms and held her for a few seconds.

"I'm so happy you're here," Caroline said using the tissue up her sleeve to wipe her eyes. "Millie loves you. She does."

Barnum gazed at Millie and took her in his arms. "I love you," he whispered. "I'm the luckiest man alive."

The last person Barnum needed to meet came up to him. "Last, but not least. Alan Brewer."

Barnum extended his hand, but Alan flicked it away and embraced him with a big pat on the back. "Thank you for what you

What About Barnum?

Binary Bounty # 1

did for Caroline. You've given me back my reason to live."

"My pleasure. You two make a great couple," Barnum said as he stared at Millie's smile.

She too was teary-eyed like her mother. "Emotions run high in this family," Millie said as she wiped her eyes.

"Did you tell this man how we went back to Puerto Vallarta to try to find him?" Alan chuckled to camouflage his deep emotions, Millie thought.

"Yes. I did. I believe this was what convinced Barnum how much I love him."

"Children," Caroline called out from the kitchen. "We're having dinner on the terrace. Dad's going to make steaks on the Barbecue. I've made different types of salads to accompany the meal. Hope you all brought your swimsuits."

Millie thought life strange yet delightful. Here she was back at her parents' house with Jonah, only, this time she wasn't alone. She would never be alone again. The magic enveloped her, and when Barnum squeezed her against him and pecked her lips, she shivered from their touch. Staring deep into his eyes, she admired their shade of indigo which she realized meant their souls lived in synchronicity.

Millie and Barnum will return …

They will be there in future adventures and you will learn more about Barnum's planet, and his customs.
You will be able to travel with them to other worlds and encounter new foes, and new friends.
Jonah will continue to grow in strength and wisdom and will have some tough choices to make.

All in all, this little gang will keep you enthralled and won't mind at all if you wish to tag along.

Other books by Joss Landry:
Mirror Deep, a mystery with romance
I Can See You, from **Emma Willis Series # 1**
This is a paranormal and urban fantasy mystery
I Can Find You, from **EmmaWillis Series # 2**
This is also an urban fantasy thriller.
Exhale and Reboot, a mystery with romance
Ava Moss, A cozy mystery with romance.

What About Barnum?

Binary Bounty # 1

Keep the faith. When all appears lost, there lies beyond another path that will lead you home. Joss Landry

Joss Landry

CPSIA information can be obtained
at www.ICGtesting.com
Printed in the USA
LVHW01s1353110918
589745LV00001B/2/P

9 780995 956803